CW00853396

The Leopard Man
Anne Ousby

Dedication

Thanks to my children, their families and my friends – for
their love and unceasing support. Especial thanks and
gratitude to
Wendy, Avril and Gillian, to Brenda my grammar whizz-kid
and Anne for giving me the confidence to persevere.

And thanks to Cath, Craig and family for sharing their little
slice of amazing South Africa and all the wonderful creatures
that inhabit it, both human and otherwise.

.

'Velvet footsteps two and three

Padded gravely after me.

-There was nothing, nothing there.

Nothing there to see.'

Leopards at Knole by Victoria-Sackville West

The Leopard Man

8 a.m.

The leopardess lies on a ledge, her eyes never leaving the activity in the valley below. She has been watching since first light. Her body is tense, her senses heightened and her breath comes in staccato bursts. Two young cubs lie pressed against their mother's flanks – her anxiety transmitting itself to them in one jangling line of fear.

****

Quent's hand trembles as he raises the binoculars to his tired eyes. He has to grasp his wrist tightly with the other hand to steady his grip.

He sees three bakkies crawling along the base of the kloof. The fiery sun flares on their windscreens, turning them into miniature sun-spots. There is no mistake. They have found him.

They'll get as far as the rocky shelf, jutting out below the waterfall, and then they'll be on foot. Several hundred metres further on they'll pass his pick-up, stuck bonnet-first in a muddy runnel. Quent's mouth twists at the thought of the sweating, angry men fighting their way uphill through dense undergrowth. It isn't hot yet but it will be and the mozzies down there are as big and mean as bees. It will be at least two hours before they get to him. Plenty of time – time for her to come.

He leans back on the chair, easing his aching shoulders. It's been a long night and the thoughts that come in the dark are stuck to his brain like used gum. The chair creaks dangerously as he stretches his injured leg out in front of him. Even this slightest of movements sends the pain spinning away again. 'Christ!' He hurls the word into the stillness and a spiral of rock pigeons comes plummeting down the cliff-face behind him, before disappearing into cracks in the rock.

After a few moments the pain subsides but his thigh wound has opened up again and bright new blood seeps onto his trousers. He's burning up but there's nothing to be done. The antibiotic and painkillers are long gone.

He'd seen a doc in Cape Town. 'Get yourself to hospital, man,' the old guy had wheezed, in between pulls on his cigarette. 'You don't want septicaemia,' he added, unnecessarily. 'It's bloody nasty.'

Quent knows all about blood-poisoning. He's seen enough of it in the bush. Men had lost their limbs and some their lives but Quent had been careful. He'd had treatment. Christ! All those drugs had cost a fortune. No bug could live in his body – at least that's what he told himself. But he curses himself now for not stocking up with med before leaving the city. Stupid, stupid. He steels himself to probe the hard, hot flesh surrounding the wound and catches sight of his hand – a stranger's hand – the dry, dusty skin covered with liver-spots. An old man's hand. He flexes his forearm and sees the one-time taut, brown skin creasing into stringy wrinkles down its length.

He shakes his head angrily. Got to stop feeling sorry for himself – got to concentrate. He's still alive, isn't he? Still functioning? He reaches for some water and struggles to uncap it. Old man's hands, old man's grip. One time he could undo a water bottle with his teeth or was that a beer bottle? He wouldn't try that again, not if he didn't want to break his remaining few good teeth. His tongue searches his coral-reefed tooth line, probing the fissures. At last he gets the bottle uncapped and pours the liquid down his throat. While he drinks he watches the early morning mist tumbling past him and down into the valley – like some giant plug has been pulled.

A million cicadas have begun their throbbing salutation to the day while Malachite sunbirds and Cape sugarbirds add their counter-melody. The mountainside is a kaleidoscope of late summer colour. Huge orange King proteas sway on bushes close to the house and banks of flaming red disa stretch away across the mountainside like some royal carpet welcoming the sun. A Steppe eagle is frozen high in the sky

2

above him on the lookout for prey and he can hear the warning barks of baboon in the valley below.

There's a dull thudding in Quent's head like the onset of a massive migraine, but he pushes it away and concentrates on a tree-heather poking its fragile flowers through the railings. Quent takes a sprig and holds it to his nose, breathing in its perfume; then he rests a finger on the delicate bell-like bloom and watches as they tremble on the stalks – so fragile and yet so strong. Fynbos plants are tough little beauties. They have to be to survive the weather on the kloof. Summers are hot and dry with incessant winds and the threat of fire, followed by winters with prolonged storms that lash the mountainsides. But for now all is calm and Quent's breath hangs on the air like an intrusion.

Quent half-closes his eyes and remembers. *Gauta.* The leopard will have been hunting and maybe got lucky and stashed a klipspringer high in some tree beside the river. Now she's heading home to her still-suckling cubs that have lain all night, still and quiet in the dew-wet bush, dreaming of their mother's milk, tail tips twitching to the lilt of their dreams.

Quent strains his tired eyes across the scree-covered slopes but there is nothing there, only the rise and fall of feeding birds and the soft wind rustling the vegetation. The binoculars are halfway to his eyes before he remembers. There will be no leopards on this kloof. Not today or tomorrow – not ever. He has seen to that. He swears and sends a stone skimming away. It bounds and clatters down into silence.

It's all over for him. He's a dead man and he will be judged. Nothing is left, nothing good, or honest, or worth a shit. Something like a sigh escapes from his mouth and he looks up at the summit, so beautiful in this perfect light. He squeezes his eyes tight shut and when he opens them again there's moisture on his cheek. Wiping his face with the back of his hand he dislodges the heavy quilted blanket that is draped across his shoulders and it falls onto the dog at his feet. The animal shifts its huge weight and groans.

'Hey, Bullseye? Okay, man?'

As he bends to retrieve the blanket the morning explodes about him and the juddering in his skull becomes a huge clanging bell. A wild wind sends a maelstrom of vegetation, blossoms and small sharp stones spiralling about him. The dog leaps up, barking furiously, and Quent flings his arms around the railings to stop his chair from toppling backwards.

Through the choking, swirling dust Quent sees the outline of a helicopter rising slowly above the escarpment in front of him. For an instant he and the look-out guy eyeball each other. The chopper hangs there for a moment and then rears up and sweeps away over the shack and the surrounding terrain before clearing the peak and chattering angrily away into the valley beyond. Within seconds the only discernible sound is the humming of bees in the heather. Maybe he's dreamt it? But no, there goes Bullseye charging up the kloof after the intruders and the hillside is a battle-ground of severed flower heads and broken plants.

Quent's hands are shaking as he picks up the water bottle. Bastards! What are they playing at? There's no place to land up here and where do they think he's going? There's only one safe route up and they have that covered. Quent can't be sure but he thinks the guy in the chopper was carrying a rifle. Maybe they were going to shoot first and ask questions later? Just one clean shot would do it. But he doubts their ability.

He watches as the frustrated dog comes bounding back down the mountainside towards him, barking hoarsely, his muzzle garlanded in slather.

Farnie's Birthday

From the road it was easy to see why Pig's Snout Kloof was so called. Halfway up the mountainside two precipices of immense limestone had fallen away from a huge rock shelf, making the snout of the pig, while above and on each side dark scrub dissected the white rock. The *eyes* were gouged out during some ferocious storm, long ago, when two massive boulders had come crashing down into the valley. Forest trees now grew in the craters where leopards once hunted. Baboons roosted in these trees. Fear of leopard was part of the baboon's genetic memory, passed from mother to baby.

It was midday and unseasonably hot for the time of the year. The collared doves were silent, conserving what little energy they had for each breath. Even the incessant throbbing of cicadas was muted and the tall eucalyptus trees stood motionless, their silver leaves flickering in the paralysing heat.

Suddenly, the sound of a baby's laughter prodded into this stillness, incongruous in the sticky torpor. A woman knelt beside the peaty stream which ran alongside the trees. Her skirt was hitched up around her waist exposing lean brown legs and thighs. She was washing a baby boy who was splashing happily in the water. The woman's heavy long black hair swung across her face as she bent to scoop up the honey-coloured liquid and ladle it over the delighted child. Then she sat back on her heels and watched as the water meandered silkily down the boy's body. Some water splashed into his eyes and he blinked in surprise. His mouth was wide, hoping to catch the sparkling drops.

'You're so beautiful, my Farnie.' They were alone but the woman's voice rang out. The loud sound startled the collared doves from their perches. It was as if the woman wanted the whole world to hear her and she did, because today was her baby's first birthday.

Farnie closed his mouth and stared up at his mother – his large blue eyes wide with astonishment. He'd never heard his

5

mother shout before. Two tiny frown-lines appeared on the little boy's forehead and he looked so solemn that she laughed and picked him out of the water, swinging him high up to the sun and showering them both in an arc of golden, wet beads. Then she planted a kiss on top of his head and felt the flickering pulse beneath her lips. 'Beautiful, beautiful boy,' she murmured into the soft down of his hair.

Raki had been brought up in a Christian boarding house where any public show of emotion or pride was regarded as a sin. She was encouraged to talk softly, walk slowly and pray loudly. Her mother, Sofia, ran the business while her father reared sheep. He wasn't a very good farmer – so his wife kept telling him – and too often the crops failed or the sheep got sick, so Raki's mother was the main bread-winner.

A procession of boarders came and went throughout Raki's childhood. The house was more like a church than a home. It even smelt the same, from all the fusty clothes the boarders wore. Most of them were earnest young men preparing for the ministry or eager young couples planning to be missionaries.

Henrik Morgan was one of the boarders but Raki barely noticed him. His head was usually bent over the Bible or saying grace before meals. Even when he talked directly to people he didn't look at them. He and Raki's mother got on well and when Mr Morgan took over as pastor of the Birkenheadbaai church he moved into the church house with his mother. No one could speak to Sofia for a few days after that without her snapping at them.

Mr Morgan's mother came from Stellenbosch and made it clear – to anyone who cared to listen – that the little old-fashioned Birkenheadbaai was not what she was used to at all. She was a city girl and shopped in Cape Town. She had shoes especially made for her by a craftsman in Jozy. Raki had always preferred to go barefoot and could never quite understand the envy her mother obviously felt for Mrs Morgan's made-to-measure shoes. Sofia was often heard telling her cronies that poor Henrik didn't have much money and it was such a shame to see it being wasted but Raki noticed the way her mother looked at the older woman's feet.

Henrik Morgan had never shown the slightest interest in Raki and it was difficult to say who was the most surprised when they got married. On their first morning as man and wife Raki woke to discover him bending over her and staring – much as if he was reading a difficult passage from the bible.

After drying the child Raki slipped a faded T-shirt– several sizes too large – over his head and fastened on his sun hat. Then, hitching him onto her hip, she shouldered her backpack and headed for home. It was a steep climb to the house and he was a big boy, but the woman's slender body gave a lie to its strength. She walked quickly, eager to give him his presents. She wouldn't be sad today. It didn't matter that there would only be Farnie and her at his party. They didn't need anyone else

8.05 a.m.

Bullseye has been down to the flat water run to drink and is panting back up the slope. When he reaches Quent the animal rests his nose briefly against the man's hand, and then moves on. This is the nearest Bullseye ever gets to being affectionate.

The dog pads towards a large flat rock marking the boundary between the fynbos-covered mountainside and the boulder-strewn mountain top. This is Bullseye's favourite spot. Here he has a perfect view of the gap in the rocks where the track comes up over the edge of the kloof. The dog leaps effortlessly up onto his viewpoint then he lies down, head on paws, and within moments his fawn-coloured coat merges with the colour of the rock.

Quent is in awe of the way Bullseye adapts to any new circumstance. Raki had never learnt to trust the dog like he did. He told her until he was sick of it that the dog would never hurt her, that she was as much a part of the dog's life as he was, but she didn't believe him. 'No, he's your dog, Quent,' she would say. 'A one man dog and that's the way I like it.'

Quent had come up the kloof yesterday. He didn't know how close they were behind him but one thing was certain – they were on their way. He'd left a trail wide enough to drive a tank through.

He'd chosen the petrol station with care. The place was shiny new and well staffed. The immaculately dressed petrol pump attendants all wore identical corporate uniforms with identical corporate smiles. These slipped when they saw the huge dog standing in the back of the pick-up, watching their every move through narrowed, suspicious eyes.

'Oil need checking, boss?' One guy asked as he washed the windscreen and windows with enthusiasm. 'Water need filling, boss?'

'Yeh, man,' Quent smiled. 'Check it all.'

Quent's rifle was propped on the passenger seat and when he got out for a piss they saw a hand gun tucked into his trouser waistband and the blood on his trousers. The clincher came when he emptied his pockets of loose change into their hands before he left. That was when he told them that the cops were after him. One man had smiled nervously. 'Sure they are, boss,' he agreed sensibly. 'You're a bad man.'

Quent certainly looked the part even without the camouflage trousers, combat boots and three-day stubble. His torn-away T-shirt revealed the tattoo of a leopard which covered his right upper arm. It was a magnificent creature caught in mid-flight leaping towards its prey, fangs exposed, claws unsheathed. When Quent flexed his arm the animal moved too.

Quent turned the key in the ignition and nodded to the attendant. He decided not to tell him where he was heading. There had to be something for the cops to work out – an opportunity to use their brains.

As Quent swung out onto the highway he watched in the mirror as the men shouted excitedly to each other and pointed after him before running inside to spread the word.

Quent drove his vehicle as far up Pig's Snout as he could, then he slung the rifle and small back-pack across his shoulders. Everything else was strapped to a pannier across the dog's back. There was a hessian sack, a carton of water bottles and a few basics. Quent was banking on there being some biltong in the shack. Raki always kept a supply of the dried meat for emergencies, even when she was down the mountain. It was highly unlikely she'd be there and he told himself that's the way he wanted it – she mustn't get caught up in his shit – but he couldn't stop himself from hoping. If he were truthful, that hope was the only thing that kept him putting one foot in front of the other through that long, agonising climb.

He wasn't sure how he'd ended up at Pig's Snout. One minute he was at Jaco's and all hell broke loose and next he was passing a sign saying *Birkenheadbaai 100 kilometres*. God knows what happened to the 600 kilometres in between.

When he reached the kloof it was getting dark but he could have climbed this kloof blindfold. All he had to do was keep to the track with the waterfall on his right. Bullseye whined urgently whenever Quent got too close to the falls. He grasped the dog's tail and let the animal pull him up on the slippery sections. He stumbled and slid on the loose shale and once, when he felt suddenly dizzy and nauseous, he grabbed at an overhanging branch to steady himself. It had broken away in his grasp and he had slithered sideways towards the edge. If the dog hadn't got between him and the sheer drop it would have been the end of him.

The last trace of the dipping sun vanished as he heaved himself over the rise and sank down, exhausted, into the scrubby fynbos. He was afraid to look at the house. Please God let there be smoke coming out of the chimney.

Steeling himself, he grabbed his stick, pulled himself upright and looked – nothing. No smoke curling out of the chimney. The front door swung backwards and forwards in the wind. The windows were blind. She wasn't there and he tasted disappointment like sour cherries in the back of his throat. But what had he expected? Did he really think she would be waiting for him, like she always did, with that resigned, gentle smile? Like all those other times he'd climbed the kloof, full of remorse and vowing never to hurt her again? She had always taken him back, looked after him, never asked where he'd been or who he'd been with.

While he gazed about him Bullseye went off to explore the familiar terrain, reclaiming his territory, glad to be home.

Raki and Quent had built the kloof house together. They'd used timber from the *Pig's Eye* and hauled it up the kloof by hand. Everything had to be carried up here. "A labour of love", she called it. It was his first real home, ever, but now it was an empty, dry shell and he hated it for still standing there, defying the elements. If he'd had a grenade he would have tossed it inside.

The Kloof House

As Raki struggled up the kloof two Hadedah ibis bickered noisily overhead. Raki stopped so that Farnie could watch them. 'See the funny birds, Farnie? They've got floppy wings haven't they?' Farnie nodded wisely. 'Like a pair of old black gloves? And listen, my love. What are they saying? *Ngahamba, ngahamba – I travel, I travel.* Silly birds, we know they're travelling, don't we? But they quarrel about everything.'

Farnie was sucking his thumb, preparing for sleep, but he took out his thumb and waved at the birds. He loved birds and monkeys and ants and anything that moved.

Raki thought about birthdays as she climbed. She was seventeen before she found out her birth date. As a child she thought she didn't have a special day and it was hard not to be jealous of her friends who had parties and presents on their birthdays. She began to think she was adopted or perhaps, more romantically, she'd been abandoned like a foundling in one of Charles Dickens's novels. But none of her family had birthdays either, not her two sisters nor her father or mother. She must have been about ten when she finally plucked up the courage to ask her mother.

Sofia van de Venter was at the kitchen sink washing spinach for dinner. Her back was to her youngest daughter – a very expressive back, her mother's. Raki waited patiently while she continued to rinse a spinach leaf to within an inch of its life. Disgusting black millipedes called shongalongas liked spinach and it wasn't nice to find one stuck between your teeth. When at last Raki's mother spoke, her voice was cold. She didn't look at her daughter. 'Do you know when our Lord was born, child?'

'The nativity, Moeder, everyone knows that but – '

'– That's the only birthday you need remember, girl. Your birthday is unimportant, just as you are.' And no more was said.

11

It was only when she needed her birth certificate to apply for a driving licence that she found out. Sofia didn't approve of young women driving but Raki's father, Desmond, taught her on the dirt roads that meandered through their farm. Eventually he gave her the old Renault that had stood in their yard for years gathering spider's webs and rust. Raki loved that car.

She and Farnie had crested the steep incline now and were on the level and almost home. At that moment Farnie shouted and pointed at the sky. Looking up, Raki saw a Jackal buzzard drifting on the thermals. She put down the struggling child and as soon as his feet touched the ground he clung onto her skirt with one hand and flapped the other one like a bird. As he flapped he screeched, *'Ka, ka ka,'* imitating the buzzard's call.

There was always a wind on the mountain and it caught the child's voice and flung it away. Raki's thin top was glued across her body and a long switch of black hair whipped across her face. She caught the child's excitement and added her own *'Ka, ka, ka'* to the sky.

Farnie shrieked again – more confidently this time. Raki pretended to be shocked and stuck her fingers in her ears. The boy was almost hysterical now and repeated the call over and over, drunk with the power of the sound. He attempted to flap both arms but fell forwards onto the springy turf and Raki snatched him up and carried him into the safety of the kloof house.

The house was plugged, mushroom-like, into the one slice of level ground on this side of the mountain. It was in the lee of a protective mound of rocks. The wind could blow as much as it liked up there but the Kloof house was secure.

It was a single-storied Cape Dutch building with two rooms facing downhill: a kitchen and a bedroom. There was a door and two windows opening out onto the stoep – a large patio area with a wooden veranda and railings surrounding it. There were shutters at the windows and the house had a

12

pitched roof and chimney, supported by timbers dragged laboriously up from the forest below. It was thatched with reeds from the stream. The kitchen had an open hearth and a Dutch oven with iron bars to hang pots on. The floor was compacted earth and the walls were made of clay and sealed with lime mortar ground from crushed sea shells. She and Quent had spent two days collecting shells from the nearest beach, ten kilometres away. There were still shards of shell embedded in the surrounding turf. Some were abalone and they shone out like milky pearls in the moonlight.

Sometimes at night Raki was sure she heard the far-off pounding of the sea.

They lived in a tent for the year it took to build the house. During that time Quent was often away, working in the next valley on Maarten Broot's farm. It was a sheep farm. There were five farm hands and Quent was farm manager.

Raki never minded being on her own. It was a hard life but she flourished. All the water had to be carried up from the stream and there was no sanitation. Eventually Quent built a compost toilet, although Raki never objected to going in the open air. They bathed in the stream and Raki washed up in a bowl on the kitchen floor. Every drop of waste water was saved for Raki's small veggie plot. She grew mealies, sorghum, potatoes and onions – anything that could survive the climate on the mountain. It was tough but Raki loved the freedom. There was no one to tell her what to do.

When she had time she would lie on her back in the fynbos and read one of her precious supply of books. She'd read them all many times but it didn't matter that she knew what was going to happen. The words were sweet to her. She'd wanted to go to college and teach literature but her mother wouldn't hear of it.

'A girl's destiny is to learn how to be a good housewife in preparation for the day a man chooses her to be the mother of his children,' she lectured. 'What do you need a job for? And besides, men don't like clever women.'

Raki never argued with her mother. It was pointless.

When Raki moved in with Quent, the kloof house and the mountain were her refuge. The only thing she dreaded were the occasional trips into town for provisions. She would do her errands as quickly as possible and escape. Once she saw her mother in the Spar and hung about, trying to pluck up the courage to speak to her, but when her mother saw her she looked straight through her, as if she didn't exist, and Raki abandoned her full trolley in the middle of an aisle and fled.

Raki and Quent weren't rich but they got by. Quent trapped game for the pot and Raki dried the meat for biltong. She cured the hides and made hand-worked leather bags, belts and boots, which her cousin, Mari, traded for her at the market in Birkenheadbaai. Raki couldn't face doing her own, she might bump into her mother or, worse still, she might meet her husband.

8.10 a.m.

Quent stares down into the valley. The baboons are quiet now; so the men must be through the *eye*.

He would have bet good money on them making their move last night. The whole of the valley had been lit up by a dazzlingly bright full moon – a Blue Moon. Folks said a blue moon was guaranteed to bring good luck to anyone who saw it but Quent had never had much faith in what *folks said* or *good luck*, come to that. From his look-out the light from the moon had thrown the profile of the *pig* into sharp relief, deepening the eye sockets into black, bottomless pits.

Why any sane person would choose to climb the kloof in the killing heat of day was a mystery to Quent. He had come up in the late afternoon, when the sun was going down. Of course, he thinks, smiling wryly, there's always the outside chance that they're frightened of him – of the old hippy. But he has few illusions. His days of scaring people are long gone and he sees himself through their eyes – a small, wiry man with weathered skin and long, thin, greying hair drawn back from his hollow cheeks into a straggly pony tail, his once-bright blue eyes now so sun-bleached they look almost white.

More likely, he reasons, they're frightened of climbing the kloof at night. They're strangers to this mountain, whereas Quent knows every stand of trees and jagged low branch. He remembers where the path becomes too overgrown and slippery to follow; where the safe places are to cross the waterfall and which bushes to avoid, where puff adders moon bathe.

Grabbing his stick, Quent heaves himself upright. The wound hurts like hell. A few years ago an injury like this would have healed in days, but not now. He waits until the pain subsides and then he hobbles to the door of the shack, where a flitch of muslin-covered biltong hangs. She hasn't let him down. The door is wide open but he hasn't been inside yet.

Quent hacks off a thick piece of kudu and tosses it to the dog. Bullseye jumps down from his rock and demolishes the meat. Quent cuts a small piece for himself and chews on it. It's an effort to swallow but he forces it down. Got to keep his strength up. Another glimmer of a smile.

He'd discovered a crate of booze pushed under the veranda. Maybe she'd been saving it for him. She was tee-total but she'd never stopped him drinking. Maybe it would have been better if she had. He's been drinking all night, anything to stop himself from thinking because every time he relaxes his guard, there it is again – that terrible jagged, bloody hole. That's when the wave of nausea hits him again; he's sweating, his mouth salivates and the blackness closes in around him.

The Christmas Market

Raki put the little boy on the floor while she filled the kettle and put it on to boil. She stowed the shopping and Farnie settled down to play with his stones. He had two buckets full and spent hours taking them out and arranging them in long lines across the kitchen floor. Sometimes he put them in order of size, sometimes by colour or whatever took his fancy. Raki was always stubbing her toes on them.

She unzipped her boots and stood them side by side. The sunlight warmed the soft leather into beaten gold. She loved those boots. Farnie had filled them up with his stones a few days ago and had had a huge tantrum when she emptied them out. 'No, Farnie,' she scolded, strict for once. 'These are Mama's best boots. See? I made them. Aren't they beautiful? Can you see the pretty stones down the side? Mama's going to make you a pair just like this one day. You'd like that wouldn't you?' But the child wasn't impressed.

She'd never throw those boots out. It was how she and Quent had met.

The Birkenheadbaai Christmas Market was held on the first Sunday in November. Mari traded there. She sold homemade pickles and preserves. This particular Christmas she asked Raki if she wanted to go halves with her on renting a stall. Raki's leather goods were very popular. However, it was the weekend she was supposed to make the family Christmas cake. Her mother had been pressurising her to get on with it.

But Mari was a very persuasive woman. 'You can make the stupid cake any time, Raki,' she coaxed. 'Come on, it'll be fun. We'll have a laugh and you can earn a bit of pocket money for Christmas. You don't have to tell Mr Turkey.'

Mari had always called Raki's husband Mr Turkey. Raki needed cash to buy all her nieces and nephews nice things for Christmas. Her husband didn't believe in wasting money on gifts for other people. However, he let it be known that he

17

had his eye on a particularly good first edition of Baden Powell's *Aids to Scouting*.

'A very acceptable Christmas gift,' he remarked on more than one occasion.'

Raki let Mari talk her into it. She'd always loved the Christmas market. When she was a child it had been the start of Christmas for her. The stalls were stocked with pretty Christmas gifts, and Father Christmas – a black man in a cotton-wool beard that kept slipping sideways around his ears – duly arrived driving a donkey cart. Gangs of unruly little kids played tag amongst the stalls while Father Christmas gave out little packets of sweets and water balloons and Bing Crosby's *I'm dreaming of a White Christmas* crackled out of ancient loudspeakers – as it had done all of Raki's life. It was always hot and the men stood about drinking beer while their women and children went from stall to stall.

Raki and Mari were doing a roaring trade – Raki had made children's purses, belts and bracelets in different colours and Mari had her special Christmas-edition preserves and chutneys. There was a beer and wine stall next to theirs where a group of men had been getting steadily rowdier and rowdier as the afternoon wore on. Raki had been brought up in a tee-total household and felt uncomfortable around drinkers. She didn't look at them and tried to ignore their loud, boisterous behaviour. Mari was the opposite and waved and shouted to them. Raki loved her cousin but she knew she was a flirt. One man came over with some beers. Mari took one and he offered one to Raki but she shook her head and looked away.

'My cousin doesn't drink,' Mari explained. 'She's the pastor's wife.'

The man laughed. 'What? Old Morgan? She definitely needs a drink then, maybe two.'

Mari laughed and tapped the man on his hand. 'You're a very naughty fella, Pierre. I'll tell Trudi if you're not careful.'

Raki watched the man return to the group and say something to his cronies. They all laughed and looked at her. She felt herself blushing. How dare they? She knew Henrik wasn't popular in the town but she didn't like them making

18

fun of him. She glared but they had forgotten all about her. They were grouped around a man who was telling them some story. He was smallish but well-built, dressed in army fatigues, boots and a black T-shirt. His long hair was tied back in a pony tail and he had a wide leather strap on his upper arm. When he raised the other arm to make some point she saw a tattoo of a leopard on his brown muscular arm. She had never seen anyone like him before and she must have been staring because he looked up suddenly and caught her eye. She felt something like an electric shock run through her. He smiled lazily before turning back to his cronies.

She was uneasy for the rest of the afternoon. Why on earth had she looked at him? What would she do if he came over and spoke to her? She looked around guiltily. Thank God none of her family was in sight and Henrik was out of town on one of his camping trips.

'Did you see that one giving me the eye?' her cousin asked. 'Cheeky devil.'

'Who?' Raki asked.

'Him, the old guy?' her cousin pointed to the man with the tattoo. 'Who does he think he is? Ruddy Rambo?'

Mari watched all the Hollywood movies.

'All he needs is one of those bandanna things wrapped round his head and he'd be the spitting image.'

'How old d'you think he is?' Raki asked casually, putting more belts and purses on the stall.

Mari shrugged, 'Ancient. Must be about fifty I'd say. Why?'

'No reason.'

He didn't look old to Raki. In fact compared to Mr Morgan he looked young. The man didn't come near her and by the end of the afternoon she knew she'd been stupid. Why would he be interested in her? It was ludicrous.

Mari was busy packing cartons of preserves into her car and Raki was struggling with a big box of her things when a pair of boots slipped off the top and fell to the ground. And suddenly there he was beside her.

19

He picked up the boots and examined them. 'Nice,' he said turning them over in his hands, examining the stitch-work. 'You make these?'

She nodded and waited for him to give them back.

'Beautiful workmanship,' he said, and smiled.

His teeth were so white and his eyes deep blue.She felt light-headed. *Please God, don't let me faint.*

'What size did you say they were?'

He was standing so close she could smell his faint, musky, male smell. He squatted on the ground at her feet and took off one of his boots and then pulled on the new one. It was too big for him but he pulled on the other one and scrambled up, looking down admiringly at them. 'How much?'

'But they don't fit,' she said. 'I could make a pair your size if I took a pattern of your feet.'

'No, these are fine,' he said, smiling again. 'They fit like a glove.'

She was sure he was making fun of her and she blushed with embarrassment. 'I've got to go. Can I have them back, please?' She felt her eyes pricking with tears.

He saw her awkwardness and immediately took off the boots, put on his own and tucked the others down into the box. 'Allow me,' he said, taking the box off her. 'Where's your car?'

'I live over there,' she said, pointing across the street.

Without another word he marched ahead of her and left the box on her doorstep before giving her a mock salute and striding away to join the group of men heading for the pub.

She didn't expect to see him again but in the following week he seemed to pop up everywhere. First time was in the Spar, then the post office, the library...on the street. They never spoke but she knew he was watching her and if he caught her looking at him he always smiled. The biggest surprise was when he came to church the following Sunday and sat directly behind her. Mr Morgan was preaching and Raki was trying to concentrate. Mr Morgan liked to have a post mortem about his sermon afterwards, not that he wanted the truth, he just

20

needed to know how marvellous he was. All she had to do was get the general gist – nothing too detailed – and he would be satisfied. That Sunday, however, she was having problems even remembering to breathe. She could feel the man behind her as if there was some electrical charge connecting them.

He was dressed in the same clothes he wore when she saw him at the market and was totally out of place in the church. She could hear the *buzz* as people whispered behind their hymn books. Raki was ashamed of her fellow parishioners and plucked up the courage to smile at him when she passed him the offertory plate. He took the plate and winked at her.

When Raki came out of the church the man had disappeared.

Groups of women were gathered in the sun for their usual Sunday gossip. There was only one topic on the agenda that day. Raki stood with Mari, while Raki's older sisters, Gloria and Madre, made spiteful remarks about the man. All of the men except for Pastor Morgan and Raki's father were in the pub opposite, watching the rugby. Desmond van de Venter wanted to be there too but he knew better. Mr Turkey was in the middle of a bunch of admiring women. Sofia was holding court and congratulating the pastor on his wonderful sermon. Thank goodness someone had been listening.

Her oldest sister Gloria's loud voice intruded on her thoughts.

'– And did you see that dreadful tattoo on his arm? What does he think he looks like? You'd think he would have covered it up in church. I don't know what Mr Morgan must have thought. The man should have – '

'– Shown some respect,' Madre, her other sister, added. She always finished off her older sister's sentences for her.

'It was that guy from the market.' Mari hissed in Raki's ear.

'Really?' Raki pretended to blow her nose.

But Mari wasn't going to be put off. She dug her friend in the ribs. 'Raki? I'm talking to you. Has he been bothering you?'

Raki gave her cousin a surprised look and shook her head. But inside she wanted to shout *yes*, at the top of her voice. This man was definitely 'bothering' her, only not in the way her cousin meant. He hadn't spoken to her since that day at the market but she thought about him all the time. And when she saw him her heart lurched and her mouth went dry. She lay awake for hours each night imagining what she would say to him and what he'd say to her. For the first time since she was a teenager and had that crush on Anton she had a sexy dream. Yes, he was definitely bothering her.

'Raki? Are you sure?' Mari looked worried. 'Only Quent Byrant's got a bad reputation. Pierre's wife Trudi says he runs a string of women. He especially likes blacks. Raki? Why are you smiling? This isn't funny.'

Raki bit her lip and tried to look serious, but the corners of her mouth kept twitching. Quent Byrant. She liked the sound of it. It suited him. It was unusual. He looked like a Quent. She wondered what he would think of her name. Maybe he wouldn't like it? But he could call her whatever he wanted. She didn't care.

Gloria's voice rose from the group. '– And did you see the size of that knife stuck in his belt? Wearing that in –'

' – in God's House. Disgusting.' Madre's mouth turned down at the corners as if she was eating something extremely unpleasant.

For the first time in years Raki felt happy and while her sisters' voices droned on she concentrated on the cobbled path. The sunlight bounced off the whitish stone and swallows spiralled overhead, gorging on air-borne insects. Summer began when the swallows arrived. They nested in the eaves of the old barns around their farm. It never ceased to amaze Raki that such small creatures could travel all the way from England to South Africa, through raging storms, drought and dodging trigger-happy Europeans to get to exactly the same dot on the map every year.

Raki had never been further than Cape Town when she went for her grandmother's funeral. She'd been too young to remember much about the city except that they had strawberry milkshakes and pizza and her feet hurt because she had to wear shoes.

'I'm only thinking of you, Raki,' Mari hissed in her ear. 'Please be careful. He's the sort of guy to avoid, believe me. I know.'

But Raki wasn't listening. She was somewhere else on a cloud of her imaginings. Surely he must like her if he'd followed her into the church? She was saying his name over and over in her head. Quent Byrant. *Raki loves Quent. Quent loves Raki. Raki=Quent.* She knew she was behaving like an adolescent but she couldn't help it.

'He's bad news,' Mari droned on. 'And I know what a little innocent you are.'

Suddenly Raki had had enough of Mari's lecturing. 'For goodness sake, Mari,' she snapped, turning to face her cousin and frowning. 'I can look after myself.'

'I'm just warning you. Don't be so bad-tempered.'

Raki was indignant. 'I'm not bad tempered but what gives you the right to lecture me? I'm a married woman in case you've forgotten.' And then she'd stalked off with her nose in the air.

The next day Raki left the house early to do some shopping. Mr Morgan was out visiting his parishioners and she was in a hurry to buy the ingredients for the Christmas cake. She must make it today. It was only the second year that Sofia had entrusted her with this special job and she was still a bit nervous, although, of course, she followed her mother's recipe down to the last currant, soaked for twenty-four hours in sherry – medicinal of course.

She locked the front door and as she turned around there he was, Quent Byrant, sitting on the wall, waiting for her. She almost went straight back inside but he must have seen her hesitation because he jumped down from the wall and came towards her, smiling.

'I've decided to order a pair of boots, Mrs Morgan. You will need to take a pattern from my feet.'

Her throat felt dry and she wasn't sure she could speak. 'Yes,' she managed. 'But...' and she coughed to clear her throat, 'but I can't make them before Christmas.' Her courage failed her then. 'And I'm afraid I have to go shopping now. Maybe you could come back later?' she added, 'when my husband's in?' She was safe in the knowledge that Mr Morgan would never allow a man like Quent Byrant across his threshold. Then she walked quickly down the steps. She had to get away from him.

'That's okay, I can wait,' he said, following her. He swung open the door of his bakkie and held out his hand to her, smiling. Those eyes again. She looked away, unable to return his gaze. 'Maybe I can offer you a lift to the shops, Mrs Morgan?'

They both looked across the street at the Spar supermarket – the only food store in town -- and then back at each other and Raki felt the moment stretching away. Finally, someone said, 'That would be nice.'

She took his hand and allowed him to help her up into the passenger seat. Her hand was trembling but his grasp was warm and strong and she felt a tingling sensation shoot right through her body. Mari had told her about the first time she'd held Anton's hand and how it was the sexiest thing she'd ever experienced. Back then Raki had no idea what she was talking about, but now she knew.

'Where to?' Quent asked as he got in beside her and leant across her to close the door. She smelt the maleness of him and as his hair brushed against her lips she had an overwhelming urge to kiss it. He sat back in the seat and looked at her. 'Cat got your tongue, beautiful lady?'

'Beautiful'? He'd called her beautiful. Her smile was dazzling. 'I don't care where we go, Mr Quent Byrant, just drive.'

He touched his fingers to his forehead in a mock salute. 'Whatever you say, Mrs Raki Morgan.'

As they drove slowly down the high street she saw several people she knew and waved. It was hard not to laugh at their slack-jawed incredulity and she watched them in the side-mirror as they dispersed in all directions like clucking chickens after a genet raid on their coop. *Pastor Morgan's wife is in Quent Byrant's bakkie and they're heading out of town.*

Raki wasn't sure what was happening to her but one thing was certain. Her life would never be the same again. She was so glad.

8.15 a.m.

Quent is running: oblivious to everything but the need to escape from the thing that is crashing through the undergrowth behind him. It is close, very close, and his body tenses, waiting for the slashing claws. *Never run from a predator. Never run...* Thorns rip at his flesh and panicking birds erupt about him, lobbing their frantic alarm calls into the sky. He is barefoot and devil thorns have punctured his skin. Each time his foot hits the dirt an excruciating pain shoots up his leg and into his brain. His long, sweat-sodden hair whips into his eyes and his thirst is terrible. His swollen tongue lies stranded at the bottom of his mouth. If he doesn't find water soon he's done for, but he can't stop running, he must never stop running. His heart is hammering so loudly he's certain the whole world must hear.

His backpack is too heavy – 30 kilos of red-painted bricks – and the shoulder straps dig deep into his flesh. If he can only get rid of that weight everything will be okay, because then he could run faster. But the pack is part of his orders and you have to obey orders or... He's forgotten what happens if you disobey, all he knows is that it's something very bad – worse than the nightmare behind him, worse than his thirst.

If he'd been looking where he was going he would have seen the overhanging branch but he doesn't and it knocks him off his feet. He lies stretched out on the ground with the burning sun drilling into his eyes. He throws up an arm to shield his face and that's when a black shadow passes across the sun, blotting it out, and he is staring up into the eyes of a large animal. His terror disappears. No more running, no more anything, just a quick end. *Thank Christ it's all over.*

The animal shakes its massive head, releasing a crown of biting flies and Quent hears a bell – a cow-bell. The animal lowers its head to sniff inquisitively at him and then skitters away, spooked by Quent's rank smell. Another, smaller face takes the animal's place – a boy's face.

A young slender child stands over Quent. He is holding a switch and he flicks it against the cow's rump. The animal lumbers away. 'Hi, Quent? Got some cola?'

'No,' Quent groans. 'Leave me be.'

'Quent,' the voice wheedles. 'Got some cola? You promise. If I was good. You promise.'

'No...' Quent buries his face in his hands. 'You're not real. For pity's sake. Leave me.'

But the child is relentless. 'It's me, Quent. Tabo. Have you forgotten your boy so soon?'

'No more, I beg you.'

'You're my friend. Quent. You said you'd look after me, remember? Nothing bad will happen to me, not if Quent is my friend. Why don't you look at me? Remember your boy. Look at my face.'

'Dear Lord, no.' His eyes focus on the child's face. All he has to do is concentrate on the smiling mouth and white, even teeth then everything will be okay. But Quent feels his concentration slipping...

'I am so thirsty, Quent. Give me some drink.'

Quent's gaze is slipping upwards, past the smiling mouth and the white, even teeth, then onto the small perfect nose and now... and now, he's staring into that jagged bloody hole, where the boy's eye should be.

When Quent comes to he's lying on his back in a pool of vomit, reeking of rancid beer. It's the terrible pain from his leg that wakes him but he's still in the nightmare and is fighting to remember what's real. He turns his head apprehensively, expecting to see the boy, but there's nothing. He feels the dog pressed up against him, whining and scratching at his hand.

'No, man,' Quent orders weakly.

His heart is pounding but he rolls over and struggles into a kneeling position. He waits a few moments gathering his strength and then presses down on the boards. But when he attempts to stand his hands slip on the puke. The dog is beside him still, his worried eyes fixed on Quent.

'Okay, Bullseye. I need you, okay?' He feels the dog stiffen as he rests one hand on the animal's broad back and presses down. 'Okay boy.' Then he places his other hand around the veranda support and heaves himself up to standing. Once upright he feels sick again but he lowers his head and waits until the nausea passes. Bullseye is still beside him. 'Good boy, lie down now.' The dog obediently drops on its haunches a few metres away, head resting on his paws, eyes never leaving Quent.

Quent pulls off his vomit splattered T-shirt, balls it up and tosses it over the railings. What's happening to him? He's never passed out when he's thrown up before. The taste in his mouth is foul. What he needs is a wash and to find something clean to wear but first he needs to rinse his mouth out. Hooking his stick into the torn plastic on the carton of water bottles he drags it to within reach. Ten bottles left. Enough, if he goes easy.

He drains one bottle and sticks another under his free arm, then he hobbles towards the house. It will take a lot more than a drink of water to get rid of the nightmare. He stands in the doorway for a moment swaying in the half-light, waiting until his eyes adjust to the dim light; then he shuffles inside. There is a curling tongue of dried-up soap by the washing-up bowl and he pours a small amount of water into his hands and works the soap until he manages to squeeze out a few weak suds, enough to wash his face and hands with.

After drying himself on a scrap of old towel he walks further into the kitchen. He feels like he's trespassing. This is Raki's place now, her home. He tries to remember her message. She needed money urgently? A lot of money – R10,000. No mention of what it was for, just that she had to have it as soon as possible. He guessed the money would be for the kid. Raki would never ask for money for herself.

It's obvious that she'd left the place in a hurry. There are dirty pans in the washing-up bowl and unwashed dishes on the table, now crawling with ants. Raki hated mess. Everything had to be just so for her. She had standards. *We may live in a shack on top of a mountain, Quent, but there's no need for us to live like*

28

pigs. She was a very methodical woman. Sometimes it drove him crazy. She was forever putting things away so he could never find anything. She made plans and wrote lists.

There's one of her lists pinned to the central wooden pole. He takes it down but the flowery writing is faded. On the floor beside the pole are Raki's best boots. They are placed carefully on the threadbare mat, heel to toe, heel to toe, just like she'd been dancing when she took them off. She always wore those boots, made them herself from the softest Bok hide. She had a nasty scar on her wrist where the heavy-duty needle had sprung out of the leather. It must have hurt like hell but she didn't cry at things like that; it was only people that made her cry. People like him. He picked up one boot and kneaded the soft leather between his thumb and forefinger and then held it against his nose. The rich smell of leather helped mask his own stink. His spirits rose. It was a good sign, wasn't it? She must mean to come back if she'd left her best boots behind.

That's when he sees it, a mirror – on a nail, hanging beside the list. A mirror with a gilt frame. He turns the glass towards him and sees the look of incredulity on his face. That is his face, isn't it? But his hair isn't so grey. Okay, he has a few grey hairs but this old guy is almost white. Quent puts his hand up to the glass and there it is. He recognises the mottled skin and the slight tremor. He grabs the mirror and hurls it against the wall. Shards of glass explode in all directions and he feels the slash as one piece cuts into his leg. What in Christ's name has Raki got a mirror for? She never cared what she looked like – not even for him. So, what was this about? Was there some new guy? Someone she needed to impress? That's when he started to laugh. It wasn't a nice sound: it was hysterical and high pitched. He'd heard mad people laugh like this and he made himself stop.

Quent goes further into the room, crunching over the broken glass and something else. He looks down. There's a line of shiny pebbles, covered with leaves, bisecting the floor. You left a door or window open in the Cape and South Africa blew inside. He can smell her in this room. It's a warm, musky scent, not exactly perfume but pleasing. In the early days he

29

had bought her some proper scent. Thought she'd like it. It was in a pink bottle with imitation roses on the top – crap. He bought it for the packaging. In his experience that's what women liked. But it didn't take him long to discover that Raki wasn't "women". He still remembered the look she'd given him when he handed it over. She had pushed it back into his hands. 'Save it for one of your fancy women, Quent,' she'd said, without a trace of malice.

And he had.

But why the mirror? He had no right to question how she was living, he knew that. He'd given up any claim when he'd walked out on her. And even if she'd been here what would he have said? Sorry? You could be forgiven anything in the new squeaky-clean *Justice and peace* South Africa: gang-raping little kids, torturing old women, killing and maiming anyone who looked at you in the wrong way – anything – just so long as you said you were sorry. But *sorry* didn't do it for Quent. He knew there were some things that could never be forgiven. *Mea culpa, mea culpa, mea maxima culpa.*

Disgrace

Bored with the pebbles, Farnie was doggedly pursuing a trail of ants across the kitchen floor. Raki gave him a rusk while she poured their tea.

As she watched her son her mind drifted back to the day when her life changed forever. Quent had driven her to Pig's Snout Kloof. He had put some loud music on in the car and sang along to it – very badly. When she looked at him he turned his head and grinned. 'Opera trained, my voice.'
'I don't think so,' she said, smiling.
'You okay? Want to go back?'
She shook her head. 'No. Lead on Mcduff.'
He laughed out loud at that.

It was the first time she'd been to the kloof. She'd seen it from the road, of course, but had never explored it. Quent showed her where he and the old woman had once lived and the rondavel which was still standing, belonging to his old maid, Eunice. Quent's voice softened when he talked about Eunice.
They scrambled up the path until they reached the place where the waterfall divided and plunged down into a deep reddish-black foaming pool at the base of the cliff. They sat on a hot, flat boulder in the sun as the torrent swept down on either side of them. He had brought some *wors*, bread and beer. She drank the beer – her first. It was nice.
After they'd eaten he stripped off and clambered down to the pool. Raki didn't have time to be shocked. He did it so quickly she barely had time to take it in. He swam like a fish, his body plunging through the red peaty water, the sunlight flickering on the bubbles clinging to his lean, strong limbs.
She had never undressed in front of a man, not even her father, and certainly not Mr Morgan. Her husband had never been in the bedroom when she got into bed. But she wasn't embarrassed with Quent and even though she knew he was

watching her she pulled her clothes over her head, left them in a neat pile on the rock and climbed down into the cold, orange water. He opened his arms and she stepped into his embrace as naturally as if she'd been waiting all her life for this moment. He took her hair out of its tight band and then they made love. Raki knew for sure then that what she and Mr Morgan had done for all those years was not making love at all. Compared to this banquet of sensuality her marital sexual encounters were a poor, undernourished cousin of meagre necessity.

Back in Birkenheadbaai Sofia had spent the day comforting poor Henrik, who had returned early from his pastoral duties, only to find that his wife was missing. He was very upset, so much so in fact that he could only force down one bowl of the delicious soup that his mother-in-law had made, plus two avocado and chicken sandwiches and a small slice of her coffee-torte. Sofia hovered over him while he forced down a schooner of sherry – *for shock*.

Sofia was as near to desperation as she was capable of. Nothing like this had ever happened in her family before and she was so outraged by her daughter's behaviour that she wished the girl was gone for good. Mr Morgan didn't say much but she knew he was suffering dreadfully.

Sofia had begged the pastor to come and sleep at the farm that night but he refused. He couldn't leave his home, he told her, not where his beloved mother had died, not even for one night, it wouldn't be right. If truth were told he also hoped that Raki stayed away. He should never have married the woman in the first place but he had thought it was his charitable duty to take her off Sofia's hands. Raki van de Venter stood little chance of getting a husband otherwise.

'You're too good for your own sake, Henrik,' his mother used to say on a regular basis, patting his hand. 'Much, much too good.'

He went to bed at the usual time and was just dropping off when he heard a vehicle draw up outside. He sighed heavily, turned off the light, and lay there planning her punishment.

The town had been seething with gossip all day at the wanton behaviour of the Pastor's wife and Quent Byrant – of all people. Those that knew him said *Bad blood will out* and those that didn't had heard rumours about Quent from people like Trudi and other women of the town.

Several citizens of Birkenheadbaai stayed up late in the hope of witnessing Mrs Morgan's return. However, they were in for a disappointment. There were no passionate embraces and certainly no fond farewells or blown kisses, not even a wave. No, it was all extremely unsatisfactory and hardly worth the inconvenience. Mrs Morgan and *that* man didn't even speak to one another. She got straight out of the bakkie and went inside without a backward glance. He drove off immediately.

By morning Henrik Morgan had planned appropriate chastisement for his erring wife. They ate their breakfast in silence with neither of them looking at each other. He didn't ask any questions or yell at her; it was as if nothing had happened. But if she thought for one moment he was going to forgive and forget she was badly mistaken.

Raki's *punishment* began on the first Sunday after Raki's jaunt with Quent. She was always the first in church and sat in her customary place in the front pew – the Van de Venter pew. That's where the family always sat but not today. This Sunday Sofia and the others sat several rows behind Raki and most of the rest of the congregation followed suit. Some brave ones felt sorry for Raki and moved into the pew behind her.

Pastor Morgan chose to base his sermon on *the woman taken in adultery* and he delivered the text directly at his wife. This Sunday set the pattern for each subsequent Sabbath. Raki suffered the humiliation stoically.

Mari wasn't a keen churchgoer. She went when she felt like it but, when she got to hear about what was happening to Raki, she went to church the next Sunday and sat close beside her, glaring at Morgan whenever he looked their way. Raki didn't want her cousin to suffer for her sake but Mari refused to leave her friend. It was Raki's secret that kept her going and not one of these so-called Christians would ever get it out of her.

Raki lost count of how many slights she had to suffer during this time but she didn't mind because she didn't regret one single second of that wonderful day with Quent. She would have gladly born the shame and humiliation for the rest of her days.

Desmond van de Venter stood by her in the only way he could. He stopped going to church. He never spoke to Raki about what had happened but it was comforting for Raki to know that in his own quiet way he was on her side. Her mother and sisters totally refused to speak to her or have anything to do with her. But the worst thing that happened was that she was deprived of the company of her little nieces and nephews. Raki loved all of the children so much and they loved her.

The town had been awash with gossip ever since the pastor's wife had driven off with *that man Byrant* but when her husband didn't throw her out the whole thing was soon forgotten. Raki never told anyone what had happened that day, not even Mari. Sofia and Mr Morgan refused to demean themselves by demanding an explanation. It wasn't necessary. She had been judged and found wanting.

Some of the more forgiving members of the community thought that the Quent-thing had been a moment of madness on Raki's part. *'Maybe she's starting the change early'*, one said – not unkindly. The menopause often made women act strangely.

The town might have thought it was a *storm in a teacup* but Sofia wasn't fooled. She kept a wary eye on her daughter, especially when Mr Morgan was out of town. She made sure that the entire Van de Venter clan were on red alert. Raki's sisters dropped by the pastor's house for no particular reason and stayed for hours. They had never visited before. Unlike their mother they made it clear that they didn't like Mr

Morgan. He took far too much of their mother's time – *time* which rightly belonged to their families.

Raki seemed oblivious to what was going on and settled back into her normal routine. No one would have guessed that she had a secret. She was going to run away with Quent. It was all planned. Outwardly she might appear to be the same, calm, quiet person she had always been, but inside she was like a wild animal waiting for release. She had perfect trust in Quent. He had told her he was coming for her and she believed him. He had promised. The only thing Raki had insisted on was that she chose the day.

Pastor Morgan enjoyed the new respect his parishioners gave him. He had proved himself to be a good man, almost a saintly man, although that wasn't for him to say of course. Outwardly he treated his erring wife in much the same way he had always done, except now he didn't speak at all. If he wanted to communicate something he wrote her a note and left it pinned on his notice board. Inside the house he made it perfectly clear that she was a non-person. Raki acknowledged that she had sinned and it was right that she should be punished. This was what she had been brought up to believe. You reaped what you sowed.

The run up to Christmas went on as usual. Quent had disappeared from the neighbourhood, to the general relief of all those concerned, and Pierre wouldn't be drawn as to his friend's whereabouts.

He's had his fun and moved on. That was the general consensus.

But how wrong they were, because Quent wasn't very far away at all.

Farnie had finished his rusk now and was scuttling towards his mother as fast as he could. 'Mama,' he said, pointing at the tin. She watched as he did his funny crawl-thing, putting one hand down and shuffling sideways on his bottom. He'd been doing this particular variation of crawling for a week or two. She was going to the free baby-clinic in town tomorrow and she thought she might mention it to the nurse. It was probably nothing but it wouldn't do any harm to ask.

The boy was side-tracked by some ants carrying away the crumbs from his rusk. He put a plump finger across the marching line and it divided into two, then four, and on and on. There was such a look of concentration on his little face it made Raki smile. She went to the cupboard and put three packages on the floor in front of him. He sat for ages, staring at the gifts as if he wasn't quite sure what he was supposed to do with them. Finally he looked up at her and she nodded.

'Yes, Farnie. They're yours. Shall Mama help you?'

She had wrapped the presents in some glossy pages from an old magazine. Once the child had exhausted all the play possibilities of the colourful paper, he discovered what was inside. There was a book about animals that Mari had found on the second-hand bookstall at the market, some wooden blocks and a leather satchel that Raki had made for him to collect things in. He was always picking up stones, seed heads and flowers and now he would have somewhere to store them. He examined each item minutely, turning the bricks slowly over, as if expecting to find something amazing on the other side. She built brick towers for him and he knocked them down as if it was the funniest game in the world. When at last he'd had enough he put the bricks in his satchel.

Raki knew her family wouldn't give Farnie anything but there was a bag of hand-me-down clothes from Mari and a card with a glittery 'One' on it with a R50 note tucked inside. Raki's cousin was the only member of her family who still talked to her. Maybe it was because she was the only one who wasn't scared of Sofia. Mari wouldn't stand any nonsense from anyone. Raki had always been closer to Mari than her own sisters who were much older than she was and had married and left home before she was a teenager.

The cousins went to the same school, sat behind each other in class, started their periods in the same week and at fourteen had fallen in love with the same handsome boy. But that's where the similarity ended. Mari was voluptuous, even back then, and had a pretty face with blonde, almost white hair, blue eyes and skin that tanned beautifully. Raki was slender with bee-sting breasts. Her black hair was straight and thick and she usually wore it scraped away from her face in a pony-tail. Her nose was aquiline, her mouth strong and her brown, almost black eyes were deep-set and wary. When the cousins were twenty Mari married Anton, the boy they'd both fancied at school, and five years later Raki married Henrik Morgan.

Raki fetched a milk tart and set it down in front of Farnie; then she placed a candle stub in the middle and lit it. Farnie's eyes widened in delight and Raki saw the flame's twin image in his pupils. He clapped his hands together and shouted excitedly while she sang *Happy Birthday*. The little boy gazed at the flickering spurts of light in amazement; then he thrust his hand out to touch the flame. Raki held his fingers and kissed them. 'Blow it out, sweetheart,' she encouraged. 'Blow it out and make a wish.' She made a *whooshing* noise and the candle flame flickered.

Farnie copied her. *Whish, whish*, he puffed, and the candle was out. He was mesmerized for a moment and then shrieked with laughter. 'Again, again,' he ordered, and she lit the candle and he blew it out until it disappeared in a pool of wax on top of the tart. The little boy's face was bright with joy. Such a small thing and yet it had given him so much pleasure. This was the moment to cry but Raki sniffed back the tears and smiled at the boy.

Farnie was laughing. He had picked up his animal book again and was holding it upside down, looking at the picture of a pig.

'Oink, oink,' said Raki, helpfully.

The child gave her a look that was almost scornful. He pointed an imperious finger out of the window, towards the valley below. His pig didn't say *oink oink* at all.

8.20 a.m.

Quent hitches up a chair and sits down heavily. His legs are trembling. The urge to find something clean and warm to wear is strong but he doesn't have the energy – not yet – and the nightmare is still there in his head, like a rolling-news report.

Me and Pierre had been on night patrol. It was daybreak. We were a kilometre out from camp when we spotted a cloud of dust coming towards us down the hillside. As it got nearer we saw it was a young kid driving some scrawny cattle. He looked innocent enough but we were taking no chances. We followed him through the bush. He had ten cows – all that lean, rangy breed that were popular in the bush. These animals would eat anything and could survive the worst of conditions. Not much meat on them but they were the village's wealth, supplying everything needed for survival: milk, meat, skins for clothes and sinew for ropes.

We were on high alert since John Dreyer was killed. He was our corporal – a solid guy. A couple of weeks back two village boys had wandered into our camp. They seemed friendly enough and we let them stay. We made contacts where we could. The kids shared food with us and then they went back to their village. That night we got hit hard and John Dreyer died. He'd been in the SADF with Pierre. A fair man and a good soldier. The guerrillas knew our exact position and that information could only have been passed on from those kids.

After Dreyer was hit we broke camp and high-tailed it – putting as much distance as we could between us and the ambush location. We left Dreyer. No time to bury him. Eventually we holed up and radioed base. There were four of us left, Pierre, me and two blacks – Herbert Chalapo and Abel Charous. Pierre and I trusted those guys, we'd been through a lot together but suddenly we were suspicious of everyone. I even caught Pierre giving me a sidelong glance, like he wasn't sure about me. We thought things couldn't get any worse but then the new corporal showed. He was an Afrikaner called Jaco du Plessis.

On the morning in question, we were taking no chances and trailed the boy. He was thin and small, about nine or ten by the look of him. He had this T-shirt on with some Heavy Metal rock band on the front and a pair of shorts with his backside showing through the seat. He stood in a clearing, one foot resting against the other leg, picking his teeth with a piece of twig. We watched him pee against a termite mound and followed him to a pool where he let the animals drink. Then he led them to a swathe of new fresh vegetation to browse. All the time he was moving closer and closer to our camp.

There's no way he could have pretended the shock on his face when he ambled into the clearing and found himself surrounded by five heavily-armed men. He hid his face behind his hands for a moment and then he clicked his tongue and hit the lead cow a resounding whack on her rump with his bendy switch, trying to get her to turn and lead the other cows away.

But he wasn't going anywhere. All exits were blocked. He gave us a grin and held his hands up, palm facing outwards, in a gesture of friendship. He said something in some local Shona dialect and Abel — our interpreter — translated. He said his name was Tabo and he had to get back with the cows before it got too hot. He looked down at the ground as he spoke but he was taking everything in. He didn't seem afraid. This boy was used to war.

Du Plessis ordered us to drive the cattle back along the path, in the direction where the boy had come from. As soon as the kid saw what we were doing he went wild. He ran after us beating at us with his fists and screaming hysterically. I didn't need a translator to know what he was saying. The cows were his responsibility; he would be shamed if he lost them and his village would be ruined. I grabbed him and hustled him back to the camp.

Du Plessis was waiting. He had a length of rope in his hands and he'd made a noose in one end. He thumped it down against the palm of his other hand as he spoke. 'You shut his trap now, private. Or we string him up. Understand?'

This man's reputation had gone before him and we knew he wasn't bluffing, so I unknotted the bandanna around my neck and gagged the boy. It had to be very tight. It hurt him but I couldn't take the chance of him making a noise. After that I tied his hands behind his back.

We broke camp quickly. The boy refused to stand and his frightened eyes were huge as I swung him onto my shoulders. Pierre and me took it in turns to carry him. He seemed to have given up hope and lay limply across our shoulders like a rooster on its way to market.

39

We kept going all that day, taking on water and chewing dried meat as we went. I tried to get the boy to drink but his lips were clenched tight shut. It was dusk when we halted on the outskirts of a 'friendly village' but Du Plessis wasn't taking any chances and he sent our two black guys in to do a reccy. I put the boy down on the ground and he curled himself into a ball — like a centipede.

We set up camp and when Abel and Herbert returned they had the village elders with them. They brought food and water. One of the men noticed the boy and said something to Abel. Apparently he recognised the child and said he was from a neighbouring friendly village. He vouched for his good name.

Jaco told us to untie the boy and give him food and drink. The man promised to keep the boy and return him to his own village the next day, but Jaco wasn't having any. He said we'd keep the boy with us. None of us liked this new swaggering corporal but we knew to our cost that we couldn't trust anyone.

The boy was happy to see the villagers and when we took his gag off he ate the mealie-pap and gulped down some water. As he ate his eyes darted first from me and then to Pierre, as if he still couldn't quite believe he was alive. I smiled and got a can of coke out of my backpack. I handed it over and from the look in the boy's eyes I knew I'd made a friend for life.

Abel was on watch that night. At dawn we found him dead, with his throat cut. He wore a collar of black flies and his sightless eyes were smiling up at us. The boy screamed and he wouldn't stop so we had to gag him again. I thought we'd leave him there but Du Plessis had other ideas. Pierre and me hustled him along between us, until he couldn't run anymore and then we carried him. He was muttering something into my neck, the same phrase over and over again. I think it was a prayer.

They could have killed all of us that night and taken the boy but they were toying with us, showing us their strength, wanting us to know fear. And they succeeded. We were all scared shitless. Du Plessis was in front as we jogged away from that camp. We left Abel to the flies.

At last we got within a few kilometres of our unit's base camp and Du Plessis halted in a clearing. We were under a baobab tree. No one spoke. We just sank down onto our haunches and stared at the ground. Du Plessis was busy. He got out the rope and flung one end over a branch of the tree. We all watched him but it didn't register. It was only when he kicked the boy and told him to sit up that I saw the look in his eyes.

I tried to stop him, Pierre tried too, but it was no good. He was going to hang the boy. He ordered us to do it, but none of us moved, so he grabbed Tabo and made him stand while he put the noose around his neck. He was like a man possessed. I couldn't let him do it could I? I couldn't let that little boy suffer and be left there swinging from that tree for the vultures and hyenas to feast on? And suddenly the gun was in my hand. He turned his face to stare at me and I shot him in the head – through his eye.

I murdered a child.

Jaco swore and screamed, said the gunfire would bring all the terrorists down on us. Said he'd get me court-marshalled. But I didn't care. I dug a hole, wrapped Tabo in my blanket, and laid him to rest.

Then we moved on, to the next village, to the next child– who liked coca-cola and smiled at me though trusting, big eyes.

Mari to the Rescue

The over-excited little boy refused to close his eyes that night until he'd 'read' his animal book over and over again. He finally fell asleep sitting bolt upright with the book propped beside him on his pillow and his satchel clutched tightly in his hands.

Raki went outside and sat in the old chair, watching the sunset. She was exhausted but happy and rested her head on the back of the chair as the white-hot sun plunged from sight. The sky was a shifting, dissolving pattern of coloured light. If Raki altered her gaze slightly that seemingly indestructible band of orange became a pink fluffiness that bled into a green stripe that became a dark mouth that spewed out gouts of brick-red cloud. It was an amazing evening. One to be hoarded against the days and nights of wild battering wind, rain and mist that would surely come now it was autumn.

Raki tried not to think too much about what lay ahead. It was already hard work carrying Farnie up and down the rock-strewn path to her house, but in the winter, with the threat of flooding and mud-slides, she knew it would be well-nigh impossible. Added to this Farnie would be walking by then. Last winter he'd been a baby and she was breast-feeding so it was comparatively easy. They had stayed warm and dry inside the house while the tempests raged about them.

While she was pregnant she'd collected and chopped wood so that the wood-pile was stacked high. She also made sure that there were adequate food supplies. The money that Quent left her had to last a very long time but now it was gone. Mari traded Raki's leather goods at the market but the tourist season was over now. Next summer she would have nothing to trade because she'd used all the animal hides. She couldn't bring herself to trap game. The last flitch of dried meat hung on the veranda and their diet had become almost vegetarian, except for the eggs and cheese she bought and the bits and pieces Mari gave her. Raki saw to it that Farnie never went hungry.

Looking back it was hard to imagine how she'd got through those first terrible months after Quent left her. No one knew she was pregnant. Everything seemed hopeless and the panic she felt overwhelmed her. But bit by bit she managed to drag herself out of her apathy and one day when her morning-sickness was slightly better, she scrambled down the kloof to where her car was parked on the old CLP site. She could get reception down there and she rang Mari. Mari didn't answer so she left a message.

Er...are you there, Mari? A long pause *I'm having a baby, Mari.* Raki's voice broke and she cleared her throat. *Don't worry. I'm fine. I just wanted to tell you. Bye, Mari.* Silence. *Oh, and it's me. Raki.* Then she switched off and sat in the car, breathing in the old comforting smells of warm leather. It always soothed her. It was safe and warm and she got in the back seat, settled down and closed her eyes.

When she married Mr Morgan her car was left in one of her father's barns. She wanted to keep it but Mr Morgan insisted that running two cars was an unnecessary expense and where would his wife want to go anyway? Everything she needed was provided in Birkenheadbaai.

After she moved in with Quent it was a different story. He often went off for days on end and she had no way of getting into the local shops when she needed supplies. Quent said she should get her car back but she couldn't face confronting her parents. The only way was to get it while they were out.

So, she and Quent made a plan to steal her car. Well, it was Quent really, because she would never have had the nerve on her own. They waited until one Sunday morning when she knew her family would be at church. Quent drove them to the farm in his bakkie with a can of petrol. They pushed the Renault out of the barn and filled it up. It seemed to take ages and Raki was a nervous wreck, expecting to see her father's car any moment. She kept walking to the end of the lane where she had a good view of the road coming out of

Birkenheadbaai. She made Quent promise that if she saw them coming he would leave everything and take her home.

Fortunately, they were back on the main road before she spotted her parent's double bakkie coming towards them. Quent was driving in front and she was tucked in behind, in the Renault. Her parents swept past without noticing her.

Raki lived in a state of high anxiety for several weeks afterwards. It didn't matter how often Quent told her it was her car and that no one would arrest her. But it wasn't just the car that made her anxious. It was a very hard time for her. Leaving Henrik Morgan had been the easy part but the loss of her family was terrible. She missed her quiet, kindly father, but most of all and despite everything she missed her mother. When she lived with Mr Morgan she saw her mother almost every day. Raki helped Sofia clean the church and do the flowers. They used to shop and bake together. Sofia was a good cook and she passed on her skills to Raki, who loved to make special cakes for her nieces and nephews. Raki had become that great institution in any family – the childless favourite aunt; the one who had time for everyone. She was always there for them and their problems; the aunt who would never pass judgment on them or betray their confidences; the aunt who gave her love freely without any constraints.

When Raki ran off with Quent all that came to an end. She occasionally glimpsed her sister's children in town but when they saw her they avoided her. Most of them were young adults by then but she had one little four-year-old niece, Karuna, who was an especial favourite of hers. One day the child was with her older brother in town and when she saw Raki she squealed with delight and ran towards her, arms wide, shouting, *Tannie, Tannie,* but the boy grabbed the little girl and dragged her away. Raki drove home in tears.

For nights afterwards she would lie awake and hear the little girl sobbing, *I love you, Tannie. I love you.* In those early days she cried herself to sleep most nights. She knew it was pointless and self-indulgent but she couldn't help herself.

'Raki!' her mother used to scold, fixing her with what her father called a mega-gimlet glare. 'Who do you think you're impressing with those crocodile tears? It's showing off. And the Good Lord despises show-offs.'

Quent hated it too. 'What is it with you, Raki?' he'd say, when he caught her weeping into her pillow. 'Christ, woman, am I making you that unhappy? I thought you wanted this.'

And she would wipe the tears away with the back of her hand and sniff loudly.' I do, you know I do, but they're my family, Quent...'

That always did it.

'...Your family?' he'd yell, white-faced and furious. 'For chrissake woman, your precious family hate you. None of them speaks to you and that holy hypocrite of a mother of yours cursed you in front of the whole church. Remember? She said you'd burn in Hell's fire – we both would – and she'd be glad.'

'I know, Quent, don't shout, please, I hate it when you shout...'

'...And I bloody hate it when you're like this. How d'you think it makes me feel?'

'I can't help it. I love them.'

'Why? What've they ever done for you?'

'Love isn't like that, Quent. It's unconditional.'

'Well, maybe you should go back to them then. I'm sure your husband would forgive you if you went down on your knees and licked his holy boots.'

And then he'd bang out of the house, Bullseye at his heels, and not come back until the early hours. She didn't ask where he went on nights like that. Sometimes he didn't come home until the next day.

Eventually she learnt to control her tears and waited until he was out or she was sure he was asleep. Then she would creep outside, sit on the stoep, and let the tears come. She couldn't go far from the house because the dog patrolled at night and she was frightened of Bullseye. Afterwards she would slip back into bed beside Quent and watch him sleeping.

He slept like a child on his back, with his arms thrown wide, fingers twitching in his sleep. His sleep-breathing was shallow and she would edge closer and closer, not wanting to

45

wake him, until she could see his chest rising and falling and be reassured. He slept naked and she loved to watch the moonlight gleaming on his taut, brown shoulders, making his tattoo three-dimensional.

The leopard looked as if it was about to leap out at her, eyes wild and jaws twisted into a snarl. She loved that leopard. It didn't frighten her. She used to trail her finger around the animal's shape and Quent would turn towards her in his sleep and pull her into his arms, cradling her head against his chest. Quent wasn't a tender man and she stored those precious moments against a bad time.

When Mari didn't get back to her she went back up to the house. She was disappointed but not surprised. She wasn't expecting anything from her cousin. Mari helped her sell her produce but that was it. Their close relationship had ended when Raki moved in with Quent. Mari loathed Quent — even more than she hated Mr Turkey. Mari wasn't nasty to Raki, just cool. Raki missed her cousin's friendship and support but she wouldn't give Quent up, not for Mari, not for anyone.

The next day Raki was outside attempting to salvage some potatoes from her neglected veggie-patch when she heard someone scrambling up the last bit of steep track to the edge. There was no mistaking Mari in a foul mood. No one could swear like her cousin.

Raki went to the top of the rise and grasped Mari's hand, pulling her onto firm, flat ground. Mari's pretty face was fiery-red and her blond hair was stuck to her pink scalp. She dropped the assorted shopping bags she'd been carrying and sank to her knees amongst them, trying to get her breath back.

When she was able to speak she turned a furious face to her cousin. 'For God's sake, Raki! Why can't you live down there like the rest of us mortals?' As she scrambled to her feet she switched her attention to the house. 'So? Where is he? I've got a thing or two to say to Quent Byrant.' Mari waited for a response but when she didn't get one she looked at Raki. Raki had on an old skirt and top and some hideous walking boots, caked in mud. She hadn't washed or changed her clothes for days, her hair was matted and straggly and she was thin and stooped. She looked ten years older than when Mari had last seen her. Well? That's what living with a bastard like Quent Byrant did for you. Mari felt a surge of irritation. Christ. You'd think she could make some effort. She looked like white trash.

Raki stood patiently, head bowed, her long fingers laced across the incongruous little bump sticking out of her matchstick frame.

'He's...he's left me, Mari,' Raki said, the tears running down her face.

'Oh my God. Raki, you poor thing. Come here.' Mari pulled Raki into her arms and they stood there locked together while Mari rocked her cousin like a tiny baby. 'No, no, don't cry, honey,' she crooned, kissing Raki's hair. 'I'm here. Everything's going to be okay, I promise. '

And Mari was true to her word. She organised Raki's ante-natal care, provided stuff for the baby and gave Raki her old maternity clothes. She even struggled up the kloof with a mirror. Raki had laughed at that. Of all the things she needed? A mirror? Mari also invited Raki to stay with her and Anton, before and after the birth. And best of all she never lectured Raki about how stupid she'd been.

Raki shivered. It was dark outside now and the wind had picked up. Going inside the house she tucked Farnie down under his warm blankets. The little boy murmured in his sleep and found his thumb. Raki leant over him and brushed her lips against his eyes. 'Sweet dreams, my baby.' Then she took the heavy blanket off her bed and went outside again. She wrapped the quilt about her and settled down to watch the stars.

8.25 a.m.

Quent can't move out of the chair. He is as weak as a kitten and there's nothing to do but wait for his physical body to obey his commands, Until then he allows his thoughts to go where they will. He couldn't stop them even if he wanted to.

How long is it since he's spoken to Raki? Six months at least. A long time. She'd texted him a couple of times since then, thanking him politely for the pitiful amounts of money he sent to her, c/o her P.O box in Birkenheadbaai, but he'd never replied. What could he say? Tell her he should never have left her? That he'd been a stupid prick? Too late for any of that.

The irony of the situation wasn't lost on him. The exciting, supposedly better life he left Raki for hadn't materialised. He hated the work and he despised his boss. Most of his wage went on drink or gambling and what was left was spent on women. He wasn't choosy, just so long as they didn't ask too many questions or expect anything from him.

The day she rang him he thought it was one of his drinking buddies so he left it. Jaco had been giving him a hard time about some cock-up with a shoot and he was trying to sort it. Anything went wrong on the Du Plessis place it was Quent's fault. Maybe Jaco had hired him to be his whipping boy. *I'll break you, Byrant.* Jaco's bullying voice followed him everywhere. *I give you a job out of the kindness of my heart and how do you repay me? Eh? You bloody waste my time and my money. When I tell you I want the bloody zebra and Bok ready to work at six sharp, I mean six, not ten past.*

But whoever was trying to contact Quent wasn't giving up and after about the tenth time he answered. He'd need to do some drinking to get Jaco out of his head. 'Yeah?' he snapped. 'What?'

'Quent?'

It was a woman. Her tone was soft and guarded. He couldn't place it at first and yet the voice was as familiar to him as his own. It was from somewhere else, another time.

'Is that you, Quent?'

'Yeah,' he'd replied warily. He didn't like women calling him. You never knew what they were after. 'Who's this?'

'It's me,' she said, laughing. 'Raki.'

It was her laugh that did it. She had a great laugh. 'Raki?' The sheer surge of pleasure he experienced took him by surprise. 'Hey, man, this is great. How are you? Are you doing okay?'

'I'm fine, Quent, absolutely fine.'

'Good, that's good. Listen, Raki, I'm sorry about that. Not recognising you.'

'Don't worry,' she said, doing what she always did, making it easy for him. 'Reception's terrible up here.'

'Where are you?'

'Halfway down the kloof. Remember there's that rocky ledge where you can get a bit of reception if you hold the phone over the water? It's too hot to climb all the way down just yet and I've got...I've got a lot to carry.'

'What are you doing up there?'

Her laugh again. 'It's where I live, Quent. Have you forgotten?'

'Come on, Raki. You're joking, aren't you?'

'No. Where else would I be?' Her tone was sharp now.

'In Birkenheadbaai, of course, with your family.'

'The kloof house is my home, Quent. I don't have any other.'

'No!' he was angry and shouting now. 'You can't live up there, not on your own.'

'I'm perfectly capable of looking after myself. It's a case of having to.'

Quent didn't like this one little bit. He needed to have Raki safe, amongst her people. It had rained solidly for two months last winter. It must have been hell up there. And what if she'd got sick, or had an accident? 'So?' he said, at last, guilt making him cruel. 'Wouldn't Mr Turkey take you back?' He regretted it the moment it was out. 'Shit, me and my big

49

mouth. Raki? Sorry, hey? I didn't mean…I'm just worried about you. Please, say something. Raki. Please. I'm sorry.'

'Look, Quent,' her voice was cool now, matter-of-fact. 'You're breaking up. I wanted to tell you something but it can keep. I'll ring some other time.'

He was desperate now. 'No, no, please, don't go. What is it? Tell me.'

She was silent.

'Please. I promise to keep my big mouth shut. It's the shock, that's all. I want everything to be sorted for you and that doesn't include living hand-to-mouth on Pig's Snout. I thought I was doing you a favour walking out on you.'

'That's what you thought, was it? You were doing me a favour?'

'I just want everything to be okay for you.'

'No, you want everything to be okay for you. But that's all right because as it happens I'm the happiest I've ever been.'

'But what d'you do for money and food?'

'The Good Lord provides,' she murmured, but he caught the edge in her voice. 'Really, Quent,' she continued. 'You don't have to worry about me. It's not your problem.'

'What's happened to you, Raki?' he was puzzled. 'You're different. '

'Am I? Maybe it's because I'm a mother now.'

'Sorry, say again.' He'd heard what she said but he was playing for time. 'Didn't quite catch that last bit.'

She spoke slowly and clearly. 'I've had a baby, Quent, the most beautiful baby boy. I've named him Farnie.'

He couldn't think of anything sensible to say.

'You still there, Quent?'

'Yes, I'm here.'

'So?' they both said in unison.

There was a long pause before Raki spoke again. 'The birth was fine. Mari and Anton let me stay with them and a midwife came out from Hermanus. It was good. Not too much pain or anything considering Farnie was so big – '

He cut across her. ' –So? Where was she?'

'Who?'

'Your mother? Didn't she offer to look after you, you and your...baby?' He couldn't bring himself to say the name.

'You don't get it do you Quent? That part of my life is over and that's fine. Nowadays I don't lose any sleep over it. I have to save all my energy for Farnie. He's all that matters.'

'But you need a proper home if you've got a kid.'

'The kloof house is our home and he loves it.'

'But what about your husband? Raki? He must want you back now – '

'– My husband? What are you talking about?' Her voice was shrill. 'You think...' she spat at him, 'you think my Farnie is Mr Morgan's? How dare you.'

'Hey, Raki man, calm down. I only meant...'

'...D'you have any idea how insulting that is? You think I went back to that man ... and we made Farnie? You knew how much I hated him, Quent, how could you think such a thing?'

'But? If it's not his then...?' Quent was floundering and this time she wasn't going to help him. But then he understood what she meant. 'No way, Raki. You're not catching me like that.' He spoke without thinking, forgetting in his panic who he was talking to. There had been other women, other threats of paternity, some true but most not. Those women were looking for a meal ticket. Well, he wasn't about to get caught busting his guts out for some other guy's bastard.

She said nothing but he heard the shocked intake of breath and he winced at the pain he'd given her. 'Raki, please, don't switch off. I'm sorry. I'm sorry. But what am I supposed to think?' As he talked he was trying to make sense of it all. It wasn't possible. This child wasn't his. It couldn't be. He wouldn't allow it to be.

'He's six months old, Quent, and whether you like it or not he's your son. I wouldn't lie to you. I don't lie.'

Her voice had a tremor in it and he wondered how much courage it had taken for her to ring him.

'I wasn't going to tell you, ever, but you're his father, Quent, and you should know. Come and see him,' she was begging now. 'If you saw him you'd know he was yours. He's got your eyes. Come and visit us, Quent. He's such a happy little soul. I'm teaching him all the animal and bird names. I know you'll love him, please...'

That's when Quent switched off. He wouldn't think about what she'd said. That was how he'd always dealt with bad stuff. But the image of her up there on that kloof through the long, hard winter wasn't so easy to push away. And there was the child too. Without someone to protect her how would she survive? Her people would never take her back with an illegitimate child, He should have illegitimate child.Heshould have promised anything...everything, but it was too late for that, all that was over now and they both knew it. There were too many broken promises.

It wasn't his fault, he told himself. She should have prepared him for what was coming. At least that's what he kept telling himself. It was easy to forget what she'd said but it wasn't so easy to get the image of her out of his head. He could see her shocked, white face and stern, almost squaw-like, profile turned away from him. Her deep brown eyes would be fixed on some other light and suddenly he remembered her arms about him, her mouth on his neck and the warmth of her breath on his skin. Her passion. It had been so surprising from a woman like her. He could still smell her when he smelt the warm sun on new fresh shoots. He had faced dangerous men and animals all his life but he would never have this woman's courage and dignity. He would never be good enough for her. He was sorry for what he'd said but fatherhood wasn't for him, now or ever.

He went into the local town that night and got blind drunk with Johannes. When he'd sobered up and had time to think about it he'd texted her several times, but she'd never replied. He told her he was prepared to help her financially and he did – whenever he remembered. There were her stilted texts acknowledging the money but nothing else until a week or so ago when she'd contacted him asking for money. He'd been going to sort it but then the world went crazy.

Quent looks back at the kitchen, at the jam-jar full of dried proteas and the bunches of rosemary, thyme and oregano trailing from the rafters. There's a long plait of garlic hanging from a nail on one wall beside a sack of potatoes and an overturned bag of rice. Looks like the baboons have been having a feast.

A small hard-backed book of animals lies open on the table. The page has a monkey on the front. There are dirty finger-marks all over the animal. Something very sticky is smeared across the page. There's a child's T-shirt on the back of his chair. He holds it to his nose and breathes in. There's a powerful smell of earth and sweet rusks dipped in hot tea but there's something else too, something totally alien to him. This is proof, isn't it? Because if the boy was his, surely he would recognise his smell? If only Raki were here, then he could explain to her. Explain that he wasn't being cruel but he can never be a father.

The night Quent left her

Raki sat outside all that night. She couldn't sleep. Despite her best efforts Farnie's birthday had brought back all the bad stuff.

The night Quent left her was still raw in her mind – as bloody and agonising as ever. It was like some old movie playing over and over again while threadworms of dust gyrated across the screen.

The day it happened Quent had taken some foreign students out on the kloof, eager to see their first leopard.

Raki remembered her grandfather sitting her on his knee, when she was very little, and telling her that a friend of his great uncle's had shot the last leopard on Pig's Snout. 'He got the bugger good, Raki. Used the skin for a rug.' She remembered the pride in his voice.

Raki was preparing a special meal. Maybe Quent would come home in a good mood. Something was wrong with him lately. He'd relished the leopard conservation work to begin with but now he was irritable all the time. The more she did for him the angrier he became. It got that she was frightened to open her mouth. That's why she wanted this particular evening to be special. Raki smiled a secret smile as she laid the table. She'd made potje pot – his favourite – got in some Windhoek lager and picked a jar of yellow, pin-cushion proteas for the table. It was to be a celebration.

But Quent was so late she began to think he wasn't coming at all. It was a dark moonless night and she worried about him coming up the kloof. She opened the door, so that the lamplight shone out across the mountainside to light his way home, then she got out her drums. Playing the drums always soothed her. She could lose herself in the complex, repetitive rhythms. She and Mari used to go to a drum group when she was a teenager. They played at parties and family gatherings. She'd given it up when she married but she kept her two small drums. She'd taught Quent.

She wasn't sure how much later it was but suddenly she heard the dog. She picked up the drums and stepped back inside the house. The animal came and stood a few metres away sniffing the air. He could smell meat. Bullseye never attempted to come inside, which was fine by Raki. Quent had constantly reassured her. *You're part of his family, Raki. He'd never hurt you. All he wants is to protect you.'* But she remembered the time she'd first met him and tried to pat him and he'd leapt away barking furiously at her and wouldn't stop until Quent appeared.

'It's okay, Bullseye, this is Raki.' Quent soothed. 'Calm down, man.' 'They don't like being touched, Raki,' he'd warned her. 'When he gets to know you better he'll let you scratch his ears.'

But Raki wasn't about to touch that dog ever again.

She was adding some hot water to the stew to try and salvage it when Quent trudged wearily inside, slamming the door behind him. 'For chrissake woman, d'you want to get us eaten alive?'

He dumped his gear on the floor and sank into a chair. His shirt was dirty and torn and his face was grey. One of his fingers had an old rag wrapped around it and she could see blood seeping through the cloth. She knew better than to say anything. He hated fuss. She would wait until he was in a better mood and then she'd dress it for him. She opened a beer and gave it to him. He took it without a word and drained it in one.

'Everything okay?' she asked, handing him another bottle. He ignored her and turned his chair away from her while he drank. She wasn't going to talk to the back of his head so she busied herself getting the food and putting it on the table. She had a heavy, uneasy feeling in the pit of her stomach but she tried to ignore it. He was tired. All he needed was time to unwind. As she dished up she said brightly, 'Good day?'

Quent banged his empty bottle down on the table, thrust back his chair and went through to the bedroom. Raki put the plates down, waited a few moments, and then followed.

His rifle and some boxes of cartridges were on the bed and he was stuffing clothes into his rucksack.

She was trembling so much she had to sit down.

'Quent?' She couldn't disguise the terror in her voice. 'What's happening? Where are you going?'

'Got a job up country,' he muttered, as he jammed his climbing ropes and pitons into a large canvas haversack. 'Good money. Don't know how long I'll be gone. Couple of weeks, maybe more. I'll let you know.' He got up and brushed past her on his way back into the kitchen. He dropped his gear on the floor by the door then he took out his wallet and laid a pile of crumpled R100 notes on the table. 'This should be enough to see you through.'

'But I've made your dinner, Quent,' she said desperately. 'You must eat.' If she kept talking maybe this wouldn't be real. 'It's your favourite. Please, can't you stay tonight, just one night? There's something I want to tell you.'

'No,' his voice was too loud. 'I promised the guy. Sorry.' He spread his hands out in a helpless gesture.

They stood awkwardly either side of the table, not looking at each other. The food had congealed around the edges of the plates and Raki's stomach heaved. She took the plates and scraped the meat outside for the dog. Bullseye appeared immediately and they watched as he gulped down the food.

'What's going to happen to him?' she said.

'He comes with me.'

'But I thought he belonged to the farm? Martin Broot paid for him, didn't he?'

'I said he comes with me. He's my dog, okay? I trained him...he's mine.'

Raki forced herself to focus on the proteas. Up close she saw that the tiny yellow blossoms were covered in frothy, grey webs crawling with tiny spiders. She looked up and met Quent's eyes.

'I've got to be straight with you, Raki. I owe it you. I'm moving out – for good.'

Raki's mouth was open and her eyes wide with shock – the tears made them shine in the dim light.

When he spoke again his voice was soft, almost a whisper. 'I'm sorry, Raki man, but there's no nice way to say this. It isn't working for me. It's got nothing to do with you. It's me. I'm…crap. I can't handle all this …' and he waved his arms about, as if the room was somehow to blame.

She smiled but her lips were trembling. This was one of his jokes. He was always playing jokes on her. 'You're tired, Quent. You need some sleep. Tomorrow everything will be fine. You'll see.'

But he wasn't listening. 'I never made any promises, did I? You knew the score. I told you I wasn't the sort to settle down. I've been on the move all my life. That's the way I like it. You knew, Raki. You said it was okay.' The words exploded from him like they were forced out of a corked-up bottle.

Raki decided not to think about what he was saying. This was some nightmare and she'd wake up any minute. 'But you love the Project,' she said at last. 'You said it's what you've always wanted,' she laboured on. 'And one day you'll find your leopard, I know you will.'

Quent laughed. It was an ugly sound. 'I found her today.'

She thought she must have misheard. 'What?'

'I saw the leopard today. She's living somewhere up here, under the cliff, maybe got cubs stashed up here too.'

'A leopard?'

'Yeah, a leopard.'

'But that's amazing, Quent. It's what you've always wanted. I don't understand. Why aren't you happy? Quent? A leopard on our Kloof? It's a miracle. Robert must have been so pleased.'

'Du Toit? He didn't believe me, none of them did.' His voice was dead. 'They think I made it up to make myself look big.'

'But you didn't…you wouldn't. She's there, you said so.'

For a moment he forgot his anger. 'Yeah, she's there all right. I don't know how I missed her all this time. She was waiting for me, right under my nose, Raki. That's where that side of biltong went. Remember? I told you it was too big for a genet to take.'

'And she's really here? On our mountain?'

'Yeah,' his voice was dreamy. 'A beautiful, golden leopardess.'

'And you were the first to see her?'

'Yeah. ' There was an edge of irritation in his voice now. 'Didn't I just tell you?'

'Yes, sorry, it's great, Quent. Well done.'

'Great?' he mimicked. 'It's bloody marvellous. I never thought I'd see a leopard in these mountains, thought they were finished – like me.' His eyes shone as he spoke. 'Thought they were gin-trapped or poisoned, or spooked by the bastards with their vineyards and orchards and *private keep out*, their fancy 4 x4s, quad-bike trails and golf courses, but they're still here – in the secret places. Not the game reserves or wild-life estates, the real thing...and there's still hope because not only is she a beautiful specimen but maybe she's got young. I wish you could have seen her.' For a moment he was the old, passionate Quent but then the light in his eyes died and he hung his head. 'But it's no good.' He shook his head violently. 'I'm sick of it. Sick of all those do-gooder kids, with their rich mummies and daddies and their private education and their bloody arrogance. They laugh at me – I heard them – calling me *the snake eater*, like I was some pathetic old tosser. They think they know it all but they know...' he searched for the right word, '...they know bloody squit. Put them down in the bush without their fancy satnavs and land-cruisers and they'd be up shit-creek before the sun went down. I promise you.'

'Of course they would, Quent. You're the best there is.'

He turned a furious face to her. 'Will you stop being bloody nice, Raki. Shout at me. Scream at me. Stop bloody agreeing with me. I'm leaving you, you stupid bitch. Didn't you hear what I said? Why aren't you angry? God, I can see why your old man was glad to see the back of you.'

She felt for the chair and sat down heavily. She was crying.

There was a long silence before Quent spoke again. 'See? All I ever do is make you cry. I never wanted to hurt you, Raki.' He almost touched her then but at the last moment he drew away and stood rigidly as if standing to attention. 'This time with you has been the best...I promise ...I've never felt like this about any woman before but...' she had to strain her ears to hear what he said next, '...but it isn't enough. D'you understand? I'm sorry.' He was silent for a moment but then his face brightened. 'But we can still be mates? I'll come by when I can, see how you're getting on?'

She sat slumped, hands clutching the arms of the chair; the tears ran unchecked down her cheeks and into her mouth. She was ugly but she didn't care.

He picked up his bag. 'One day you'll thank me for this, Raki. You'll be able to go back to your folks now. That's what you want, isn't it? Your old woman warned you about me and she was right. I'm not to be trusted. Hey?' he attempted a grin. 'You'll be an honest woman again.'

'I love you, Quent. What will I do without you?'

He shut his eyes and screwed up his face as if he was in pain and then he reached for the door.

She put out a hand blindly. 'Please, don't leave me, Quent.'

'You'll be okay, Raki. No harm done, eh? It's not as if there's a kid or anything?'

There was absolutely nothing to say.

His back was to her. 'I love you, Raki, but it's no good. I'd destroy you in the end.' Then he swung his backpack over his shoulder and stepped out into the night.

She stumbled to the door and watched as he walked quickly away. The moon had come out from behind a bank of clouds and she saw him raise a hand in farewell. He didn't look back. She ran to the edge of the mountain and watched as he strode down the track, leaping from boulder to boulder towards the flat-water run. The dog danced beside him like a firefly flitting in and out of the shadows. He was barking excitedly, as if they were at the beginning of some great new adventure. She couldn't hear but she knew Quent was humming. He did that when he was happy. When he reached the stream he stopped beside a crippled, wind-blown tree that clung tenaciously to a huge boulder. It was *their* tree. They never passed by without touching it. Reaching across, Quent snatched a leaf and then he was swallowed up in the night.

Raki stood where she was for a long time. Any moment now he would come bounding back up the hill towards her, laughing, telling her that he didn't mean it...she wouldn't let him mean it. She waited and waited but he didn't come and finally she dropped down onto the damp earth and closed her eyes. She would die. There was nothing else to do. Her life was over.

She must have fallen asleep then because when she opened her eyes she was freezing cold and stiff and lying face-down in the scratchy vegetation. The wind howled across the mountainside and it was drizzling. She didn't attempt to get up. This was what she wanted, wasn't it? One arm was trapped beneath her and she had pins and needles in her hand. She turned slightly onto her side so that she could straighten it out. Is that what you did? Made yourself comfortable before you died?

She began to laugh, great gulping hysterical blasts that came from somewhere deep inside her. Her body twisted painfully with each paroxysm and that's when it happened – a rippling sensation across her belly. She froze. Nothing. But then, there it was again, a sudden spasm as if the baby had fallen off a step in his dreams and put out a tiny hand to save himself.

Raki sat up carefully, cradling her belly in both hands. She forced herself to take deep, long breaths. 'Shh, shh, baby,' she whispered. 'Everything's going to be fine. Mummy's here… I'll always be here.'

'Quent,' Raki whispered into the night.

The stars and moon were incredibly bright. The constellations laid out above her like a child's picture book. When Farnie was older she would teach him all about the night sky. She would tell him everything there was to know in the whole of his world.

No more bad thoughts. She had her son, her house, and she lived in all this beauty. What more could she expect from life? There was the promise of a new, precious day and she would go to the clinic and then visit Mari.

8.30 a.m.

Quent's still holding the child's T-shirt as he goes into the bedroom. He lets it drop on Raki's bed, which is strewn with piles of clothes, spilling out and over, onto the floor. The other bed is neatly made up, as if waiting for someone to jump in. This was his bed. He remembers the first night they made love on this bed and how shy she'd been when he pulled the two beds together. When he saw her watching him he'd smiled and taken her in his arms, kissing the worry-lines away from her eyes.

'You're a strange woman, Raki. We've been sleeping together in the tent for a year, and that never seemed to bother you.'

She'd looked up at him. 'It's silly I know, but this seems so final, somehow.'

'Well? What did you expect, Mrs Morgan? A separate bedroom?'

'No, but this is like we were married or something.'

'Christ!' he said, in horror, stepping away from her. 'Don't say that, woman. I'm allergic to matrimony, didn't I tell you? Makes me come out in a rash.' But he must have seen the hurt in her eyes because he pulled a funny face and made her laugh.

Quent rummages through the clothing until he finds a faded, misshapen T-shirt that had once belonged to him. They had used it to carry sea-shells up the kloof to grind into lime-mortar for the walls. They'd threaded the arms through two long poles and then tied the bottom edges further down, making a cradle. It had been Raki's idea and had worked well. She was always the practical one.

After pulling the shirt carefully over his head he places the hand-gun down beside the bed – in easy reach – then he lies flat, lifts his backside and peels off his stained trousers.

Mission accomplished, he relaxes back on the pillow, breathing deeply, but as he does so something catches his eye on the wall above his head. There's a brightly coloured birthday-card sellotaped there. It has a glittery number *One* on it. Quent takes it down and his fingers are frosted in sparkle. The message reads, *Happy First Birthday, little Farnie, from Tannie Mari, Anton and the boys.* Maths was never Quent's strong point but even he can work out this particular sum. He's been away for a year and a half.

Too late, he understands what Raki had been trying to tell him the night he walked out on her. She was pregnant. Would it have made any difference if he'd known? Of course not. It was all about him. It always was. You had to look after number one, because sure as hell no one gave a shit about you. Quent was so full of rage and self-pity that night. Escape was all he could think of. He tears the card in half then quarters and then into tiny fragments, until all that remains is sparkly confetti which he tosses into the air. He watches as it flutters down onto the bed and surrounding floor.

The Clinic

On the surface everything seemed perfectly normal at the clinic. Raki was pleased she'd made the effort to be first in the queue, even though Farnie didn't want to be hurried and insisted on taking his presents with him. On the way down the kloof to the car he dropped his book in a bush and she tore her one good shirt on some thorns retrieving it.

The baby clinic was held in a pleasant, brightly-lit room with white walls and long creamy curtains that billowed out in the warm, soft breeze. The patio windows opened out onto a lawn edged with jacaranda and bougainvillea. Raki looked forward to her clinic visits. She was on speaking terms with some of the mothers and Farnie loved being with the other children. He got very excited as soon as Raki parked outside the building.

Today, after her session, she would drive down to the harbour and see Mari and they'd have cake and drink coffee and gossip. She would thank her cousin for Farnie's card and the money; then she planned to go to the Spar and buy crayons and paper. Farnie loved to draw.

This was her plan but it had all gone horribly wrong.

At the moment Farnie was sitting on the floor by her feet, playing happily with some Lego blocks while Raki watched the clinic nurse writing on an official looking form. The woman's lips were a thin line of disapproval as she stabbed the pen at the paper. She was having trouble with the biro ink and kept shaking the pen angrily to get it to write.

Raki sat still, hardly daring to breathe, hands folded neatly in her lap. Her smile felt as if it had been stitched on her face. She glanced out of the window. There was a man working on the borders, adrift in an ocean of impossibly blue fallen blossoms. Raki watched the sun glinting on his machete as the blade rose and fell amongst the weeds. Bees drifted like smoke on the lavender and a *Jacky Hanger* was making its *swizzling* cry from somewhere nearby. The bird had skewered a tiny vole onto a piece of rusty wire on the fence and was on the lookout for more prey for its butcher's spike. From the waiting room next door came the sounds of babies grizzling and the murmur of voices, playing like the same low note on a piano. The pungent smell of the nurse's deodorant hung heavily in the air. Surely Raki had misheard what the woman had just said? There was something wrong with Farnie? Something serious that needed urgent treatment? Raki thought she was joking at first. But the normally smiley woman looked very stern. And she had hurt Farnie. Raki glanced down at her little boy. His eyes were still red and puffy from a few minutes ago when the nurse had examined him.

The woman looked up from her writing and saw Raki's smile. 'I can assure you that this is no laughing matter, Mrs Morgan.'

'Sorry,' Raki stammered.

'Dysplasia of the hip is a severe condition and should have been dealt with at birth, or at least before baby was three months old.'

Dysplasia was the only word Raki heard.

'Didn't you notice anything unusual while you   were carrying baby?'

Raki didn't know what to say. As far as she was concerned the whole being-pregnant thing was highly unusual.

The nurse sighed. 'For example, were baby's limbs in a strange position? Did you feel them digging into you?'

'Not really, although towards the end he seemed to have one foot jammed against my waist. It was quiet uncomfortable but I thought it was normal?'

'Ah,' said the nurse, cutting in. She looked pleased with herself. 'That will be when the dislocation occurred.'

'The dislocation?'

'Of the hip.'

'So? Dysplasia means he's dislocated his hip?' Raki waited for a reply but the   woman was busy writing again.

Farnie was trying to pull himself up to standing on Raki's skirt and she put her hand out to help him. He leant against

65

her and made a grab for her cell phone, which was sticking out of her bag. 'No, Farnie,' Raki said. 'That's Mama's.'

'See what he's doing?' The nurse pointed to the way he was leaning against her with all his weight on his left leg. 'You do know why he does that don't you?'

'Because of the dysplasia?' Raki guessed.

'Because, Mrs Morgan, that child's right leg is shorter than the left.'

'Oh my God!'

The nurse wasn't going to waste time feeling sorry for this neglectful mother. 'Who attended you during your confinement?'

'My confinement?'

'For God's sake woman don't you understand English? When you had the baby! Who was the doctor?'

'I didn't have a doctor, nurse. It was a straightforward birth.' She saw the woman's eyebrows shoot up. 'There was no need,' she said defensively. 'My cousin was with me and a part-time midwife. I was so lucky, everything went really well and the midwife was very professional.'

The nurse tut-tutted under her breath. 'Okay, no doctor present at birth,' she wrote fiercely, 'and a home delivery.' She said the *home* as if it were a dirty word. I don't suppose you can remember who you saw when you went for your post-natal examination?'

Raki looked away but she felt the blush creeping up her neck. 'I had to miss my appointment. It was winter,' she explained. 'I couldn't get down the kloof. The path was washed away and it would have been too dangerous.' She heard the nurse's contemptuous *huh*. 'But I was well, we were both well, and Farnie has never had anything wrong with him. You know that, I've had him weighed and checked regularly ever since he was born, never missed. He's a healthy little boy. You said so, many times.'

Everything was happening too fast for Raki. It seemed like only a few moments ago she was telling the nurse about Farnie's strange crawling technique and how he'd started to stand on tip-toe on one foot, while the other was placed flat on the ground. Before she knew what was happening the nurse had Farnie up on the examination couch. Raki hadn't been prepared for the rough way the woman had handled her son. She made Raki hold him while she pulled his legs this way and that until the little boy cried out in pain.

'Did you hear that?' the woman said triumphantly at last, ignoring Farnie's tears. 'There was a definite *clunk* sound.'

ll Raki heard were her little boy's sobs.

The nurse stopped writing and slapped the piece of paper down in front of Raki so that she could read what it said. The woman's finger stamped down on the words as she spoke. 'First thing tomorrow you take this to the paediatric unit at the Provincial. Understand? No excuses — whatever the weather. This matter must be dealt with as quickly as possible, before any more harm is done.'

There were a hundred questions that Raki should have asked but her brain was in free-fall and it was as much as she could do to get unsteadily to her feet, pick up the letter, and hitch Farnie onto her hip.

'No!' The irate nurse jumped up and snatched the little boy out of Raki's arms. 'Didn't you hear what I just told you? Don't carry that child on your hip.'

Farnie opened his mouth and howled. 'Mama' he shrieked, holding out his arms to Raki. She took him back and made a cradle, so that his body was against her chest and his legs hung over her arms.

'I expect this sort of feckless behaviour from them.' The nurse jabbed her thumb at the waiting room which was full of black women and their babies. 'But not from someone like you. If he has a limp for the rest of his life he will know who to blame.'

8.35 a.m.

It had been coming on for weeks, the feeling of dissatisfaction, like some unbearable itch that was just out of reach from his probing fingernails. Quent imagined a reddened, raised mozzy-bite nestling just between his shoulder blades and it was driving him nuts. Everyone and everything irritated him and Raki was first in the firing line. He hated himself for doing it but it was her fault for being such a victim. Maybe he was testing her, seeing how much she could take before he drove her away. Because that's what he wanted, wasn't it? They always left him in the end, all of them – the ones who said they loved him.

If he was honest, most of his discontent arose from his work on the Cape Leopard Project. At first he'd loved it; the pay wasn't brilliant but he would have done it for nothing if they'd asked. Quent was passionate about leopards, always had been. No, the problem was Quent's boss, Robert du Toit – a brash, fresh-faced young guy with a bum-fluff beard, just out of Stellenbosch Uni. Sure the boy-wonder had brains, trouble was he didn't use them and he treated Quent like some pathetic old tosser. Quent had years of experience in Rhodesia tracking game in the bush but Du Toit never asked the older man for advice or insight. To say Quent was humiliated by this treatment didn't come close.

Quent got all the duff kit and Pig's Snout was his allocated sector, even though a leopard hadn't been officially logged on this kloof for a generation. His sighting of a leopard when he was a kid couldn't be corroborated. This was galling but the worst part for Quent was that he got the useless eco-tourists too. Wild-life volunteers came from all over the world to experience CLP work and they paid a lot of rand for the privilege. The revenue they brought to the project was crucial and they had to be treated well. Their job, supposedly, was to help track and monitor leopard and other predator populations in the Cape. The small leopard was one of a unique species that only occurred in this region – the Cape Kingdom. The leopard was high on the conservation danger-list and eco-virgins vied with each other to get one of these rare animals crossed off their *must do, must see* lists. Quent got the fat kids, the unfit and the poseurs – dressed in their designer safari gear – who couldn't keep up and demanded time-out to take pretty pictures.

There were three camera-traps and one cage-trap on Pig's Snout and all four had to be checked daily. The memory card in each camera had to be retrieved and replaced and any animals caught in the walk-in trap had to be catalogued and released. It was boring, repetitive work, made worse by the certain knowledge that he would never see a leopard.

Quent had a title - not that he gave a shit about stuff like that. He was designated *Biological Field Assistant* and guide. The 'guide' tag was okay – he knew every blade of grass on Pig's Snout but the 'biology' thing was embarrassing. Quent and biology had parted company very early on in his education. Fortunately, the enthusiastic young ecologists didn't expect any science from this old guy with the leopard tattoo. They were the egg-heads, weren't they? They had the degrees and the enthusiasm and most importantly of all, they had the money.

Even with all the irritations, Quent still preferred CLP work to his job on Maarten Broot's sheep farm. The only good thing about this was that he had met up with his childhood friend, Willem. Quent thanked God or fate or whatever it was that had brought them together again after so many years. Quent had often thought about his old friend but that was as far as it got: that is until the day he started work as farm manager and came face to face with Willem.

Willem had been Broot's head stockman for years. What he didn't know about merinos wasn't worth knowing and by rights he should have got the manager's job. But even in post-Apartheid South Africa whites still got the plum jobs in rural areas – not the same in the cities. A good enough reason to steer well clear of them, thought Quent.

69

If Willem resented his friend getting the job he didn't show it. Willem wasn't political, but there were plenty of blacks who were – especially the young – Willem's younger brother, Johannes, for one.

Quent and Willem worked side-by-side on the farm. Quent could always rely on Willem to cover for him when he messed up or when he forgot to do something. Willem never let you down. Whatever happened he was there. Any of the stock went walkabout Willem was the man to check them out.

Quent's friend hadn't altered at all except that his once wide, trusting smile had become guarded. He was still tall and rangy. Quent would have known him anywhere but Willem had more trouble placing him. The first day they met Willem had hesitated for a few moments, as if he couldn't quite believe his eyes, and then suddenly his serious expression had changed into one of sheer delight.

'Is it you, bra?'

Quent smiled, 'Yeh, it's me, man.'

Willem touched Quent's greying hair gently as if he was afraid it might rub off on his fingers. 'You are old now.'

Quent winced but Willem had always been direct. 'Only two years older than you, Willem,' he managed a grin, 'but life's treated me bad.'

'Maybe,' Willem said, looking away from his friend.

Quent soon discovered that his life had been a blast compared to Willem's. There'd been a bad fire on the estate where Willem lived and word was he and his family had to run for their lives. They spent the night in the dam until the fire swept over them. When they crawled out the next morning everything was gone – their house, garden, chickens, possessions – the lot. The estate was destroyed too, so there were no jobs to return to and they had to move on – start a new life.

Willem's old man had gone to work in the apple-growing region in the mountains. He promised to send money home for his wife and family but neither he nor the money ever showed up. Those were the days when apple-pickers were 'paid' in wine or beer.

Willem's mother got work where she could but it was never enough and the older children had to do whatever they could to earn a few rand. Willem had tears in his eyes when he talked about his mother. She had died when she was forty two and his once happy, beautiful mother was reduced to an old, old woman, stooped and bent with the years of back-breaking washing and cleaning.

Willem had to leave the school and when he was fourteen Willem and his younger brother, Johannes, were taken on by old man Broot. They'd been there ever since. Broot was a good employer but Quent hated sheep. He hated the stink of them, the taste of them but most of all he hated their stupidity. Most animals, you had some idea how they would react in different circumstances but not sheep. The one thing you knew for certain with a sheep was that if there was a way to kill itself then it would find it.

Quent was passionate about wild animals and even as a small boy seemed to have an affinity with them. Apparently, he'd lived on a farm in Rhodesia once — although he was too young to remember anything much — and he moved to South Africa when he was three with the old woman and Eunice. They had a small-holding at the bottom of Pig's Snout. Eunice was their black maid and had been with the old woman all her life. Quent loved her. The old woman kept a few calves, sheep, chickens and ducks and there was a kitchen garden in the backyard but she made her living by sewing clothes for wealthy whites. Quent's childhood wasn't happy but he could always escape up the kloof when things got tough.

Another good thing happened while Quent was working for Broot. He was put in charge of the Anatolian.

In the old days Broot's grandfather had used gin-traps to protect his livestock from predators. There were still a few leopards about back then. Nowadays there were some animals in the Cedarburg's and numbers were increasing, thanks to the CLP and more enlightened farmers. True, the leopards had been hunted, trapped or poisoned out of Pig's Snout, but there were other, smaller predators on the mountain, like caracal and genet. These animals could take lambs and weak calves. The conservation guys were looking for a more humane way to control predators and asked Maarten Broot to take part in a programme introducing Anatolian shepherd dogs to the area. They had been used successfully in Namibia to protect livestock from cheetah. Quent was the obvious choice when Broot looked about for someone to take charge of the dog.

When the Anatolian was delivered to the farm Quent was the first person he saw. *It was love at first sight*, Raki said. Maybe she was right. Quent should have stuck to dogs. They didn't have expectations. They were never disappointed in you and never gave you grief. They were on your side.

Quent named the pup Bullseye. The animal was a light creamy-yellow, with a black muzzle and ears. Raki asked Quent why he called the dog Bullseye but he just shrugged, pretending it wasn't important. Raki had learned to recognise that tightening of his jaw and let the matter drop.

Quent spent a lot of time on the De Broot computer researching Anatolians. He used to come home with pages of the stuff and read them to her. *"The large Anatolian is firstly a guard dog,' he told her, his eyes shining. 'The animal is loyal, fiercely possessive and protective towards its family and surroundings. It is not an outgoing dog, like a Labrador, and will not greet you if you are unknown to it. The dog is normally aloof and suspicious of any unknown person or animal coming into its territory. Once you have been introduced to the dog by its owner it will approach you of its own accord and after smelling your hand might allow you to scratch its chin. Anatolians are unlike sheepdogs that herd sheep or livestock according to instructions from their owners. They have been bred to work independently with little interference from men. Its instinct allows it to bond with all the animals and people in its home range. This protective drive is so strong that it has difficulty sharing its herd or family with another guard dog".*

'Isn't this amazing? Raki? Are you listening?'

His two jobs meant that Raki saw very little of Quent. Luckily she didn't mind being on her own, loved it in fact. He'd get back at night, tired and hungry, and there she'd be making some food and singing at the top of her voice, her voice echoing eerily up and down the kloof. She sounded a bit like a choir boy before his voice broke. Maybe it was because she always sang hymns? Didn't know any other songs, she used to say, smiling at him. So, he'd taught her some African songs learnt in the bush in Rhodesia. She would sit outside the house at night, play her drums and sing to the stars.

Amazingly he'd been living with her for two years by then. He'd never stayed that long with any woman before this but Raki was undemanding and never put pressure on him, not like most of the women he'd had relationships with. Also Raki was still married. He'd tried marriage once but it had been a huge mistake.

Quent stretches out on the bed and feels his eyelids drooping. It wouldn't hurt to have five minutes, would it? Sleep didn't wait for permission.

What to do?

A limp for the rest of his life?

Somehow Raki got Farnie into the car. She was sobbing and Farnie was hysterical. He hated it when mama cried. She rocked him until he'd cried himself into an exhausted sleep then she put the sleeping child in his car-seat and drove along the coast road until she found a spot facing the sea. It was windy and grey and the waves were rolling in. Black-headed gulls swooped and soared over the choppy sea. She wanted to walk along the beach but she couldn't leave Farnie so she wound her window down and leant out, trying to clear her head. She didn't know what to do but she was too upset to go to Mari's.

After Farnie's birth, Raki and her little son had stayed at Mari's for a few days. They had all been so kind to her. Even Anton was on his best behaviour.

There was only one thing that Mari and Raki fell out about – well, two if you counted Quent, but that was an on-going battle. No, the major row occurred one morning when Mari was going through yet another bag of baby things – her most precious. Mari loved kids and had always wanted a little girl but her youngest son was twelve now so she was finally parting with the carefully stored treasures.

Mari was holding up a baby-gro. It was black with white stripes. 'What d'you think? Anton used to call Ben his little zebra in this.' She buried her nose in the tiny garment before handing it over to Raki.

Raki smiled, 'It's sweet. Are you sure?'

'Yeah, yeah' Mari was busy in another bag. 'Here, you'll need these.' And she tossed several packs of disposable nappies to her cousin. She saw Raki's expression. 'You weren't thinking of using towelling nappies were you? Okay, disposables are expensive but the baby can have a bare bum in the summer.'

Raki didn't mind having to wash nappies and said so but Mari wasn't listening. She was babbling, a sure sign that she had something on her mind but didn't know where to start. Eventually, she stopped folding and re-folding the baby things and looked her cousin straight in the eye. 'Look, sweet-pea, don't take this the wrong way, but have you thought about letting Sofia know – about the baby?' Mari had always called her aunt by her Christian name. Sofia didn't like it but that didn't deter her niece.

Raki felt the blood draining from her face.

Mari saw her reaction but ploughed on, determined to have her say. 'I mean, she is your mother and the baby's Grandma, Raki. Raki? Say something, for God's sake.'

'No!' Raki shouted, jumping to her feet. 'No, no, no.'

'I'm sure she'd be okay about it, once she got used to the idea.'

Raki paced the room muttering.

'Come on,' Mari said. 'What could she do? She wouldn't turn her back on an innocent little baby. Okay, I know she can be a bit...rigid about morals and stuff but I'm sure in the end she'd be reasonable.'

Raki stopped her pacing and glared at Mari.

'Reasonable? You know my mother, she's never been *reasonable* in her life. Didn't you hear what she called me?'

Mari nodded, 'Yeah, but that was a gut reaction; she's had time to get used to the idea since then. I'm sure she misses you.'

'Did she say so?'

'Not exactly, but I'm sure she does. She must. You're her youngest child and you were always close.'

Raki shook her head. 'She isn't close to anyone except God and that man.'

'She's a tough cookie but surely – '

'– You don't understand. When my mother makes up her mind that's it.'

'But what about your dad?'

Raki turned away for a moment and when she turned back to look at Mari her eyes were bright with tears. She sighed and shrugged her shoulders. 'He won't do anything to upset her. Now please, Mari, I don't want to talk about it anymore. If you're fed up with having me here maybe it would be best if I went home. You've been really kind but I can manage now. I really can.'

'Home?' Mari's voice was hopeful.

'Pig's Snout.'

'For God's sake, woman, get real. You can't live up there with a new born baby. Winter's coming.'

Raki grabbed Mari by her wrist. 'You've got to promise you won't tell her. If you do I'll walk out of that door and you won't see me, ever again.'

'Ow, that hurts,' Mari said, trying to loosen her cousin's grip.

But Raki wasn't letting go. 'Promise me, Mari.'

'Okay, okay. Whatever.' Raki let go and Mari rubbed her wrists. 'But I think you're wrong. They'll find out soon enough. You know what the gossips are like in this town? What they don't know they make up.'

'Maybe, but it mustn't come from you.'

'I've said I won't, haven't I? Don't you trust me?'

But Raki wasn't satisfied and made Mari swear on the Bible.

When Farnie woke he was his normal, good-natured self again – all trauma forgotten. Lucky him.

She made her mouth smile at him. 'Shall we go and buy something nice in the shop, Farnie, um? What would you like? Tell Mama.'

'Num num,' Farnie replied, without hesitation. This was his version of sweets.

The Spar had just opened when she got there and Raki was glad. She would get a few things and go straight home. No visiting Mari today.

As she drove she tried to blank her mind but there was a voice in her head the whole time asking the same question. *What are you going to do now?*

8.40 a.m.

Quent didn't know how long he'd been asleep but he wakes with a start. There is a fierce light shining in his eyes. He props himself up on his elbows and moves slightly, so that the laser of sunlight coming through the window isn't drilling into his eyes any more.

He's had a very bad dream – the sort you only get when you've had a bad trip or a really big shot of morphine. He still has the taste of nightmare in his mouth.

He had dreamt about a dog.

When he was nine Quent found an injured dog on the side of the road. He was on his way home from school with Willem. His friend had just crossed over to his house and Quent was alone.

He saw something white, lying in the long grass against the fence and when he looked he saw a small pup lying there, hard to say how old but very little. Dogs were always getting knocked down along this road. Quent hoped it was dead. He and Willem had found one a few weeks back. It was smashed up but still alive. Quent was squeamish about killing things back then so Willem found a heavy rock and bashed the dog's brains in.

Quent tried not to look at the pathetic bundle as he hurried past. *Please God let it be dead.* He glanced apprehensively over his shoulder. Good. The animal wasn't moving so he could relax and he went back to examine him. Death held a fascination for the nine year old. The pup's muzzle was tucked between its front paws as if it was asleep. Quent couldn't see any blood but one leg was twisted beneath its body. Not a bad way to die Quent thought. Little thing like that, he wouldn't have suffered. The black settlements were full of unwanted dogs; they ran in packs until someone got out a shotgun and killed a few. The old woman called them vermin. 'Always after a free meal,' she said 'Waste of space, dogs.'

He was beginning to breathe normally again and stood up to go home. He had to get back to do his chores or she'd be after him. As he turned to walk away he heard a sound. He stood still listening; there it was again – a faint whimper. His heart was pounding but he knelt down beside the animal and gently touched the dog's leg. It was sticking out at a strange angle. The dog screamed with pain. It must be badly broken. Quent panicked. He should kill it. That would be the good thing to do. He could go and get Willem but he remembered the look on his friend's face when he'd hidden his eyes the last time. He picked up a rock and weighed it in his hand. Was it big enough and heavy enough? It looked bigger than the pup's head. Maybe if he closed his eyes and smashed it down he could do it. He must do it. He took one last look and raised the rock over the small head but as he did so the animal turned its face and looked straight at him. One of his eyes was surrounded by a black circle, just like a bulls-eye. Quent held his hand out towards the dog and the pup licked his finger.

Quent wrapped the injured dog in his shirt then he carried it back to Pig's Snout. He hid behind the chicken coop until he was sure that the old woman and Eunice weren't about. Eunice was kind but Quent knew she wouldn't do anything to upset the old woman. There was an old outhouse that was only used in the winter to store firewood so he hid the pup inside. Quent got some water and a few scraps of food that wouldn't be missed and made a bed of straw in a dark corner behind an empty barrel.

Quent had never loved anything as much as he loved little Bullseye. The time he spent with the animal, nursing him back to health, was the happiest he could remember. Bullseye was still quite sickly and content to sleep all day but when Quent talked he would watch him as if he understood every word.

Quent kept Bullseye there for weeks, sneaking out bits of food. He made a splint for the injured leg and eventually the pup was able to stand. Quent knew the old woman wouldn't let him keep Bullseye and it was only a matter of time before she found him. He couldn't expect the dog to keep quiet now he was getting better. All it would take would be one bark. He told Willem and he said he'd ask his mum if they could keep Bullseye for Quent. They had loads of dogs – one more wouldn't matter – and Quent said he'd work for her at the weekends to help pay for his dog's keep.

He was so relieved when Willem's mum said *yes*. He was going to take Bullseye over there that night, after he'd done his homework and chores. He ran home as fast as he could so that he'd be finished early. He was so happy. Bullseye was going to be safe. But when he got back, the outhouse door was wide open and the dog was gone.

He ran into the house. It was empty and the old woman wasn't in the garden. He ran around their land searching everywhere he could think of. He didn't dare shout in case the dog had somehow managed to get out on his own, but deep down he knew the old woman had found him. He clung on to the hope that she'd chased him off the farm, so he went down on the main road and walked up and down calling. Then he climbed up above the farm. He was crying and it was getting dark and the old woman would kill him for being late. But he wasn't going back, not until he found his dog.

He heard the vultures before he saw them. They were in a feeding frenzy around a stunted apple tree halfway up the slope past the waterfall. A large raptor circled lower and lower overhead looking for somewhere to land. Quent picked up a stick and ran screaming towards the tree. The birds looked up and hopped backwards, assessing the threat, before hopping forwards again.

But Quent was driven by a fiercer emotion than mere hunger. He swore at them and hurled rocks and heavy sticks until he made them retreat. He would have done anything to chase them away from that pathetic little white thing swinging from the tree, with a length of cord tied about its neck.

He buried Bullseye up there by the tree. He only had his hands to dig with and the ground was rock hard but he finally managed to scoop out a shallow hole. It wasn't deep enough and he knew the scavengers would be back but it was the best he could do. He held the little dog in his arms and kissed his muzzle before he laid him gently in the grave. 'Good boy, good boy,' he crooned. 'Sleep tight.' He'd heard Willem's mum say that to her little baby. It seemed a nice thing to say. He wanted to say a prayer but he couldn't remember any about dogs.

When he got back to the house the old woman was waiting for him, arms folded, triumphant. Eunice stood behind her, head down, unable to look at him. The old woman didn't beat him; she was enjoying herself too much to be angry. Eunice placed a plate of slop in front of the boy and then retreated to her own little rondavel in the garden.

The old woman sat down to watch him. He ate the food, although every mouthful made him want to puke. He knew if he didn't eat it she would only serve it up again and again until he did. And he didn't cry – he wouldn't cry – he wouldn't give her the satisfaction.

But when he'd finished and swilled off his plate under the tap he couldn't stop himself from asking one question. 'Why didn't you shoot him?'

'What?' she'd laughed. 'Waste a bullet on a mangy little runt like that?'

And he'd climbed up the ladder to his room in the eaves with the sound of her laughter in his ears.

She had one parting shot for him. 'You try that again, boy, and I'll make you string up the next one yourself. Got it?'

When Willem asked him where Bullseye was he said the dog had got out and run away.

Quent closes his eyes again. All he wants to do is sleep. Maybe this time he won't dream. Maybe.

The Diagnosis

Raki was on the road to Cape Town very early the next morning. However, when she got to the hospital she waited for hours before she was seen. They sat in a long, airless corridor on chairs made for extra-terrestrials and magazines printed before she was born. At first Farnie had been fascinated by this new big place with all the noise and bustle but pretty soon he was bored, tired and fractious.

At midday they were shown into a tiny cubicle where a young coloured man took Farnie's details. Raki wasn't sure that this medic was a doctor and he never introduced himself, but she was very relieved when he didn't examine Farnie. After a cursory look at her notes he got someone to show her to yet another long corridor with chairs down each side occupied by people wearing identical dazed expressions. This was the queue for the x-ray department. It was teatime before Farnie had his x-ray done and another hour before a nurse showed them into a small room where a man sat behind a desk, studying Farnie's x-ray.

Mrs Morgan?' the man said at last, looking up. 'Please.' He indicated a chair and held out his hand. 'I'm Mr McNeil the paediatric orthopaedic consultant for this unit.'

Raki said *hello* but she didn't have a free hand to shake with because she was carrying the sleeping boy in her arms. She sank wearily down into the chair. Only a few minutes ago Farnie had been hysterical with hunger and tiredness. She was totally exhausted. She hadn't brought enough food or drink for him and she had been frightened to go and look for something in case she lost her place in the queue. The doctor smiled and she felt the tears coming. 'Long day?'

She nodded.

'Try not to worry, Mrs Morgan,' he said cheerfully. 'The x-rays show the CDH isn't too far advanced and with prompt treatment your little boy should grow up perfectly normally.'

'CDH? I'm sorry, but what is that?' She was determined to ask questions this time.

'Congenital dysplasia of the hip, Mrs Morgan. Is he your first child?'

She nodded.

'Ah,' he said, writing something down, 'and is anyone else in your family affected by CDH?'

She shook her head, 'I don't think so, but my family don't talk about things like that.'

'Good, good,' he said, cutting her short, the smile switching on again. 'I'm sure that young...' he read the notes, '...Farnie will make a full recovery once he receives treatment. But the sooner it's done the better. I think we can get away with a closed reduction at this stage. We'll save the open reduction as a fail-safe option, shall we?'

'I'm sorry,' stammered Raki. 'But what does it mean? Closed reduction? Open reduction?'

The man didn't exactly sigh but he spoke very slowly and clearly. 'Closed reduction is when the head of the femur is manipulated into its correct position in the pelvis. But if things have gone too far we use open reduction, which is a small operation to do exactly the same thing under a general anaesthetic. '

Raki flinched as she remembered how rough the nurse had been with Farnie. The man saw her fear. He hadn't expected a mother of her maturity to be quite so emotional. 'There's nothing to worry about I assure you, Mrs Morgan. Farnie won't feel a thing. It's a simple, straightforward procedure. I've done thousands of them.'

Raki felt sick.

'After the procedure he will be placed in a spica – a body cast to maintain the proper hip position, which will have to be changed every six weeks or so, to allow for the healing process to work and to gradually encourage the hip to work normally again.'

'How long? How long will it take to work normally?'

The consultant looked at the notes again. 'He's one?' Raki nodded. 'Then it will take a year or thereabouts. These things can't be rushed, Mrs Morgan, and during this time you will have to come for regular check-ups to see how he's progressing. But it will all be worthwhile once he's running about, won't it? Try not to worry, children are most resilient. Believe me; you will suffer far more than he does. For him it will be just a minor inconvenience. It might even be fun – a new experience.'

'But I live on a mountain, how will I manage?' It was out before she could stop herself.

'A mountain?' he said. 'Interesting. Do you have a 4X4?'

'No. I have to walk up and down carrying Farnie.'

'Ah,' he said, making a pyramid with his fingers and holding them against his mouth. 'You live on your own?' He was beginning to get the picture.

'Yes.'

'I suggest you move somewhere more appropriate while he's getting better. Umm?' He was pleased with himself. Why did these people not think for themselves?

Raki nodded. She couldn't think of after, not yet. 'But he will get better?'

The man smiled reassuringly. 'He seems a perfectly healthy little boy so there's no reason why he shouldn't make a full recovery. And even if he doesn't, children are great at adapting. You see they don't have any preconceived ideas of what's supposed to be normal, like we adults do.'

'But what happens if he doesn't make a good recovery?'

'He may have a slight limp but I'm sure it won't come to that. Now, if you would like to see my secretary, second door on the left down the corridor, and give her your details. She will arrange to have the boy admitted as soon as there's a bed available.'

'How much will it cost?'

'My secretary deals with that side of things.' The man was already putting her notes to the bottom of the heap. 'But it's not expensive. You'll pay for the procedure, then follow up appointments and the traction beforehand.'

'Traction?'

'Didn't your doctor give you any information?' The consultant's patience had run out and now he was irritated by this woman's ignorance.

'I didn't go to a doctor, the nurse sent me straight here from the clinic.'

'I see,' he said. 'Well, your son will be admitted to hospital three weeks before the procedure and put on traction. You, of course will be with him for the entire time. We believe in keeping mothers and babies together. You will have a bed beside him and it will be just like being at home. You will care for him. The only difference being, he will be in traction. Very simply, traction can prevent the necessity for surgical intervention. We're trying to lengthen the affected leg, so that it will match the other. Don't worry, it doesn't hurt.' He'd seen the mother's face. 'I'm sure you can see the advantages of that.'

'Three weeks is a long time and I expect this traction is expensive? Only I don't have med-Care.'

'Ah,' said the doctor. 'Not to worry. Your son will be put on the waiting list.'

'How long will we have to wait?'

'We pride ourselves in this hospital that no one waits for longer than a year for treatment. Now, go and have a nice chat with my secretary. She will be most helpful I'm sure. Any questions just ask her.' And with that he ushered her out of his room and pointed her in the right direction before going back inside and firmly closing the door behind him.

8.45 a.m.

Thank God, no dreams this time, but he's so cold. It's this that has woken him. He's naked from the waist down and needs to find something to wear. Last thing he wants is to be caught with his pants down when they walk in on him.

As he hunts for something his thoughts are on Willem. He hopes his friend got back home okay and wasn't in trouble. Willem had always been a great friend to him – shame Quent hadn't returned the compliment. He took and Willem gave. God knows why the man hadn't given him up a long time back. Quent was nothing but trouble. But he'd written the letter, hadn't he? Last night – by the light of the moon and a lamp. Or was that part of a dream? He'd check in a minute, when he got outside again.

Willem worked with him on the leopard project too - didn't earn as much as Quent but any extra was appreciated by Florentina – Willem's wife – who had five kids plus Willem and Johannes to feed. Quent and Willem had some great times roaming the kloof together, just like when they were kids, but then things started to go wrong.

It was always the same for Quent. Nothing held his attention for long before he got bored and restless. It wasn't just Du Toit. All the scrimping and saving was doing his head in. There was never enough money for drink and smokes and there was always something needed fixing in the kloof house. Quent was becoming a 'married' man whether he liked it or not. He needed space and when he was back in the house Raki was always fussing around him, second-guessing what he wanted to eat or drink, always smiling and happy and...annoying. He knew he was being unfair, she was a great woman, an uncomplaining, surprising woman, but the whole ...'couple' thing was hard to take.

Some days he saw the years ahead spiralling down towards death. He was well into his fifties now and any small injury took twice as long to heal as it used to. Even the work for the CLP took it out of him. The arrogant kids working on the project saw his exhaustion when he came down the kloof at the end of the day. They thought he was past it, but he wasn't, not yet. That's what this was all about, even if he wouldn't admit it. Even making love took it out of him. Sex was very important to Quent. It was what made him a man, what gave him his confidence, but Raki was fifteen years younger than he was and it was beginning to show.

That's when he started getting messages from Jaco du Plessis. They were always the same. *Was Quent available for work? Did he want a job on Jaco's estate?* And lastly, *where the hell was he?* Pierre, his mate in Birkenheadbaai, filled him in with details. Apparently Du Plessis ran a wild-life farm up North, the sort where the animals were used by film companies for nature documentaries. Everyone knew that Quent had a way with animals, including Jaco. He used to call him *The Leopard Man* to wind him up.

Quent hadn't heard from Jaco since he was chucked out of the Scouts, over twenty years ago now, and to say that Quent was surprised to hear from his old enemy and ex NCO was a massive understatement. It was hard to credit the cheek of the man, acting as if everything was okay between them. Quent would need to be crazy to work for that bastard and he wasn't quite that desperate yet. Nevertheless, he was intrigued. Quent was bored and it gave him something to think about.

After the fourth message Quent decided to put the guy out of his misery. He wanted to find out why Jaco du Plessis was bothering to track him down after all this time. It must be something important to keep him ringing and getting no response. Jaco didn't like being pissed about. He'd always been a single-minded bastard; liked getting his own way.

When Quent rang Jaco, the man picked up immediately. 'Yeah? Du Plessis. What?'

Quent smiled wryly. Always the charmer our Jaco. 'Hi, it's me, Byrant.'

'Byrant?' Jaco said, pretending not to recognise the name. They both knew he was playing a game.

'Quent Byrant, Jaco. You've been trying to get hold of me? You've messaged me. What? Five, six times.'

'If you say so. Remind me, man, what was the gist?'

So Quent told Jaco what he already knew. It was worth playing along if he got some entertainment from the conversation.

Jaco interrupted before Quent had strung a sentence together, 'Ja ja, I remember. So? Where've you been all this time? Prison?'

Quent laughed. That was what you did with people like Jaco. Quent had learnt this when he was in the Scouts, because if you didn't laugh you might just have to stick a knife in his fat, Afrikaner guts. 'Not prison, Jaco, busy. Had a commitment, you know, busy, busy.'

But Jaco wasn't listening. Apparently he needed a manager for his business, to oversee the care and handling of the wild animals for the photo-shoots. It was exactly the sort of work that Quent loved. If it had been anyone else but Jaco he would have said *yes* straight away but Quent liked playing games too.

'Umm,' he said when Jaco was finished. 'I might be able to help you out, but I've got a few things to sort before I can take on anything else.' He made his voice sound non-committal. 'But I'll keep you posted, yeh?'

'Don't keep me waiting too long, boy.'

And that was as far as it got. Quent felt pleased with himself. He'd never really intended working for the man, even though the work sounded very interesting. He wasn't to know that a week or so later he would be talking to Du Plessis again, telling him he would take the job.

Du Plessis stopped messaging Quent after their conversation so Quent had nothing left to distract him from the killing boredom of his life. The outcome was inevitable. The question wasn't *if* he dumped Raki but when.

R10, 000

By the time Raki pulled out of the hospital car park the evening rush-hour was easing. She was in no fit state to drive but what other option was there? She hadn't the money for an overnight stop.

She was sure that the knocking sound in the engine was getting worse. The thought of breaking down in the mountains at night with no money and a small baby filled her with dread. She'd been brought up on horror stories of the wild blacks who lived in the mountains and preyed on women like her, alone and unprotected. Car-jacking would be the best she could hope for.

She'd always had this problem about black people. The ones she knew were lovely, like Willem and his wife Florentina – who visited the kloof house with their family. Raki and Florentina got on really well. Raki and Quent weren't rich but she always managed to find the little ones something to take home – some of her leather work or vegetables from her garden and they loved to watch the baboons. Then there were her black friends who worked on her father's farm, men and women she'd known all her life, more like extended family than paid employees.

It was the others she was frightened of – the strangers. When Nelson Mandela and the ANC took over in South Africa her mother made Raki pack an emergency bag for when the blacks rampaged through their area, killing and raping all the whites. Raki had left that bag behind when she moved in with Quent but it wasn't so easy to leave behind the fear.

As she drove she glanced in her mirror and saw that Farnie was fast asleep. His face and hands were covered in biscuit mush. She'd managed to buy rusks and juice at the petrol station where she'd filled up. She hadn't eaten all day but she wasn't hungry.

Had the secretary really said it could cost R10,000 plus for Farnie's treatment? Where on earth would she get that sort of money from? It was impossible but so was the alternative. If Farnie had to wait for a year for treatment he might be a cripple for life and it was all her fault.

She nursed the car up and over the Sir Lowry Pass and when she was on the easier road she pulled off the main highway and parked on the hard shoulder under a dense, spreading tree.

It was a risk stopping but she needed to ring Quent. She knew he wouldn't be able to give her the full amount but surely he would give her something? He'd been sending her small amounts of rand since he left her. It was guilt money but she didn't care. She'd vowed she'd never ask him for anything ever again but this was different, this was for Farnie. What did her pride matter where her little boy's future was concerned? She'd have gone on her knees to the devil if necessary.

Quent must be earning big money now and it was the least he could do. She had no preconceptions about him anymore. He didn't want anything to do with her or Farnie. He'd made that perfectly clear in that horrible phone call. She wished she'd never rung him. She'd vowed not to. She hated Quent for what he'd done to her and she continued to hate him until the day her baby gave her his first radiant smile. His beautiful almost sapphire-blue eyes flashed with love and a tiny dimple appeared in one cheek. Quent had an identical mark. The pain of the similarity made her weep. Even then it had been six months before she'd plucked up the courage to ring Quent and tell him he had a son. It had been a huge mistake but here she was again texting him, asking for money. But this was different she told herself this was for Farnie. He would get back to her, he had to. *But what,* said the little worm in her brain, *what if he doesn't? What would she do then?*

It was dark by the time she'd finished messaging Quent but there was still some light traffic on the road. She was undecided about what to do next. Maybe she should try to get back to Pig's Snout? But would she have the strength to climb

90

the kloof in the dark with a sleeping child in her arms? No, of course not, much better to stay where she was. The car was out of sight. She'd chance it. A couple of hours sleep - that's all she needed – then she'd drive on. Maybe she'd go to Mari's? Her cousin would know what to do, she always did. Mari couldn't help her financially, Anton was often out of work, but she was full of good sense. Raki made herself comfortable and shut her eyes. She should really change Farnie's nappy but she didn't want to wake him. Yes, she would go to see Mari first thing in the morning.

She shut her eyes but the headlights from passing vehicles raked through her car and she knew for certain she would never sleep. She had a pounding headache and all she could think about was Farnie. There must be someone she could go to for the money? Her mother? No, never. Who else was there if Quent didn't ring back?

A thought kept nudging at her but she kept pushing it away. She could never go to that man. *But he is your husband. Maybe he'd like to buy you off?* But no, why should he? *Because then he could show everyone what a saintly, forgiving man he was.* He would make her suffer but maybe she deserved it? It would be a small price to pay. Hurt pride in return for Farnie's future happiness.

8.50 a.m.

On the day it happened Quent had taken two Scandinavian women up the kloof. Willem was back on the farm dipping merinos.

The tall female spent her time scanning the mountainside through her latest, high-spec glasses while the other little plump one buzzed annoyingly around Quent.

Only one of the cameras was working properly and the cage trap was falling to bits. If they ever trapped a leopard it would never hold a mature animal. The strategy was to trap, dart and put a GPS collar on any leopard they caught. Then they could track its home range. If any of the guides got a leopard they were supposed to get word to the project vet immediately, who would come out and dart it.

This particular day they found and released a couple of small *Bok*, a porcupine and several dassies or Rock Hyrax – large quarrelsome, hamster-like creatures. One of the ungrateful bastards had bitten him on his finger when he'd turned it loose. If the fat female hadn't been there going, 'Oo, isn't he sweet,' he would have kicked the little runt into touch, but he let it go. In his experience happy volunteers tipped well.

'Shame,' Du Toit had goaded him that morning, slapping him on the back like they were best buddies. 'You wouldn't have a clue about a GPS or a satnav would you, fella?' He smiled broadly at his assembled adoring groupies. 'Smoke signals more your style, eh? Maybe we should invest in some carrier pigeons? So you can let us know when you get a leopard?'

Oh yeah, very funny; Quent laughed all the way up the kloof.

Quent was well aware that if the miracle happened and he trapped a leopard he would have to climb all the way down to where he could get transmission on his cell phone. That was on the road side of the trees and a good hour and a half hike from the cage trap. But as it happened, unknown to Du Toit, Quent had sorted this particular problem. He and the project vet went back a long way and Quent had a few darts put away, just in case. It was all a waste of time, of course, but it pleased him to put one over the smug little prat.

The Swedish girls saw a caracal and two klipspringers. The baboon troupe was nowhere to be seen. Quent had no idea where they were. Maybe moved to new territory he thought. No leopard, but Quent knew, everyone knew, there was as much chance of seeing the illusive animal on this kloof as there was in discovering gold in the sea. And besides, if there was any leopard-glory going Du Toit wanted it for himself. He patrolled the mountains east of here, where leopard had been sighted recently.

There had been a leopard once, when he was a kid. He and Willem had seen it. They'd climbed to the top of the kloof after dassies. They were good meat for the pot. The boys used slings and Willem was a dead shot. There were already two plump animals strung together across Willem's shoulder but they'd seen some more disappearing at the foot of the rocks and went after them. They'd nearly reached the rocks when Willem froze and put his finger to his lips.

The sun was setting and there she was, standing in the shadows, scenting the air for prey. A beautiful Cape leopard. Even in the dim light she had blazed out at Quent, her coat gleaming like looted gold from the tomb of some Egyptian king. He must have made some sound because her ears flicked and she was gone. The two boys stood for a moment hardly daring to breath. That was when Quent fell in love for the first time.

The boys didn't speak on the way down the kloof. It was like if they talked about her it wouldn't be real. She was the last leopard Quent ever saw on his kloof. He didn't tell the old woman, not even Eunice, they wouldn't have believed him.

It had been a long, very hot day, trekking up and down the kloof and it was late afternoon by the time he'd checked everything and he and the women were on their way back down to the campsite. Quent needed a drink badly. They'd almost reached the wooded valley, where the path levelled out through the trees for a bit, when the smaller of them, the dassie-lover called Birgitte, decided she needed another drink. She must have the bladder of a camel Quent thought.

Tilsa, the tall one had a big green nose. She perched herself on a rock and swept the surrounding terrain with her binoculars. She had been 'spotting' leopards all day. *There's one. Oh no, it's a tree. Over there, quick. I'm sure...no just a shadow. Where are your leopards?* she demanded finally, as if Quent was some bloody magician who could wave his magic wand and conjure up the animal. Stupid, stupid bitch. But at least she was quiet now while she concentrated.

Quent loved this crepuscular time of day when the daytime creatures went to sleep and the predators and night-feeders came out. The sun was setting behind the trees and he shielded his eyes as a large white hunting-owl swept low overhead. It landed on a tall tree further down the valley. The wind had dropped and everything was quiet as if nature was drawing breath while it waited for the drama of night time to begin.

'Oo, look!' Birgitte shrieked suddenly, wrecking the moment. There was a small yellow frog swimming frantically away from her. Quent had sympathy for the frog. The girl was crouched down beside the stream, exposing her blotchy, sturdy thighs. She cupped her hands and took a long, noisy slurp of water. She was prettier than her friend but that wasn't saying much. She had freckles and disproportionately large breasts which swung beneath her like twin hammocks. Her glasses were steamed up with all the sweat that ran freely down her face, so she had taken them off. She saw him watching her and smiled short-sightedly at him. Maybe she thought he fancied her. She pulled her unglamorous sun hat further down over her ears and stood up. These fair-skinned girls always ended up so red-faced you could have fried an egg on their skin. Little Birgitte was a mess but at least she didn't have a green nose-guard like her friend.

'To stop the cancer.' Tilsa had informed Quent when she caught him staring. 'You should wear one. Old people are susceptible. You will have skin carcinoma for sure, in fact that,' and she pointed to a nebula of moles on his arm that were in danger of joining up, 'pre-cancerous without a doubt,' she predicted, with an unsympathetic curl of the lip.

'My God, I think I'm melting, Tilsa,' Birgitte moaned, sitting down on a rock and mopping her face with the edge of her shirt, exposing the rolls of pasty-white flesh on her midriff. 'Look at me.'

Not if I can help it, thought Quent.

'When I take off this hat I am going to look such a freak.' She tried to catch Quent's eye, as if she expected him to disagree, but Quent was busy filing his report for the day. Du Toit insisted on a detailed run-down of the proceedings — which animals had been caught in the traps or photographed, at what time, the weather conditions, etc etc.

'Doesn't your dog want a drink?' Green Nose asked suddenly, destroying his concentration. She was glaring at Quent

Everything this female said was confrontational. Quent had thought it was a language thing to begin with but as the day wore on he realised it was just the way she was — plain, bloody belligerent.

'The dog drinks when he wants,' Quent replied and glanced at Bullseye, who was lying down a hundred metres or so away from them, staring down into the valley. On these jaunts he would appear every now and then, as if he was checking up on them, making sure they were treating his territory with respect.

'And what about food?' the girl snapped. 'In my country we look after our animals properly.'

That made Quent laugh. 'Bullseye catches his own dinner.'

Birgitte was on her feet and walking towards Bullseye, her hand outstretched. 'Who's a beautiful boy, then? He is so big. A monster dog.'

'I wouldn't touch him, if I were you.'

'Why on earth not? Who's a lovely boy,' she crooned to the dog, standing in front of him with her hand outstretched.

'He'll go for you.'

The girl turned a frightened face towards Quent. 'Really? You're not teasing?'

'No, I'm not teasing. Anatolians are not like other dogs. They're working dogs and they take their work very seriously. They don't wag their tails or roll over to be petted and they hate being touched, particularly on the head.'

He noticed the girl's hand had dropped to her side and she had taken a step backwards. Bullseye was watching her intently with more curiosity than malice – but she wasn't to know that.

Tilsa jumped down from her rock. 'This is foolishness. Man and dog have a special bond, he would not hurt me.' She took a step towards Bullseye. 'You are the sort of man who likes to frighten people with your stories. I have known many men like you before.'

'Okay, you know best.' Quent's smile was lazy. He was beginning to enjoy himself. 'Go ahead, give your theory a go. Touch him.'

'No, Tilsa, don't,' Birgitte squealed. 'I think our guide is right.'

Quent was watching Green Nose. 'Just remember, if anything happens I did warn you. All I hope is that you've got good cover.'

Green Nose took another, smaller, step towards the dog.

'No!' Birgitte was frantic. 'Please Tilsa. Leave the dog alone.'

'It's okay, I'm sure your friend knows best. It's up to her if she wants to upset an animal that weighs 60 kilos and stands as tall as her waist.'

On cue the dog began to growl. It was a low vibrating sound, not loud, but impossible to ignore. Tilsa stopped dead in her tracks, wheeled about and hurried back to her rock where she busied herself adjusting her backpack straps. Quent had the satisfaction of seeing her hands trembling as she did so. He knew Bullseye wasn't growling at the Swede but he didn't tell her that.

Quent looked through his binoculars to where the dog was staring. The animal's hackles were raised and he continued to growl. 'See something, Bullseye?' he asked, but there was nothing down there but the owl. Quent put away his notebook and checked his watch. 'Okay, time to move, unless you want to be stranded up here all night, with just me, the dog and the snakes.'

He heard Tilsa's contemptuous snort but even she kept close behind him as he continued the scramble downhill. Bullseye didn't go with them.

Quent had a strong urge to ditch the women. Let them find their own way back to the CLP camp but Quent knew Du Toit would have something to say about that. He was considering going into town tonight, maybe have a few beers, a game of pool. He might go to the shebeen; see if Willem was there. Raki wouldn't mind. Didn't matter if she did. She'd said something about cooking him something special but it could keep. He wasn't hungry, just thirsty, very thirsty.

'D'you want to hear a story about the Cape cobra?' he said suddenly, determined to get some reaction from the big Swede. Good name for her.

'Oo, yes,' gushed little Birgitte, trying to keep up.

Quent had several snake stories in his repertoire but he always used this one with women. It was the one about the time he ate a Cape cobra — not the best thing he'd ever stuck his teeth into but passable if you were very hungry and he had been. Green Nose kept quiet but the other one squeaked and squealed her way down the mountainside. She stuck to Quent like glue and he breathed in the sweet smell of her sweat and felt her hot, clammy breath on the back of his neck.

'Oh, my God. How scary,' she gasped. 'Did it try to bite you?'

'Sure, but I've been handling poisonous snakes all my life. I was brought up on a farm in Rhodesia — before it became Zimbabwe. We had green mambas on our land. '

'Green mambas?' Birgitte shrieked again, nearly deafening him.

'Keep it down, for God's sake, Birgitte,' Green Nose ordered. 'How can we hope to see a leopard or anything else with you making all that noise?'

'One came for me once,' Quent continued, ignoring Tilsa. 'They rear up on the back of their tails and come straight for you like an express train. This one certainly intended getting me. Its mouth was gaping, its fangs dripping and it stood way above my head...'

'...That wouldn't be too difficult,' Green Nose muttered maliciously.

'My God. What happened?' He had Birgitte in the palm of his hand. Maybe he would claim his reward later? Maybe she wasn't a lesbo and even if she was, so what? It wouldn't be the first time he'd bedded one of these eager little girls and he was sure it wouldn't be the last. Maybe, he thought, it might soothe that itch? 'I sliced its head off with my machete,' he said modestly.

'Oh my God,' Birgitte was nearly wetting herself. 'You are so brave, Quent.'

Gotcha, thought Quent and gave the girl one of his lop-sided grins. 'Not brave, Birgitte, lucky.'

'Why?' Green Nose interrupted, 'why did you kill it?'

What was it with this woman? 'Because,' he said slowly and deliberately. 'It was gonna bloody kill me.'

'No, not the mamba,' she said dismissively, as if she was talking about a kitten. 'Why did you eat the cobra? Was it a threat to you? It is silly to eat an animal like that. A waste of a wonderful creature.'

"Silly?" He was startled. They weren't supposed to say things like that. They were supposed to think he was macho. But then, in that instant, none of it mattered. He froze. 'Nobody fucking move!' He was pointing downhill to where the stream disappeared into the wood and his finger was trembling.

'What?' Birgitte began, but Quent made a slashing motion across his throat.

98

He pointed again. 'Over there,' he whispered, 'on the other side of the stream.'

Tilsa had her binoculars focused on the place he was indicating. He didn't need to use glasses, he could see the animal clearly with his bare eyes. It was a leopard – a glorious, golden animal, oozing in and out of the shadows. He was confident in calling her a 'she'. The female Cape Leopard was smaller than the male. 'Have you got her?' his voice shook.

Green Nose shook her head.

The sun was sinking behind the trees and throwing a chequered quilt of shadow and sunlight over the surrounding bushes and vegetation. Light and shade pulsed in the dying sun as if it was alive and the beautiful rosette markings on the leopard's coat were one with the leaf patterns. He'd never seen an animal with such a light pelt before. She looked like a shaft of lightening on the darkening mountainside. Why couldn't the Swede see her? 'Beside that boulder. There. You can't miss her.'

'You are mistaken,' the woman said, eyes glued to her binoculars.

'Are you blind, you stupid bitch? Follow the line of my finger. There. For God's sake, quick, before she disappears.' He followed the path of the leopard. 'On the far side of that patch of reeds. Christ! She's so beautiful. There...there. Got her?'

The animal was moving swiftly, she would soon be lost in the band of trees.

'No, nothing.'

Before entering the wood the animal stopped and scented the air and then she turned in their direction and looked directly at Quent. She was magnificent. He felt his eye-lids prickling. Leopards were living on Pig's Snout again. He was so happy he could have kissed Birgitte. For a moment he was even tempted to hug the other one. He couldn't believe his luck. To see a leopard on Pig's Snout was nothing short of miraculous. A bloody miracle. Maybe life was worth living after all?

He stood still watching the achingly empty space where the creature had been, only a few seconds ago, before

99

vanishing into the trees. Quent's heart was beating so fast he felt it juddering in his teeth. He'd forgotten the girls; he'd forgotten everything, the irritation, his dissatisfaction, everything except that incredible, mind-blowing leopardess. When Tilsa spoke again he jumped.

'I think it is time we descend.'

And for once she was right. It was almost dark now. Quent turned on his head-light and indicated that they should do the same. No one spoke on the way down.

Mr Turkey

The first time Raki actually noticed Henrik Morgan was at one of her mother's formal tea parties, to raise money for the church and *to cheer up their pastor after the tragic death of his dear mother* – or at least that's what Sofia told her. Normally Raki steered well clear of these shindigs but her mother was most insistent that she attended this one. That should have made Raki suspicious but, as her cousin kept telling her; *she was a babe in arms* when it came to the ways of the world.

Sofia told Raki that the older women needed help serving the teas. This was unlikely because the same ladies had been making the teas all their adult lives. Mrs Veiser was in charge of the tea urn and the Misses van der Merwe always washed up. The tablecloths had to be folded in exactly the same way, the teacups arranged in a certain pattern, the chairs put in exact semi-circles; everything was ordered and each woman had her task, often passed down from mother to daughter. The Misses van der Merwe had inherited the washing up from their mother and her mother before her. If Raki had tried to do any of these jobs she would have been sent away with a flea in her ear. The one time she'd attempted to help it was a disaster. There'd been a raffle and afterwards Raki had grabbed a rubbish bag and swept all the used tickets inside, only to be swooped on by at least three irate ladies. Apparently, Mrs Veiser's sister-in-law from Hermanus always made confetti out of these tickets – painstakingly cutting each piece of paper into horseshoes, lucky cats and the baby Jesus.

Raki should have heard alarm bells ringing that day, especially when her mother complained about what she was wearing. It was only when Raki looked back that she realised this was the day when Sofia van de Venter had decided Raki would be the pastor's wife.

Sofia's teas were famous in the area and the church hall was packed out with women and children. There were only two men: one was Desmond van de Venter, who was only there because his wife said so and the other was Pastor Morgan, surrounded by adoring females. It was a strange phenomenon but any new pastor, married or otherwise, young or old, always attracted a group of women, married or otherwise, young or old, who competed with each other for the pastor's affection. Pastor Morgan was very young – in their eyes – and *otherwise*, which made him doubly eligible.

The refreshment table was in danger of collapsing under the weight of food. There was every conceivable type of sandwich, sausage rolls and plate pies, cakes, rusks, gateaux, milk tarts and *koeeksisters* – the ubiquitous gooey, honeyed plaits of dough. Mr Morgan's plate looked like a mini volcano. He had taken a piece of everything – not wanting to offend any of the good ladies.

Raki stood by the door keeping a low profile. Her father lurked beside her and kept saying things to make her laugh. They both watched Mr Morgan eating; it was hard not to. He didn't stop gobbling until every morsel had disappeared. His protruding Adam's apple moved in a strange way when he swallowed. Raki couldn't take her eyes off that wobbling wattle. That was how the *turkey* thing came about. It was Mari who coined it, of course. At one point Raki caught her father's eye and he winked at her.

Fortunately, Sofia wasn't the least bit interested in what Raki or her husband were doing; she was homing in on her prey. They could hear her strident voice from where they stood. 'We are so terribly sorry for your sad loss, Henrik,' she said, offering him yet another sausage roll. Sofia was the only person who called him Henrik. 'Your mother was a fine woman – a pillar of the Church and this community and a great help to you in God's work. Your loss is our loss.'

'Umm,' was all the man could manage.

'Our only solace is that she has gone to a better place, Henrik. She is in the arms of the angels.'

'Um, um,' came the reply.

There was a slight pause while Sofia offered another plate of food. 'That big house must seem so empty and lonely without her. We all know what a wonderful home-maker she was.' Sofia only lied when there was no alternative. It was well known that Mrs Morgan Senior had done nothing all day except lounge about eating pastries and crocheting jam-pot covers.

Sofia offered the man a large piece of cheesecake. 'My daughter made this, Henrik,' said Sofia, glancing at Raki. She caught her daughter's eye and beckoned her over. 'She has a very light touch, wouldn't you say?'

The man flicked a glance at Raki. 'Umm.'

Raki's mother pressed home the advantage. 'I regard myself as an adequate pastry cook, Henrik,' she said modestly. 'But I must give credit where credit's due and my daughter has a lighter touch than I do. It's the cool hands you see and, unfortunately, mine are always hot.'

Mr Turkey put down his plate at this riveting piece of information and took a long, thoughtful drink of tea.

8.55 a.m.

It was dark when Quent and the girls got back to camp. Du Toit was waiting for them. He looked pointedly at his watch as they came within the perimeter lights. All the volunteers were gathered around the braai pit drinking beer and shouting and laughing together. The smell of barbecued meat made Quent's mouth water. Suddenly he was very hungry.

'Just about to send a search party out for you three, Quent.' The boy-wonder said. 'It's dangerous up there when it gets dark.'

'Is that so?' Quent smiled, refusing to rise to the bait. 'But we knew our brave leader would come and find us if we got lost, didn't we, girls?'

'You look very pleased with yourself.' The boy didn't miss much.

'Yeah, well that's because I am, son.' He relished that 'son'. 'Thirty minutes ago I saw a leopard on this kloof, just the other side of the pig's eyes. I'm pretty certain she was a female – smaller build than the male. She was heading up towards the cliff. Maybe she has young up there in the rocks.'

Everyone had stopped talking and was listening intently to what Quent was saying. He heard their whispered, 'A leopard? Did he say a leopard?' Du Toit was silent for a moment and then he managed a sort of smile. 'You're sure? That's...amazing. Who would have thought it? Yeah, great work, Quent.' By this time Quent was surrounded by people congratulating him and wanting to know all the details.

Normally Quent went home as soon as he'd dumped his volunteers but tonight he decided to stay. Someone thrust a bottle of beer into his hand. They all knew this was an amazing coup for the project and there was much back-slapping and genuine elation. They toasted the new leopard in beer, several times. Quent felt relaxed and somehow vindicated for all the slights he'd suffered. He was happy, definitely happy.

'Excuse me.' Green Nose was standing beside Du Toit. 'I hate to be a party-pooper,' she said, loving every minute. 'But unfortunately my friend and I aren't able to corroborate the alleged sighting of a leopard by this guide.'

There was a stunned silence. 'Ah,' said the boy, allowing himself the tiniest of smirks.

'Alleged? What d'you mean alleged?' Quent glared at the woman.

'Exactly what I said.' Tilsa had removed her green nose. 'Birgitte and I were there but neither of us saw anything.'

'I did,' piped up Birgitte, not looking at her friend. 'I definitely saw something.'

Tilsa snorted. ' – What? You can't even see your hand in front of your face without your glasses, Birgitte, and you weren't wearing your glasses were you? You are too vain to wear them.'

'No, but...'

'Look,' Quent said, still on a high and prepared to be magnanimous. 'I know you must be pig-sick missing out but the fact remains that I saw a leopard and it's living on the kloof – no question.'

'Then why didn't I see it?'

Quent bit back the retort he'd liked to have made and smiled. He turned to the boy-wonder. 'It's a huge pity that this...lady didn't have time to get her very expensive high-tec binoculars focused correctly before the leopard disappeared from view.' He heard the muffled snigger from the other volunteers and so did the Swede. 'But hey, that's her loss. I saw leopard. No argument.'

But Green Nose wasn't about to give in. 'I think our designated guide is mistaken, Robert. He likes to tell stories. He thinks he is a good story teller. Isn't that so, Birgitte?'

The little girl ducked her head. 'But that doesn't mean he didn't see the leopard, Tilsa. And I think I saw it too. My long sight is much better than my short sight. It's true, don't glare at me.'

'If there was something there I would have seen it.'

Quent's voice was dangerously low. 'So? Let's get this straight. You're saying I'm lying?'

Tilsa saw the fury in Quent's eyes and stepped behind Du Toit. 'I am not judging. I am telling the truth.'

Quent made a lunge at the woman. 'You bitch,' he yelled. 'You lying bitch.'

The boy grabbed Quent before he could get to her. He was surprisingly strong. 'Chill, man,' he warned, his hands flat against Quent's shoulders. 'There's no need for anyone to get excited. This will be proved one way or another within the next few days. The CLP will concentrate all its resources into this kloof and the leopard, if it exists, will be found and collared. Okay? Okay, Quent?'

Quent was breathing heavily and he felt the blood pounding in his forehead but he managed to keep himself under control. He nodded and Du Toit stepped away from him.

'I saw a leopard, Du Toit, no question.'

'I'm sure you did but first law of science, Quent, prove your hypothesis. Now lighten up for God's sake,' he said, and gave Quent a friendly punch on the arm. But then he went and ruined it all. 'Just a thought though. Maybe the old eyes aren't as keen as they used to be? Perhaps an eye check would be in order?'

This time the others didn't even try to disguise their laughter.

"D'you know how long I've been tracking leopard, Du Toit? Longer than you've been alive, boy.'

'Hey, man. It was a joke, okay? I rate you, you know I do. That's why we took you on. The project values the knowledge you old guys have. But we've got to do this by the book. If the leopard's there, then we'll see it soon enough. All we need is corroborated evidence. You know that. Otherwise any old Tom Dick or Harry could say they've seen a leopard, couldn't they? And we don't want to put out incorrect data. We'd lose all credibility. Make ourselves a laughing stock. It was hard enough getting international funding for this project and we can't afford to lose the overseas support.'

'A simple question, Du Toit,' Quent was trying desperately to hang on to his temper. 'Are you telling me you that you believe a woman, just out of school with no field experience, to someone who's spent the last thirty years in the bush?'

'For God's sake, man. Write your report up tonight and we'll look into your claim.'

'Answer the question.' Quent's voice was icy.

Du Toit turned to walk away and Quent grabbed his arm and spun him around. 'I know what this is really about, man. You're jealous.'

Du Toit brushed Quent's hand away. 'Go home, old man, before you say something you'll regret. Have an early night. You old fellas need your sleep.'

The boy was lying in a heap at Quent's feet before Quent realised he'd hit him. Everyone just stood, open-mouthed, staring first at Quent and then down at Du Toit. Green Nose was the first to recover and helped the boy to his feet. She muttered something obscene at Quent. He barged his way through the silent circle of people and disappeared into the night.

Birgitte ran after him. She was breathing heavily by the time she caught up with him. 'I'm glad you hit Robert,' she puffed, 'he was horrible to you.' He turned and faced her. She blinked owl-like at him in the dim light. 'Don't be angry with me, please. I told them I saw the leopard didn't I? I could have agreed with Tilsa.'

'What d'you mean?'

She moved closer to him. 'Come on, Mr Leopard Man. Say 'thank you' properly to little Birgitte.'

'Are you saying you didn't see the leopard?'

She shook her head. 'Of course not. How could I see a leopard? I'm registered partially-sighted.'

'Then why did you say you did?'

'Because I didn't want her to make you look like a fool. Tilsa's such a bully. Sometimes I don't know why I'm friends with her.'

He turned away but she put out a hand, detaining him. He removed her sticky fingers from his arm.

'Please, Quent, don't be cross. I did it because I like you. And I don't think you're old at all. I like...mature men. I could bring us some steak and beers out here if you like; we could have a picnic under the stars.'

'Go back to your friends, little girl.'

'I'm twenty-two,' she said. 'Not so little.' He knew she was his for the taking. She smiled in what he supposed she thought was a sexy way. 'If you don't want any food maybe there's something else I could do for you?'

He grabbed her and forced her down onto the ground. His hands and mouth were everywhere. She struggled at first but then he felt her relax and she moaned a little and wriggled her body into a more comfortable position beneath him. 'Umm, naughty leopard man.'

That was when he jumped to his feet pulling the girl up beside him. 'Luckily for you,' he said, 'I'm particular about what I eat.' Then he smacked her rump and pushed her back towards the firelight. She burst into tears and stumbled away and he walked quickly in the opposite direction. The dog detached itself from the shadows and followed Quent.

The girl's tearful voice pursued him into the trees. 'Loser. Go eat some snake, you pathetic old man.'

And that was the moment it happened. In that instant he knew exactly what he was going to do. He kept walking – he wanted them to think he'd gone home but after five minutes he doubled back to where his bakkie was parked. They were making one helluva noise, laughing and shouting at each other as he skirted the campsite. Du Toit's voice was the loudest and Quent heard him shouting *Leopard Man* and the responding hoots of laughter.

Once in the bakkie Quent let the handbrake off and coasted down the hill towards the main road, only firing the engine at the last moment. He drove into Birkenheadbaai, past the brightly lit main street, past the expensive holiday homes with their razor wire and Rapid Response Unit warning signs and on into the RDP, where his friend Willem lived with his wife and kids in one small concrete box.

Wedding plans.

The whole thing was totally bizarre – a black comedy, a farce that had nothing to do with Raki. Surely her mother didn't really expect her to marry someone like Mr Turkey? This wasn't *Pride and Prejudice*. She wasn't *Elizabeth Bennett* and he wasn't *Mr Collins*. This was the Twenty-First Century.

Of course, everyone knew that Henrik Morgan was on the lookout for a suitable Mrs Morgan Junior. According to Mari, who knew everything, he wanted someone to cook for him and bear him a child – a boy preferably. That's why he'd been doing the rounds interviewing likely candidates. 'Measuring their child-bearing hips,' Mari told Raki gleefully.

Sofia dropped very heavy hints about the pastor's large house and Raki's ever diminishing hopes of getting married and having a home of her own. She made it known that it would make her very happy to welcome Henrik into the family.

Raki knew her mother well enough to realise she was serious about this but there was no way Raki would marry the pastor. She would never be that desperate. But she didn't like arguments so said nothing to Sofia. Anything for a quiet life and she could stop this madness whenever she chose.

9.00 a.m.

As Quent drove towards Birkenheadbaai that night the plan was taking shape in his head. What he needed now was to talk to Willem. Without him there was nothing.

It wasn't unusual for him to call in for a drink with his friend after work but tonight he didn't want Florentina and the kids listening to what he had to say, so he suggested that he and Willem went to the local bar.

'Ok, but do not bring my husband home drunk, man,' Florentina warned, waggling her finger at Quent. She was smiling but they both knew she wasn't joking. Quent was Willem's friend and if he was her husband's friend then he was hers also, but she knew the score. Quent wasn't the most reliable of men.

In the bar Quent wasted no time telling Willem about the leopard on the kloof. It was easy to talk because the shebeen was full of noise, everyone shouting to each other and music pounding in the background.

'A leopard, bra?' Willem was surprised. 'On Pig's Snout? Are you sure? How big was she? Where was she? Did she have young?' Many, many questions.

Quent was in a hurry to get to the main business so he rattled through the details about the sighting and a little about Du Toit's reaction — he didn't dwell too much on his humiliation, although there was anger in his voice. Willem listened intently and when Quent was finished he sighed. 'If it is God's will I pray I will see this beautiful creature before I die.'

'You're gonna see her sooner than you think, Willem. And it's got nothing to do with that guy on a cloud up there.'

Willem and Florentina were staunch church-goers and Quent never passed up an opportunity to have a go at his friend. Willem ignored him. He knew what he knew.

Quent was off again, machine-gunning the words at Willem. The man wore a dazed expression as he tried to follow what Quent was saying. Something about Quent catching the leopard and selling it to Jaco du Plessis– who Willem had heard about many times from Quent – and for them to leave Birkenheadbaai and work on Jaco's wild-life estate and make a pile of money to take home. Willem was used to Quent's wild ideas but this one was the wildest yet. He said nothing but his face said plenty.

Quent eventually took a breather and they drank their beers in silence. The noise of the bar, was reaching a crescendo. But the laughter and stamping feet, the smell of spilt beer and sweat receded into the distance. The two men were alone in a quiet place with nothing but the leopard and Quent's plan in their heads.

Quent could be very persuasive when he wanted but he knew he had to tread very carefully with Willem. It was crucial that he had a totally reliable, right-hand man to make the whole thing work and Willem was that man – a guy you could trust with your life, However, Willem was cautious by nature and he had scruples. Okay. He got in trouble when he was a kid – like all kids – but as an adult he followed a strict moral code. As far as Quent knew he'd never cheated on Florentina or done anything remotely criminal.

But Quent held a trump card because his friend was unhappy with his poorly paid job with Broot. All he had to do was convince him that he could earn a shed-load of rand if he helped Quent. He had to lie a bit because nothing was sorted yet, but Quent was confident that he could deliver all that he promised. And he was right because all it took was one phone call to Jaco du Plessis. He did it there and then so that Willem could hear the whole thing.

It took longer to get through to Jaco this time but Quent persevered and eventually the man answered.

'Yeah, what?' There was a whole lot of stuff going on in the background, people yelling and Jaco bollocking someone at the same time as he talked to Quent.

'Yeah, well do it!' He yelled down the phone, nearly deafening Quent.

'Jaco? It's Byrant. I've been thinking about your offer and I've decided to come on board.'

Jaco was silent for a moment. 'Bad timing, boy. I'm up to my eyes in shit here. I SAID OVER THERE!' he screamed suddenly, and then in the same breath, 'maybe I don't need you now?'

Quent was smiling as he spoke. 'Okay, man, that's cool. I won't waste any more of your valuable time. Sounds like your operation's running smooth as clockwork so I'll – '

Fortunately, Jaco didn't do sarcasm. '– Hang on. Not so hasty, Byrant, I'm thinking. I might be able to fit you in somewhere, for old time's sake. I like to help old comrades out when I can.'

Quent managed to stop himself from laughing outright. The only person Jaco ever considered helping was himself.

Jaco took Quent's silence as acquiescence and, satisfied at last that he was in the driving seat, was ready to talk business. 'I'll let you know when I want you to start.'

'I'll be with you tomorrow.'

'What?' The man bawled above the racket.

'I said I'll be with you tomorrow, late evening, at a guess.'

'Wait a minute, wait a minute. I'm running a bloody business here; you don't just drop in when you feel like it. I'll tell you when I need you.'

'It's tomorrow or never,' Quent insisted.

'Got to go, Byrant. Ring me some time next week and we'll sort a date.'

'Okay, no sweat. I can take my Cape Leopard to some other game farm if you're not interested.'

There was a pause on the other end, just long enough for Quent to know he had his man hooked. When Jaco spoke again his tone was friendly, almost matey. 'Cape Leopard you say?'

'Yeh, but you're obviously not interested so – '

' – Hold your bloody horses. Christ, you choose your moments don't you? I've got a big shoot on this week. It's a bloody madhouse here but yeh, okay, I'll expect you and the leopard tomorrow. I'll get an enclosure sorted. Is she a good specimen?'

'Only the most beautiful leopardess I've ever seen.'

112

'She'd better be.'

And that was that. No questions asked.

'I'm bringing a guy with me – excellent worker. And before you ask, yeah he's black.' Quent shot an apologetic look at his friend but Willem just shrugged.

'Wait a minute, boy. I'm bending over backwards for you. I don't need any more boys.'

'He's part of the deal, Jaco. No Willem, no me...no leopard.'

'Okay, okay. Just get yourself here. Now bugger off.'

Quent couldn't resist a parting shot. 'Yeah, see you, man. Oh, and I'm bringing my dog. Okay?'

'Bring them on, Leopard Man,' the man shouted above the din. 'Bring the whole bloody shebang. Tomorrow.'

Quent put his cell phone on the table and clinked his bottle against Willem's. 'Sorted,' he said and took a long swig. 'I knew he wouldn't be able to resist it. Got a nose for a quick profit has our Jaco.'

Willem was silent.

'Everything okay, man?' Quent touched Willem's shoulder but Willem ducked his head and wiped his hand nervously across his mouth.

Quent groaned. 'Please, I need you, man. Don't let me down.'

Willem's voice was very quiet when he spoke and Quent had to lean closer to hear him above the racket. It was very late and the noise in the shebeen had reached maximum decibel level. 'I want to help you,' Willem said. 'But it's happening too fast. I have to tell Florentina and my kids...you know. It will be tough for them if I come with you. My father...'

'...But you're not your father, man. You love your family and this is going to make a difference in their lives, in all your lives. Come on.' Quent's voice was gentle, persuasive. 'Jaco's expecting us tomorrow. I can't do it without you. This is your chance to make some proper money. A year or two and you'll bring home a pot of gold. Think about it, enough rand to put those kids of yours through school. That's what you've always wanted isn't it? Hey,' he said, thumping Willem on the back. 'They could be running this country one day.'

Willem attempted a smile. 'Florentina would like that.' Another pause. 'There's something else, Quent.'

'Yeah, what?'

'Why? Why are you doing this? Why are you selling a beautiful creature to a man like this Jaco?'

'Does it matter? Let's say it's too good an opportunity to miss. A chance to make something of ourselves. Maybe start our own businesses when we get back? We could open a store, or a bar...anything. It's got to be better than what we're doing now. Christ, man! The stink of those sheep. So? What d'you say?' He held out his hand. 'Come on, shake on it.'

'Florentina's going to give me a hard time.'

'Yeah, well she's a woman, isn't she? But you're the boss, man. Tell her about the money. You'll be able to afford a new house. Move to a better area. Have some fun.'

'Yeah, that would be nice, bra. Some fun.' And Willem smiled and shook Quent's hand.

Quent pulled his stool nearer. 'Okay, now we get down to business.' Quent's plan was to transport the animal down the mountain on a cradle with four poles attached. Four pairs of hands. 'We need two guys to help get her down the kloof once she's been sedated. I was thinking Johannes for one? Tell him I'll pay him R500 for the day. He could keep his mouth shut, couldn't he?'

Willem nodded. 'For that sort of money he would keep his mouth shut for ever, man.'

'And one more? We need someone we can trust, Willem – a non-drinker if possible. Another family man maybe.'

Willem thought for a moment. 'There's the little man from Lesotho? He always wears his blanket?'

Quent had noticed the small man about the estate wrapped in a brightly coloured blanket. Like a lot of migrant workers he was desperate to send money home to his family. He was unskilled, did the worst jobs on the farm and earned very little. Willem said he slept in the bush to save money. Good choice, thought Quent. This man would keep his

114

mouth shut. Willem said he'd get Johannes to go up and see him as soon as he got home.

With the men sorted Quent went through the timing in detail, making sure they'd covered every angle. At last, when he was satisfied, he stood up and held his empty beer bottle towards Willem, 'One more for the road?' he asked.

Willem shook his head. 'There is much to do before morning.'

'Yeah, sure.' Quent nodded. His friend was right. They'd need clear heads for the morning and there was something that had to be done tonight. They walked out into the warm, silent night. Quent was still talking. 'D'you want me to run through the plan one more time?'

Willem touched his head. 'No, I have the plan written in here,' he said. 'I drive your pick-up to the track on Fern Kloof, on the other side of Pig's Snout; then I climb up to meet you and the other boys on the Pig's Snout side at 5.30a.m?'

As they approached the pick-up they heard Bullseye's warning growl. Quent never had to lock his car with that animal around. 'Okay, man,' Quent said, opening the passenger seat door and handing Willem the keys. 'In the back, boy,' he said to the dog, who'd been keeping the passenger seat warm. The animal jumped out and sprang into the back of the vehicle. They drove in silence, both caught up in their own thoughts.

Bullseye stuck his head through the small window behind their heads and breathed his stinking breath all over them. 'Christ, dog, what have you been eating?' Quent pulled the pane of glass across the small window, shutting the dog out.

'What will happen to him?' Willem asked.

'He comes with me,' replied Quent. 'We're a team.'

'And Mrs Morgan?' Willem always referred to Raki as Mrs Morgan. It was a mark of respect.

'She's fine about it,' Quent lied.

'Um.' Willem said, concentrating on the road ahead.

Willem was silent after that and when Quent glanced at his friend's face he could see how worried he looked. Willem had a lot to lose if things went wrong. See? That was the problem for married men with kids – heavy commitments.

Willem loved his family and would really miss them, and they him. The affection in that family was so strong you could almost taste it the minute you walked through the door. Quent almost envied Willem his life and family – almost but not quite. He couldn't imagine himself as a family man. No, he would have no regrets when he left. Raki knew the score. He hadn't made any promises. They'd had a great time but it was over.

Willem drove them to the CLP campsite turn-off and a little way up the track. They didn't want to wake anyone on the site. Willem cut the engine and switched off the lights then they walked up the track to the campsite. It was a cloudless night but they didn't need torches to find their way to Eunice's place. The CLP used her rondavel to store the larger bits of kit like animal cages. Quent used his knife on the old rusty lock. They found the largest cage and carried it back to the pick-up and stowed it in the back.

Willem climbed up into the driving seat and started the engine. Just before he drove off he leant out of the window and whispered softly into the night. 'Hey, bra? You sure you will find her again?'

'I promise you, Willem. There's a leopard and I know exactly where she is. 5.30 tomorrow? And don't be late.'

Willem did a thumbs-up.

'Timing is crucial.' Quent added unnecessarily.

'I am never late, Quent,' Willem said simply.

'And I'll expect those two guys to be waiting for me at the foot of the cliff? Five on the dot or they don't get their money. Tell them that.'

'Yeah, yeah,' Willem's voice was tired. 'They are good men,' he said before reversing down the track and out onto the main road where he turned for Birkenheadbaai Quent watched the pick-up lights until they disappeared. He didn't blame Willem for being pissed off with him. Quent was the unreliable one. It was Willem who covered for him when he was late for work – usually hung over – or when he'd forgotten to do something important. It was Willem – always

116

Willem. Yeah, he owed Willem and this job with Jaco was his way of thanking his friend. It pleased Quent that Willem would earn enough to send his little kids to school. He felt good about that.

It was very late and he had that long climb ahead of him. He would grab his gear and sleep out on the other side of the stream. There was no need to wake Raki, he told himself, he could text her once he was on the road to Jaco's place. Bullseye padded along a few paces behind him and Quent began to hum very quietly. It was some stupid pop song from when he was a kid. This was the start of the rest of his life. His chance to make something of himself before it was too late.

The campsite was eerily quiet. He walked straight through the centre, side-stepping the empty beer bottles that littered the ground. They'd all be having a long lie-in tomorrow. That suited Quent perfectly. They could sleep all day as far as he was concerned, little Birgitte, the big Swede, Du Toit, the lot of them.

The braai pit was still smouldering as he passed by and he watched little sparks of flame shooting up into the darkness, like static electricity. Didn't the brats know it was dangerous to leave a fire burning? One sudden gust of wind and they'd have a bush fire on their hands. There was something quite pleasing about the thought of Du Toit and his students getting fried, but nevertheless Quent picked up a plastic container of water and poured it onto the embers, dousing the flames. He'd experienced too many of the Cape's raging wild-fires to take any chances and his leopard was up there. The last thing he needed was her spooked by fire.

There was one large perimeter floodlight still on gathering an army of flying bugs which clung to the light like one huge bee swarm. It was the dead of night and yet the thumping beat of the generator as it worked overtime and the pulsing of cicadas were incredibly loud. Quent felt as if he were the only person awake in the whole world. Everything felt a bit weird, like he was in some surreal dream.

What had Willem said? Things were happening too fast. And the other thing? Was Quent sure about the leopard? Oh yes, he was sure and he knew exactly where he'd find the animal. It was like he'd dreamt it. This dreaming was something he'd always done, since he was a kid. It was something he could never tell anyone about. He'd tried to tell the old woman once – big mistake.

'Just like your father, you. Full of bullshit. Well it doesn't wash with me, understand?' And she swiped him across his head to make the point.

He didn't care whether she believed him or not. He knew it was true. In his dreaming he could imagine a place or an occasion so vividly that he could actually see it and most times he was right.

On the other side of the stream, about 1km from the kloof house, there was a rocky ledge, halfway up to the summit. This was where the leopardess kept her cubs. The ledge was strewn with large boulders and there were clumps of grass and a few bushes growing on it. It was the perfect safe place for the cubs when the leopardess was out hunting. In the evening she would leave them, then in the morning she would return to the ledge and suckle her young. That's where she'd be tomorrow. He knew it.

Quent was dizzy with tiredness and elation as he climbed the rock-strewn path up to the house. Yesterday he'd been a loyal member of the CLP and now he was about to betray everything he believed in and for what? For sweet, sweet, revenge. God, he'd love to see the Boy Wonder's face when he found out what he'd done. Du Toit wouldn't be sneering at him then, would he? He would be the incompetent fool who'd let the one Cape leopard living on Pig's Snout kloof slip through his fingers – right from under his supercilious fat nose.

Quent had expected Raki to be asleep when he got to the house – in fact he was banking on it – but then he heard the drums. Whenever he heard drums he thought of Raki and saw her profile again, stern with concentration, with the tip of her tongue showing between her white teeth.

But that night the last thing he wanted was her waiting up for him. He had planned to leave some money and then hightail it before she woke. It would have been kinder that way, he told himself. When he got near the house he saw that the door was wide open and the welcoming lamplight spooled out across the ground towards him. A million flying insects were homing in on this beacon of light.

Going inside he slammed the door hard behind him. 'What d'you want to do, woman? Get us eaten alive?' His voice sounded ugly, even to him.

Quent starts suddenly. He hears the *thud* of that door as it slams shut behind him.

The new Mrs Morgan

Gradually the sky was lightening and it wouldn't be long before Raki could drive on to Birkenheadbaai and her cousin. She had been awake all night. However much she tried to stop herself from thinking about the past, there it was, hammering to be let in.

Henrik Morgan asked Raki to marry him two Sundays after her mother's tea party. At least that's what must have happened, but he made it sound more like a business proposition than a proposal of marriage.

'He's looking at you, Raki,' her mother whispered urgently as they stood together outside the church. 'No, don't look.' She pushed her knuckles painfully into the small of Raki's back. 'For goodness sake, girl, straighten up.'

Raki shrugged her off. 'That hurt, mother.'

'Go and say something to him.'

'Why?'

'He expects you to speak to him.'

'But why? What am I supposed to say?'

'Anything. Say you liked his sermon.'

Sofia had never mentioned the word 'marriage' but Raki was under no illusions as to what her mother wanted. It wasn't what Raki wanted – no way – so why hadn't she told her mother straight away? And why was she now walking towards the man? Good question.

The pastor watched Raki out of the corner of his eye as she approached. He excused himself from the group of admiring women he was talking to and took Raki by the elbow, leading her back into the church. His fingers dug into her flesh and she wanted to pull her arm away but didn't. The women were watching them. She saw their raised eyebrows and knew she was blushing. This was getting out of hand. She must tell him immediately that it was all a silly misunderstanding. She could never marry him.

He began speaking as soon as they were alone. He used that nasal drone that many clerics adopted and while his voice buzzed around her like an adenoidal bluebottle she rehearsed what she would say. She didn't want to hurt his feelings. He was a fool and she despised most of what he spouted in the church but he was her pastor and she owed him some respect.

She didn't hear most of what he said, not until he'd almost finished. ' – I think that would be in order.'

'I'm sorry,' she stammered. 'I missed that last bit.'

'The wedding,' he said, obviously irritated by her inattentiveness. 'I don't think there's any need for...' he hesitated, searching for the right word. 'There's no need for any undue fuss. Wouldn't you agree? I thought a simple service and then a small gathering at your mother's house. Um?' He didn't wait for a response. 'It's so soon after the death of my dear mother it would be unseemly to make a fuss. Um?'

No her brain screamed. *No. No. No!* She was so shocked by the suddenness of it that all she could do was stand there with her mouth open like some stranded fish. Her mother had bustled up by then and Mr Turkey told her that everything had been settled and Sofia had hugged her. Raki was probably almost as surprised by that as the proposal. Her mother never hugged anyone. Afterwards Sofia led the slightly smirking Mr Turkey and the shell-shocked Raki out into the clear, sparkling Sunday morning, where the congregation were frozen like a waxwork tableau, only brought to life by the arrival of these three people.

In the flurry of kisses and congratulations that followed her mother's announcement Raki remembered catching sight of her father and Mari. They were standing side by side on the church steps, both wearing the same horrified expression. She wanted to shout. *No. It's not real. I'm not marrying him. I'll never marry him. It's only a dream – a nightmare.* But she kept quiet while the wedding plans were discussed and the banns read and the ceremony arranged and the guest list drawn up.

If Raki was honest, what kept her mouth shut was fear – fear of dying an old maid in her mother's house, with nothing to do but cook and clean and talk about which flowers to put on the altar that week. Life was frustrating and boring and she longed to escape from Birkenheadbaai, get away to the city and do something with her life. But her education had ended when she was sixteen. She had never had a job and had been brought up in a god-fearing household where females were expected to learn the skills of home-making then get married and bring up a family. A family which would follow the strict biblical and Christian principles of the Reformed Church of South Africa, the NGK – Nederduits Gereformeerde Kerk – where they would prepare for The New Jerusalem.

She had a secret hope that she clung to. If she went through with this wedding, Mr Turkey might possibly be her passport to a new life where she might find the freedom and intellectual stimulus she craved. Pastors were moved to different parishes so it was likely she would live in different places, maybe even be able to continue her studies; have the opportunity to write. At least that's what she hoped. And there was the other hope – that she would have a baby. She could put up with anything if she had a child.

When Raki asked Mari to be her bridesmaid her cousin took her by the shoulders and shook her hard. 'Are you mad? My God, woman, you can't marry that creepy bugger. Have you seen his eyebrows?'

Raki shook herself free. 'He's not very pretty, I'll give you that but – '

'Bugger *pretty* he's got murderer's eyebrows, Raki. They meet in the middle. It's true, don't laugh. I saw a documentary about it.'

'He's not that bad, Mari, really. When you get to know him.'

'I'm warning you, Raki, you marry that man and I'll never speak to you again.'

But Raki went through with it anyway and Mari was her bridesmaid.

9.05 a.m.

Quent gives up trying to find something to wear. He's too exhausted, so he piles more of the clothes behind his head and makes a soft pillow. Easing his bad leg up onto the mattress he lies back with both legs straight out in front of him. It's the first time he's been totally relaxed for days and his body feels as if it's dissolving into the mattress. The need to sleep is almost unbearable. Shifting his head to make himself more comfortable, a swirl of red and orange catches his eye and he pulls out a long skirt from the pile under his head. It's tie-dyed in vivid colours. He's never been a man to notice what a woman wears but he remembers this skirt. Raki was wearing it the first time he saw her

After the Scouts Quent drifted from job to job. For several years he'd worked as a game-tracker for wealthy trophy hunters. It paid well and Quent loved the freedom. It seemed like the good times would never end but then Nelson Mandela was released from Robbens Island and it all came to an abrupt end.

In the last ten years Quent had been living from hand-to-mouth and he was sick of working in yet one more deadly, badly paid job. Okay, he'd never agreed with Apartheid, it was wrong, but things had been easier for whites before. You could earn big money, no questions asked, but now the conservationists were making it hard for people like him. The only work he could get was on farms or estates. He'd always worked for himself and didn't like being told what to do. At the ,moment he was staying with his old oppo, Pierre, in Birkenheadbaii. The town bored Quent to death. There was nothing there for him. He had no family and Eunice and the old woman had died years back. He was in the army when the old woman died. He was surprised by how shocked he'd been that she was gone.

Quent had grown up in Pig's Snout Kloof, not far from town. He and Pierre went back a long way. They'd been at school together and later met up in the Scouts training camp in Rhodesia. It was either that or be conscripted into the South African forces fighting the Nationalist terrorists in their own country. Quent wasn't a liberal but he had no wish to kill black South Africans. He wasn't comfortable with Apartheid and knew the political scene would have to change one day soon. It just took a lot longer than he predicted.

At the moment he was waiting to hear if he'd got a job on a game reserve in the Little Karoo. He'd decided if he didn't get it, he'd high-tail it for Cape Town or Jozy. He still had a few contacts there from his army days. He hated cities but there was always if you weren't too choosy about what you did.

It was definitely time to move on because Trudi was making it abundantly clear that she wanted this non-paying, beer-swilling, rude bugger out of her house. It hadn't helped when he'd laughed at her the night Pierre was out and she came onto him. He had a reputation with women. Some of it earned, the rest of it sheer imagination. Trudi was one of those women who believed she was every man's answer to a prayer.

Ever since then she'd been on at Pierre to get rid of him. Tomorrow he was moving out so Pierre and some other guys had got together to give him a good send off. And while they waited for the local Inn to open they filled in the drinking time at a beer stall in the farmers' market on the Green.

The field was crowded with the usual florid-faced Boer men and women and their children dressed in their Sunday best, eating cake and *wors* while the men drank beer. There were a few coloured women selling produce and one black man selling trainers and sun hats.

Quent turned his attention to the women. The best looking female there was a busty blonde with china blue eyes. When he caught her eye and winked she didn't look shocked or glare, she put her head on one side and stuck out her

124

tongue. Very encouraging, he thought, maybe he'd follow that one up later. She turned to say something to a woman standing behind her. Quent hadn't noticed her at first. She had long black hair and a slender body. She was different from all the identikit blonde Afrikaner women dressed in their fussy clothes with their pink fleshy faces.

Blondie had her stall set up in more ways than one and her jars of homemade preserves and pickles were selling like hot cakes. The dark-haired woman was selling leather goods. There was one very handsome pair of men's boots on display. The blonde was enjoying herself, flirting with the men and joking with the women, but Quent found himself watching the other one. There was something about her.

She was smiling as she showed a red leather purse to a little girl who clutched a few dirty coins in her hand. The child held out the money but the woman shook her head. The child's face crumpled and she scrubbed away a tear with the back of her hand. The woman was immediately down beside her, arms around her and wiping her tears away. Quent didn't need to hear what was being said to know that the kid was going to win this particular transaction. When the woman stood up the child was waving the red purse triumphantly over her head and shouting to her friends who were watching and giggling. The tears had miraculously dried up as the little girl ran back to them.

The blonde woman said something to the woman but she just shrugged and smiled. She was wearing a black sleeveless T-shirt and her slim arms were brown and muscular. She wore a leather bracelet around her upper arm, with a piece of pink-quartz sewn into it. Hard to guess her age. Probably not as old as she looked. Quent saw boots sticking out from underneath her long, flowing, black tie-dyed skirt. At that moment she looked up and stared him straight in the eyes. Her gaze was steady and calm and she smiled, then she dipped her head and pretended to be busy.

It wasn't a come-on smile it was like she knew him and liked him. Quent didn't move for a few seconds. He didn't believe in love. That was for kids in Hollywood movies. It didn't apply to him. Did it?

Married Life

Raki never loved Mr Turkey. She didn't even like him and from the look in his eyes when he spoke to her, the feeling was mutual. Over the long years of their marriage this antipathy grew into icy dislike, especially when she didn't get pregnant. Raki was sad that they didn't have a child. She had always adored children. It might have been possible to bury herself in motherhood and ignore everything else.

It didn't surprise her that she didn't conceive. Mr Morgan's frantic fumblings in the dark, while she lay as rigid as a lump of stone, were hardly conducive to making a baby. Her sex education had been poor to say the least, even after Mari, her cousin, had given her the gruesome details on the eve of her wedding.

'It's fun,' Mari had said, 'when you get used to it, but it made me want to laugh at first. But you mustn't do that, they don't like it.'

Laugh? Raki had wanted to cry. She wasn't really sure that Mr Morgan had ever penetrated her properly and he had certainly never touched her on purpose. If their bodies accidently met while he was mounting her, she felt his shudder meeting her shudder and becoming one. The moment he thought he'd performed he would roll off her and scuttle back to his bedroom without a word. He slept in the large bedroom at the front of the house that used to belong to his mother. He still kept her false teeth in a small porcelain pot on the dressing table. He changed the water every day and cleaned the teeth with foaming Steredent.

In the early days, when she still felt a modicum of gratitude towards him for choosing her as his wife, she suggested that they should go to the doctor to be checked out.

'Checked out?' he'd hurled back at her, as if she'd said something obscene. 'I don't need any demeaning medical investigation to prove my manhood. Look to yourself, woman. You are barren and you must accept it as God's will.'

And that was an end to it as far as he was concerned. At least her 'failure' to conceive meant that he never needed to sleep with her again, either in the practical or biblical sense. Sex was for procreation only as far as Mr Morgan was concerned. This arrangement suited Raki perfectly and her bedtimes became her special time. She would light the candles – Mr Turkey forbade the use of electricity after 6pm – and read.

The pastor was a disappointed man and made it widely known. He had married Raki in good faith, provided a comfortable home for her, where she would want for nothing. All he asked for in return was that she was a proper wife. It didn't seem a lot to ask to a man who had always got his own way. Not only was she barren but she refused to take any part in the life of his church.

On this one matter Raki had decided to make a stand. She wouldn't join any of the church women's organisations, or help with parish teas and barbecues, or sell raffle tickets, or visit the sick. She told Mr Turkey that she was too shy to be involved. On consideration he thought she was probably right. There were other women in his parish more than eager to help him out of his little difficulties. Besides, he liked to remind his wife every now and then how useless she was.

Just as Mr Turkey was disappointed in Raki, so she was with him. He was never offered another ministry. They remained in Birkenheadbaai and that was where he intended staying he said. He wished to be buried in the town. 'To lie beside my mother in death.' He would tell her, eyes moist, wattle wobbling.

Raki had to find something to occupy her time. She had always made things and was a clever needlewoman so she began to make leather goods. She made some lovely things and gave them away as presents to her sisters and nieces and nephews. It was Mari who suggested she traded at the weekly farmers' market in Birkenheadbaai.

Mr Turkey baulked at the idea when she mentioned it to him. 'It isn't the done thing for a minister's wife to trade,' he lectured. But it wasn't too long before he realised her goods were very popular and the money she earned was substantial, so he turned a blind eye. 'It amuses her,' he would tell the sharp-tongued, eagle-eyed women of his parish. These were the very same women who had hoped that their unmarried, plain daughters might marry this personable young minister. 'I'm a modern man,' he would add, modestly flexing his large, soft fingers, 'and we must allow our ladies their freedom.'

Henrik was very careful with money and allowed Raki the bare minimum to run the household. But Raki was her mother's daughter and a very good manager and she had few personal needs. He insisted she keep a ledger and write all the expenses down, so that he could go over it at the end of the week. There was always something to complain about. 'Six candles, Mrs Morgan?' he would query, his bushy eyebrows clashing together with exasperation. His eyebrows were the only lush part of Mr Turkey. They looked too heavy for his otherwise small, pale face. He had a habit of stooping forward, ever so slightly, to enjoy the shine on his highly polished boots, and Raki wondered if it was the eyebrows that were weighing him down.

'Why do we need six new candles?' he insisted.

'It's for the power-cuts, Mr Morgan,' she would explain patiently. They had a lot of power cuts. 'I need light to sew with.'

She didn't mention that she also needed light to read with. He thought reading an unnecessary and dangerous pursuit, especially for women. There was everything a woman needed to learn in the Bible – lessons to be digested about morality and women's role in a Christian household. You never knew what sort of influence a book might have on an untutored mind.

Mr Turkey's house was a two-book house – The Bible and Baden Powell's 'Chief Scout of the World.' He took troops of scouts on adventure weekends to properly regulated campsites, of course, where experienced trackers took the boys out to see the wildlife. Mr Turkey stayed at base-camp preparing the evening's fun around the campfire. This began with a small service to the glory of God and included several rousing hymns to be followed by hilarious scout songs and cocoa and rusks. If the boys were very good they would play *the pick a text game*. The pastor would write down well-known extracts from the Bible and put them in a mug. Then the boys would choose one and say which chapter and verse the text came from. If they were successful they would be allowed an extra half an hour around the campfire before going to bed. It has to be said that the pastor was disappointed by the number of boys who went to bed very early on such nights.

Raki loved it when her husband was away and she could read in peace. She spent as much time as possible in the small local library. Raki read anything and everything and sometimes Mari lent her modern bestsellers. Of course she kept these hidden from Henrik. The sex parts both intrigued and horrified her.

Raki never spent money on herself. She had no interest in looking 'nice.' She had grown up in a household with two attractive older sisters and she gave up trying to compete with them at a very early age. What would have been the point? 'Of course,' she'd overheard her mother telling her aunt, Mari's mother, one day. 'Raki is such a good girl. She'll make a splendid companion/housekeeper for us when we're old.' Raki's school wanted her to go to Stellenbosch University and train to be a teacher, although Raki would have preferred to be a writer, but her mother wouldn't hear of her going away.

The pastor took charge of everything, even Raki's Sunday clothes. It was important that the pastor's wife be suitably dressed on the Sabbath. These clothes hung in a specially made sliver of a wardrobe in his bedroom. It was kept under lock and key. This amused Raki. What did he think she would do with the clothes if she had free access? Her Sunday-best collection was two old-fashioned dresses, buttoned through from the throat to her ankles, a cotton one for summer and a wool one for winter. They were both in some greeny colour which she couldn't put a name to and made her normally glowing dark skin look sallow. There was a three-quarter navy-blue coat of heavy wool for cold days and a shiny, blue hat, too small for her, that had belonged to her husband's 'blessed' mother along with a pair of creaky, tough leather shoes that hurt Raki's feet. She went barefoot by choice but when she needed shoes she had made herself a pair of soft leather boots that held her feet in their gentle grasp.

After a year of being married to Mr Morgan, Raki stopped thinking about what she wanted from life.

She lived in Mr Morgan's house for ten years but she would have been hard pressed to tell you anything that had happened in that time. The political tsunami that was the new South Africa swept over her. She was dumped high and dry somewhere far away from home with no thought about anything but the long days that had to be endured – each one identical to the one before. Nelson Mandela, the ANC, terrorism, the race-laws, and the end of apartheid, a black president and the Truth Commission were phrases she recognised but didn't register as she trudged wearily towards lonely old age.

As the years crawled by she came to expect less and less and that was exactly what she got. By the time she was thirty-five she had given up on love.

But then she met Quent.

9.10 a.m.

Quent runs his hands down the length of the skirt. There's a long jagged tear from the hem almost up to the waist and he shakes out the length of material to cover his body. The coolness of the fabric on his flesh quenches the fire surrounding the wound.

Raki always wore long skirts, always, no matter how hot it was. He could never understand why. Especially as they lived up here on the mountainside, where thorns and razor-edged vegetation lurked, ready to cut and slash any unsuspecting passer-by. Trousers or shorts would have been much more practical and Raki had good legs, very good legs, so why cover them up? It wasn't that she was ashamed of them because in the house she often walked about in just a T-shirt and pants.

He asked her about it once. It was early and the melodic low cooing of doves had roused him. He had lain there watching the early morning light poking its tentative fingers further and further through the shutters, until they dissected the interior darkness of the house into a draughts-board of light and shade. Too soon he would have to get dressed for another day of grafting at the farm and he wanted to put it off for as long as possible.

Raki was lying with her head resting in the crook of his arm. She was naked. He felt her cool breath on his skin. She was always cool, however hot the day. He traced a finger lazily up and down her leg – from her heel right up to her thigh.

She mumbled something and turned away from him. He followed her and kissed her shoulder, running his fingers up and down her spine. He could feel each individual vertebra. There wasn't the slightest trace of fat anywhere on her body. 'Please, Raki,' he coaxed, 'I want to talk. Wake up.'

She sighed heavily and turned to face him. 'What?' she wasn't exactly grumpy but as near to it as Raki could manage. She would be the first to admit she didn't like mornings.

'Why d'you always wear long skirts?' he asked. 'It's stupid.'

She pushed him away a bit, so that she had space to spread herself. 'You've woken me up to ask me that?'

'I've been lying awake all night worrying about it.'

'Liar,' she said and closed her eyes again.

'No, no, no, woman. You've got to stay awake or I'll be thinking about it all day. Not all of us can laze in bed till midday.'

She opened her eyes a crack. 'I wish. I have to do the shopping, take the car in to get the brakes fixed, plant out the tomatoes and spinach, collect kindling for the fire, heave water up from the stream ....and that's before midday. Then I have to cook and clean and – '

He stopped her with a kiss. ' – Now you're awake you can answer my question.'

'Why do I wear long skirts? Well, I like them for one thing and...' she stopped and smiled at him, 'you'll laugh at me.'

'What, me? Never. Come on, Raki, man. You know I'll get it out of you one way or another.' He cupped her face between his hands and kissed her eyes. 'Please.'

'Okay, you win. I wear them because I don't want to have to shave my legs,' she moved closer to him and buried her face in his neck.

He did laugh. 'You what?'

'You heard me. It's embarrassing.'

'But you don't care what people think about you.'

'Sometimes I do. And this is embarrassing, believe me.' She whispered into his neck. 'You know what they'd say if I walked about with hairy legs?'

He was finding it hard to concentrate with her erect little nipples brushing against his flesh. 'No. What?'

'You know.'

'No, I don't. Tell me.'

'No, Quent, I can't.'

'Of course you can. Look at yourself, woman. You're in bed with a man who isn't your husband; we're going to make love in a minute and you're acting like a little virgin.'

Her giggle against his chest tickled him. 'Isn't it time you got up?'

'I have,' he said moving closer, proving it to her. 'Now tell me, for chrissake.'

'They'd say,' she hesitated and then took a deep breath. 'They'd say I was a...a lesbian.'

He leant away from her so that he could study her face. Her eyes were lowered and her beautiful long black hair hung down over her breasts.

'No way. My woman is definitely not a lesbo,' he murmured, smoothing the hair out of her eyes. He knew he had to tread carefully. She was only just beginning to talk about sexual things with him. Her mother had brought her up to think that homosexuals were destined for the eternal burning fiery-pit of Hell, along with divorcees, prostitutes, non-believers, masturbators; women who swore, people who denied that God had red hair, blue eyes and was White, and the thrice-cursed fornicators who lived in sin, especially if they enjoyed sex – namely Raki and Quent.

'How do you know? I might be both,' she told him, looking up and meeting his gaze. 'Bi-sexual? Mari told me,' she added, her cheeks flushing.

'Your cousin's a bad influence on you.' Quent's good mood had vanished. He didn't like Mari knuckling in on Raki's education. She was too full of herself, that woman. It was Anton's fault – always been a weak guy – didn't know how to keep his woman in line.

Raki sensed his annoyance and moved closer, wrapping her arms about his neck. 'You're the one who's a bad influence on me.' And then when he didn't respond. 'I'll shave my legs if you want me to.'

He was probing the soft, warm spot behind her knee with one hand while he circled her strong, brown thigh with the other. She groaned with pleasure. He didn't give a sod whether she shaved or not and besides, part of his male ego liked the thought that he was the only one who saw her lovely, strong brown legs and felt them wrap themselves around him when they made love. He had never thought much about the Muslim faith, or any other come to that, and he would tell you he liked the idea of women being equal – at least on paper – except for soldiering, of course, and drinking and rugby and men's stuff. But the thought of her legs being his private property was definitely a turn-on.

Quent takes a deep breath, letting it out in one long sigh, and closes his eyes. He can't think any more. Exhaustion is coming down like a steel shutter and there's nothing he can do about it. He is warm and comfortable where he lies and the need to sleep is so strong he doubts he can fight it. He glances at his watch – a few moments, that would do it, a few precious minutes of oblivion. What harm can it do? Bullseye will wake him if they come.

Just before he loses consciousness Quent sees the deep plastic tray with blankets tucked inside, down on the floor beside the bed. It is the type of box used by fishermen to market their catch in. This is the boy's bed. It must be. And with that thought his eyes close.

Birkenheadbaai

Raki did sleep. She dreamt of crying babies and lines of flickering candles lighting the way up to a house on the top of a mountain.

It was the familiar sound of Farnie attempting his version of *Twinkle, twinkle little star* that woke her but nothing else bore the slightest resemblance to normality. It was morning but she wasn't at home in her bed and Farnie wasn't on the floor beside her in his cot. Instead she was slouched uncomfortably in the driving seat of her car and Farnie was in the back.

Her neck hurt and she had to turn her head carefully to smile at Farnie. 'That's a lovely song, sweetheart,' she said, handing him the last rusk out of the bag. She was trying hard not to show her rising panic. Just then a wagon sped past with very bright headlights and Raki found her cell phone – 5.30am.

When he'd finished eating she got in the back with him and changed his nappy. He lay on the seat pulling her hair and kicking her in the chest with his chubby little feet. 'Mama's feeling hungry,' she said, pretending to bite his toes. He screeched with laughter and suddenly the enormity of her problem slammed into her like a fist in her solar plexus. The horror of what was happening was too much for her and for a moment she couldn't move. It was only when Farnie yanked her hair so hard and she cried out in pain that her brain kicked in.

She looked at her cell phone. No messages. Her hands shook as she finished fastening the nappy. She straightened out Farnie's legs and kissed each dimpled knee. When she let go they snapped back into their normal frog-like position. All baby's legs looked like that though, didn't they? His limbs and body looked perfect to her; how could there be anything wrong? Maybe they'd made a mistake but no, she'd seen the x-rays.

She picked Farnie up and held him tightly against her – too tightly. 'It's going to be all right, my baby. I promise.' Farnie hated being constrained and protested very loudly until she released him and put him back in his seat. He hated that even more and went rigid, arching his back so that she couldn't get his seat belt done up.

'No, Farnie,' she pleaded. 'Be a good boy for Mama. We have to go to Mari's now. You'd like to see Tante Mari wouldn't you? Maybe Katchy will be there? Um?'

But the child wouldn't be distracted and Raki was forced to hold the screaming child down while she fastened the belt.

'I don't want to hurt you,' she wept. 'Oh, no, please. Farnie. Be good.'

They were both bawling by the time she was ready to start the car. She sniffed back the tears and wiped her face with the back of her hand. Why hadn't Quent got back to her? She considered leaving another, more urgent message but her battery was low, so she plugged the phone into the charger and turned the key in the ignition. Nothing happened. She switched off and made herself count slowly to twenty. If she flooded the engine she'd be stuck. Her thoughts returned to Mari. She was the only absolutely trustworthy person in Raki's life and had never let her down. She would know what to do.

Raki turned the key again. The engine fired for a second or two and then died. She switched off and tried to stay calm. What would she do if she was stranded there? It was like a mini miracle each time the Renault wheezed into life, something to thank God for. Raki hadn't stopped believing in God even though she didn't go to church anymore. It had never seemed like the place for the sort of kindly God she believed in. She wasn't sure if He still cared for her, after what she'd done, but she had to trust in something.

At the third attempt the car stuttered into life like a chesty old man. She let the revs build up slowly before she eased out onto the deserted road and headed for home. One day the car would just die on her but thank God that day wasn't today.

She nursed the car along, despite every fibre of her being screaming for her to put her foot down. At last she left the apple-growing regions and descended onto the plain of the Kleinsrivier valley and on towards Birkenheadbaai and Mari. The knocking sound in the engine grew louder and louder.

136

She turned on the radio and found a very loud music station to drown out the noise. At least Farnie had stopped crying now and was shouting along to the music and kicking his feet into the back of her seat.

The consultant's secretary had urged Raki to put Farnie's name on the waiting list. Raki had agreed but there was no way she would make him wait for a year. Whatever it took she had to give him the best chance. The woman advised her to ring as soon as she got the money together and they could book him in.

'Try not to worry,' she said as Raki left her office. 'He's a healthy little boy, I'm sure he will make a good recovery, even if he has to wait for the procedure.'

9.15 a.m.

Quent is on the beach with Raki. They stand on the tide-line, bare-legged, collecting seashells. Their brown skin is dusted in an icing-sugar layer of white sand. Raki holds her turquoise *kikoi* bunched up about her waist, making a pouch for the shells. As the tide rushes in and out, little bi-valves spout from the sand clinging on tenaciously. The fierceness of the retreating water sucks Raki's and Quent's feet into deep holes, cementing their ankles in wet sand. They rock from side to side as the waves come roaring in and when the water sweeps out again the force of the rip-tide threatens to topple them. They hold hands, laughing – crazy with love.

This beach is close to Cape Agulhas, the southernmost tip of South Africa, and the gigantic rollers come straight from the Antarctic. The foaming water is full of rage and the memory of ice. The thunder of the waves is deafening. They have to scream at each other to be heard.

Quent wakes with a start. The booming of the waves has woken him but it's not in his dream, it's here, somewhere close by, and it's getting louder. Confused, he struggles up onto one elbow and attempts to pin point where the noise is coming from. Eventually it takes on the shape of a hard, deep, rumbling bark – Bullseye. Quent focuses on his watch. It can't be them, not yet. No one can make the climb that fast and in his experience most cops are fat.

Quent swings one leg and then the other off the bed and tries to stand but the room tilts crazily and he puts out a hand to steady himself. He waits until the dizziness passes and then he hobbles to the window. From here he has a clear view down to where the path plunges over into the valley below but his vision is blurred and Bullseye is frantic now. Quent grabs his stick and shuffles outside. Each step jars his thigh and sends the pain ripping through him.

The dog is positioned at the back of the house, head back, barking furiously, eyes glued to the track leading up to the mountain peak.

'Maybe it's the old fella baboon, boy? You never liked him did you?' But now Quent comes to think about it he hasn't seen any baboons since his arrival. They used to hang out on the rocks behind the house. Must have moved to new territory. So if it isn't the monkeys what is it? Bullseye continues to bark.

Quent uses his binoculars but sees nothing unusual. 'Okay, Bullseye, man, I believe you. You saw something but there's nothing now.' A sudden thought strikes Quent. What if they tried climbing over the ridge from the next valley? It would make one helluva trek – he knows this from his own experience. He's only done it once and he never wants to repeat it. A nightmare journey. Of course, if they wanted to catch him unawares it would be the best route but why would they want to do that? He knows they're coming – they know he knows they're coming – hard to miss a bloody great chopper.

He examines the terrain again, more closely this time. Was that a moving flash of brighter colour amongst the dark green vegetation? Adrenalin jags through his body. Lowering the glasses he scrubs at his eyes and looks again. His hands are shaking and his heart is pumping but there's nothing moving up there now, only the usual suspects – raptors sweeping overhead and the occasional scuttling dassie.

The dog lopes away uphill and when he's gone a few hundred metres he stops and looks back at Quent. He is making soft, urgent yelping sounds. 'Shut it, Bullseye. Come, lie down.' The dog doesn't want to but at last he turns and comes back, head down and legs dragging.

Quent leans on his stick, getting his breath back. The dog has seen something for sure but there are plenty of small predators about – or maybe it was a porcupine, yeah, that would be it. Bullseye has always had a thing about porcupines, ever since that time he had a painful encounter with one when he was a pup. There are several bits of broken quill still embedded in his muzzle. You didn't forget something like that. Quent watches as the dog leaps onto his boulder and lies down again facing uphill.

Quent hobbles back to the shack and as he does so he sees a movement in the corner of his eye. He swings the binoculars up and glimpses a largish animal disappearing behind some rocks. Could be a caracal or even a big genet, but the colour – the golden flash of brightness – makes is heart pound. A leopard? No, it can't be? He's hallucinating. *But it might be - if there was one then why couldn't there be another? Wouldn't that be something?* He stands absolutely still for several minutes, the binoculars glued to his eyes, but whatever it is has gone.

He shrugs off the hope. Of course there isn't a leopard. And even if there was he and the Cape leopard are set on the same course – extinction. There's no place for either of them in the new South Africa. One thing Quent has learnt is that you don't get second chances in this life especially if your name's Quent Byrant. Screw it up once and that's it.

Back at the house he hooks the hessian sack out from under the veranda. He drags it into the bedroom, sinks down onto the bed and upends its contents onto the blanket. There are two boxes of cartridges, a hunting knife in a scabbard and a fob-watch on a chain.

He eases the knife out of the scabbard. Raki made it for him. The leather is soft and three crystals are sewn down its length. The blade of the knife is very sharp. Maybe she could give it to the kid when he's older? He turns it over and over in his hands. He's known about this knife all his life. As a boy he had been allowed to see it occasionally – *a tantalising glimpse* the old woman would say before hiding it away again.

'Is it mine?' he asked once, his fingers curling in anticipation of grasping the hilt in his hand.

'Yours? Why would it be yours, boy? D'you think someone special gave it you?' And then she'd laugh that horrible laugh and walk away.

But it must have been his, he told himself. Why else would she keep showing it to him? When he was a kid she said he was *too young* to have it and when he was a teenager she said he was *too wild*. In the end he took it. It was the day he walked out of the old woman's life forever. His dog was dead and so was Eunice. Willem was gone too. There was nothing left for him.

Quent joined the Rhodesian army in the late 70's when he was nineteen and at twenty-two he was transferred to the Scouts. He had that knife with him throughout the Bush War. He loved the Scouts. He was the sort of recruit they were looking for. He'd been a big-game tracker and hunter and he was in love with all the wild places of Southern Africa and especially the animals.

The Scouts battalion was led by a maverick C.O. who chose men who could work in a unit but also think and act on their feet. The *spit and sawdust* of the regulars had never suited Quent and he slotted into the new regime as if he'd been born to it.

Everything about the Scouts was different. It was a mixed-race force, including the first black African commissioned officers in the Rhodesian Army. In addition the Scouts recruited from enemy forces. Captured guerrillas were offered a choice between prison, a trial and possible execution, or joining the Scouts. The ones who "turned" were called *"tame" terrs*. Abel Charous was one such and he was in Quent's *stick* – a group of five or six men.   Quent did his training at Wafa Wafa, a camp near Kamba, where he met up with Pierre Montes. Pierre had been recruited from the South African Police Force. There were quite a few South African police in the Scouts. Pierre had been a long-haired guitar-playing hippy when he was young and had liberal views. He was also a tough guy. You had to be to survive Wafa Wafa.

The training was seventeen days long – *seventeen days of hell*. It was tough even by SAS standards and concentrated on preparing the men for survival in the bush, they had to exist for long periods without any back up, and often disguised as guerrillas. The ethos of the training was to starve, exhaust and antagonize the rookies until they either broke or made the grade. Out of the sixty men, when Quent was at Wafa Wafa, only seven made it, including him and Pierre.

141

The Scouts' critics described them as bandits and ruffians while their supporters saw them as a group of experts providing the eyes and ears of the security forces. They were known affectionately as the *armpits with eyeballs* because they were encouraged to grow long beards and dress in filthy, often ragged clothes. Quent didn't care what the world thought. It was the first time in his life he felt valued.

The Scouts' job was to locate the enemy, ascertain its strengths and intentions and pass this information back to the conventional units so they could pin-point their attacks. In their reconnaissance role they needed to be undetected by the guerrillas. It was not unknown for a *stick* to follow an enemy detachment for anything up to a week, moving only in the morning and the evening when the slanting rays of the sun tended to highlight the minute signs of human movement for which they were looking.

In Quent's *stick* there was Pierre Montes, the NCO John Dreyer and two black guys – Abel Charous and Herbert Chalapo. Herbert was from the Rhodesian army. John Dreyer was a brave, just man but after he was killed in an ambush everything went pear-shaped.

'The Scouts' days were numbered. The local tribes' loyalty swung to the guerrillas. Villagers patrolled the bush to locate the *sticks*. These people were known as *Majabis* and many were young boys who were on the hills tending the herds of cattle. If in their wandering they discovered an observation post they would deliberately move the cows into the camp and identify the exact position of the Scouts.

In 1980 Zimbabwe became independent and the Bush War came to an end. Soames was about to hand over power to Robert Mugabe's ZANU party and Joshua Nkoma's ZAPU party and Soames was getting ready to hightail it back to Britain.

Pierre and Quent were considering their future too. Quent just wanted out. Something terrible had happened to him and the sooner he got away the better. Pierre decided to go home to Birkenheadbaai and join the South African Defence Force. 'There's nothing here for us now, man,' he told Quent. 'Anyone can see there's trouble in store for the new Zimbabwe. Come back with me. Join up.'

But Quent had had enough of the military. There were other options for a man like him. Southern Africa was still a good place if you were white and didn't care too much what you did. Maybe he'd land some great job, handling animals, and forget what had happened?

He was almost looking forward to the future when they heard that they'd been selected for special duties at the hand-over of power in Harare. *Special duties* had an ominous ring about it. God knows why they chose the Scouts but the military mind was something Quent didn't pretend to understand. He only found out the details the night before the ceremony. They were at Wafa Wafa having a drink when Jaco du Plessis walked in. He was smiling – always a bad sign.

'Right, listen up.' Jaco bawled. 'I don't want to have to repeat myself. I've got better things to do with my time.' He produced the orders like a magician pulling a rabbit out of a hat. 'We have been selected as part of the guard of honour at the hand-over ceremony. It's a great honour and you'd better not let me down. That's it, except for one little detail. You leave your guns at base, okay? We are to be unarmed.' When the corporal was finished there was a stunned silence – each man looking at the next, unsure that they'd heard correctly.

It was Quent who spoke first. 'Sorry. Didn't quite catch that.'

Jaco's lip curled contemptuously. 'Sorry what, boy?'

Quent tried to keep his tone neutral, almost apologetic but not quite. 'Sorry,' there was an insolent two second beat before he added, 'Corporal.'

There was unfinished business between these two but Quent was a patient man and he had no wish to spend time banged up in a military prison for assaulting an NCO. However, it didn't stop him dreaming about what he'd do to Jaco du Plessis one day. Oh yes, he'd get the bastard for sure. That was a promise.

Jaco flushed and took a step towards Quent. 'We're there as peacekeepers, Byrant. Got that? No firearms, that's orders.

If a big black buck takes a potshot at you then you show him your ass and run for cover. Got that? All of you?'

Pierre and the others muttered, *yessir*, but Quent was silent.

The corporal drilled the words into Quent's ear. 'We don't retaliate whatever happens. If anyone fires, you take evasive action. Is that understood?'

When Quent finally spoke, his voice bristled with anger. 'Can't speak for anyone else but I'm a Scout not some pathetic no-brain squaddie. I haven't spent five years in the bush fighting to stay alive only to get shot in the back by some trigger-happy bastard.'

The next morning Quent was marched in front of their unit's C.O. He stood to attention beside Jaco while the officer finished writing something. Quent had always had a lot of time for this man. The colonel never expected any man to do anything he wouldn't do himself. When he was ready he pushed his glasses up his nose, put down his pen, and looked at Quent.

'Private Byrant, isn't it?'

'Yessir.'

'Good man. I understand there's some problem over the orders you've been given concerning the hand-over?'

'Yessir.'

'They're not negotiable, private. We all obey orders. That's what being in the army is about. If you don't obey you know the consequences?'

Quent nodded. 'I'm prepared for that, sir, but I'm not prepared to run away from teenaged-psychos toting Kalashnikovs.'

'Speak when you're spoken to, Byrant.' Jaco hissed.

Quent ignored him and continued. 'Sorry, sir, but I can't do it, won't do it. Not for Soames or any bloody politician.'

'Not even for the Scouts?'

'Especially not for the Scouts. We've lost good men, sir, too many good men and....'

'...I'm warning you.' Du Plessis was a very nasty colour.

144

'No, Corporal. Let the man speak.'

Quent looked the officer straight in the eyes and spoke slowly and clearly. 'If someone takes a potshot at me then I will return fire. Sorry,' he added. 'I don't want to make trouble for you.'

The man stood up. He looked very tired. 'Sadly, Private Byrant, you and the Scouts must part company as from now. All your military details will be expunged from our records. As far as the Rhodesian army is concerned you never enlisted. In fact you never existed. You will collect your back pay and leave before morning rally. Take one of the pickups and load up your gear. The corporal here will see you off the compound.' With that the officer handed the documents he'd been writing to Jaco and gave Quent a brief salute.

Jaco marched him out and onto the parade ground. .

'Right, Byrant. Ten minutes to get sorted. Some of us have work to do. Now bugger off. '

Quent piled the vehicle with his possessions. He was very angry, not so much with the commander – he was just obeying orders – no, he was pissed off by the stupidity of it all. All those years in the bush, all those people dead on both sides, and for what?

Quent puts the knife back in its scabbard and picks up the watch.

The fish dock

Raki drove on through the cold, dead light of early morning until she reached the outskirts of town. Her cousin lived down by the harbour in a small one-storey house beside the fish quay. As Raki drew up, fishermen were unloading their catches of schnook and yellow-fin into tubs of ice on the dockside. When she opened her door the overpowering smell of fish hit her. The stench hung like a coarse net curtain over the harbour and surrounding low-lying houses. Sea birds dived and screeched amongst the rocking boats. The water was choppy, even here in the inner harbour, and drifts of trembling spume piggy-backed against the harbour walls.

Raki found an old jumper on the back seat and pulled it on then she unstrapped Farnie. She was careful to hold the child in front of her with her arm around his tummy. As she hurried across the road to the house, the brisk wind caught at her hair and clothes and she tasted salt.

Mari's house was in darkness and in any other circumstance Raki would never have dreamt of disturbing them. She knocked gently on the door and waited – nothing. So she tried again a little louder this time – still no response. She made herself wait for a few moments and knocked again and this time she didn't stop until a very bleary-eyed Anton yanked back the door. His sleep-tousled hair stood up on end and he looked like he hadn't shaved for days.

'Yeah, yeah, yeah,' he muttered. 'I'm coming, man.' He didn't look at Raki. All his attention was focused on the job in hand which was to get into his fire-fighting over trousers. Birkenheadbaai's fire department was made up of local volunteers and this was the height of the bushfire season, the end of summer. The fynbos was tinder-dry at this time and all it needed was one careless tourist to flick a cigarette butt out of a car window and they had a fire on their hands. The men were on 24/7 call-out.

At last Anton looked up and saw Raki. He was so surprised he let go of his trousers and now he was standing there in his Springbok boxer shorts. 'Shit, Raki. What are you trying to do, give me a heart attack?'

At that moment Mari appeared and elbowed her husband out of the way. She opened the door wide and gave Raki as near a smile as she could manage. 'My? Someone's up bright and early.' Her voice was friendly but Raki knew her cousin and there was a brittleness to her smile. She was smartly dressed and had on full make-up and immaculate hair. Her gold bracelets jingled against her smooth brown arms. She looked fantastic but Raki could see that she'd been crying.

Raki hesitated. 'I'm sorry, Mari. It's not a good time but I –'

Mari waived her apologies away. ' – Come in if you're coming. Let's get this door closed or the house will stink of fish all day and it's bloody freezing.' Farnie was watching Mari through hooded, worried eyes. This wasn't his normal Tante Mari. Mari saw his face and her expression softened. She took him out of Raki's arms and put him on her hip. 'Shall we go and see what Katchy's doing, sweetheart?'

Raki grabbed Mari's arm, swinging her around, then she took the boy out of the bewildered woman's grasp. 'You mustn't hold him like that!' Raki's voice was shrill, almost hysterical.

'What on earth's the matter? Raki?'

'I'm sorry.' Raki looked pleadingly at her cousin. 'I'm so sorry, but he mustn't be carried like that. His hip...it's...' and that's when she broke down.

Mari put her arms around her and pulled her inside. Anton was still standing beside the door. As Mari swept past him she jabbed him in the ribs. 'For God's sake, Anton, shut that door. You're making a spectacle of yourself.'

'What time is it, for God's sake?' he grumbled, closing the door and shambling back towards the bedroom, leaving a trail of fire-fighting clothing in his wake. 'Only chance I get for a decent lie-in and she turns up.'

147

'Only chance?' snarled Mari. 'You can fester in that pit every morning from now on. Stay there all day as far as I'm concerned. Stay there for the rest of your life.'

He slammed the bedroom door hard.

'Look, Mari.' Raki turned to go. 'I'll come back another time. You're busy.'

'No, no, you're okay. I've got half an hour before I have to leave.' Mari looked very serious for a moment and then she made a face. 'Men, hey?' She led the way into the kitchen and steered Raki to a stool at the breakfast bar, then she put the kettle on and gave Farnie a big kiss. 'How's my birthday boy? Have you come to town to buy something nice with your money? Give Tante Mari a smackeroo, beautiful boy,' she crooned, hugging the now happy child. 'I wonder where that biscuit tin's got to? Ah here it is, honey. Would you like one of my special biscuits, um?'

'Mama,' he said conversationally and gave her a wet sloppy kiss.

Mari put him on the floor and he crawled off with his biscuit to 'talk' to the dog, Katchy, who was wearing that long-suffering look that all dogs have when coping with the unwanted attention of a small child.

'Be gentle, Farnie' Raki warned. 'Don't pull his ears, he doesn't like it. Good boy.'

The two women watched the antics of the child and the dog in silence, neither wanting to be the first to speak.

'So? What's wrong with Farnie's hip, Raki?'

It took a few moments for Raki to get started but then the words tumbled out of her in an unintelligible jumble. Eventually Mari held up her hands to stop the flow. 'Whoa. Slow down, woman. I've got no idea what you're talking about. Start again only slower this time, from the beginning. Okay? You took Farnie to the clinic and then?'

This time Raki got the story out coherently and when she was finished Mari sat very still for a moment and then went and got down on her hands and knees beside Farnie. She kissed him on the head and then sat back on her heels and looked up at Raki. 'Oh my God, Raki, you have such bad luck.

The poor little thing.' She came back to the breakfast bar. 'I know it's no consolation to you at the moment but Trudi Montes's oldest had CDH, or whatever it's called, and he's absolutely fine now. You'd never know there was anything the matter with him. He doesn't have a limp or anything.' She drank her tea and then put her hand on Raki's knee. 'It's bound to be a terrible shock for you but I wish to God there was a simple operation for my problems.

'Anton?'

'Who else?'

'What's happened?'

Mari dabbed at her eyes with the edge of a hanky, careful not to smudge her mascara. 'He's lost his job again.'

Raki held Mari's hand. 'I'm so sorry.'

'Yeah, well so am I.' Mari got up and made the tea. 'But it's not exactly world news is it, Anton losing a job? Wouldn't make the front page of the local rag.'

When she brought the tea her hands were shaking so much it slopped about. Raki took the cups from her and set them down on the table.

'Guess how many jobs he's had in the past five years? Thirteen,' she said, not waiting for a reply. 'I lay in bed last night and counted up. Thirteen! Bloody thirteen. Unbelievable. And it's never his fault he gets the push, oh no, it's always someone else, or something else, or bad luck, or the boss's got it in for him or it's the credit crunch or the ANC or...or God hates him...' Her voice had reached a shrill crescendo and the dog and boy were watching her with identical puzzled looks on their faces. 'I can't go on like this, Raki. I've had enough.'

Mari sat down suddenly and rested her head on her hands. Raki didn't know what to do. It shocked her to see Mari so upset. Her cousin was the strong one, she never got emotional. It was one of those unwritten rules. Mari didn't cry. They used to joke about it when they were young. Raki had too much emotion and Mari had none.

Raki drank her tea and waited until Mari sat up, took out a handkerchief, blew her nose loudly and wiped angrily at her tears. She raised the cup to her lips and looked at Raki over the rim. She attempted a smile. 'Well? Better out than in, they say.'

'I'm so sorry.'

'I'll survive. I've got to. My life may be falling to pieces but there's no way I'd give up. While I can still put lippie on and have my bikini-line waxed, the world won't come to an end.'

They smiled at each other. 'So? What happened?' Raki asked.

'He was rude to some customers, told them to f... off. At least that's the official version. Doesn't surprise me; he's a rude bugger. Problem with my husband is he can't take orders. Likes to give them, oh yeah, very happy to play the little Hitler but he can't hack it when the tables are turned. The boss told him to apologise to the people, who just happened to be black, but guess what? He told his boss to f...off too; so *goodbye* Anton.'

'Maybe it really wasn't his fault, Mari? You know how difficult people can be?'

Mari shrugged. 'Whatever. He's got the sack and we're all paying for it. He takes it out on all of us, especially the boys. They can't do anything right. If he carries on like this they're going to walk out of this house and never come back. I can put up with him but they can't. If only he'd go to the doctor, Raki. You know what he gets like? He needs professional help but, oh no, there's nothing wrong with Anton. He's perfectly okay; it's the rest of us with problems.'

'Will you be able to manage? You've got the boys and the house and everything to pay for?'

'I'll work all the overtime I can get, get thoroughly pissed-off and probably have a nervous breakdown. But what's new?'

'Staffords?'

She sighed and made a face. 'Yup. I'm in the estate office, doing the books. I can't be late, or madam will be cross.' She glanced at her watch.

'But you said you'd never work for her again.'

'I know but needs must, honey. And apparently Madam van de Poop can't do without me. ' Mari made up funny names for all the people she didn't like.

'I'm so sorry...'

Mari held up her hands, 'Please, please, please, no more bloody apologies.' Mari saw her cousin's face. 'Look, Raki , I'm not angry with you, I'm just angry with life, but I'll sort it, don't worry. Okay, that's enough about me,' she said, squaring her shoulders. 'Your turn now. I can give you...' and she squinted at her watch, 'exactly ten minutes. After that I've got to re-apply my war paint and get to work. Madam insists that her staff are well groomed. *I set high standards here, Marianne. Clothes are so important. Yis?* Mari was a great mimic. 'Anyway there's plenty of time to sort what we're going to do about little Farnie,' and she pressed her cousin's knee. 'It'll be all right, you know. I won't let anything bad happen to my favourite little boy.

9.20 a.m.

The fob watch is for Raki. Eunice told him it had belonged to his father. He should have been satisfied with that – Eunice didn't lie – but he had to double check. He wanted it so badly.

'Did my daddy leave it for me?' He asked the old woman.

And she'd made that *whooping* sound that was halfway between a laugh and a curse. She was crazy with delight at his gullibility. 'God, no, boy. You don't have a *daddy* do you? You're a bastard.' He wasn't sure she really knew anything about his parents and what had happened to them but when he asked the question, she'd smile, touch her nose and wink her leathery eyelids.

The watch is pretty and delicate, not clunky and grandfatherly. The back is intricately decorated with silver curlicues on the gold case. It is old gold, almost orange. If he's honest he can't imagine Raki wearing such a thing but she would enjoy holding it up to the light and seeing the sunlight glinting on the precious metal. He holds the chain loosely and lets the time piece swing backwards and forwards. Then he holds it to his ear and hears the steady heartbeat. He sets it to the correct time.

He wishes he has something else to give her but he knows she won't mind. Fine things don't impress her. She thinks they're a waste of money. She has a cell phone to tell the time so why would she need a watch? This surprising sortie into the technological age is one of the things that amazes him about Raki – a woman with no desire for luxuries, happiest when shitting in the open-air and revelling in gathering wood for the fire or water from the stream – ten, twenty times a day if necessary, with no complaint. A woman like her, used to hard graft and even harder words, to be attached to her cell phone, like it was a favourite son? But what would he know about *favourite sons*? He drops the watch back on the bed and covers his face with his hands. He mustn't think about the boy.

He makes himself concentrate on the day he was kicked out of the Scouts. Of course he'd been stupid he should have gone along with what they wanted. Now he was losing a good pension, references and his good name – not that he cared about that. The important thing was he'd stuck to his principles and he was free.

He'd had no idea what he was going to do or where he was going. He'd managed to grab a few words with Pierre and Herbert before Du Plessis hustled him off the base. Quent could see how much the little man was enjoying his humiliation but he refused to give him the satisfaction of showing how he felt.

He was cracking jokes with his mates one minute then driving straight at the corporal the next. Du Plessis was standing just inside the compound gates waiting to close them behind him and Quent had the satisfaction of seeing the man's fear as he leapt out of the way.

Quent had money in his pocket and hadn't been on R&R for a long time. He toyed with the idea of going to Jozy or Cape Town to rest up a bit – have a good time, see some friends but somehow it didn't appeal. He needed to go somewhere quiet, get his head straight. He was going to miss the Scouts. For the first time in his young life he'd felt as if he belonged somewhere and that people cared about him. And now it was over.

He didn't plan to go back to Birkenheadbaai, it just happened. Pierre had promised to help him find work when he got home, so Quent decided to hang out in the area until his friend was demobbed. He hadn't been back to Pig's Snout for nearly ten years. The old woman had died shortly after he left but maybe he could doss down in her place, if it was still standing.

It was a long drive and he slept in the pick-up. It was like he was on holiday. No routine, no orders, no Du Plessis. Maybe it wasn't as bad as he thought? He was still young, popular with women and could turn his hand to most things.

He had the rest of his life to look forward to. And he would forget, eventually, wouldn't he?

It was nearly dark as he approached the turn-off leading to Pig's Snout but he took the opposite sharp right instead and bumped down an overgrown track to where Willem and his parents had once lived. Taking his torch, he went to explore.

It felt weird being at Willem's place. Surprisingly there were still some burnt timbers sticking out of a huge mound of ivy and Port Jackson willow; half a door frame rose drunkenly out of a jungle of weeds. Quent had spent so much time here when he was a kid. Willem's folks hadn't had much but the little they had they gladly shared with their son's friend. Their house had been so full of family and laughter and warmth – unlike the old woman's house. He had spent as much time at Willem's as he could. Quent had often wondered what had happened to Willem after the fire. Maybe he'd look him up. He was beginning to get good vibes about coming back to his old hunting ground. He still had connections here. Memories too, but he could handle them.

He returned to the pick-up as night settled down around him. He had a beer, ate some food. It had been a very long day. He stretched out in the back of the vehicle and stared up at the stars. They were very bright. Was it his imagination or were they in slightly different positions here than in Rhodesia? He'd never get used to calling the place Zimbabwe. He wondered what they'd call South Africa when the blacks took over. And they would, he was sure of that.

Willem had always been interested in the stars. He used to point out the constellations to his friend but Quent never took much notice. He could do the Southern Cross – any fool could spot that one – even worked out how to navigate using this constellation. The rest was a mystery to him. Long as he knew where the sun rose and set he was okay.

He hadn't thought about Willem and his family for years. They were Catholics. Willem's mum had gone to the mission school. There were seven kids if he remembered right – three girls and four boys. Only one went to school and that was Willem, the oldest. There was no money for the rest of them.

That's where Quent and Willem met up. They sat beside each other on the first day. There were only two blacks in the school and they had a rough time of it. Quent was regarded with suspicion by most of the white kids for befriending a black but Quent didn't care about being popular or losing friends. He liked Willem and that was all there was to it. Besides, they were alike. Both outsiders. Quent was born in Rhodesia and Willem came from the black settlement on the outskirts of Birkenheadbaai, which could have been the end of the world as far as the white residents of the town were concerned.

To begin with the two boys were picked on by the others. Quent was small for his age but what he lacked in height he made up for in pugilism. First time some bigger boy pushed in front of him in the dinner queue Quent let fly with his fists – two punches to the belly – nobody tried it on with Quent again.

Willem survived because he had an amazing gift. He could run like the wind. Every school Sport's Day all the kids – even the meanest, biggest boys – went crazy to have the black on their team. They would bribe him with sweets and food to run for them. They wouldn't talk to him or play with him for a whole year and then suddenly he was this amazingly popular kid. Quent said he should tell them to *bugger off* but Willem would just smile. He loved running, you see, and he also liked being the number one kid, even if it was just for one day a year.

Soon as dawn broke the next day Quent crossed over the road to Pig's Snout.

The old woman's house had totally disappeared in a mound of young saplings and ivy. Surprisingly, Eunice's little rondavel was still there, wrapped snugly, like a gift in a velvety blanket of vegetation. He fought his way inside. He would doss down there for a few days. Quent mooched about for a day, looking for something, anything to remind him of his childhood. It surprised him how desolate he felt when he found nothing. It was like he'd been cheated. He was trying to shake off the feelings of deep loneliness that had been with him since leaving Wafa Wafa but it still clung to him. He'd remembered a kid at school who had to stay in the hostel because his family lived in Pretoria. He used to cry himself to sleep each night. One of the kindlier priests said he was 'homesick.' All the other kids, himself included, used to take the piss out of him, but Quent had always remembered that 'homesickness'. Is this what it felt like?

Quent took a few days making the rondavel habitable. There were some battered old pots and pans lying about but everything else had been recycled by people passing through. Nothing went to waste in South Africa. He dug out the fire-pit outside the rondavel and there was plenty of wood for braais. Quent liked being in Eunice's house and exploring his kloof again. But there were ghosts on the kloof. Quent believed in ghosts.

One day, out on a walk, he came across an old crooked tree. A frayed piece of rope flapped on a branch. He searched for the grave but there was nothing there. Quent returned with a can of petrol and stayed until there was nothing left of that tree but scorch marks on the fired earth. He had never felt so cold and alone in all his life.

Shortly after this Pierre returned home and Quent stayed with him for a few weeks. Pierre had some celebrating to do and Quent was happy to help him. Everything was coming up roses for Pierre Montes. He was genuinely pleased to see Quent and tried not to gloat too much about the nice little pension he had from the Scouts and his glowing testimonial – no such thing for the disgraced Quent. It didn't even please Quent to find out that Jaco had got blind drunk before the handover and spent the night in the clink.

In time Pierre joined the SADF, married his childhood sweetheart, Trudi, and had two kids – both boys – retired from the SADF, built a house and a business selling agricultural machinery. He had it made.

Quent was one of the boy's god parents, or *God-awful-parent* as Pierre laughingly called him. It didn't seem to bother

Pierre that Quent never remembered to bring presents for his son. The same couldn't be said for Trudi.

In the years that followed, Quent tried his hand at most things. There weren't many tourists about back then so a lot of the game reserves were having a lean time. The ANC was gaining support worldwide and the fear of terrorist attacks kept the European and American tourists away. Fortunately, there was still money in the white man's pockets and he still preferred white employees rather than black or coloured ones.

He tried a bit of garden design. He worked on building sites doing plastering plumbing...anything. He joined a mate in a business venture running tourist boats up the creek. He did a spot of shark-diving and whale-spotting, he worked on sheep and ostrich farms and wine estates. The years rolled by.

Advice

'So, Raki? Fire away.'

Raki put down her cup and stood up. 'No, Mari. I'm going. I just wish there was something I could do to help you for a change.'

Raki's cousin raised her eyebrows. 'What? You help me? That's like Father Christmas putting out a stocking on Christmas Eve and expecting someone to fill it with goodies.'

Raki hung her head, 'Am I that pathetic?'

Mari leant over and patted Raki's face. 'Yeah, but you're lovely *pathetic* and if there's anything I can do to help, I want to, okay? Now sit down and tell me how much it's going to cost.'

'Are you sure?'

Mari nodded.

Raki sat down and took a big breath. 'The consultant's secretary said I could pay in instalments – first payment for the three weeks traction including my staying with Farnie in hospital, next payment for the op and finally for the follow-up appointments. Apparently they have to take measurements every six weeks to allow for growth and alter the spica accordingly.'

'Spica?'

'The plaster cast they put his legs in to correct the displacement.'

'How long does that go on for?'

'The consultant said a year.'

'So? A lot of cash?'

Raki nodded. 'R10,000 at least, plus all the extras – the towels and bed-linen, the supply of disposables and food while we're there... the list gets longer and longer all the time.'

'And what's gonna happen afterwards – when he's all better?'

This question made Raki sit up straighter. 'I haven't thought about that, Mari, but I can't live in the kloof house anymore.' Her voice trailed off. 'It's hopeless, isn't it?'

Mari smiled brightly at her cousin. 'Hey. Never say die, Raki. We've been through worse than this.'

Raki shook her head miserably. 'I don't think so, Mari. This is the worst thing that's ever happened to me.'

'What? Worse than that man walking out on you? Or marrying that creep?'

'Yeah, worse, much worse.'

Mari sipped her tea thoughtfully and when she looked at Raki again she was very serious. 'You know I'd do anything for you and Farnie, don't you?' she said. 'But now it's my turn to say *sorry*, honey, because I don't have that sort of money, in fact I don't have any sort of money. I wish I had'

Raki flushed. 'Oh God, no, I haven't come to you for money. You and Anton have done so much for me. I can never repay your kindness as it is. You've both been brilliant. No, I just thought, well hoped actually, that you might be able to think of something or someone who might be able to help me...?' Her voice trailed away. What was she doing here? She didn't want to upset Mari, not now. She knew how hard it was when Anton was going through depression. Mari was the one who needed help not Raki. She stood up and this time her voice was firm. 'I've chosen the way I live, Mari, and I'm just going to have to get on with it. I've been in touch with Quent and I'm expecting him to call me any time, so you don't have to worry about it. He won't let me down, Mari.' She'd seen her cousin's look of disbelief.

'Have you actually spoken to him?' Mari's mouth curled contemptuously around that *him*.

'No, but I left a message on his phone. He'll get back to me.'

Mari snorted. 'His sort never rings back, Raki. Don't you know that by now? Look how he reacted when you told him about Farnie.'

'Yes, but he's had time to get used to the idea now. He's not a bad man, Mari.'

'That's debatable. Forget him, Raki. He's never going to deliver.'

'That's not fair. None of you gave him a chance. He was so special to me.'

'Like you were special to him?' Mari's voice was hard.

Raki put her hands over her face.

Mari rubbed her cousin's arm. 'I don't want to hurt you but you've got to be realistic. Quent Byrant is no good. He did you a favour walking out on you.'

Raki raised a tear-stained face to her cousin. 'That's what he said too but the only time in my life I've been truly happy was with him. He gave me so much.'

'Yeah? But don't forget what he took.'

'He never meant to hurt me, Mari. And he didn't know about Farnie – not then.'

Mari banged her cup down hard and the liquid shot out all over the work top. She grabbed the cloth and mopped angrily at the spilt tea. 'D'you know something, Raki? I'm so sick of hearing about the wonderful Quent Byrant. When are you going to stop protecting the creep?' Mari was shouting now. 'He's not worth it. He was never worth it. My God, woman, he wasn't faithful to you, not even when you were together.'

'D'you think I don't know that? I'm not as stupid as you think I am but it makes no difference. He's the only man I'll ever love.'

Raki stared defiantly at her cousin and Mari had an unbearable urge to shake her until her teeth rattled but then she remembered Farnie and all the anger slipped away. 'We're bloody mugs us women. Bloody, stupid idiots.' It had been on the tip of her tongue to tell Raki that Quent had tried it on with her, not once, but many times. But she couldn't do that to Raki, she'd never do that. She touched her cousin's cold hand and then she opened her mouth and the words just flew out. She regretted them as soon as she said them but they had a life of their own. 'Listen, honey. After Farnie is discharged from the hospital you can move in with us. You'd be very welcome and the boys would love it. Farnie's their favourite.'

160

She saw Raki's expression. 'There's no problem, honestly. We'd all love to have you.'

'You're such a good person, Mari. No, I mean it. You're a true Christian.'

'Not according to your mother. She says I'm a heathen and she's given up on me.'

'That makes two of us then.'

'So? Will you come?'

Raki shook her head. 'I can't but thanks so much.'

Anton didn't like kids – not even his own. The two boys only met up with their father when it was absolutely necessary. Mari was the one they went to with their problems. Fortunately, the boy's adolescent sleeping habits and lack of communication suited Anton perfectly.

Anton had been in the SASF during the troubles and had been through a tough, almost barbaric regime of training. When he came home he had changed. For a long time Mari didn't understand but over time she realised how deep the psychological trauma of his war experiences had been. It helped to be aware of it but it didn't make it any easier. Mari was incredibly relieved that Raki had said *no* but asked again. 'He'd be okay about it.'

'No, Mari. I really appreciate it but you don't have room and you know Anton would hate it, especially now. No,' she said, stopping her cousin from having to deny it. 'It would be a disaster. Anton doesn't like me very much and he certainly wouldn't want a toddler under his feet all day.'

Mari stirred her tea thoughtfully. 'There's only one other option, Raki. You won't like it but – '

'No way, Mari. I could never ask her.'

'Not even for your son's sake?' She glanced at Farnie, who was happily lying on top of Katchy, prising his mouth open to shove biscuit crumbs inside. 'Besides, Uncle Des's got some say, hasn't he? You and he were always close. He loves you, Raki and I know how much he misses you. He drops by sometimes when Sofia's busy doing churchy things and we talk about you. Well, he talks about you and I tell him all about Farnie.'

'Does he? Really?'

'Of course. What grandfather wouldn't?'

'Then why doesn't he come?'

Mari shrugged. 'Sofia's a tough woman. Shame my mum died, she was the only one who could out-boss your mother.'

'You can handle her too.'

'I try.' Mari said. 'Look, Raki, would it help if I had a word with Uncle Des?'

Raki shook her head. 'It won't do any good. My father has always done what she wants. You know that. Anything for a quiet life, that's him. I love him but he's weak. I expect that's where I get it from.'

'Rubbish. You're the strongest woman I know, living up there with nothing but baboons and snakes for company. I wouldn't last two minutes without proper running water and a flushing loo.' She was silent for a moment while they both watched Farnie with the dog. 'They're your parents, Raki. It's their duty to help you.'

'Not any more. You were there the day I went away with Quent. You heard what she said to me. Everyone did.'

'It was just the shock, Raki. I mean. You've got to admit it, you did it in style. It was like something out of that film with Dustin Hoffman. You know? He ran off with the bride at the end – *The Graduate* – remember?'

But Raki wasn't going to be comforted by some make believe film. She remembered the look on her mother's face that day. She would never forget it.

9.25 a.m.

Quent watches the fingers of sunlight filtering through holes in the rotten shutters and picking out the shiny barrel on his hand-gun. He'd spent most of the previous night cleaning it with an oily rag. It could save your life as well as kill your enemy. He spins the barrel. Three bullets left. He likes the *click, click, click* of the silky smooth-running mechanism. Quent balances the gun in his hand, aware of its weight and seeming innocuousness. How is it that such an insignificant piece of kit could inflict such terrible wounds?

He's killed more people than he cares to remember with his knife – had to, or they would have killed him but he's never lost any sleep over it. In war people die. But the gun? He glances apprehensively at it, as if it were some sentient creature waiting to pounce. He's murdered three living creatures in cold blood with this inoffensive little weapon.

Quent puts the gun back beside the bed then he spreads out two pieces of paper. These are letters for Raki and Willem.

It took a long time for him to write them. He's no writer and, anyway, what did you say to the two people you most cared about when you'd treated them like shit?

The first one he addressed to the Birkenheadbaai police but it's really for Willem. It's a confession. He doesn't want Willem or his brother getting the blame for what he's done. Hopefully he's said enough to protect them. He takes full responsibility for everything that happened at the Du Plessis place and for the whole leopard thing. Quent has tried to be totally honest and writing the letter's made him feel a bit better, like the words have released something in him. Not that he's sorry – to hell with that – he's glad.

Confession has always been difficult for Quent. When he was seven he started at the mission school in Birkenheadbaai. It was the old woman's idea. The school was run by the Christian Brothers.

The old woman told the head priest she'd been a Catholic once, like she expected him to clap her or something. She also told him that Quent needed a firm hand. 'I've done my best, Father,' she said modestly, 'but he's a terrible liar. Gets it off his father. Needs to be taught right from wrong.' She lowered her voice and whispered something into the priest's ear. Quent didn't hear what she said but he saw the man's expression.

In the end the only thing the Brothers taught Quent was that he was a sinner. He was born in sin and would die in sin. His name would never be in the Book of Life. That was the way of it. For a child like him there was no salvation. Quent was never sure what that meant – 'a child like him.' However, all this didn't stop him from getting religion. He wanted very much to be in that Book of Life, wanted to be good and go to heaven to see his mother – still wanted to if truth were told. Everyone had a mother didn't they? There was a sort of half-memory of a woman resting her hand on his head – a gentle touch. But nothing else.

So he tried really hard to be good and confess all his sins. The boys learnt them off by heart and chanted the list every Monday morning. That was after the priest had checked their names off for those who had been at the Mass on Sunday and those who hadn't he thrashed. Didn't matter what the excuse was.

Quent never understood the difference between 'venial' and 'mortal' sins but he could still remember the words. *Venial sins were minor sins that did not deprive the soul of divine grace, either because it was committed without intent or without understanding.* Quent learnt pretty quickly to always plead ignorance. *Mortal sins were sins considered to be so wicked that they caused complete loss of grace and led to damnation unless absolved.* The quandary for the young Quent was who decided what was really wicked? He didn't consider the old priest with his bad breath and leather strap to be a good judge in such matters. He thought if you didn't have a clean handkerchief in your pocket you were already halfway to Hell.

'Filth, boy,' he'd yell, holding up some greasy, snot-smeared rag pulled out of some luckless child's pocket. 'D'you know what this means, boy? A filthy, sinner's mind.' And *thwack, thwack* went the leather-strap on the offender's legs.

The way Quent saw it was that there were times when you had to do bad things to make things right and other times when right actions had terrible consequences. The main problem with confession for Quent was he didn't know how you were supposed to feel when you sinned. Oh, he could reel off the list, like forgetting to say his morning and evening prayers, or being cheeky to his parents – easy for him because he didn't have any – being late for Mass – which he never was because if he nicked off the old woman would beat the shit out of him to be followed by the leather-strap on Monday. But after that he was stumped.

It was tricky because when he went to confession he couldn't just kneel there saying nothing. This was where the young priest, Father Martin, would jump in, after a long, exasperated sigh. "Impure thoughts, boy?" he'd prompt, his voice tired and bored, wanting to be off playing rugby with the young seminarians. The priest would drum his fingers impatiently on the chair, where he sat on the other side of the curtain, drinking his hot sweet coffee with condensed milk and dunking his biscuits. Quent knew this because he smelt it on his breath when he leant closer to the grille to give Quent his penance and then final absolution. So, Quent owned up to impure thoughts, like looking up Sister Bridget's skirt. There was no way he was going to tell some old religious fanny about his really impure thoughts. Did he look stupid?

Quent and the other boys hoped it would be the old priest, Father O'Mann, who heard their confession. He was very deaf and not as bad as the rest. 'Enunciate, boy,' he'd encourage, the moment a child knelt down on the other side of the confessional. 'I can't hear what you're saying if you mumble.'

'It's been three days since my last confession, Father.' Quent shouted back.

'Well?' the old man would respond.

So he would bellow back, 'I've had impure thoughts twenty-five times, Father.' That would set off all the other little sinners outside waiting their turn and when he came out they'd be rolling around on the benches wetting themselves. It got so that each boy would make up terrible sins just to make his friends laugh. Father O'Mann handed out the strangest penances in the school. You had to sweep the Presbytery or help the house-keeper with the washing or polish the benches. It was only years later, after Quent had long given up on religion, that he discovered that Father O'Mann had been having it off with his housekeeper for years. In the end she was chucked out and he was sent to another school in Pretoria. So, Quent and the priest weren't so different after all. However Father O'Mann taught Quent a very important lesson and that was how to say *sorry* and be very convincing.

The second letter was for Raki. He doesn't need to see it to remember what it says. The writing is a scrawl and his vision is blurred. 'SORRY,' it says, right across the page in big letters. *I'm so sorry, Raki. Forgive me. I should never have said those things about Farnie. He is my boy. I know it. You deserve a good life. I loved you. Quent.'* It's not enough, he knows that. There's so much he wants to tell her – to make her understand how sorry he really is but he can't – not on paper.

'You see, Raki.' His voice is weak and reedy. 'I did something terrible – and the plain truth is I can never be a father – not to your boy or any other. You see, I murdered a child. His name was Tabo. Did I tell you? I gave him a coke and then...and then I killed him. May God forgive me, because I never will. Could you? Or my son? Will you be the one to tell him his father killed a little boy?'

He tucks the two letters he's written beneath the fob watch then he hobbles outside and lowers himself carefully onto the chair. His wound isn't throbbing quite so much. Maybe he's over the worst of it – there's no harm in hoping.

Bullseye sits motionless on his rock, his back to Quent, staring intently up the mountainside. One ear flicks backwards

166

acknowledging Quent's presence. The sunlight is so bright Quent has to shield his eyes. He opens a bottle of water and drinks slowly. Suddenly he's very hungry and slices off a piece of biltong.

'Bullseye?' Quent holds out a piece of dried meat. 'D'you want this?' The dog doesn't need asking twice.

Quent hopes he's done everything he needs to. It's important to cover every angle but he can't think any more. He's bushed. What he needs to do is sleep on her bed and breathe in the smell of her. Nothing else seems to matter much

Leaving

It was Christmas morning and Sofia had been up since daybreak in order to get the huge turkey in the oven. When Raki arrived to help, the kitchen was already a fiery furnace even with all the windows and doors open. Sofia insisted on cooking traditional Christmas fare – turkey, pudding, the lot. It didn't matter that the weather was too hot to eat such a substantial meal and that she and Raki were nearly as cooked as the turkey by the time they'd finished. It was what she did – what she always did – and in Sofia van de Venter's mind tradition was the second most important thing after her blessed Dutch Reformed Church.

When Raki was nervous she was clumsy and that morning she dropped a lot of things. She had just smashed her mother's favourite gravy-boat. This china was an heirloom from Sofia's great-grandmother.

'That went all the way with her on the Great Trek,' her mother complained bitterly. 'Through pot-holes bigger than hippos, across rivers in flood, through hostile native territory and trigger-happy Brits. It even went into the concentration camp with her and now you break it.'

'I'm so sorry,' Raki said, sweeping the china fragments into the dustpan.

'Never mind, never mind. Leave that now.' Sofia was torn between the need to get on and the period of mourning that the demise of her heirloom demanded. But she would find time for leisurely recriminations later.

Part of the problem for Raki was that Sofia was watching her out of the corner of her eye. It was the same look she'd worn almost permanently since Quent had come on the scene. Sofia was pretty certain that Raki hadn't been with that odious little man again but she was still suspicious, even though her spies informed her that Quent Byrant had cleared off for good. Apparently there was some irate husband on his trail from a liaison with some other woman. He was a womaniser.

Came from bad stock. The old woman who brought him up was little more than a tramp and he had been allowed to run wild as a child and mixed with a rough gang of children — mainly blacks. There was no sign of any parents. Of course, Sofia hadn't known him then, she didn't mix with such people but she had heard various things over the years. You only had to look at the man to know he was up to no good — a middle-aged man wearing a pony-tail with animal tattoos all over him? Ridiculous. It was obvious he was devoid of moral scruples. He'd had his *bit of fun* with her daughter and moved on to the next poor, weak woman. Of course it still enraged her that he'd had his *bit of fun* with her daughter — her married daughter — the one married to Henrik Morgan, a man she greatly respected.

As long as Quent Byrant was gone for good Sofia could just about deal with it. Raki would be forgiven in time but her sin would never be forgotten. The pastor had dealt with the whole situation in an exemplary fashion. He was a truly saintly young man. It was such a shame that their union hadn't produced children. That would have made all the difference. Sofia knew it wasn't a 'happy' marriage in the accepted sense but there were worse marriages. You only had to read the newspapers or listen to the news. The world was full of promiscuity and adultery and it wasn't just the blacks.

Sofia wouldn't have been quite so unperturbed if she'd known the true whereabouts of Quent Byrant, because he hadn't gone anywhere. He was living at the top of Pig's Snout Kloof, lying low, waiting for Raki.

Raki could have told her mother why she was so desperately ham-fisted that morning. In a few hours time she was going to leave her husband. After the service Quent would be waiting in his bakkie outside the church and Raki would climb in beside him and they would drive away.

Quent had laughed when she told him her plan. He thought she was joking, but she wasn't. If it was left to him he would have just taken off with her when no one was about. But it was very important to Raki that her family saw her go. She didn't want it to be a sordid, hole-in-the-wall, affair. It had taken all her courage to agree to leaving Mr Morgan but she wasn't ashamed of what she was doing. She was proud and she wanted them all to see her pride, especially her mother. This was the moment she'd been waiting for all her life.

'But why, Raki?' Quent had asked. 'Who gives a sod what they think? Especially that bastard, Morgan? Just walk away.'

'I'm not going to creep away in the dead of night like we're doing something wrong, Quent. I love you and I want them to see me get in the car with you and drive away, with my head held high.'

'Your mother will go crazy.'

She knew he was right but however much he tried to talk her out of it she refused to budge. In the end he agreed. In a way he admired her even more because he knew how she hated upsetting people. Yet here she was, prepared to stand up to the terrible Sofia van de Venter. It didn't matter a toss what they thought of him. All he wanted was to have Raki to himself on top of that mountain and make love to her.

Raki's concentration collapsed at about the same time she realised she'd turned the potatoes for roasting into mush.

'What on earth's the matter with you, girl?' Sofia snapped. 'Now you'll have to get some more potatoes peeled quickly, before we leave for church. And where are those chestnuts?'

'Nearly done, Mother.' Raki looked down at her fingernails. They were dirty and chipped from the hard, chestnut shells. You could buy cans of ready-prepared chestnuts in Woolworths but Sofia insisted on the real thing. Raki wouldn't have minded if anyone actually liked chestnut stuffing, but nobody did – not even her father, who ate everything.

'For goodness sake, pull yourself together,' her mother lectured. 'Or this Christmas feast is going to be ruined.'

Raki had a quick look at the kitchen clock – only a half an hour and they would be on their way to church. She'd packed her small bag days ago and had hidden it early that morning behind the veranda on Mr Morgan's stoep, while he was sleeping and before her father picked her up to take her to the farm to help Sofia.

She had planned to write a note to her husband, it seemed the right thing to do, but in the end she couldn't think of a thing to say. He had never loved her and she certainly didn't love him, in fact she thought she might hate him for all his petty slights to her. So, on Christmas morning, she'd written that week's inventory of expenses and left it on her pillow along with a R100 note to cover the cost of the candles that she took with her.

Raki and her father didn't talk on the drive to the farm that morning. She spent the time watching his gentle face. It was like she was storing up an image of him. The idea of the new life stretching out in front of her was frightening as well as exhilarating. What if her father never wanted to speak to her again? She leant over and touched his hand. She would see him again one day but she had a lump in her throat all the same.

At one point he glanced at her. 'Happy Christmas, Raki,' he said, and squeezed her knee. 'Life treating you okay?' he asked. He was smiling but there was concern in his eyes.

'Yeah, everything's good, thanks, Dad. And Happy Christmas to you, too,' she added, picking up his free hand and kissing it. 'I hope you have a lovely day.' Should she tell him? This would be the ideal opportunity. The words were on her lips but just then a baboon ran straight out in front of the car and they had to swerve onto the hard shoulder to avoid it.

'Bloody baboons,' he yelled out of the window.

It was a youngster and Raki watched as its mother stood on the far side of the track screeching at it.

Raki's Dad smiled. 'Someone's going to get an earful when she gets him home, ja?'

Raki nodded. The moment was gone and soon they were turning onto the farm track. 'You do know I love you, don't you?' she asked, as they pulled up outside the house.

'I certainly do,' he said. 'And the feeling's mutual. Now I think you'd better get in the there, quick.'

Raki could see her mother's shape rushing backwards and forwards in front of the kitchen windows, already busy. How many times had she been part of this? The ritual of Christmas morning? She had helped her mother when she was quite small. Her sisters and mother made the dinner while she laid the table. Raki loved getting all the special Christmas china out and laying the table with the big damask tablecloth and matching serviettes. She used to polish the best knives and forks until they shone. When the table was done she would pick blue and white agapanthus flower-heads and float them in a special silver dish. Then she'd place it in the centre of the table alongside the little wooden tableau of the nativity, with the baby Jesus, who got burnt accidentally one year and was badly charred. Raki had always loved Christmas.

'Raki?' her father was waiting for her to get out. 'Penny for them?'

'Sorry, Dad.' She'd made some desserts and had them on a tray on her lap. He took it from her and led the way inside the house.

'Are you sure you're okay?' he asked, as he held the door open for her. 'You seem – '

' I'm fine, Dad, honestly. You know me, I always get emotional at Christmas.' And she'd led the way into the kitchen.

'What've you got to smile about?' her mother snapped, noticing Raki's expression. 'You may think it's funny breaking my special gravy boat but I don't. Now, have you got that pudding in the steamer yet? It takes a good four hours. Wake up for goodness sake.'

No one knew what Raki was planning, not even Mari. Now the day had finally come, Raki was nervous and excited and terrified in equal measure. Her emotions roller-coastered and her guts were in turmoil. She had to keep running to the loo. Sofia was perplexed. Her daughter didn't look ill, in fact she looked surprisingly healthy and her skin glowed. On rare occasions Sofia's youngest looked surprisingly presentable.

'Is something wrong with you, Raki?' she asked, after Raki returned from her most recent dash to the toilet. 'Only I don't want you handling food if you've got a bug. This is

Henrik's busiest time of the year and we can't have him incapacitated, can we? You're still smiling. What on earth's the matter? Raki? Has something happened? You might as well tell me. You know I'll find out in the end.' And she did.

After the Christmas service Sofia led the way outside into the warm soup of a summer's day. She was looking forward to wishing all her friends a *Happy Christmas* and distributing all the little homemade gifts she was famous for. Her hand sewn, religious-tract book marks were much sought after.

The smile froze on her lips as she saw the old, muddy bakkie parked outside and the man lounging inside it. The vehicle was directly in front of the church at the end of the church path. Quent had his window down and he was smoking. One of his brown muscular arms rested on the window ledge, his long fingers tapping out the rhythm of loud rock music coming from the bakkie's music system. The man's leopard tattoo seemed to leap away from his arm. It only took Sofia a moment of open-mouthed astonishment before her brain kicked in and she sprang into action. When she couldn't see Raki she sent Desmond off to search for her.

Raki had slipped out of the church by the back door and had run across the street to retrieve her bag. She put it by the church wall and then she joined the people outside the church as if nothing had happened. After the first shock everyone was trying to behave normally and the people pouring out of the church had no idea what was going on. They were too busy wishing everyone a *Happy Christmas* and exchanging gifts. Raki saw Sofia moving towards her, her face grim. Raki was smiling and talking to her nephews and nieces and wishing them a *Merry Christmas*. They were clustered about her hugging her and thanking her for their presents. Raki looked so happy. No one could have guessed that her legs were like jelly and she felt as if she was going to be sick.

Quent was there, just like he promised. She felt his eyes on her and she waved to him and gave him her most dazzling smile. She felt about sixteen again when she'd had that crush on Anton. She remembered how her heart had seemed to beat faster and her hands sweated when she saw him. It was just like that only a hundred times more intense. Quent was so handsome. She could hardly believe that he loved her and that in a few moments she would be with him forever. It wasn't possible.

She caught Mari's eye as she turned back to the children. Her cousin looked stunned. Raki smiled encouragingly at her and Mari beckoned at her, furiously.

Sofia was beside her now hissing urgently in her ear. 'I want you in the car, right now, girl? Are you listening to me? Don't look at him. I forbid you to look at him. He's the devil trying to tempt you.'

'Oh Mother,' Raki said, laughing. 'Do you ever listen to yourself?'

Sofia grabbed her daughter's arm, her fingers digging in, as she tried to pull her away. It hurt. 'If you'll excuse us? Raki and I have things to do,' she said, moving through the astonished relatives and friends. Her voice was brittle with panic but she was making a huge effort to stay calm. 'We can't have the Christmas pudding drying out, can we?' she laughed. 'Come along, Raki. We'll see you all at 1.30 sharp.' And, as she attempted to hustle her daughter towards the car she called over her shoulder. 'Henrik? It's time to go.'

Henrik looked up in surprise. It was unheard of for his mother-in-law to interrupt his time with the parishioners. He was still in the middle if wishing them a *joyous Noel* and receiving their little tokens of esteem. He flapped a subtle, grey and brown home-made scarf in Sofia's direction. 'You go on, Sofia. I'll be with you shortly. There's no rush. I don't think the turkey is going anywhere, do you?' His little joke went down very well with his ladies.

Up till then Raki had refused to move but suddenly she tore herself away from her mother's vice-like grip and faced her. 'I'm sorry, mother, but I'm not coming with you.'

Sofia was sweating and she mopped at her face with a lace-edged hanky. It didn't do the job. 'Don't be silly, Raki,' she said. 'We must get back. There are things to be done. I need you, Raki.' Sofia was pleading with her.

'I'm sorry, mother, but I'm going with Quent.' Raki's voice was clear and assertive and several people gave up all pretence of having normal conversations with their friends. This drama being played out in front of them was the only thing they were interested in. They all knew that the pastor's wife was a shy, timorous kind of woman and that her mother ruled the roost. They watched mother and daughter with a growing sense of anticipation. There was definitely something incredible happening here.

'I'm leaving him,' Raki announced, flicking a glance in Mr Morgan's direction. Her voice was strong and clear. 'Quent and I are going to live together.' Even Mr Morgan heard her this time.

'Don't be ridiculous, girl,' Sofia's voice was shrill. 'Come with me now and we'll say no more about it.'

Raki shook her head slowly. 'I can't do that, mother. It's over...all of it.' Everyone was watching. Even the children were silent. Raki pointed at the pastor. 'I'm leaving him and I'm starting a new life with Quent. Please, try to understand. This is what I want. I'm choosing it, not you or anyone else – me. I'm going with the man I love and who loves me and there's nothing you can do about it.'

Then Raki spoke directly to her husband, 'Everything's in order. I'm taking the clothes I stand up in. I think I've earned them, don't you? The accounts have been done up to the end of the month. I wish you well, Mr Morgan, even though you have never cared for me. Goodbye. Goodbye everybody, goodbye Birkenheadbaai,' and then she'd walked quickly to the bakkie, picked up her bag and got in beside the smiling Quent.

Quent wound up the windows and started the engine.

That was the moment when Sofia finally managed to engage her brain and she charged the vehicle, wrenching at the door handle but it was locked. She pounded on the side of the bakkie. 'Let her out, you bastard, you fornicator,' she screeched. 'Leave my daughter alone.'

Raki's father was the first to get to Sofia. He put his arms around her. 'Leave it, Sofia,' he begged, taking one last despairing look at his daughter. 'She's a grown woman, we can't interfere.' But Sofia tore herself out of her husband's grasp.

As the vehicle moved away she ran beside it beating on the door. 'You Jezebel,' she screamed at Raki. 'You whore, you wanton hussy. God will punish you. You're not my daughter. I disown you, d'you hear me? I never want to see you again – in this world or the next. You're dead to me; you're dead to all the family. You're worse than dead. I wish you'd never been born.'

As the bakkie gathered speed Sofia fell to her knees in the road. Raki watched the outraged tiny figure in the middle of the dusty road, gasping for breath with both fists raised heavenwards, calling down vengeance from her God.

Mari leant towards Raki and nudged her. 'Raki? Are you still with me?'

'What? Oh yeh, sorry Mari. I was...thinking.'

9.30 a.m.

Quent and the dog stare up the mountainside.

Quent's attempting to make some sense of it all. He won't be leaving the kloof again. He should never have left it in the first place. Another insane thing to add to the long list of unhinged stunts he's pulled off in his lifetime. Why couldn't he see he'd been happier here than anywhere else? Too late now but he knows he should have stayed with Raki; looked after her, her and the kid. But back then all he could think about was his need to escape, from her, from responsibilities, from the whole leopard thing but most of all from Du Toit and his contempt for him. Quent had always craved respect and when the man treated him like a dog turd he retaliated like some pathetic little school kid with a grudge.

The night he left Raki, Quent bivouacked on the other side of the flat water-run. It had been relatively easy for him and the dog to wade across the stream from the kloof house side. In late summer the water flow was weak. The winter was a different matter. The rainwater came rushing down the mountainside and was funnelled into a narrow chasm before it leaped down the falls to the forest below. In times of spate there was quite an undertow, even up here where the stream was shallow.

He hadn't told Raki anything about his plans. The less she knew the better for her. he knew that if he got away with it Du Toit would be paying her a visit. Knowing him, he'd probably involve the police too. Raki was one of those people who couldn't tell a lie. He'd told her a lie to protect her – at least that's how he reassured himself. But he knew it wasn't true. Did that make him feel guilty? Leaving her to face the music all on her own? No was the simple answer, Raki didn't come into the equation at all.

He'd lain awake for what was left of that night, watching the stars and going through the plan in his head, over and over again, anticipating anything that might go wrong. He'd planned it like a military exercise. In and out fast; each guy knowing exactly what his job was. Quent lost track of how many times he'd checked the shotgun and the rifle. Quent would use the rifle to dart the leopard and Willem would carry the shotgun in case of emergencies. Willem was a good shot. Quent has seen him take out a caracal at 100m as it streaked away through a dense thicket, a goat kid in its jaws. Yeah, he could trust Willem to cover his back.

The box of tranquillising darts was safely stowed in Quent's backpack. This was the supply his mate the vet had given him. The big man had grinned when he handed them over. 'Don't forget, man,' he'd shouted, waving a pudgy finger. 'When that bloody angry she-leopard comes straight for your jugular, forget the bloody darts, use the shotgun.'

However, Quent's self-belief waned as the first tentative shafts of morning light prodded into the darkness. Last night it had all seemed so easy but maybe that was the alcohol and anger talking - a potent cocktail. His unswerving confidence and excitement had even persuaded the normally level-headed Willem to go along with his plans. Quent remembered the way his friend's eyes had shone in the dim light of the shebeen when Quent talked about a new life with loads of money to send home to his wife and children.

But, as he lay on the mist-shrouded mountainside, with his teeth chattering in the cold, he had a reality check. Christ. What had been thinking of? Just about anything could go wrong. Point one and most important, he might never find the leopard again. They were elusive at the best of times, so what made him think he would just stroll out and catch her? It could take days of tracking before he even got a glimpse and he didn't have days, he didn't even have a day. He had five or six hours max. Point two, Du Toit might decide to make a very early start to track down the leopard. Point three, even if Quent caught the animal they might not be able to get her down the next valley to the waiting pickup. And what if the sedated leopard suddenly woke up halfway down the kloof?

Quent forced himself to get up and fold his bed roll. He made his way through the thigh-high, dew-wet vegetation to the stream with the four water bottles. He was trying desperately to blank his negative thoughts. If it didn't pan out for them they could always go back to the Broot farm as if nothing had happened. He felt a bit bad that he was leaving Maarten Broot in the lurch. He'd been a good boss. The other option was to still go to the Du Plessis place. Quent was pretty sure Jaco would take him on, with or without the leopard. He wasn't so sure about Willem.

Bullseye rose silently out of the fynbos and followed Quent to the stream. He stretched and then sniffed at Quent's hand before wading into the water and lapping up the icy liquid with his spade-like tongue. The grey outline of the man and dog shrouded in the white, dead-light of early morning, side by side in the black, peaty water, was like a monochrome tableau. Quent filled the water bottles. There would be no time to do this later and it was going to be very hot work. When he was done he sluiced his face and head in the water, attempting to clear his head. Too much to drink last night. Stupid.

When Quent returned to his camp, he stowed the water bottles and then made himself eat a piece of bread and cheese, even though his guts protested. Afterwards he swung his pack onto his back, testing the weight. On the ground beside his blanket was a heavy-duty climbing rope and pitons. He slung his rifle across his shoulders.

4.30 a.m. Willem would have the pickup at the bottom of the kloof by now and be halfway up the mountain to meet him. The thought of his friend gave Quent a lift. They were due to rendezvous in an hour. He knew how tough it would be getting the sedated animal down the mountainside but with four of them it should be possible. If Willem hadn't agreed to come in with him he would never have considered taking such a chancy route. It would have been far easier to take the direct track straight down Pig's Snout but he couldn't risk meeting Du Toit and his cronies coming up the kloof. No, over the mountain into the next valley was the only way.

Options

Raki looked at Mari and saw her cousin was smiling. 'I wanted to cheer when you drove away with your nose in the air and that smile on your face.'

'All I wanted was for her to understand, Mari.' Raki shook her head sadly. 'For the past three years I've dreamt of her holding me in her arms and saying that she loved me and wanted me home, but it will never happen. You grew up beside us, you've heard and seen how she's acted all our lives. She makes her mind up about something and that's it. She can't change.'

'Can't or won't?'

'Either way it's the same.'

'Yeh, maybe you're right. I've never seen her as angry as she was that day. She was hysterical after you left. Spent all her time with Mr Turkey or on her knees in the church –'

' – Praying that something terrible would happen to me and Quent?'

'I wasn't much help either, was I?'

Raki shrugged. 'You hated, Quent. You thought I was making a terrible mistake.'

Mari said nothing.

'Anyway, none of it matters now, does it?'

Mari squeezed her cousin's hand. 'I suppose you could always try your sisters. Maybe they'd chip in a bit each?'

'No way.'

Madre and Gloria were under Sofia's thumb and they had families and commitments of their own. Raki had never been close to either of them and they disapproved of the way she lived – almost as much as her mother did.

'Okay, that leaves Mr Turkey.' Mari didn't look at Raki, she knew what her reaction would be. 'You're still married to him, Raki. If anyone should help you it has to be him. My

God, you were his slave for all those years. Has he ever given you any money since you left?'

'Why should he?'

'He's still your husband.'

'But I left him, Mari, for another man, and I humiliated him in front of all his parishioners.'

'So what? He owes you big time.'

'I suppose I could ask him. I've got nothing to lose but it's going to be difficult. He'll probably refuse to see me and even if I speak to him he'll say *no*. He's bound to.'

'Yeah, I agree, he'd say *no* if you asked him just like that but he couldn't refuse if you said you were going back to him.' Mari was talking fast to stop Raki from butting in. She could see the look of horror on the other woman's face. 'He's your best hope, Raki. He'd have to take you in wouldn't he? He's a man of the cloth and you're still married and now you've got a little boy to support he couldn't leave you destitute. He's loaded.'

Raki felt suddenly faint and held onto the edge of the table to stop herself from falling. 'I can't go back to him, Mari.'

'He wanted a child, didn't he? A boy? To carry on the family name?'

'Yes, but he wanted his son not somebody else's.'

'If he saw Farnie, saw what a gorgeous little boy he is, maybe he'd reconsider and – '

'You think I want that man to be my son's father? To bring him up in that miserable dark house? So that he could make my Farnie into an emotionally-deprived religious freak like him? Never.'

Mari got off her stool and took the cups to the sink. She talked as she rinsed them. 'If Farnie doesn't have the operation soon he might be handicapped for life. Is that right?'

Raki nodded miserably. 'Yeah.'

'Then, what are we thinking about? Surely anything's better than seeing him grow up as a cripple? You'd still be his mother, even if you lived with Mr Turkey. And you're stronger now. You wouldn't put up with any of his nonsense.'

'He'd never accept him, Mari, I know him. He may have money but people like him have money because they don't spend it. You think he'd part with a single cent to pay for an operation on my bastard son? I know that's what he'd say. He'd say let him be a cripple. I can hear him. He'd say it was God's Will – a punishment for my sins. You think he'd tolerate someone else's child living in his house? My God, Mari. What would all the old nanny- goats make of that?'

Mari came back to the table. The two women looked at each other and Raki knew it was hopeless. So that was an end to it. Farnie would just have to wait his turn and she'd have to hope and pray he had it done before the defect was too serious to correct. This time Mari didn't try to stop her when she stood up and called Farnie to her. She held out her arms and he crawled towards her, pulled himself up on her stool and she lifted him onto her lap.

'Time to say bye bye to Tante Mari. Give her a kiss and say *thank you* for the biscuit.'

The boy did as he was told and Mari kissed him..

'Before you go, Raki, there's one other option.' Mari looked nervous. 'This is a last resort if all else fails, and remember I'm only suggesting it because I love you – both of you.' She talked rapidly as if the sheer momentum of the words would carry her along. 'In the long term it might be the only solution. I've been worried about you and Farnie for ages, about what's going to happen to you both. I don't mean because of what you've just told me, although of course that's another problem, but what are your plans for the future? You can't go on living up there on the mountain, you know that. When the food and money run out, then what?'

Raki was puzzled. 'I can't think about all that now. I'm concentrating on Farnie's op. I'm fine, we'll be fine just as soon as he's better. We don't need much.'

Mari banged the table with her fist. 'For God's sake, woman, you won't be fine. What about when things go wrong - like they have now? What if you get ill or fall or, heaven forbid, you die up there? Who's going to find you and look after Farnie?'

Raki was shocked by her cousin's anger. 'Don't say things like that, it frightens me.'

'And so it should.'

'We get by.'

'Listen to me. The world isn't a lovely, happy, secure place. God won't provide all the time. You must think about your future. Yours and Farnie's.'

Raki lived from day to day, that's how she thought she'd always live, but she recognised the truth in what her cousin was saying. And she'd been worrying about it too.

Mari hesitated before she spoke again. 'You love Farnie, you're a fantastic mother and you'd do anything for him?'

Raki was surprised. 'Of course.'

Mari spoke slowly, head down, staring at her hands. 'Have you ever....have you ever thought about putting Farnie up for adoption?'

Raki recoiled as if Mari had punched her.

'Please, hear me out. There was something on the telly the other night about hundreds of childless white couples who are desperate to adopt white babies. These people have loads of money, Raki, and if Farnie was adopted his new family would have the money for the operation wouldn't they? God forgive me, I know it would be terrible for you, for both of you, but Farnie's only little and given time he'd forget...' Mari couldn't continue.

'Forget? Forget me? Is that what you're saying? In time he'd forget his mother?'

'If you really want him to grow up a healthy, able-bodied child, then you have to think about this seriously, Raki. Please God you won't have to but you have to face facts. You don't have any money. That's the problem. Look at you? What are you going to do? Wait until your clothes are so old they drop off your back? For God's sake, you can barely look after yourself let alone a child. Even if you got the money for the op, what then? Hey? Your car's falling to bits, you don't have med care, you live from hand to mouth and winter's coming. Finally there's this.' She looked at Farnie. 'Anton and me may be up shit-creek without a paddle but we've got a roof over our heads, I can work and we've got a bit of savings to tide us over until he gets another job. You have nothing.'

Raki stood up abruptly, scooped up her son and marched out of the kitchen. Her hand was on the front door pulling it open by the time Mari caught up with her and got between her and the outside.

'Don't be like this, Raki. I'm only trying to help.'

'Help?' Raki turned a furious face to her cousin. 'You think that's helping? You're crazy. You want me to give my baby away to strangers? So I'll never see him again, ever? So he'll grow up calling some other woman mama?'

'D'you know something, Raki? You say you love him but you have to prove how much you really love him. Giving him up might be the most motherly thing you could ever do for him.' Mari raised her hand to try and touch Raki's face but her cousin knocked it away. 'Please, Raki. I only meant to help. '

' Goodbye, Mari.'

'But where are you going? Raki? Please. Please, speak to me.'

Raki's voice was a whisper. 'I'm never giving him up. I'd rather die, I'd rather we both died.' And then Raki pushed past her stricken cousin and went out onto the street.

Mari watched her helplessly as she ran across to her car, put the boy inside and drove away.

'Has she gone?' came Anton's complaining voice from the bedroom. 'Mari? I'm talking to you. What did the bloody female want now? Coming here at the crack of dawn? She's got a screw loose, that one. No wonder that guy ditched her. Mari? Bring me a coffee, man, I've got a thirst on me like a camel.'

'Shut up,' Mari hissed and then more loudly each time until she was screeching. 'Shut up. Shut up. Shut up!'

9.35 a.m.

Quent drains another bottle and tosses the empty away. His cell phone clatters onto the boards. Hooking his stick around it he manages to pick it up. No signal up here but he can't understand why she didn't answer his texts. It doesn't make sense. If it was something urgent she would have had the opportunity to ring him by now. Soon as he got to his mate's house in Cape Town, after Jaco had sacked him, he'd sms'd her, once, twice, all that day and all the next but there was nothing. Soon as his leg was better he intended coming to the kloof house to see her. But he had to be up to making the climb. He had enough sense not to go looking for her in Birkenheadbaai There was the small matter of the leopard and he didn't want to make trouble for her or Florentina.

But then suddenly, out of the blue, he did get a text but it wasn't from Raki, it was from Madam du Plessis. That was a week ago now. Longest week of his life.

Quent lost track of where his thoughts were going and his mind drifted back to that other day – the day he found his leopard.

While he waited for Willem's brother and the other guy to turn up that morning, Quent counted out his remaining money. After what he'd given to Raki there was just enough to pay the men and have some over for petrol. He would be cleaned out but as soon as he got to Jaco's he would be paid for the leopard. That was the deal. Cash on delivery. Jaco was a hard-nosed businessman and refused to say exactly how much he'd part with for the animal but he'd promised it would be substantial. Cape Leopards were rare and both Jaco and Quent knew their worth. If Jaco tried to cheat him Quent would move on – simple as that.

Quent put the money in his shirt pocket to make it easy to get out in a hurry. When they got the leopard down the mountain there wouldn't be time to hang about.

His guts went into spasm again and he relieved himself in the bushes. His insides always tied themselves in knots when he was nervous. Shortly after this, two men emerged out of the morning mist. Fortunately, Bullseye recognised them and after the ritual sniffing the satisfied dog disappeared into the undergrowth to find his breakfast.

Johannes was a rangier version of Willem but he lacked his brother's easy charm. There was something in the boy's expression that reminded Quent of himself and he wasn't sure that was such a good thing.

The other man was older, small and bent, and when Quent raised a hand in greeting he ducked his head shyly in response. Quent wasn't looking at the man's face he was staring at what he was wearing. He'd seen him in the distance on the Broot farm but never up close. The man was wrapped in a threadbare blanket – a Basotho blanket. Although the jewel-like colours were dimmed, it was still very beautiful. The last time Quent had seen a blanket like that was...a lifetime away.

Eunice used to knit blankets in kaleidoscopic colours and had made one for him. That blanket had gone everywhere with him. It had warmed him on chill nights in the bush and comforted him when the bad dreams came. Now it was rotting in a shallow grave in Zimbabwe.

When Quent thought about his childhood at all Eunice was always there. There was a hazy recollection of a man being around when he was very young but it was nothing tangible. He was the smell of stale tobacco smoke drifting on bright sunbeams or the thin-lipped, eyebrows-raised glance between Eunice and the old woman that meant someone had done something bad – and for once it wasn't Quent. There was one time he remembered the piano playing and Eunice dancing, with her skirts held high around her waist and the old woman singing in a sweet, high voice that seemed so wrong coming out of her mouth.

The two women grew up together in Rhodesia. Eunice was the old woman's playmate, then her maid and finally her confidante. They moved to the Western Cape in South Africa when Quent was little. The old woman's family were Afrikaners. Apartheid was part of her life, of all of their lives. Outside the house Eunice was bound by the race laws but inside she was second only to the old woman.

Her rondavel was just one room, a bedroom-cum-living room with a cob-oven outside. Quent learnt never to disturb her when she was in her house. It was her private place and she retreated there when things got bad, like when her nephew was shot in the Soweto riots or the time her brother 'disappeared' one day and never came home. The police took her away after that and when she came back Quent had to keep quiet while the old woman nursed her.

Quent remembered Eunice sitting at the kitchen table when he came in from school, a pot of tea on the go, elbows resting on the table, knitting needles clacking. She'd grab Quent and Willem too, if he was there, and hug them both to within an inch of their lives. Quent pretended he hated being hugged and he'd fight her off so that she'd laugh and take a swipe at him with the dishcloth. She was always there for him and he went to her with all his troubles. You didn't disturb the old woman with your problems.

Eunice had a repertoire of proverbs for all occasions. Like when Quent hadn't got anything much for Christmas and she lectured him. *It is greedy for a person who carries an elephant on his head to pick up a snail with his toes.* Some of her mottos were incomprehensible to him, still were, but they had always made him laugh. *'If you don't want the monkey-tail to touch you, don't go to a monkey dance.'* She'd said this once with grim satisfaction when he'd run in from school with a bloody knee because some big kid hadn't let him play football in the Big Boy's playground.

Quent must have been staring at the man because he took a step towards Quent and said something softly to him in Sesotho.

Quent looked at Johannes.

'His name is Elias,' the boy said, and yawned.

Quent hoped Elias was stronger than he looked. Given the choice he wouldn't have chosen either of these men for such a difficult job but Willem was a good judge of character and besides they were all there was.

He looked at his watch. Five or six hours, that was all he had. Last night it had seemed enough – more than enough. In the clear light of day he just had to hope luck was on his side because he would surely need it to be. Everything revolved around when Du Toit began his search of the kloof. Quent was banking on it being late morning at the earliest.

While they waited for Willem they made the stretcher for transporting the leopard down the mountainside. Quent had already cut two straight long poles and these had to be threaded through both sides of the tough webbing sling. Ropes were attached to the webbing which would secure the animal in the cradle. Each man would take an end of the pole, two in front and two behind. The men seemed glad to be doing something. Quent watched them as they worked. Maybe they were shit-scared too? Johannes yawned again showing a mouthful of white even teeth. He saw Quent looking and said, 'You got any food, man? He needs something.'

Elias's hands were trembling as he attempted to thread the pole through the webbing. Quent had thought he was cold but maybe not. He opened his backpack and offered the remains of the bread and cheese to the little man. He wouldn't take it but Johannes broke off a sizeable chunk of bread and cheese and forced it into the man's hands. Then Johannes got up and walked away as if he was going for a pee. After a moment Quent followed the youngster's lead and when they came back Elias was busy working away and the food had disappeared.

They were finishing off when Willem showed up, smack on time. Rocks came clattering down the mountainside long before Willem arrived, red-faced and breathing heavily. Dirty channels of sweat ran down his dusty face. He wiped it out of his eyes and smiled at Quent. 'Am I on time, bra?' Quent grinned back acknowledging his friend's mockery. Willem was carrying a shotgun slung across his shoulders. He took it off

188

and gave it to his brother; then he went and stood in the stream, scooping up great handfuls of water and lapping like a thirst-crazed dog. He drank and drank and when he returned he was dripping wet but smiling.

Willem squatted down beside Quent and the others while Quent went over the plan. Johannes translated for Elias. When Quent was positive they all knew what they had to do he got to his feet and pulled the backpack on. He took a huge lungful of air and let it out slowly. 'Okay, guys, time to get moving. No unnecessary noise, okay? And spread out. Walk slowly, yeh?'

He shared out the gear between the four of them. Johannes and Elias were to carry the rope and the stretcher between them, while he and Willem carried the guns and backpacks. As they moved off. Bullseye emerged from the fynbos and joined them. His muzzle was stuck with blood and feathers. He rubbed his face in the vegetation as he trotted along, getting his face clean.

Shark

Raki didn't go straight home after leaving Mari. She went to the Spar and sat in the car park until the store opened. She wouldn't think about what Mari had said. She made herself concentrate on Farnie. His needs were the only thing that mattered and she was out of milk. He was onto cow's milk now but he liked to drink weak rooibus with a lot of milk.

As soon as the store opened she hurried inside and grabbed what she needed plus some sweeties. She was through the check-out and on her way out when she noticed the coloured man, leaning against the wall by the exit. She recognised him. He was often there in his blue track suit, smiling that smile and having whispered conversations with the poor blacks who were huddled outside the shop, some of them begging, most of them just passing the long tedious hours. He must have sensed her watching him because he gave her a friendly smile; then he sidled up to her.

'Have you got money, madam?' he asked politely.

Raki pretended not to have heard.

'Money?' he repeated. 'Have you got money?'

Raki always tried to save a few cents to give to the beggars who waited patiently outside the store. But this man was no beggar. She turned her back on him and walked quickly out of the shop, only too aware that he was watching her. Outside, she glanced back and saw to her relief that he had switched his attention to a wizened black woman, with most of her front teeth missing. She had a small child clinging to her skirt. While he talked she nodded her head vigorously and held out a hand. He produced a small pile of notes and briefly rested his hand on the child's head before handing over the money. She took the money and disappeared inside the store.

It was Mari who'd told Raki who this man was. 'See that guy?' she said one day, jabbing her thumb in the man's direction and pulling a face. 'He's a loan shark. Look at those poor bastards. There should be a law against blood-suckers like him. Promise me you'll never get involved with him,' she lectured. 'You never finish paying off a debt with someone like that. The interest just keeps going up. You'd have to be crazy to get mixed up with a guy like that.'

'Or very desperate,' Raki added.

She remembered that conversation now as she watched the old woman filling her basket with bread and milk.

'Poor people,' she'd said to Mari. 'What happens if they can't pay the money back?'

Mari frowned. 'Bad things, Raki, very bad.'

Raki sat in the safety of her car and watched the money lender at work. He was outside the shop now doing business with three young single women. They were dressed in tight jeans so Raki knew they weren't married. Married black women never wore trousers. There was a lot of pushing and shoving and giggling amongst the girls as he talked to them. He had his arm around one of them. She was the one he handed the money to and she took it and tucked it provocatively into her tight back pocket. He smacked her on the backside and the three of them ran off like naughty children stealing candy. Next, the man moved on to a couple of men in baseball caps hunkered down on the pavement beside the supermarket door, drinking from bottles in brown paper bags. The man's smile disappeared. When the men saw him they jumped up but he grabbed one before he could escape. Raki didn't need to hear what he was saying to know he was threatening him. When he was finished the two blacks sauntered off down the middle of the road towards the squatter camp, pretending nonchalance, and the man shouted something in Xhosa after them and waved a fist. They picked up some stones from the road and hurled them at him.

As she drove home Raki thought about the money lender. If she had the money she wouldn't have to ask her mother or Mr Turkey, or, heaven forbid, put Farnie up for adoption. Anything would be better than that wouldn't it? She had her cell phone on the seat beside her and she glanced at it – no messages. She felt the panic rising. Quent must deliver but if he didn't what then? She almost turned around, there and then, to talk to the money lender, but Farnie was hungry and the weather was getting worse by the minute.

She drove in a daze. The rain was lashing down and the spray from oncoming cars was too much for her windscreen wipers to deal with. It was like driving underwater. Several cars flashed her and sounded their horns as they sped past and she made a determined effort to concentrate on her driving. But it was difficult because her mind was so full of what Mari had said.

When she got to Pig's Snout she stared blankly ahead towards the grey, forbidding mountain top. The wind was even stronger on the kloof and the car shuddered as each new gust hit it. The thought of having Farnie adopted was raw and ugly in her head. She needed to sleep; needed to clear her brain and think.

Of course she was in trouble. The little money she had left would soon go on petrol and food. There were a few provisions in the kloof house, a whole side of biltong, and vegetables to be harvested, but how long would they last? 'Oh God,' she said out loud. 'Make Quent ring me, please.' Her cell phone rang at that exact moment but it wasn't Quent, it was a text from a frantic Mari. Raki deleted it unread and shoved the phone in her pocket.

For the first time since she'd lived on the kloof, she dreaded the trek up that mountain. The elements had joined forces against her and by the time she reached the house she was just about done in. Amazingly Farnie had slept all the way up, and his dead weight hung like an albatross in her arms. However, as luck would have it, the minute she put him down he woke, determined to play and shout and have a good time.

When Raki eventually fell into bed that night she was too tired to undress. She lay in the dark staring up at the moon's flickering reflection on the ceiling while the wind made eerie, discordant music in the chimney.

Bad thoughts come with the night. The money lender was a very bad idea – she knew that. She'd be in debt for the rest of her life. She'd always be frightened, and what if that man hurt her son?

The longer she lay, listening to the wind and rain, the more Mari's words filtered into her brain. To give up her beautiful son for adoption was unimaginable but what if that was the only way he could get the operation? Her life would be over if it happened, but what mattered was Farnie, not her.

And even if she did manage to scrape the money together for the op, what was she going to do after that? Her savings were almost gone and her life was insecure to say the least. Something would have to change if she were to go on living on the mountain. And if she was being totally honest she knew her saviour wouldn't be Quent. Even if, by some miracle, he offered to pay the whole R10,000, she knew he wouldn't be willing or able to support them in the long term.

She tried to think rationally. A beautiful child like her Farnie would soon find new parents. He was very young and would forget her and grow to love his new mummy and daddy. Maybe he'd have brothers and sisters. He'd be part of a proper family with grandparents and uncles and aunts and friends. He could go to a good school and university and do something with his life. She'd had a year of happiness with her baby. Maybe that was all she deserved?

Raki made one definite decision that night and that was that she would do nothing for a few days. This would give her time to make a proper reasoned decision. There would be no half-baked knee-jerk reactions to the problem. In the scale of things a few days would make no difference.

She promised that she would make these last few days special for them. And she wouldn't cry all the time. She was going to be strong like Mari and, when and if she had to give him up she wouldn't let Farnie see she was upset. She was going to be very brave.

9.40 a.m.

The four men moved slowly and silently uphill. They came together at the foot of the cliff where a tortuous, narrow path led upwards to the summit. This was where Quent had 'dreamt' his leopard would be. It was no more than an animal track. Johannes and Elias stayed at the foot of the cliff and Quent made Bullseye lie beside them. Quent didn't want Bullseye spooking the leopard.

He and Willem laboured on upwards, finding footholds where they could and grabbing onto anything that gave them leverage. Several times Quent chose the wrong hand-hold and went sliding and slithering back down the small distance he'd only just managed to scramble up. Willem was a lot fitter than his friend. He was one of those effortless walkers who didn't seem to have an unnaturally long stride and yet within minutes of a walk would leave any companion a long way behind. Now, he was waiting for Quent beside a rocky outcrop where the path disappeared into the solid cliff face. As Quent reached him he offered his hand but Quent heaved himself up the last few metres. Once beside Willem he stood with his hands on his hips, trying to get his breath back. They were about 50m from the summit. Quent stared about him. The cliff had closed in around them like a tight fist and he felt his chest tightening in the airless pressure of the place. Willem started uphill again and Quent took a deep breath and stepped forward. As he did so something moved in the periphery of his vision. Quent crouched down and whistled to Willem who instantly fell on his knees and crawled back to him.

Quent was grinning and Willem looked at where his friend was pointing. Thirty metres down from the top of the kloof was a ledge and there, partially hidden by scrubby bushes, was a leopard. Unbelievable. No mistake – she was the leopardess he'd seen yesterday. Her markings were identical and her magnificent coat gleamed in the rays of the rising sun. Quent had to fight the urge to raise his fists to the sky and yell triumphantly. He felt light-headed with relief. He had seriously begun to doubt that he'd really seen the big cat. Green Nose had got to him but now he was vindicated. It felt so sweet.

Quent glanced at Willem expecting to see the same exultation on his face but he was surprised to see how worried his friend now looked. Willem caught Quent's eye and pointed to the ledge again. Quent swept the area with his binoculars and saw what Willem had seen. There was more than one leopard there, another furry head, maybe two, but much smaller – a cub or cubs? There was a sudden movement in the bush and the vegetation thrashed about for a moment before everything went quiet again. Quent held up two fingers but Willem shrugged.

There was something else there, glinting in the rays of the early morning sun – something metallic. Quent swore under his breath. It was the trap anchor of a gin-trap. If his leopardess was in a trap that was it – end of story. This was one problem he hadn't considered. He prayed it was the cub that was caught and not the mother but he would need to get closer to find out.

He signalled to Willem that they should go higher. They crawled painfully up the track until they were opposite the ledge. From there they could see the female lying beside a cub, flank to flank. They were so close it looked like one animal. Quent thought they must both be in the trap but then he saw the cub properly. One of the small creature's paws was terribly mangled, almost amputated in the steel claws of the trap, and there was blood and gore everywhere. The mother's attention was concentrated on her cub. There was no sign of another cub.

The cub looked dead. Quent hoped it was – if not it would be in terrible pain. His first reaction was to grab the rifle and put the pathetic creature out of its misery but with the mother so close he couldn't risk it. He chanted obscenities under his breath at the farmer who had laid this trap. Now he was nearer he could see how rusty it was. It must have been there for years. Maybe Broot's old man had set it. No

195

livestock farmer would have thought twice about trapping predators back then. There were some farmers who still used them. 'Kill the bastard, vermin.' He'd heard this said so many times by the old guys. You couldn't blame them. It was their livelihoods at risk if a leopard was living in the area. It was a reason to celebrate if they caught a thieving caracal in their traps but how much better if it was a leopard? Quent was thinking fast. He needed to dart the mother before he could do anything about the cub. However, it was obvious that if he tried to approach the leopard on foot the animal would attack. There was only one way onto the ledge and that was the escape route for the frantic leopard – not a good combination. Looking up, Quent spotted a very narrow ledge sticking out above the leopard's ledge. If he could get down to there from the summit he would be able to shoot a dart straight into the animal. He needed the rope.

He signalled urgently to the men to come up and bring the gear. Quent cursed himself for not bringing the rope himself. More time would be wasted as they waited and then Willem and Quent still had to get to the summit.

But Quent wasn't the only one thinking on his feet. Willem pointed to his brother who was tying the rope around Bullseye's broad shoulders. As soon as it was secure Bullseye sprang away from Johannes and came charging up the path towards Quent. The two men toiled behind carrying the stretcher between them.

The dog knew there was a leopard and was in a frenzy of excitement. Quent jumped up. He had to stop the animal from attacking the leopard. 'Bullseye.' He yelled. 'Down.' And he brought his hand down viciously, stopping the dog in his tracks. Then, when he was sure the animal was watching him and not the big cat, he beckoned the dog on, holding his hand out flat to stop him from coming on too fast.

'Quent. Be careful, man.' Willem was on his feet beside Quent, his shotgun aimed at the ledge. The leopardess was snarling like a chainsaw. It was a long leap to reach them from where she was but leopards could spring halfway up a tree with an adult Bok in their jaws. The men froze.

'If she comes for us try not to kill her, Willem,' Quent whispered.

He saw his friend's finger tighten on the trigger.

The animal was standing over her cub now, still snarling, but Quent saw the indecision in her eyes. After a few moments she lay down again, her fierce, bright eyes never leaving the men.

'Can your brother handle a gun?' Quent asked Willem, and when his friend nodded he held up the shotgun for Johannes to see and then he propped it beside his and Willem's backpacks.

When the dog reached them they set off for the summit. Quent carried the rifle and the box of darts. As they began the ascent the sun chose that precise moment to leap up over the rim of the mountain and drill its fierceness into Quent's eyes, blinding him. Time was flashing by. He wasn't just sweating from the heat now. Most of it was fear.

It took them nearly an hour to work their way up to the top and once there Quent saw that the ledge he was aiming for was even narrower than he had first thought. It was less than a boot's-width deep. At best he would have nothing more than a toe-hold. He tied the rope around his waist and gave the other end to Willem who secured it around his waist and then onto a rock. Quent loaded a dart into the rifle and stuffed another in his pocket. Then he slung the gun over his shoulder. Willem carefully fed the rope out as Quent lowered himself over the edge but the ledge came sooner than Quent expected, his knees buckled and he swung out into space. The rope twisted and he came back facing the rock. He jammed his boots against the ledge. When he was sure he was steady he stood up, praying that his legs would hold him. They felt like jelly.

'Okay, bra?' came Willem's worried voice from above.

'Yeah,' Quent lied.

He was breathing heavily, his face pressed into the warm rock. He allowed the smells of sun-baked earth and vegetation to calm him. There were clumps of heather and thyme in the crevices and a tiny red insect with long black legs and waving antennae paraded in front of his nose.

The next part was the worst because he had to turn around and face outwards. Somehow he managed and then he was standing there looking down on the leopard beneath him. He had an overwhelming urge to step out into the abyss. He closed his eyes for a moment and the pounding in his head gradually subsided. The rope jerked twice and he looked up to see Willem peering worriedly over the top of the cliff. Quent forced a smile. He made himself look down again to where the leopard crouched over her cub.

'Okay, man?' Willem whispered.

Quent raised his thumb but he was aware of the huge yawning chasm beneath his feet. Somehow he had to position himself so that he could use his rifle, not an easy matter when there was barely enough room to move his feet. Finally he managed to lean back into the rock and turn slightly sideways so that he could take aim.

The animal was about 20metres beneath him, lying stretched out full length beside her cub. All her attention was centred on Johannes, Elias and the dog. Bullseye was standing up facing the big cat. Quent knew from the way the animal stood that every fibre of his being was calling out to him to chase the leopard. Quent dreaded to think what would happen if the dog lost control. It was up to him to act fast. He raised the rifle to his shoulder. He didn't think, he just aimed and fired. The shot was perfect, the dart landing in the leopard's rump. Perfect shot. She reared up snarling at the pain, ran to the cliff edge and disappeared from view behind some bushes that were clinging to the sides of the edge. Quent could see the bush thrashing about as she fought the effects of the dart. Within moments everything went quiet.

'Get me up, Willem,' he yelled, adrenalin surging through him. He couldn't quite believe it. She was sedated – or at least he hoped she was. They'd still have to be extremely careful when they approached her but he'd done it.

Willem was already heaving him up and as Quent's head appeared over the edge of the cliff he shouted, 'Good shot, bra. You are good shot.'

They were both on a high as they took off down the cliff path. They jammed their boots sideways and 'surfed' down to where the others were waiting. They arrived beside Johannes and Elias in a cloud of dust and small rocks. Johannes was grinning widely but there was no time for talk. Every second was precious. Willem and Quent knew what they had to do. A wounded leopard could be very dangerous. This particular animal was protecting her injured cub and if she wasn't totally unconscious they were in big trouble. The men exchanged glances then they scrambled across the scree and pulled themselves up onto the ledge. Willem was in front carrying the shotgun and Quent came behind with the dart gun. The leopardess's head suddenly appeared over the top of a bush and she got unsteadily to her feet and turned her snarling face towards them. Both men braced themselves for the attack but the animal's legs suddenly gave way and she toppled sideways. They waited until they were absolutely certain that she was out cold.

Quent could see her clearly now. She was a young animal in absolutely prime condition with a plump stomach full of meat and a glowing, golden coat. It was his leopard, no question.

Unexpected Visitor

Raki woke to a beautiful day. Farnie was still sleeping and the bedroom was awash with the blueness of the sky and the brightness of the sun, warming the walls and furniture. Yesterday seemed like the worst sort of nightmare but she wasn't fooled. She knew it was all horribly real. It would take more than a bit of sunshine to solve her problems.

It was already warm when Raki stuck her head out of the door and looked up at the mountains. The air was still. It would have been easy to imagine that summer had returned to the kloof but Raki knew better. This was the lull before the storm. The long, grey days of autumn and then winter would soon be upon them.

After breakfast she and the excited little boy went down into the Pig's Eye and bathed and splashed in the pool. She washed some clothes and spread them on a hot flat rock to dry. She had taken a picnic with them and after eating they'd picked wild flowers, looked at insects and played hide and seek amongst the trees. Raki would put Farnie behind a tree and then he'd cover his eyes and she'd creep away. After a few moments she'd return and walk past the tree and he would scream with laughter. He thought if he sat with his hands over his eyes his mother couldn't see him. Eventually he would snatch his hands away and shout *boo* very loudly and she would pretend to be very shocked. It didn't matter how many times they did it he thought it was hilarious. Raki wished she could bottle his hysterical giggle. It made her so happy but then she remembered and wanted to cry.

She spent the days of their holiday see-sawing between tears and laughter.

She had come to accept that Mari had only been trying to help when she mentioned adoption but it had been such a shock — it still was. She wanted to ring her cousin and apologise for walking out on her but she'd lost her cell-phone. It must have dropped out of her pocket when she came back from Mari's. She searched up and down the path but didn't find it so there was no way of contacting Mari. More crucially she didn't know if Quent had responded to her text. She tried not to panic. He'd send the money to her P.O. Box in town, wouldn't he?

When the dawn broke on the fourth day of their holiday it promised to be yet another peerless day. The bokmackeries woke Raki early and the sky was cloudless and brilliant, transforming her white bedroom ceiling into a rippling, cobalt silk sheet. She had promised herself that this would be the day to decide what she was going to do. But not yet, not until she'd been into Birkenheadbaai for milk and to check her mail. Everything depended on that. She also planned to take some mealies and tomatoes to the store and trade for eggs and cheese. That would mean she would see the money lender again. There were lots of choices she told herself, but the feeling of dread grew and grew.

She played a lot of strenuous games with Farnie that morning, determined to tire him out. If she tried to harvest vegetables with him it would be hopeless. His idea of helping was rolling the vegetables down the mountainside and trashing the tiny seedlings. Some days he refused to take a morning nap, so she was keeping her fingers crossed.

Luckily, he did fall asleep and after she'd put him down she hurried outside, pulling on her boots as she went. She never gardened barefoot. There were too many spiders, scorpions and the occasional snake amongst the plants. Raki loved gardening. Messing about with plants always had a soothing effect on her. But not today. She tried to ignore the sick feeling in the pit of her stomach as she attacked the weeds but she couldn't. This was the day, the day she'd prayed would never come, the day she might have to give her baby up for adoption. And how would that work? Did she have to advertise in the paper? Or take Farnie to an orphanage until they found a couple who wanted him? *An orphanage* like in Oliver Twist?

She was numb as she plaited the garlic, her nimble fingers suddenly big and clumsy. When she was finished she hung half the garlic on a nail on the kitchen wall where Farnie and the young baboons couldn't get at them. She'd take some to sell in town and she might call at Mari's with some bulbs – a peace offering?

Raki moved on to the vegetable plot. The sunlight bounced off hundreds of CD's that she'd attached to wires, strung along each row. These were to scare off the monkeys and birds. Anton had got the freebie discs from the music store. Quent used to fire his rifle to frighten off the baboons but Raki preferred this kinder approach. She hated guns.

Raki loved the monkeys and didn't mind too much when they stole food from the house. It was a small price to pay for their company. It was hard to be lonely with a bunch of rowdy baboons living nearby. The troupe slept in the forest at night but came up the kloof during the day. Usually they hung out in the mound of rocks behind the house. Mothers left their babies there in crèches and the inquisitive youngsters often visited Raki's house on their way down to the flat-water run to drink. Raki kept the door and windows open during the day. Immature baboons were like all young animals, curious and keen to explore anything new but they didn't like to be trapped inside with no exit. As long as Raki kept an eye on Farnie everything was fine and the little boy loved baboons. Raki treated the dominant male with respect and he would often come and sit on a boulder close by and watch the young baboons playing by the kloof house. He was like some benign policeman.

She and the baboons had learned to live with one another, although just lately they seemed to be in a perpetual state of agitation. The least thing seemed to set them off screeching and baring their teeth at each other. Raki supposed that there was a new kid-on-the-block trying to usurp the dominant male. It had happened before; it would happen again. It was nature but she felt sorry for the old baboon.

When she'd harvested the vegetables Raki collected the watering cans and went down to the stream. The plot needed a lot of water. There were no trees up here to protect the earth from the hot summer winds, and the thin top soil blew away if it dried out. Any compost she had was dug into the soil to retain the moisture but it still needed a huge amount of water. Fortunately, there was never any shortage in the stream. It sometimes snowed on the mountains in the winter and there was a lot of rain. Raki toiled backwards and forwards with the cans for an hour. It was hard, hot work, but it kept her mind off things.

She was just coming back up the kloof with the last can when she stopped to wipe the sweat out of her eyes. As she looked down the slope she saw a figure clambering slowly up the kloof towards her. She wasn't frightened. Anyone climbing up here in this heat had to have a good reason.

Her first thought was that it was Mari, but no, she could see it was a man, dressed in shorts and shirt with a hat pulled down low over his eyes. Raki allowed herself the tiniest sliver of hope before shaking her head at her stupidity. It wasn't him. She un-tucked her skirt and shielded her eyes against the sun, trying to get a better view, but as she did so the material caught on a vicious saw-toothed aloe. As she wrenched the material free there was a ripping sound. The skirt was torn from the waist to the hem but she barely noticed. All her concentration was fixed on that figure trudging wearily towards her. She wiped her dirty hands on her skirt and waited. At last, whoever it was saw her and raised a hand in greeting.

That was when she knew who it was.

9.45 a.m.

Up till that moment it had been all about paying Du Toit back and showing the arrogant prick that Quent Byrant wouldn't take shit from anyone. But now it was different because now Quent saw how beautiful the animal was. Was he really going to sell this amazing creature to that bastard Jaco? He didn't have to. He could walk away now, let Du Toit find her. He and Willem could go back to the Broot farm as if nothing had happened. They wouldn't be missed – not yet. He could go back to Raki.

When Quent looked up Willem was standing over the broken body of the cub. It had been dead for some time. Quent prised the trap off what remained of the cub's leg and broke the steel jaws with the butt of his rifle before tossing it over the edge of the cliff. They heard it clattering down the mountainside. The noise seemed to go on for a very long time. Maybe that hadn't been such a good idea.

The cub was big, almost big enough to leave its mother. Maybe there was another one hiding in the undergrowth? Quent pushed some branches aside with his rifle but there was no time to search thoroughly.

'We must go, bra.' Willem's voice was urgent, 'Our new life is coming.'

That's when Quent's legs began to shake. He was trembling so much he thought he might fall over.

'Is something wrong, bra?' Willem rested his hand on Quent's shoulder. 'Are you ill?'

'No, no, I'm fine.'

'We must hurry.'

Quent nodded. Willem was right. There was no going back. If he chickened out now he would always regret it. He made himself grin at Willem, 'Yeah, sure, sorry. Okay, good work everyone. Bring the stretcher, Johannes. Let's get her loaded.'

The four of them man-handled the leopardess off the ledge and onto the stretcher. She wasn't as heavy as a male but her dead weight must have been 30kgs or so. As soon as she was safely tied down they grabbed a pole each and heaved the stretcher off the ground. Elias and Quent were in front, the taller men behind. Bullseye circled them as they began the ascent, trying to get at the leopard, but Quent yelled and he backed off.

The climb up that mountain was the stuff of nightmares. For every step they took they slithered two steps back. Quent began to think they'd never make it. The men slipped and stumbled on the loose shale as they inched upwards trying not to fall over or let go of the poles. No one spoke and they didn't look at each other. They were all in their own private hell. All Quent heard was the leopard's sturterous breathing.

It took two hours to reach the summit and when they got there they lowered the stretcher and sank to the ground. Willem and Johannes were grey with exhaustion and the little man from Lesotho was bent double, spewing up. Quent handed around what was left of the water. Surprisingly it was little Elias who was on his feet first and the others were shamed into joining him. They grabbed the poles and set off downhill.

The journey down was easier in some ways but harder in others. The shale was like a layer of ice on top of the bed rock and they fell continually, scraping their knees and elbows, and once or twice the stretcher was thrown sideways. They almost lost the leopard over a huge boulder. Quent knew he was wearing the same look of fear as the others. They had to concentrate on where they were placing each foot but there was something else that was worrying them. The leopard had begun to make louder noises, as if she were waking up. If the dope wore off before they got her down and in the cage they were in deep shit. Quent and Willem had their guns but it would be almost impossible to shoot off a dart in these conditions.

Quent didn't look at his watch again because it would only have panicked him. He knew it had taken a lot longer than he had anticipated and they were in real danger of being discovered. Du Toit might be a prat but he would be very keen to find out if Quent was telling the truth and he may have discovered that the animal cage was missing.

When at last they reached flatter ground Quent saw the main road snaking away along the coast towards the Kleinsrivier Mountains. And best of all, down in a dip, just a few hundred metres away, was Quent's pick-up.

When they reached the vehicle they lowered the leopard and slumped against the sides of the vehicle. The guy from Lesotho was suffering the most. He was coughing and bringing up great gouts of phlegm. Johannes and Willem looked at each other.

'Is he going to be okay?' Quent asked.

Willem shrugged. 'It's cold at night on the farm; he's only got that thin blanket and he's been outside for three months. It could be pneumonia or TB or Aids, or all three.'

'For chrissake. How are we gonna get her in the cage with just the three of us?' He jumped into the back of the pickup and opened the cage doors.

Willem took both of the poles at the back of the stretcher while Johannes joined Quent at the front. Quent reckoned if they could get it on the pick up, then Johannes could help Willem at the back while he untied the leopard. Willem was heaving at the poles when the little man moved beside him and took his pole. Quent and Johannes scrambled up onto the back on the vehicle. They propped the stretcher against the side of the pick-up like a ramp. untied the leopard and manhandled her into the cage, slamming and locking the doors.

The leopard's lips curled in her sleep. A shuddering breath went through her and she opened one eye, then the other. She blinked, once, twice and got unsteadily to her feet. There was water in the cage but she walked straight through the container spilling the lot and stood there looking about her.

The men gathered around. Willem was in the middle of saying they should get some more water for her from a nearby stream when the animal went crazy. They jumped away as she leapt at the sides of the cage. The cage shuddered. Quent thought she might break out. Bullseye went mad trying to get at her. The leopard plunged and screamed with rage, tearing at the bars with her claws and teeth. There was nothing they could do but watch the traumatised creature until she exhausted herself and flung herself down. That's when Quent darted her again.

They were all physically and emotionally drained but Quent was elated. He'd done it. He grasped Willem's hand and pumped it up and down. Willem laughed, they all laughed, even Johannes had a smirk on his face and little Elias was smiling too.

But there was no time for congratulations. They must get away as quickly as possible and Quent felt in his pocket for the money. He was literally handing it to Johannes and Elias when he heard a shout and saw a group of men hurrying down the mountainside behind them. Du Toit had found them.

Desmond

Raki clasped a hand over her mouth to stifle the scream and stumbled down the track, not caring where she trod, going faster and faster until she was flying towards the man. He was standing still, waiting for her, his arms open wide. She rocketed into him, nearly knocking him off his feet then she grabbed him and sobbed into his shirt. They stood like that for a long time until he gently unwound her arms from around his neck and took her hands in his, kissing each palm. When he straightened up she saw the wetness on his cheeks.

'Forgive me, Raki,' he muttered. 'Please, say you forgive me. I've been such a coward – '

' – Shh, shh,' she whispered, putting a finger on his lips and smiling through her tears.

'I wouldn't blame you if you never wanted to speak to me again.'

She put her hand on his face feeling the wonderfully familiar stubbly skin. 'Is it really you? I can't believe it.'

'I wanted to come, Raki, I promise you. So many times I got up and said this is the day I'm going to visit my daughter, you've got to believe me. I even drove out here, to the bottom of the kloof, more than once, but in the end I couldn't do it. Your dad's a coward. And if it wasn't for Mari I wouldn't be here now.'

'What did she tell you?'

'Everything... She told me everything, Raki. My God, you've been through such a terrible time.'

He couldn't continue for a moment and she watched his lips trembling. He was fighting to control himself. She'd never seen her father cry. It was horrible. She took him in her arms and patted his back, like he was a small child. 'Shh, shh,' she soothed. 'It's okay, Dad. Really.'

He shook his head violently against her shoulder. 'No, it's not okay. Mari was very angry with me. I've never seen her so angry. She told me what had happened to Farnie and how you need money for an operation and you don't have it.' He hesitated for a moment and his voice was very soft when he spoke again. 'She was so worried about you. She said...she said you might do something... to yourself and the child because of what she'd said to you.'

'I'd never hurt Farnie, she knows that.'

'But she said you were desperate. She was scared for you and felt so guilty because she was the one who suggested you should have him adopted.'

'She was talking sense, Dad. She always does. I wanted to ring and tell her everything was okay and to say I was sorry, too, but I've lost my phone. She's been my best friend, Dad.'

'Better than your father, that's for sure.'

Raki squeezed his hand.

'She...your mother...was at a church but I think Mari would have yelled at her too if she'd been there. Why didn't you let us know what was happening?'

'You know why.'

'But we're your parents.'

'She cursed me, Dad, said I wasn't her daughter, said she wished I'd never been born that she never wanted to see me again, *in this world or the next*. You can't have forgotten.'

'She's...she doesn't mean to be so hard, Raki. She misses you.'

'Does she?'

Her father couldn't look her in the eyes.

'It's okay, honestly. She can't hurt me anymore. But you're here now, that's all that matters.'

They stood in each other's arms and Raki felt so at peace. Everything was going to be all right now he was here. He'd look after them. She wouldn't have to give her baby away, or borrow money from that money-lender. She could stop worrying. Thank God. Thank God. Farnie was safe.

'She doesn't mean to be cruel. But she's made her stand. D'you understand? She can't back down–'

' – It's okay, Dad, I promise you. As long as you're here, it doesn't matter. I love you.'

'I don't deserve it. All this time and I turned my back on you.' He took a deep breath. 'But that's all in the past.'

'Did you tell her you were coming?'

He widened his eyes at her – just like he used to – and she couldn't help grinning. 'It's okay, Dad, I know she hates me. I came to terms with that a long time ago. But what about Farnie? Does she know about him? Does she know I have a son? And if she does, has she cursed him too?'

'She wouldn't do that, Raki. And yes, of course we both knew about ...your son. Not much gets past the good women of Birkenheadbaai, and then of course you go to the clinic and the shops and the Post Office.'

Raki was silent for a moment and then she sniffed and straightened her shoulders. 'It must have been very hard for someone like her. Someone who is so certain about what she believes. What did she always tell us? If we obeyed God's commandments then we would be eternally blessed. *Thou shalt not commit adultery*. I tried to love that man, Dad, I really did, but all it brought me was misery. In the end we have to do what's right for us and I don't regret it. My life before Quent was...nothing, less than nothing. My marriage to Mr Morgan was a sham. There was no love, no companionship, not even a desire to make it better. If I'd stayed with him I think I would have killed myself.'

Her father stood in front of her, head bowed.

'It may not have worked out like I wanted with Quent but I've got a beautiful little son and I thank God every day for him.'

'I blame myself,' her father whispered. 'I should never have let you marry Morgan.'

'It was my decision, Dad. My fault. No one else's.'

'But I knew it was wrong. Any fool could see it was doomed from the start but Sofia wanted it so badly. She went to pieces for a while after you ran off with that man. It was like it knocked all the stuffing out of her. She was so humiliated and hurt. It was like you'd deliberately decided to punish her for making you marry Morgan. But, what's done is done, there's no going back. We've all made mistakes.'

Raki looked her father straight in the eyes. 'I'll never regret what I did, Dad. I want you to understand that. I loved Quent, really loved him, and I wanted to be with him for ever. Married or not, it didn't matter. Those two years we had were so good and a million times better than that other life. If she's waiting for me to say I was in the wrong then she'll wait for an awful long time. She's the one who's wrong, Dad, not me.'

'I haven't come here to talk about your mother, Raki. I've come to help you. You and your little boy.'

'Farnie.'

'Farnie?' Her father rolled the name experimentally around his mouth. 'I like it.' He rested his head on hers. 'I've missed you so much, Raki.'

She breathed in his dear, familiar smell. She wasn't sure how long they stood like that but it was the crying of a child that roused them both.

Her father took a step away from her. 'I think it's time I said *hello* to my grandson, don't you?' And taking the watering can from her he led the way to the house.

9.50 a.m.

There was no time to think. Quent yelled for everyone to pile in the pick-up and as they scrambled aboard he yelled. 'Hang on to your hats. This is gonna be one helluva ride.'

He drove with Willem beside him. The other two were in the back with the leopard and Bullseye. Quent raced the vehicle down the bumpy track, crashing into potholes and lurching over rocks, then out onto the main road. Once on the highway Quent drove like a maniac, putting as much distance between himself and Du Toit as he could. It would take his pursuers an hour or so to get back to their vehicles. By that time they would have lost his trail.

When he thought it was safe Quent pulled off the road and the four of them got down. Johannes was the first to speak. 'So, baas, what now?'

Quent didn't miss the mockery and he narrowed his eyes. 'I didn't want this any more than you did, but what should I have done? Um? Left you there to face the music.'

Johannes shrugged.

'I'm prepared to take you with me, whatever the consequences. You don't like that then bugger off.' Quent smiled suddenly. 'Up to you, boy, be my guest. I'm sure Du Toit and the cops will give you a warm welcome.'

Willem stood by his brother. 'Johannes will come with us. If the boss won't take him, then I will go too.'

'No way, Willem.' Nothing was going to knock Quent, not now, not now he'd stolen that leopard right from under du Toit's smug nose. 'Trust me. It'll be fine. Jaco won't be able to help himself when he sees what I've brought him.'

Quent glanced at Elias. He wasn't so confident about the little man. He stood apart from them, blanket wound tightly about him. His head was down and he was shifting from one foot to the other. It was very hot now but he was still shivering. Quent's instinct was to ditch him but he knew

Willem would never go along with that. He spoke to Johannes. 'Tell him he's coming too. He'll make better money at Jaco's and have somewhere to sleep and regular food – I'll see to that.' So many promises. But Quent would have promised anything to get on the road again. Du Toit would have alerted the police by now and no doubt they'd be setting up road blocks. They needed to get off the highway as soon as possible.

No one knew where they were heading apart from him. They all got back in the vehicle but this time Elias was in front with Quent – Willem insisted. Once back on the road Quent turned off the main road onto a track heading up into the mountains. He hummed as he drove. He felt the pain from a hundred scratches and cuts and bruises on his body, and his hands were one mass of blisters. It didn't matter, nothing mattered. This was more like it. This was life.

He slid back the window behind him. 'Everything okay back there? '

Willem stuck his head through the gap. 'We're good bra and our leopard's okay.'

'It's your bloody dog, man.' Johannes complained. 'Every time I move a muscle the bastard growls at me.' But despite his moans Johannes sounded excited. Not for the first time Quent saw the similarity between himself and the boy.

'Don't worry, he won't hurt you and it's only another 200 kms to go. What are you belly-aching about? '

Quent glanced at Elias. He had his eyes closed. Quent prayed that the little man hadn't died on him. That's all he needed, a corpse to get rid of. But then Elias murmured in his sleep and Quent relaxed.

Quent wipes the sweat out of his eyes. He's burning up again. Time for another drink. He's trying to remember what happened to Willem's shotgun. Did he take it with him to Jaco's or throw it away in the panic? It doesn't matter now but it's strange how details like that suddenly seem so important. His eyelids flicker and close. The man and dog are asleep and dreaming. One of them whimpers.

Setting Off

At last the day came that Raki was dreading and longing for in equal measure. This was the day Farnie was going into hospital for traction. It was all organised.

Things had moved bewilderingly fast since her father's first visit and Raki was having trouble keeping up with it all. It felt like she'd just woken up after a long, debilitating illness and life was beginning to make sense again. All the feverish dreams and imaginings were receding and she was able to consider her future – their future.

She'd asked her father to check her Post Office box in town but there was nothing from Quent. Her father was paying for everything – the traction, Farnie's operation, the aftercare costs and even accommodation for her. When he contacted the consultant's secretary, Farnie was offered a bed in two days' time. Raki would stay with Farnie during the three weeks of traction and if all went well he would have the manipulation procedure and his first spica fitted.

Raki didn't know how her father was managing to pay for it all. Her mother had always controlled the finances in their house. Raki vowed that one day she'd pay him back.

The night before Farnie was admitted to hospital Raki lay all night with one hand resting lightly on her little boy's head as he slept.

When she woke the next morning Farnie was sitting up in his cot 'reading' his book to the teddy bear. *Opa* had brought him the bear. Raki loved saying *Opa*. Before this there had only been Tante Mari, Anton and the boys but now Farnie had a grandfather too. And he had promised to drive them to the hospital today and would stay with Raki until she and Farnie were settled.

The plan was that he would be waiting for her down in the campsite. She tried to argue with him. It would be hard for him to get away without her mother getting suspicious but Raki was relieved he was taking her. He said there was no way she was driving his grandson to Cape Town in that *death-trap on four wheels*. They laughed but she knew he was right. They planned to set off early to avoid the morning rush-hour into the city.

She'd asked her father to let Mari know what was happening. She was so grateful to Mari for what she'd done. Apparently things were still bad with Anton. All he did was lie in front of the telly all day. Raki didn't have time to see her cousin before she went to Cape Town but she'd ring her as soon as she could. Her father had given her an old cell-phone to use.

Raki didn't know what excuse her father would give to her mother for his absence but he told her not to worry, it would be fine. Raki didn't want her parents falling out over her but she couldn't think about that now. There was only one thing on her mind today.

When she was dressed she changed Farnie's nappy, put his clothes on and gave him a drink and some bread with honey. Honey was his favourite and she had a jar of it in her backpack, along with his clothes and nappies. While he ate she pulled on Quent's old hiking boots. Her own soft boots didn't give her ankles the support she needed for the scramble down the kloof. It was still dark and she'd have to be very careful where she trod.

She got a bag of old clothes out from under her bed and spread them around her on the floor. She was searching for something. It was very early and there was barely enough light but she didn't want to light the lamps. The oil was very low. Eventually she found the large square of cloth she was looking for and when Farnie finished eating she picked him up and quickly swaddled the cloth tightly about him and then tied him against her body, facing outwards so that his back was against her chest. She needed both her hands free for the climb.

'Mama,' Farnie wailed, struggling to get his hands out of the straight-jacket.

She kissed the back of his head. 'It won't be for long, sweetheart, promise. Now be a good boy. We're going to see

215

Opa. That will be nice, won't it? Do you think he'll have some sweeties for Farnie?'

Time was flying by and she needed to get going. The house was a tip but it could wait and what did it matter anyway? She went out of the house quickly, leaving the door open. Let the baboons come, she didn't care. All that mattered was her little boy. As she set off she thanked God that this would be the last trek down the mountainside carrying Farnie. She was strong but she knew she couldn't keep carrying the boy up and down to the house, especially when he had his spica.

She and her father had discussed her move down to the campsite and he had promised to help make the little rondavel habitable for her and Farnie when he came home. It was the only structure still standing at the CLP site after Du Toit and the others moved on.

Raki had already begun to move a few personal possessions down. She'd had a day sweeping the rondavel and getting rid of all the bugs and spiders. Farnie had loved 'helping'. The old generator was still on the site and her father had offered to take a look at it for her. Electricity would be brilliant in the long winter months. The rondavel was dry and it was near to the stream and the road. She could make it comfortable and homely and her dad said he could bring some furniture and bedding to save her transferring everything from the kloof-house. More to the point, he had insisted that he give her a weekly allowance. It wouldn't be much but enough to live on. She felt very uncomfortable about taking yet more money from him but he said it wasn't for her but for Farnie, so how could she refuse? One of the best things was he offered to supply her with sheep fleeces so that she could make rugs to sell. He might even get her some animal hides for her leather work. He'd always rated her work and was sure that if she marketed her wares properly she could make a decent living.

Although she would miss the kloof-house and her garden, maybe it wouldn't be forever and the possibility of supporting herself gave her a huge boost. Originally her father had wanted to lend her the money to rent a small place in Birkenheadbaai but that was a step too far for Raki.

Farnie was still complaining as Raki started the descent. 'Shh shh, baby,' she crooned. 'Shall Mama sing you a song?' She began to sing *The wheels on the bus go round and round*,' but he was inconsolable. 'Does Farnie want a ride in *Opa*'s car? I think so, don't you?'

'Brra, brra,' Farnie said, instantly distracted.

The birds were still roosting when she set off and the sky was that flat non-colour that happens just before dawn. It was cool and Raki was glad of Farnie's warmth, snug against her, like a warm little hot-water bottle. She could hear the distant *wooshing* of the sea and frogs were calling from the stream below. The air was clogged with the incessant rasping of the cicadas. Raki picked her way carefully between the boulders. The meagre light from her head-torch flickered erratically. The battery was running low.

The eerie morning light made Raki remember another morning, much the same, after Quent walked out on her. During that long, terrible night she had decided to get herself to the clinic for an ante-natal check up. She was in the middle of getting ready when someone rapped loudly on her door. She had flung it open, her heart thumping. Maybe...just maybe... but it wasn't Quent it was Robert Du Toit, Quent's boss. She'd met him a couple of times on her journeys up and down the kloof and he'd always seemed quite pleasant and called her Mrs Morgan very politely. It was common knowledge about her and Quent.

The young man looked grim. 'Where is he?'

'Who?'

'Who d'you think?'

'You want to see Quent?'

'Yes.' His eyes were hard. 'How many men have you got up here?'

Raki winced at the insinuation 'Quent isn't here,' she said primly and tried to shut the door but Du Toit pushed his way inside. He searched the bedroom and when he came out Raki

217

was standing with her hand on the door. 'I'd like you to leave now.'

He ignored her. 'When did he go?'

'Last night, late, after – '

'Yeah? After what?'

'You shouldn't have laughed at him. He hates being laughed at, and now he's gone.'

'Did he mention the leopard?'

'Yes, but he said you didn't believe him.'

'Did he tell you where he was going?'

She shook her head. Raki was frightened now. 'Please. Tell me, what's happened?'

Du Toit glanced at the woman. Her face was tear-stained and she had bags under her eyes. She was dishevelled and dressed in crumpled, stained clothes. It was obvious she wasn't going to help him. From the look of her, Byrant had ditched her, but there were more important things to think about.

'He said he'd found her – the leopard. I thought he'd be so happy but he wasn't ...he was very angry. Is it true? Did you all make fun of him? He hates that. He does ...bad things when he's angry.'

'He must have told you where he was going.'

All he said was he was going up-country. There was a job. Has he done something wrong?'

Someone was shouting from outside. Du Toit looked out of the door. A group of people were coming up the mountain towards them. 'No joy here,' Du Toit shouted. 'Go on up the kloof. I'll follow in a minute. '

'Please,' Raki put a hand on his arm. 'Please, I must know what he's done.'

'He's stolen a leopard. Mrs Morgan. That's what he's done and he's in big trouble – '

' – Stolen? What d'you mean? How can someone steal a wild animal?'

'Look I don't have time for this. I intend getting Quent Byrant for this and he'll get prison – a long sentence if I have anything to do with it. Stealing an endangered species is a criminal offence.'

'But why? Why would he do that? What for?'

'For a big wad of rand, Mrs Morgan, that's what for.'

'No, he wouldn't, he couldn't.' Raki was indignant. 'Quent loves leopards. They're his life.'

Du Toit laughed at that. 'Ja, he loves leopards so much he's going to sell her to the highest bidder, where she'll be used by a hunting syndicate for some fat, very wealthy tourist who needs a Cape Leopard to complete his trophy wall.'

'No, he'd never do that. I promise you. Never.'

'If he comes back or contacts you, you let me know, okay? D'you understand? I said do you understand? Because if you hide him, or protect him in any way, then you are as culpable as he is and you'll go to prison too.'

'Why is it so important? It's only a leopard.'

'Do you know how many Cape Leopards there are in South Africa?'

She shook her head.

'Each one of them is precious. And the CLP is the only thing between them and extinction. The papers get hold of this and we're dead meat, no more funding and goodbye to International goodwill – bloody gone, all of it. That's what lover-boy Byrant has done and God help these leopards without someone to protect them.' And with that he left the house. Slamming the door shut behind him.

Raki watched him running up the track. In the scale of things it was one more shock for Raki to absorb, but she had decided last night that there was only one thing she was going to concentrate on from now on and that was her baby.

It went against all Raki's instincts leaving the house in a mess with dirty breakfast dishes still on the table but she wanted to have time to settle Farnie before he had the treatment.

She was full of optimism as she entered the *Pig's eyes*.

9.55 a.m.

Quent is shivering and he pulls the quilt up to his chin. There's a foul metallic taste in his mouth. He uncaps another bottle of water and takes a gulp, swilling his mouth before spitting it away. Quent drains the bottle, upending it over his mouth so as to catch the remaining few drops on his parched tongue. How can he be so hot and yet so cold? He raises a hand to wipe the sweat out of his eyes, and as he does so the hard edge of Raki's skirt catches on his wound. 'Christ Almighty,' he yells.

He waits for a moment before steeling himself to pull back the material and take a look. His whole leg is swollen and the skin is a patchwork of angry, red blotches – the tell-tale signs of bleeding beneath the skin. And the line is there too, that long line of death reaching up his leg and into his groin. Quent has seen too many similar wounds to fool himself. Blood poisoning kills quickly unless there's access to intravenous antibiotic plus a large slice of good luck. Quent starts to chuckle – it's a crazy, manic, bubbling sound and the dog lifts his head and whines.

'Did I ever tell you about the guy in the bush, a good mate of mine, Bullseye? Got a bullet in the thigh? That was the end of him.' This makes Quent laugh again and the worried dog comes closer. Bullseye's a vague grey shape. 'Good boy, good old boy.' Quent's speech is slurred as if he's drunk. He holds out his hand and feels the dog's hot breath on his fingers. He smells the animal's rankness. Everything stinks, it's as if the whole world's rotting. He puts his hand down into the vegetation growing up through the railings and tries to find a sprig of heather but his hand slips along the jagged edge of an aloe and it slices into his flesh.

He sinks back onto the chair and closes his eyes. They'll have to hurry if they want to get to him before he dies. All that effort for nothing? It would be so easy to blow his brains out. Get it over with. But he can't do it: not because he's afraid. Christ! He wants an end to it all – but he can't do it, not while there's the slightest chance she might come. There's this tiny voice of hope in his brain but it's getting fainter now as if the breeze is blowing it away. But there's no wind today. It's one of those clear, bright autumn days that comes wrapped like a gift.

Quent wants to sleep but he's in that pick-up again, driving through the ostentatious, big white gates of Jaco's estate and up the long, winding drive with outbuildings and living quarters lining it on either side. A big enterprise. Quent's impressed. Yeah, Jaco is doing very nicely, *dankie*.

They'd arrived at their destination but now what? Quent had sounded confident about Jaco's reaction to him bringing two other guys with him but it's different now he's here. What if it messes up the deal? He talked big about taking the leopard to another buyer if Jaco wouldn't play ball but they need to get the animal off-loaded and into an enclosure as soon as possible.

He couldn't have ditched the two men in Birkenheadbaai but he didn't expect Jaco to sympathise with that. Hopefully Johannes would be okay – he was young and strong – but the little guy? Elias was a migrant worker and most of these people were illegals. Quent had no idea if Du Toit or the others had identified who was with him but it wouldn't take long when the four of them didn't turn up at Broots.

He just had to hope that Jaco was in a reasonable mood. The sun was setting and they were all exhausted. They'd only had two stops, one for petrol and the other for water. They were hungry and dead-beat. But there was a more urgent problem. A few kilometres back Willem's worried face had appeared in the small window behind Quent's seat. 'She's waking up, bra.'

Quent swore. It might be dangerous to use another tranquillising dart. Quent had no idea how much of the stuff a leopard her size could take and he didn't want to kill her – not after what they'd been through to get her.

There was a deserted car park at the end of the drive in front of a large, rambling hacienda-style farmhouse with bougainvillea cascading down ornate pillars. Quent rested his hand on the horn and kept it there until a black guy came running out of a low building to one side of the main house. He was followed by two others. Bullseye barked furiously and the leopard was up and standing unsteadily. Quent didn't want Bullseye to freak the animal and he jumped down and got the dog off the back.

Jaco's men stayed well clear of the vehicle with its huge wild dog and now snarling leopard. Johannes and Willem jumped down and walked about, trying to get the feeling back in their legs. That journey had been hairy for them all but the back of a pick-up over mountain passes was not somewhere you'd want to be.

'Where's Jaco?' Quent asked the nearest man.

The man shrugged, he didn't understand.

Quent tried again. 'The baas?'

That did it and the man grinned. 'Baas,' he said and jerked his thumb towards the house; then he said something in Shona.

Willem translated. 'He says the boss is asleep and you'd better not wake him. There's a place for the leopard over there. We can drive to the enclosure and they'll help us unload her.'

The men walked in front so that Quent could follow. Eventually they came to a largish compound surrounded by high fences topped with razor-wire. There were some trees in the centre of the enclosure and a mound of rocks to one side. It could have been better but it was okay for now. There was the sound of running water from some place close by.

Willem and the men had another conversation. 'They've left some meat by the trees.' Willem told Quent. 'He says she'll be well cared for. We are to sleep there,' and he pointed to a shack further down the track. They could see lights flickering inside. Willem took Quent's arm and led him away behind the vehicle.

'Yeah, what, Willem?' Quent was in a hurry to get the big cat out of the cage.

Willem spoke softly and Quent had to lean close to hear. 'If your friend won't take all of us, bra, I must leave too.'

'Don't talk shit, Willem.' Quent snapped, too exhausted to pussy-foot around. 'They'll put you and the other two in clink if you go back to Birkenheadbaai – is that what you want? Won't be much good to your family behind bars will you? Stop worrying.' He punched his friend's arm playfully. 'I've got the baas in the palm of my hand. I'll square it with him in the morning. Okay? Lighten up, for Chrissake. You've always been a worrier – even when we were kids. Now come on. We've got work to do. This is the start of the rest of our lives, Willem. Tell the guy to sort some food and drink for us and we'll get this cat in her new home.'

They hauled the cage off the pick-up and got it positioned at the gate into the enclosure. The leopard was very much awake now and very angry. She couldn't get at them through the double-barred cage but it didn't stop her trying. After a few minutes they managed to wrestle the cage into place and Willem clambered on top so that he could slide up the outer door and then the inner door. When he finally managed it, the animal didn't move for several moments, as if she couldn't believe she was free. Then with a sudden roar she sprang out of her prison and was running. They watched in horror as she hurtled straight towards the perimeter fence on the other side of the compound. They shouted and screamed to distract her but she kept on. She must have seen how high the fence was but she kept going, as if she intended charging straight through the wire and away to her freedom. 'Shit,shit,shit.' Quent was frantic. She was going to kill herself and there was nothing he or anyone else could do about it. The *crack* as she hit the metal was like a rifle shot. The force of the impact flipped her body up and over backwards and she landed with such a thud that Quent was convinced that her back was broken. She lay stretched out full length on the ground.

Willem was the first to speak. 'The little mother has killed herself.'

Johannes shook his head. 'No, look, she's moving.'

223

And they watched as the dazed animal slowly raised herself. Her head was moving from side to side in a jerky motion. She was looking for something and they all knew what it was. At that moment she began to make a strange, low moaning sound. Quent thought he'd heard every leopard sound there was but this was a new one on him. It was halfway between a wolf's howl and a snarl – full of grief and rage. Quent turned away.

Elias said something.

Quent looked at Johannes.

'He says that the little mother is Gauta.'

'Gauta?'

'This means the colour, gold...golden in Sotho. He says we should give her this name and then maybe she will be happy again.'

Quent watched the distressed creature get unsteadily to her feet and head slowly towards the perimeter fence. Once there she stood for a moment with her nose pressed against the wire and then she turned so she was parallel to the fence and began to wearily follow the wire, as if she was measuring her grief with each pace.

Quent doubted that anything would make this animal happy again. And he was right. But they called her Gauta anyway.

In the end he couldn't watch the tormented creature anymore and he turned his back on the compound and walked towards the shack. The others saw him go and followed. No one spoke except for Johannes who was complaining about how hungry he was. Bullseye was loath to leave the leopard's enclosure and gave one last, loud challenging bark before following the men and flopping down outside the shack.

Quent was up at five o'clock the next morning.

Jaco du Plessis was already there, beside the leopard enclosure, assessing his latest acquisition. He was fatter and seemed shorter than Quent remembered but there was still that same aggressive stance. His head was shaved like it had always been but the bristle-shine of hair showing through on his scalp was grey now, not blonde.

'So?' the man said, without looking at Quent. 'This what all the fuss's about?'

They stood side by side in silence as the animal patrolled the fence. The leopard was grunting as she walked, her breath like spurts of steam in the cool morning air.

'I thought she'd be bigger.' Jaco again.

There was no *hi* or *nice to see you*, just straight to the point, like Quent remembered. A man of few words was Jaco du Plessis and most of those unpleasant.

'Bit of a runt isn't she, Mr Leopard man?' he continued, with something like satisfaction.

Quent was determined not to rise to the bait. 'She's a Cape leopard, Jaco. They're smaller than up-country leopards. It's what makes them special, man.'

'Yeah, yeah, know all that, Byrant,' Jaco interrupted. 'As long as the punters pay up who cares?' He was looking at Quent now, running a critical eye over him, as if he were a new acquisition too. 'So? You want to work for me, eh?'

Quent shrugged. 'Thought it was the other way round?'

'I like to help old comrades out when I can,' Jaco said. 'Especially when they need a leg up.'

Quent gritted his teeth. 'I've been doing okay.'

'What? Working on some piddling little sheep farm. You? The Leopard Man?' He leant closer to Quent and breathed in. 'God, they stink don't they, sheep? Like old women's piss.'

'I was estate manager and it's a big farm.' Quent hated Jaco for making him retaliate like some boastful little kid in the school playground.

'Come on, man,' Jaco smiled. 'No need to get defensive. I take an interest in all my men. You don't forget your army training when you've been an officer.'

'You were only a bloody jumped up NCO, Jaco, not some field marshal.' It was out before Quent could stop himself and he saw the flush of anger flicker across Jaco's podgy cheeks.

Both men were silent for a few moments.

It was Quent who spoke first. 'Look, I don't want to fight with you, Jaco. I'm tired, that's all. Yesterday was one helluva day. You don't know the trouble we had getting her.'

'Don't want to hear it, Byrant.' Jaco jabbed his finger at Quent. 'As far as I'm concerned I got this animal all legal and above board, right? Or you can load her on your pick-up right now and bugger off back to where you came from – you and your fan club.' He jammed his thumb back in the direction of the shack. Bullseye had joined them and he heard the anger in the man's voice. The growl came from somewhere deep in his throat. Jaco took a step backwards.

'No, Bullseye.' Quent spoke softly to the dog and the animal's head dropped back onto his paws again but he was watching Jaco now, not the leopard.

Jaco glanced apprehensively at the dog. 'You got control of that animal?'

Quent nodded.

'Right. Time I got moving. Busy day.'

'There's something we need to discuss first, Jaco.' Quent was determined to get things settled. 'A little matter of one extremely rare leopardess?'

'Um. My boy tells me you've brought three men with you,' Jaco said. 'Our agreement was one leopard, plus you and one black.

'His name's Willem.'

'Whatever. So what d'you expect me to do with the extra two, eh? More mouths to feed, not to mention that bloody great hound.'

'Bullseye finds his own food and Willem's part of the deal. I had to bring the other two. They'll work hard. I'll see to that.'

Jaco's eyes narrowed. 'You trying to tell me my business, boy?'

'No, I made them a promise, that's all, they can't go back.'

Jaco held up his pudgy hand. 'This...' and he waved his hand around his head, '...this all belongs to me. Got that? I'm

God here. And what happens here, who I employ, who I decide to kick out, that's my business.'

'We made a deal, Jaco.'

The man looked away for a moment and when he looked back at Quent he was smiling – or what passed for a smile for Jaco du Plessis. 'Why d'you think I asked you to come and work for me, boy? Because I love you? Because of that?' he sneered, pointing to the leopard.' He shook his head slowly. 'You see, the sad thing is I'm bored out of my skull. I miss excitement like we had in the Scouts. I can do this job standing on my head. Looking after animals, having to be nice to yanks with money who think they're the best film directors since Stephen Spielberg.   So? What to do? And then I remembered you, Byrant. I thought, I know, I'll spice my life up a bit, get one of my old oppos in. Have some fun.' Jaco moved closer and spoke softly into Quent's ear. 'D'you know what I decided to do, Mr Leopard man? I'm gonna break you, boy, that's why you're here. I'm going to have some...fun with you.'

Quent laughed in the man's face. 'You? Take more than you to break me, Jaco – '

'– You think so?' the man smiled again and then he laughed – a great bellowing laugh. He went to thump Quent on the shoulder and then he remembered the dog. 'You should see your face, man. Where's your sense of humour? It was a joke. Yeah?'

But Quent knew it wasn't.

'So?' Jaco was speaking again. 'This is the deal. Obviously I'll have to make some adjustment to what I pay you if I take on your two extra boys.'

'I said they'll work bloody hard.'

'Make sure they do. That way we'll both be happy.'

'You pay me the going price for her, Jaco, and I'll be happy. If not I'll take her elsewhere.' It was Quent's turn to smile because he'd seen the look on Jaco's face as he watched the leopardess.

Now it was game of chess and Jaco sensed a victory. 'Please yourself, but who else is going to take you on, plus that sorry mob?'

'Just say the word and we'll move on – all of us.'

'Christ, man. You've got a bloody nerve. You bring me one little leopard and expect me to take you all on and still pay you the going rate? Are you crazy?' Jaco glanced at the leopard again as she padded past on her lonely circuit and Quent saw greed flare in the man's eyes. She was a beautiful cat, even Jaco recognised that, and Quent guessed he already had potential clients lining up for Cape Leopard footage. He pretended not to care about the animal's endangered category but he was savvy enough to realise she was hot property in the wild-life film makers world. Quent knew he had him. Okay, he was prepared to take a little less money than he'd hoped for – if Jaco kept all three guys on – but he'd still get a good price. And after a few minutes haggling, more for form than anything else, they agreed a sum and shook hands on it.

Jaco wasn't pleased. He didn't like losing to anybody. 'We start work at six. Anyone not ready by six can sod off out of here. Most important thing to remember is timing. If I say I want ten zebra by midday then that's what I get. Don't ever let me down, understand? You've never been the most reliable guy on the planet have you, boy? There's a map of the estate up by my place, memorise it and make sure your boys do the same. Everything's planned down to the last second on a wild-life shoot. There's no room for slackers. Got it?'

'Sure,' said Quent and clicked his fingers at Bullseye, who rose out of the long grass in one fluid movement. He stood beside Quent still watching Jaco. His expression was non-committal.

Jaco saw how big the animal was. 'Is he as tough as he looks?'

Quent nodded.

'We could do with a beast like him on the estate. The area's full of thieving blacks from Zimbabwe looking for easy pickings. Most of my neighbours have been hit.' He looked appreciatively at the Anatolian. 'Yeah, let the beast loose at night, Byrant. I'd like to see any of the bastards trying to steal from me with a hound like that protecting my property.'

'Okay, but there's one thing you should know about this dog. He's an Anatolian and he needs to know you're part of his territory. Let him sniff your hand.'

Jaco laughed.

'It's up to you of course, but if he doesn't know you're a friend, there could be problems, especially at night, when he's patrolling. Everyone who lives and works here will have to do the same.'

Jaco kicked up a bit of a fuss but in the end he held his hand out to the dog. After the initial sniff Bullseye lost interest. Jaco was accepted. Quent soon discovered that Jaco and his wife Gail, especially his wife Gail, were paranoid about security and a fierce guard dog was just what they thought they needed. Razor wire and loaded shotguns were all well and good but they wanted more.

'Okay, Byrant, that's all for now.' Jaco had one last look at the leopard. 'Yeah, she'll do.' He stared at her for a moment. 'Shame you didn't get a couple of cubs too. Now, that would really have been something, man. Story of your life, eh? Never quite deliver, do you?' And with that he disappeared down the side of the enclosure.

Quent watched him go. A little bantam rooster with a big fat backside and an inflated idea of himself. *Break him?* Well, he could try.

As Quent hurried back to the shack to tell the men the good news, he was smiling. He'd definitely come out on top with Jaco and he had no intention of turning his dog into a man-eater. The dog's bark alone would be enough to scare off any trespasser.

Terror

Raki was on the slightly easier path through the 'eye' now and was able to walk more confidently. Farnie was quiet at last, sucking his thumb. The rising sun hadn't found its way into the cool, darkness yet and Raki switched on her head-torch.

She'd only walked a hundred metres or so into the trees when she had such a sudden stab of dread that she stopped dead in her tracks. Her heart was racing. There was something wrong. She wanted to turn and run but she couldn't. She had to go on. She closed her eyes and took deep breaths. This was stupid. There was nothing there, nothing to be frightened of.

'Mama?' Farnie said, sensing his mother's panic and leaning back to find her ear with his chubby fingers.

'It's okay, darling,' she whispered. 'Everything's fine. Mama's tired. You go to sleep, sweetheart' She made herself walk on. It was just the darkness. She'd never been through the 'eye' at this time before. The kloof had always been her dear friend but this morning it had morphed into something alien and frightening. Raki picked up her speed. Her eyes were getting used to the shadows now but she didn't like the way the flickering torch-light threw the bushes and trees into strange shapes that leapt out at her.

Farnie was quiet. The forest usually had a calming effect on him. Raki thought it must be the rustling of the wind in the leaves and the lacy shadow patterns that danced along the forest path on either side as they walked along. But that was when it was light and the sun was shining and the birds were singing; now there was nothing except the *pad, pad* of her feet. Farnie was still leaning back against his mother tickling her ear. She let him. It was comforting. The heat of his fingers warmed her. Ears fascinated Farnie. When he tired of her ear he explored her nostrils and then moved on to her eyes. He poked his finger into one.

'No, Farnie. That hurts.'

He hated Mama being cross with him and burst into tears, throwing himself backwards into Raki's chest. His hard little head whipped back and hit her square on the nose. She yelped and clutched at it. It was bleeding. There was nothing else for it but to untie the little boy. He was inconsolable by the time she unravelled the cloth and picked him up, hugging him to her, talking softly and trying to soothe him. His crying was too loud in this deathly quiet place. At last he hiccupped himself into silence and clung to her, his tears saturating her shirt.

It was then that she heard the sound, not loud – a sort of crackling, like twigs snapping. Superimposed on this was a shuffling, scrambling noise that came from somewhere directly above her. They were standing beneath a massive old Ironwood tree. She strained her ears but everything was quiet. Maybe she'd imagined it? Or perhaps it was the wind or a small animal or even a baboon? Yes, of course it must be a monkey. They roosted in the trees down here, although she'd never seen them in this part of the 'eye' before. Hardly daring to breath she turned to walk away. But the noise was there again, only louder this time and closer. She made herself look up into the tree. There was a black shape, crouching on the branch, darker than the surrounding gloom. Farnie saw it too and pointed upwards, tears forgotten. 'Baba,' he shouted. 'Baba.'

'Shh,' she whispered, holding him against her.

'Shh,' the little boy repeated. 'Shh, shh.'

'It's a baboon, Farnie, nothing to be frightened of,' but her voice in the stillness sounded scared, even to her. She hugged him close.

'Baba,' he said again. But he didn't sound convinced. 'Baba, Mama?'

Whatever it was wasn't moving. Raki moved closer to the tree and stood so that her head-torch shone directly upwards. There was something large, caught in the fork between two branches. She angled her head so the light illuminated whatever it was. There, in the feeble pale light, was an animal's face. The torch picked up the lustrous kohled eyes of a grysbok – its tongue lolled grotesquely out of the side of its

231

mouth and its delicate black-toed hooves hung slackly down the trunk. In the flickering light she followed a trail of bright blood beadlets down the length. On either side of the blood there were freshly-grooved claw marks.

Raki stumbled away from the tree but before she'd gone a few paces a large black shape launched itself out of the tree and landed a few paces away from her. Raki screamed, clutching Farnie tightly against her. It was too dark to see the creature clearly. It was a blurred image but Raki was aware of a smallish head, a low, strong body on four legs and a long lashing tail. Her headlight caught the animal's face and Raki saw two huge eyes glinting at her in the darkness. From somewhere Quent's voice popped into her brain. *Never run from a predator, Raki, unless it's charging you. Stand your ground. They usually lose interest and bugger off. They only eat people if they're desperate.* She made herself stay where she was and face the animal when every muscle in her body was screaming at her to run. It must have been only a few seconds but it seemed like an eternity before the animal turned and disappeared into the undergrowth.

Even if she'd wanted to she couldn't have run. Her legs shook so badly she thought she'd fall over. Finally, she succeeded in getting her legs to obey her and she staggered off down the path, stumbling over fallen logs and catching herself on thorn bushes and overhanging branches. She was sobbing and so was Farnie. At any moment she expected to hear the animal crashing behind her. Eventually she burst out of the wood and onto the track leading to the camp-site, the car park and her father. He would be waiting for them and that thought kept her going. 'Everything's okay, Farnie. Mama's here,' she soothed. 'Shall we go and see *Opa?*'

The sky was brighter now and she could see the roof of the rondavel on the campsite sticking up out of the surrounding trees. 'Dad', she shouted. 'Dad? It's me. Where are you?'

But there was no answering call and when she got to the clearing the only vehicle there was hers. She looked wildly about her. Where was he? The blood was still pounding in her head. She hesitated not knowing what to do and then her brain kicked in and she got them both inside her car and locked the doors. She sat there for ages, her eyes glued to her driving mirror, looking back into the black line of trees, never taking her eyes from the forest edge and imagining the shape of a big cat with a long swishing tail in every shadow.

As her fear lessened she tried to make sense of what had happened. Her father must have been held up. She would wait where she was until he came and then everything would be okay.

The sky was showing flashes of orange and pink and the birds were in full song before she knew he wasn't coming. He'd promised to be here, he said nothing would stop him, *Not even Old Nick himself.* They'd both laughed at that because there was no way her father would ever let her down again. So where was he? She trusted him. Something must have happened. An accident? Her hands were shaking as she turned the key in the ignition. She should drive to Cape Town but she had to find out what had happened to her father. She made herself drive slowly down the bumpy track towards the main road. Farnie was very quiet and she glanced back at him in her mirror. His little frightened face stared back at her.

'It's okay, sweetheart,' she said giving him a watery smile. 'Everything's fine. I promise. It was just a big monkey. Mama was silly. We're not afraid of monkeys are we?'

'Baba,' Farnie said hopefully.

But Raki knew he was scared and he had caught this fear from her. She wasn't frightened of the leopard, Quent had taught her not to be frightened of any living thing. She would happily share the kloof with any creature. Leopards were beautiful, secretive animals and only attacked if they were cornered or had cubs with them. She knew that, even before Quent had told her, but how could she expect a little boy to understand? She would never be able to relax on the kloof again. It would become Farnie's prison.

When she got to the main road she turned the wheel sharply and headed towards her father's farm.

10.00 a.m.

Life on the Du Plessis place was good to begin with. Quent got to handle wild animals and track game for the hunting syndicate that Jaco ran as a side-line. It was the sort of job that Quent was good at and he was pretty much his own boss, which suited him fine. There were no Du Toits to give him grief, just the Sunday trophy 'hunters' – usually wealthy Americans and Japanese. Big tippers.

No, the work was okay, Jaco du Plessis was the problem. Quent had only been there a few days before Jaco dug up all the old stuff. Quent was a fool if he really believed it was all in the past, finished with. There was no *finish* for something like that. Quent had always known Du Plessis was an unpleasant bully and nothing had changed. Quent could always push unpleasant stuff to the back of his mind but he'd been very stupid if he thought his history with Jaco was forgotten. No day passed without the man saying something, always dig, dig, digging away, at things Quent never wanted to think about, ever again. But what had he expected? This was Jaco and Quent had come here willingly to make money, to start a new life. What an idiot. What a stupid bloody idiot.

One of their major rows was about the leopard. Jaco was keen to use the animal as soon as possible but after a lot of arguing Quent managed to convince him not to work her until she was ready. It was important to get her used to the proximity of humans and her handlers. So he and Willem went into her enclosure each morning at exactly the same time, spent ten minutes just sitting where she could see them, and then exited. They did this for several weeks. At first she would back away snarling as they entered her compound; then disappear under the cover of the trees, until one day she barely looked at them before stalking off. This was the easy part but one thing they couldn't do was make her forget.

It wasn't long before Quent realised that catching her had been one of the worst decisions of his life. He should never have taken the animal away from where she belonged. After a month he knew she was never going to recover from the separation from her cub and her kloof. She wasn't eating much and lay around most of the time behind the rocks, out of sight.

'Will she always be sad?' Johannes asked Quent and Willem one evening after work as they walked past the animal's compound, on their way to the braai-pit to cook their steak. No one answered. They all knew the answer.

Shifting his weight to get more comfortable Quent's cell phone clatters to the wooden floor and he hooks his stick around it, pulling it closer so that he can pick it up. No reception up here. Useless, like him.

'How lovely to be cut off from the world,' Raki used to say with a dreamy look in her eyes. She loved the kloof and the house and she never stopped marvelling about the mountains and the sky and the wild life. Sure it was a beautiful place but did she have to keep banging on about it? In the end it irritated him beyond measure. Why couldn't she just shut up about it?

He turns the silver phone over and over in his hands, and suddenly remembers the voice message that Jaco's wife sent him. *Need to speak urgently, Quent. Get back asap. Please. Gail du Plessis.*

He was stunned by her polite, almost pleading tone. It would have been highly unusual for Jaco du Plessis to beg but it was totally unheard of for his wife, Gail – or *Madam* as she liked to be called. Gail du Plessis didn't say *please* to anyone – Jaco included. That she'd deigned to contact Quent at all was amazing but she'd also used his Christian name. There must be something really bad happening on the estate.

This *Madam* was the same person who'd strip-searched her entire female deli-staff because there'd been some petty pilfering going on. And when she found nothing on the women she handed out lollies to them, to show there was no hard feeling. When the stealing continued Madam invested in a lie detector.

Yes, she had definitely caught Quent's attention but he didn't reply – not straight away. He was still really pissed-off with Jaco and, besides, there were things he had to do– especially get his leg sorted. It wasn't healing properly and it worried him. The doc had put him on very powerful, very expensive antibiotics and advised bed rest. But this was all costing and Quent's mate wasn't that much of a mate really and wanted him out of his place. Quent had two options: to find somewhere else to stay that was cheap while his leg healed or to take a chance and go back to Jaco's straight away.

Gail du Plessis voice-mailed him six times before he finally relented and contacted her. He guessed that Jaco needed him but didn't want to ask him personally, so Madam was doing his dirty work for him. This didn't square with what Quent knew about his boss or his wife but that was the only reasonable explanation he came up with.

'Thank God, Quent. Where've you been?'

'I'm on the sick, Gail.' He enjoyed using her name.

But she wasn't listening. 'When can you be here?'

'Jaco sacked me, Gail. Told me to bugger off; never wanted to see my face around his place – ever again.'

She still wasn't listening. 'We'll pay you double, Quent, but you must come straight away.'

Double? That sounded good to Quent but he had to make sure they wouldn't mess him about again.

'My leg's still bad – '

' – It doesn't matter. The boys can do the hard work. We need you in charge.'

'What's happened? Is Jaco ill?'

'Just come, Quent, please. Come today, tomorrow at the latest.' And then she'd rung off.

So, his trip to Pig's Snout was postponed for the time being, as was his visit to see Florentina and the kids. As for Raki, he could always send money to her post office box in Birkenheadbaai. That's what he should have done straight off, soon as he got her message, because then he would have been able to send her the full R10,000 Now there were doctor's

236

bills to settle, medication to buy and money for his keep. He had about R1,000 left and that would have to do until he was back on the estate and earning again. He would send the money as soon as he could. He'd also be able to pay Willem back because the money his friend had given him for Florentina was gone too. Quent felt bad about that but Cape Town had been expensive. He'd pay Willem back with interest – double interest. Willem would be okay about it, he always was.

Sofia van de Venter

As Raki drove towards her parent's house her mother was in her dining room watching her three bible students eating their grapefruit. There was a piece of glistening glace cherry set artistically in the middle of each fruit – a nice little touch Sofia had picked up from Henrik's mother – a woman whose style Sofia greatly admired.

She liked to be with her 'boys' at breakfast. It was the custom of the house for her to choose one of them to say Grace. They never knew who she was going to select until the very last moment; so they all made sure they had a good prayer ready, just in case. Sofia thought it started the day off on the right spiritual footing for these young men. However, unbeknown to her the students used to bet on which of them she would choose. It was the only thing that made their life in this house bearable. They bet on anything...everything, from which song the maid would sing that morning, down to how many times Henrik Morgan 'dropped by' to see Mrs van de Venter in a week. They bet on who would get the fattiest piece of bacon and whose egg would have a spot of blood in the yolk. Nothing was too insignificant to make a wager on. Today's bet had already been decided.

The lady of the house was dressed in a homely wrap-around pinny, scattered with tiny red strawberries. She stood with her hands clasped loosely together in front of her as if she were praying. There was a half smile on her lips and her once-blonde now buttery-coloured hair was caught up in a tortoise-shell comb. She was immaculately groomed apart from one strand of hair that kept falling down over her plump flushed cheeks. She had to keep *huffing* at it from the corner of her mouth to keep it out of her eyes. She sincerely hoped that her boys hadn't noticed anything amiss because that one tendril of untamed hair was indicative of a seismic disturbance going on inside Sofia's ample bosom.

But they had noticed and this phenomenom was what the 'boys' were betting on this morning. They'd never seen their landlady with a wayward piece of hair before. It was unheard of and the enormity of it made them reckless. Albert put all his money on her having an affair with Morgan – none of them liked the pastor. Hans was convinced that it was Desmond van de Venter who was having an affair with Elizabeth the maid – and who could blame him? Whereas Robert, the youngest and most imaginative, had bet his entire week's pocket money that the old woman was pregnant. If they were all wrong they decided to pool the money and get drunk – in secret, of course.

Sofia glanced at her paying guests. 'More tea, gentlemen?' There was no coffee. Sofia regarded coffee as a dangerous stimulant, almost in the same category as alcohol.

They shook their heads in unison and continued to eat. The only sound in the room came from their pointed grapefruit spoons which tinkled against the sides of the delicate glass dishes. When they were finished she collected the bowls and set them carefully on the side- board for Elizabeth to clear later.

The aroma of frying bacon hung tantalisingly in the air. The maid was in the kitchen, singing as she cooked. Her singing always annoyed Sofia but what could you do? These people had minds of their own nowadays. Sofia's beautiful country was going to perdition and no one seemed to care, except for dear Henrik. Thank God he would be here soon. She needed his counsel more than ever today.

Normally, the minute the lodgers finished their grapefruit their landlady would ring the silver bell on the sideboard and Elizabeth would appear with their bacon and eggs. The young men were always hungry because their last meal of the day was at 5pm the previous evening – anything later was *'bad for the digestion,'* according to Sofia – so by morning the three were ravenous and the bitter grapefruit only made their empty stomachs complain. At that moment Robert's stomach rumbled very loudly. They tried not to look at each other, because if they did one of them was sure to laugh. As it was, they smothered their giggles in their scratchy linen napkins.

The minutes ticked by and still no breakfasts. They shifted uncomfortably on their hard seats. What on earth was happening? This boarding house ran like clockwork, as if the landlady wound it up each morning at exactly the same time. Hans took a quick peek at his watch and Sofia landed on him like a fly swat on a mosquito.

She smiled sweetly as she spoke. 'I'm so sorry to inconvenience you, Hans, but there's been a slight hiccup on the catering front this morning. I'm afraid you will have to be patient. The help is sometimes unreliable.' The fact that 'the help' had been specifically ordered to hold back on the bacon and eggs was another matter altogether.

The culprit's eyelids flickered away, ashamed, and he stared forlornly at his empty place mat embossed with scenes from the seven plagues of Egypt. His plague was locusts.

The reason for this catering 'hiccup' was because Sofia expected her husband to burst through the door at any moment and she couldn't possibly be serving the lodgers and dealing with him at the same time. That was when she heard a car stopping outside the house. She knew it couldn't be Desmond and Henrik wasn't due yet so... She hurried to the window. This morning was turning into a nightmare. There was something worryingly familiar about the spluttering noise of this particular car's engine.

Her hands were trembling as she pulled back the curtain and looked out on the familiar shape of the Renault – the car that she and Desmond had bought when they were first married. She'd never liked it – a foreign car. The Frenchness of it seemed a bit...bohemian to her and they soon acquired a more suitable vehicle. Another skein of hair had sprung out from the tortoiseshell comb.

She watched as the car came to a clanging halt outside the kitchen door and then she left the dining room at a trot, slamming the door shut behind her. The three lodgers waited for approximately ten seconds, glanced at each other and then, as one, scrambled to the window and peeped out from behind the curtains.

As they watched they saw a youngish woman with long black hair tied back in a severe ponytail climb out of the car. She was dressed in a T-shirt and long skirt, with a pair of heavy boots sticking out from underneath. It looked as if there was blood coming out of her nose. The men glanced at each other. So? This was the infamous daughter? They'd heard all about her, of course. The runaway wife of Pastor Morgan. The woman who'd gone to live with a hippie on top of a mountain. The woman who was living in sin.

Robert Delaware from Texas was sure someone back home would have composed a Country and Western song about her. The more he knew about Pastor Morgan the more sympathy he had for this poor unfortunate woman.

Despite her general appearance, she seemed very sure of herself and they watched as she marched up to the kitchen door. She put her hand on the door handle as if she were going to walk straight in but then thought better of it and knocked loudly. The door was thrown open almost immediately.

When Raki looked up she was staring into her mother's cold eyes. Sofia didn't speak, she just stood there, hands on hips, glaring. All of Raki's courage evaporated and she was that small child again, always in trouble, forever disappointing this woman. 'Is...is dad in?' she asked lamely. 'I have to see him.'

'Mr van de Venter is not at home.'

'Where is he?'

'I've no idea.'

'When will he be back?'

'I'm not my husband's keeper. Now if you don't mind I'm very busy. I have my lodgers to attend to.'

The three young men could hear every word and were bursting to shout out that Desmond van de Venter was around the back of the house at that very moment working on his bakkie. He'd been under the bonnet since first light, trying to get the thing to start. They knew this because he'd woken the entire household banging and crashing about outside their

241

bedrooms. They would have liked to tell the woman all this but they didn't.

10.05 a.m.

The return to Jaco's place gave Quent a lot to think about. For a start, how were Willem and Johannes doing? If he was honest he hadn't given much thought to them since Jaco booted him out. Out of sight, out of mind. One thing was certain though. Willem wanted to go home. He was missing his family badly, whereas his brother was happy enough. He'd got mixed up with a crowd of young tearaways in the local, small town and his money disappeared almost as quickly as Quent's. But so what? He was a young guy, having fun.

Willem disapproved of his brother's behaviour. The men had been away from Birkenheadbaai for over a year now and Willem had had enough. Florentina texted him regularly keeping him informed about what was happening. Apparently, she thought it would be safe for him and Johannes to come home soon. After the initial police interest in the stolen leopard things had quietened down. It had been headline news in the local rag for about a week but there were more important things to worry about.

Quent always knew when Florentina had been in touch with Willem, because he would go off on his own after work and refuse to speak to them. Quent wished Florentina would leave his friend alone. He had no desire to be left in charge of Johannes.

'Birkenheadbaai?' the boy would say, wrinkling his nose and spitting in the dust.

At least, Quent didn't have to worry about Elias any more. The little man had died the first winter they were at Jaco's. Quent had a lot of guilt around the guy from Lesotho.

Quent and the two brothers were treated okay by Jaco but Elias ended up sleeping in a lean-to with a roof that leaked. The animals had better lodgings than he did but he never complained. He'd found himself an old camping bed and made himself a rocking chair out of odd bits of wood and stuck up colourful magazine pictures on his walls. He didn't work with the rest of them. He did menial work around the estate, like cleaning out muck from the animal compounds, keeping the tracks clear of bushes and collecting and chopping wood for the braai pits.

Problem with Elias was he had no skills. All he had was his strength, which was pretty remarkable considering he was so small, and his stamina – he was used to harsh conditions. It got extremely cold in the mountains of his homeland. Everything would have been fine for the little man if he hadn't got ill. They never knew what was actually wrong with him but they were forced to watch as he grew steadily weaker and weaker. They tried to get him to see the doc but he refused. All his wages went home to his family and they couldn't persuade him otherwise.

Elias cooked for himself but when they hadn't seen him for a few days Quent went round to check on him. The sun was setting and it was going to be a cold night. Quent pulled his collar up and plunged his hands deep in his pockets. The bit of plywood in front of Elias's room was pushed to one side and Quent stood in the doorway looking in, with the sun directly behind him. Elias was seated in his chair facing the door. He was holding his crucifix in one hand and muttering under his breath. His head was down but Quent must have made a noise because he sat bolt upright staring in horror at the silhouetted figure. He pointed a shaky finger at Quent and jabbed the crucifix towards him as if he were the devil. Then he started this high pitched wail that brought Willem and Johannes running.

Quent looked at Johannes. 'What's up with him?'

Johannes grinned. 'He thinks you're a wicked poltergeist and you must go from his door.'

It took several minutes to persuade Elias that Quent wasn't a spook but just as they thought they could leave him, he started up again. This time his trembling finger pointed beyond Quent at something else. 'Ayee!' he screamed and fell in a faint.

They put him to bed and Willem brought him some hot food.

Before they left him Quent bent down beside the little man and said. 'That poltergeist-man come again, you tell him *go*. Elias? You tell him. OK? You say *go*.'

And the little man repeated the word until they were all laughing and shouting *Go*.

It was the last time they saw him alive.

Jaco kept them on their toes from early morning till dusk so it was another few days before they checked on Elias again. When they got to the shack they could see him inside sitting on his rocking chair with his blanket wrapped tightly about him. He was very still – too still. His crucifix had fallen on the ground.

When Quent asked Jaco where they could bury the man, he'd laughed. 'Dig a hole and tip the boy in, Byrant. That's what you did to that other one in the bush wasn't it? The boy you murdered.'

One day, one day, Quent would shut Jaco's mouth for good.

So, they wrapped Elias in his beautiful blanket, placed his crucifix on his chest and laid him to rest in a grave on top of the hill overlooking the estate. Willem said he was always talking about his mountain home in Lesotho where his wife and their two small children lived with his parents. He was so certain he would go back to them one day with much *maloti* and he would buy land. No one knew where he lived or even his second name and there was no forwarding address for his family, so they would never know what had happened to their father. Willem and Johannes knew to their cost what this meant to his wife and children. There was some back pay owing and Quent made sure that Jaco paid up. They bought a marker with the money and put a little fence around the plot to deter scavengers. Willem remembered some of the Catholic prayers for the dead and the men stood on the hillside while Johannes sang *The Lord is my shepherd I shall not want.'*

By the next morning the vultures and hyenas had made off with little Elias.

It reminded Quent of another funeral – Eunice's funeral but she had a proper funeral. The old woman saw to that.

On the day Eunice was buried every flower on the kloof had decided to bloom. The combined cocktail of scents made Quent want to puke. He hated everything for being so alive and bright and took a stick and slashed at the plants – until the old woman screamed at him to stop. His red-rimmed eyes stung from the fierce brightness of the fiery, red coral-trees, bright-eyed lantanas and jacarandas that framed the cemetery, with the purple mountains as a backdrop and the blue, blue sky. He hated the sun that day. He hated everything and everyone, especially the old woman for still being alive when Eunice was dead – his Eunice.

It was Quent who'd found her. She was in her little house and sitting in her chair, wrapped in her beautiful blanket – just like Elias, only not like him because Eunice was loved and nothing could ever be the same again. Quent used to tease her about how much time she spent in her chair but Eunice always had an answer. *What an old woman see sitting down, a young man can't see standing up.*

The silver phone slipped through Quent's fingers and onto the floor where he kicked it over the edge of the veranda and into the fynbos. He heard the *plop* as it entered the secret world of green.

Raki and Sofia

'But I have to see him.' Raki's courage was returning. 'He promised to meet me at Pig's Snout this morning.'

Sofia's expression was stony. 'I've no idea what you're talking about. Now please go.'

'He was taking me...us... to Cape Town. We have to be there by ten o'clock. It's very important, Mother. Farnie's going to hospital.'

Sofia couldn't have missed the rising panic in her daughter's voice but all she did was glance at her watch. 'In that case I suggest you hurry up or you'll be late.'

Raki felt like an animal trapped in the headlights of a car but her panic kept her going. 'I have to know where he is, Mother. Please.'

Sofia shrugged. 'I've already told you. I don't know where he is. Now, please move your car. I'm expecting company and you're blocking the access.'

Raki took a step towards her mother. 'Why won't you tell me? Is he ill?'

Sofia tried to shut the door in Raki's face but Raki jammed her foot in it. 'You must let me see him.'

'Oh I must, must I? Leave my property at once or I shall call the police. You're not welcome here. I thought I'd made myself perfectly clear on that score.'

Raki pushed at the door, trying to force her way inside but Farnie chose that exact moment to start crying. As she turned back to the car Sofia slammed the door shut, locking and bolting it.

Farnie was hysterical by the time Raki got him out of his seat. Sofia was watching from behind the net curtain and saw the child's mop of curly black hair and his chubby arms wrapped tightly about his mother's neck. That was when something happened to her – something totally unexpected. It felt as if she'd been punched in the solar plexus – the pain was as intense. This beautiful little boy was her grandchild. The urge to rush out and hold the baby in her arms and breathe in his wonderful smell was so strong she had to press her nails into her hand to stop herself.

Farnie stopped crying the moment Raki put him down in the yard. He immediately set off in pursuit of the hens. Raki was in no fit state to drive but she had to leave soon. She couldn't risk being late or Farnie might lose his bed. At least the traction was paid for. Her dad had seen to that. But where was he? She couldn't believe he'd just gone off somewhere without telling her but what other explanation could there be?

Farnie was crawling determinedly after a handsome rooster who was pecking up seeds near the bin. Each time the little boy stopped to 'talk' to the bird, it hopped away just out of reach — obviously a kid-wise chicken. While Farnie tried to catch the rooster, she tried to catch him.

Raki held out her arms and walked towards him slowly. 'Farnie. Come on, sweetheart. Please, be a good boy. Come to Mama.' She tried to scoop him up but he was having too much fun to be caught and scuttled away. He loved the way the chickens squawked and flapped their wings trying to fly.

Sofia was trembling as she made her way back to the dining room. 'Elizabeth,' she called. 'You can serve the gentlemen their breakfasts now.'

10.10 a.m.

Quent is trying to remember exactly what happened when he returned to Jaco's place. But the more he concentrates the more confused he becomes. He's like a dog worrying away at a bone that's much too big for him. The problem is he can't say for sure if Willem and Johannes high-tailed it before the shit hit the fan and it's important for him to remember. It's getting harder and harder to focus on anything.

In his mind he can see the hard-baked earth outside the shack at the Du Plessis place and his pick-up and the beat-up old run-around that Willem had bought. But was the car still there when he drove away? If they were then they were in serious trouble.

Even when Quent was okay he'd always found it difficult to keep his mind on the job in hand. If he'd been concentrating on the day it kicked off then maybe none of it would have happened.

For once it had been a great day. The shoot had worked like clockwork and Quent was feeling pretty good – they all were, even Jaco. It was late afternoon by the time the film crew got the footage they wanted on Cape clawless-otters. The animals had 'performed' perfectly and there had been a lot of back slapping and high fiving. Finally Madam had taken them all off for a slap up meal in her farm-store – at some inflated price, no doubt. Jaco was so pleased he got out the Black Label.

Quent left them to it and returned to the river compound with Willem to feed the otters. It was some way from the main house and by the time they got there the shadows were lengthening. Otters are nocturnal and this was their playtime. They bounded along the perimeter fence chattering away to the two men, eager for their food and company. There was a female, two kits and a young male who had taken a liking to Quent.

As soon as the men were inside the compound the male began his usual loud, hectoring call. It was aimed straight at Quent. All the otters dived into the stream to be fed and Willem tossed the fish in all directions. The male returned to the bank as soon as he'd had his fill and called to Quent again. This time it was louder. *Come play with me, now.* Then the animal selected a flat white pebble from the bank and tossed it into the stream. This was his favourite game. First one to dive in and retrieve the pebble was the winner.

However, Quent wasn't interested in the otter, he was thinking about the text he'd just received from Raki. It was the first time she'd been in touch since she'd told him about the boy. It was a short message but to the point. Raki was good at saying a lot with very few words. There was some major problem, she said, and she needed R10,000 urgently. She'd never asked him for money before so he knew it would be for her boy.

Quent squatted down with his back to a tree trying to decide how to respond. He had the money, no problem, but just lately he'd been toying with the idea of visiting the kloof — not to see the kid — but to check that Raki was okay. Just because he didn't want to be a father didn't mean he wasn't going to help. He felt guilty about the way he'd reacted when Raki told him she had a child. But he didn't like surprises, she knew that.

The next time the young otter called to Quent it was from the stream. The animal lay on his back in the water, holding the white pebble against its chest like an offering. Quent still didn't respond so the animal came to get him. He danced around in front of the man chattering angrily, like a nagging wife. 'Bugger off,' Quent shouted, throwing a stick at the animal.

The otter came charging at Quent, screaming with frustration. *Take no notice of me, fella, and you'll regret it.*

And Quent did, because moments later the thwarted animal pounced on him and sank its razor-sharp teeth into his thigh. Quent watched in horror as the blood spurted out of the wound and continued to pump. He was so shocked he couldn't move and would certainly have bled to death if Willem hadn't been close by. He tied his belt tightly about Quent's leg and then picked him up, put him over his shoulder and ran back to where their pickup was parked. He put Quent on a mattress in the back then drove like hell to the nearest town, where there was a small A&E department.

Quent remembered lying there, as he drifted in and out of consciousness, watching the exposed artery pumping blood. It still made him sick to think about it. The medic put fifteen stitches in the wound and prescribed antibiotics, tetanus injections and painkillers. It cost a lot of rand but it was worth it. The doctor praised Willem for getting Quent to the hospital so quickly. Yeah, Quent owed Willem, big time.

When they arrived back on the estate Quent got Willem to drop him off at Jaco's office. There'd been no time to put Jaco in the picture before they left and Quent knew he'd be fuming. Willem had tried ringing the boss on his cell phone but Jaco's line was perpetually engaged.

The man must have heard the bakkie because he was pacing the yard, waiting for them, yelling, before Quent was even out of the vehicle, demanding to know where he'd been and bollocking Willem for disappearing when he was needed. Willem was helping Quent out of the vehicle but Jaco pushed him roughly aside and Quent had to hang onto the car door while Jaco harangued him.

The veins in Jaco's thick neck bulged. 'You leave the farm I need to know – had the boys running all over looking for the pair of you. Wasting their time, wasting my time, wasting everybody's bloody time.'

Quent tried to explain but Jaco wouldn't let him get a word in. Okay, he knew he'd been stupid but he'd expected a bit of sympathy.

Eventually Jaco calmed down enough for Quent to be able to speak. 'Look, I'm sorry, okay? But there was no time to let you know. If Willem hadn't been there God knows what would have happened. The male otter took a chunk out of me, ripped the artery in my thigh.'

Willem was hovering, not knowing what he should do. Jaco spotted him. 'You,' he bawled. 'You're supposed to be over at the Bok's enclosure. Don't just stand there. Git.'

He watched as the man ran off down the side of a barn then he looked back at Quent. 'For Chrissake, Byrant. How many times? Why can't you leave those bloody animals alone?'

'It was an accident, man. These things happen.'

'Yeah, but why's it always you? Tell me that.'

'Maybe because I'm the one handling the animals, okay?' Quent tried to keep the sarcasm out of his voice but didn't succeed.

'Sure. And that's why I pay you top whack, boy, and now look at you. Useless.'

Quent kept his mouth shut. It was the best way when Jaco was full of whisky.

'Who d'you think you are? Bloody Tarzan of the Apes!' Jaco jeered. 'Thought you were supposed to be the ace-man at handling dangerous animals? And you let a fluffy little otter take a bite out of you.'

Quent clenched his teeth. 'Otters are dangerous, Jaco.'

'Is that right?' the man looked at Quent's bloody bandage. 'Thought that was just ketchup.'

Quent hated it when Jaco was right. It had been his fault. He lectured the boys over and over about respecting a wild animal's space. *To be always on your guard while you're handling them. Constant vigilance* – that was his mantra. And what had he done? Only totally ignored the animal's clear warning signs. He'd been bloody stupid and there was no excuse.

'Trust you to bugger yourself up, just when I'm busy. We're going through a financial down-turn, man, in case you haven't noticed. You think I need some bloody cripple on the crew?'

'A couple of weeks and I'll be brand new,' Quent said. 'Willem and Johannes can manage until I'm back on my feet and I'll be here to keep an eye.'

Jaco waved his podgy finger in Quent's face. 'Wrong. You're no good to me like this. Pack your gear and get off my farm.'

'Thanks, Jaco,' Quent said. 'I appreciate it. I'll be back as soon as I'm okay.'

Jaco stared at him as if he was mental. 'Let's get one thing straight, fella. I want you off the farm and I want you to stay off? Understand? I've put a lot of trust in you, and you've let me down, big time. I've bent over backwards to accommodate you and your boys. Took you all in, didn't I? Even that little runt with the blanket? Useless, the lot of you. I should have known better than employ someone like you. You were never reliable and nothing's changed.'

Quent clenched his teeth but said nothing.

'Any fool can handle a few animals,' Jaco ranted, frustrated that Quent wouldn't beg for a second chance. 'There's plenty more casual help where you came from, much cheaper and more dependable.'

Quent had worked for Jaco du Plessis for well over a year and that 'casual' rankled. But Jaco was no sentimentalist and there was a big contract coming up. Quent understood. This was South Africa; every man, woman and child for themselves. Besides, deep down Quent wasn't sorry to be leaving the Du Plessis place. He'd had enough of Jaco and his wife and the whole set up. He didn't like seeing wild animals in captivity. What a hypocrite he was.

But at the back of his mind there was a small, calm voice saying, *now you can go back to the kloof house*. He'd been dreaming about the house lately. He was always toiling up the mountainside but he never reached the top and Raki, because he'd forgotten something and had to go back to the bottom, or the path was too slippery. He would wake up with such a feeling of sadness.

But now there was nothing stopping him from going there. The kloof house was the perfect place to recuperate. The little house that he and Raki had built together. It was the nearest to home that Quent had ever known. All he needed was a week or two to rest up. Maybe he and Raki could get it together again? It would be just like old times, he thought. But then he remembered the boy. Nothing would ever be the same with a kid around.

One thing about Quent, he could change his mind in the blink of an eye. No, he'd go to Cape Town instead. He had a mate there who'd give him a bed for a few days and after that he'd find another job. He'd think about the Raki thing later, when his leg healed.

All he had to do was pack his gear, pick up his back pay and then he could be on the road. The whole leopard thing had left a nasty taste in his mouth. No, he was happy to be going.

He found Willem and Johannes back in the shack and told them what had happened. It was dark by now and they were eating in the flickering candle light. 'Hey, bra,' Willem said, touching Quent's shoulder. 'We will be sad without you.'

Quent smiled. 'At least you won't waste so much money drinking with me.'

'True,' Willem was suddenly serious. 'You will see Florentina for me?' he asked. 'Take her some money? I will give it to you before you go. I have been saving. Tell her I will be home soon.' And he smiled. 'It will be so good to see them. My little one will be so grown up.'

'Sure,' Quent promised. 'I'll see you when you get back to Birkenheadbaai. What about you, Johannes?'

The young man rolled his eyes at Quent. 'No, I've got a girl in town.' But they all knew why Johannes wanted to stay. Without Quent and Willem, he might be in line for the top job. Quent didn't like to disappoint him but Jaco would never put a black in charge.

Quent would miss them both – especially Willem – and he knew Willem would protect Gauta. She had only been used in background shots so far but Jaco was getting impatient and was always asking when she could be used. It had become a battle of wills between Jaco and Quent. The animal was highly unpredictable and dangerous. Without Quent there to restrain him, Jaco might try to use her. Quent promised himself to have one more go at the boss before he left. It was the least he could do.

But was Willem's car still there when he left? Leaning back, he closes his eyes. He's got a pounding headache and he reaches for another bottle – it's the last one. Some of the liquid goes into his mouth and the rest spills down his chest.

Oil

The young men were all back in their seats by the time Sofia returned. A door slammed loudly from somewhere inside the house and the three flinched in unison. Sofia registered nothing unless you looked very closely and saw her hands clench and unclench in front of her pinny. The slam was followed by a loud male voice. 'Where are you, woman? I'll bloody swing for you.'

The door crashed open, and the delicate grapefruit dishes clashed alarmingly against each other. Three pairs of eyes swivelled to look at the man standing there. It was Desmond van de Venter, or at least they thought it was but they'd never seen Mrs van de Venter's husband like this before. His face was flushed to an unhealthy magenta colour; he was dressed in an old boiler-suit covered in muck and grease and he was clutching an oil dip-stick as if it was exhibit A. He thrust the offending item under his wife's nose.

'Why in God's name did you do it?'

Sofia looked away.

There was a solitary bead of oil on the end of the rod and they all watched as the sphere of black treacle glooped onto the highly polished wooden floor. This floor was the pride of Sofia's life – *slippers to be worn at all times* – and the lodgers waited for the explosion. Amazingly their landlady barely registered the calamity. The only indication of agitation was the burning bright spot of red on each cheek.

'I'm waiting, Sofia. Did you or did you not drain the oil out of my engine?'

'Desmond, I...I – '

'– And don't bother denying it. Was he in on it too? That bastard Morgan?'

'There's someone outside, Desmond,' she said, ignoring his questions. She flicked a glance in the direction of the window.

Desmond was at the window in an instant. He yanked back the curtain and knocked loudly on the glass. 'Raki?' he yelled. 'Where are you going? Stay right there. I'm coming.' As he hurried out of the room he shouted over his shoulder. 'Don't think this is over, Sofia. I haven't even begun to say what I want to say to you. We're having this out, you and me, when I get back. And no, I don't know when that will be but,' and he jammed his finger at her, 'don't go to bed before I get back. Understand?'

'Desmond?' Sofia called after him, but her voice was cut off by the banging of the outside door. 'Be careful.' she finished lamely.

Raki had finally managed to grab Farnie and was attempting to get the furious little boy into the car seat as her father hurried out of the house. Within moments he was beside her taking charge. When Farnie and Raki were in the car he stripped off his boiler suit, wiped his oily hands on it and dumped it in the yard, then he got into the driving seat. As he reversed noisily out of the yard he said, 'I hope you've got enough petrol?'

Raki managed a nod and Desmond drove out onto the main road and turned towards Cape Town. They drove in silence. After about five miles two police cars raced past them on the other side of the road, heading towards Birkenheadbaai. It was only much later that Desmond remembered seeing them.

Back at the house no one spoke or moved in the dining room until they heard the car start up and accelerate noisily away. The young men ate quickly, keeping their eyes on their plates. There would be plenty of time later to discuss the fascinating turn of events in the Van de Venter household. They positively relished their bacon and eggs that morning, even though everything was a trifle overdone. It had never tasted better and they were already looking forward to the beers they would drink that evening in the privacy of their bedrooms — their haven, where their landlady never set foot.

Sofia went through the motions of looking after her lodgers but she was miles away. Her stern mouth had softened and her stiff shoulders drooped. 'Farnie,' she whispered softly into the teapot. 'Farnie,' she murmured, experimenting with the syllables. 'My sweet little boy.'

10.15 a.m.

The day Quent left Jaco's place he was up early, said his goodbyes to Johannes and Willem, and had driven up to Jaco's office to pick up his back pay. Jaco was on his phone as usual being abusive to someone when Quent walked in. When he saw Quent he motioned to a pile of dirty, dog-eared paper money on the table; then he turned his back on him and continued his conversation. There was also a pile of low denomination coins on the desk. A bonus? Looked like Jaco had raided his piggy bank. Quent decided not to stuff the coins up the man's arse, he didn't have the energy, so he pocketed the money. Jaco had already forgotten about him but Quent wasn't ready to leave, not yet. He waited until Jaco finished his call and jumped in before the man could start another one.

'A word in your ear, Jaco,' he said, keeping his tone friendly.

Jaco still had his back to him and was punching in another number as Quent spoke. He swung around in surprise. 'Still here, boy?'

'Any plans to use the leopard in the next shoot?'

Jaco's surprise rapidly turned to contempt. 'None of your business,' he said, 'Now, bugger off. I'm busy.'

But Quent stood his ground. 'Just a word of advice,' he said, keeping his temper in check. 'Be careful with her is all I'm saying.' Quent knew Jaco would do what he wanted but he felt responsible for the animal. He was the one who'd brought her here. As if he could ever forget that. 'She's unreliable.'

Jaco ignored him.

'She's...got a screw loose, Jaco. I was going to suggest that we...culled her...

At last his words registered with Jaco. He switched off the phone and turned an angry face to Quent.

'It would be the ...best option,' Quent hurried on. He was going to say "kindest" but changed his mind. 'Definitely the best thing to do. She's very dangerous.'

'The Leopard Man's frightened of a little pussy-cat?'

Quent kept his tone neutral. 'I've told you. They're supposed to be small, Jaco. She's a Cape leopard, very rare.'

'– Ja, ja,' Jaco made a yakking motion with his fingers. 'Heard it all before, man. "Endangered species", blah di blah di blah. In case you've forgotten, that animal cost me a pile of rand. I paid over the odds for her. You took the money quick enough as I remember. No talk of 'dangerous' back then.'

'I thought she'd be okay, over time, but I think she's gone mad, Jaco.... losing her cub like that – '

' – Tell you what, Leopard Man.' Jaco's smile was almost as horrible as his sneer. 'Pay me back the money, plus extra for her food and keep, and I'll put a bullet between her eyes personally, or better still I'll sell her to the canned-hunting syndicate up-country. Did I tell you? I'm thinking of going in with them. There's money to be made from useless, old, predators.'

Quent knew his hands were shaking, but he put them behind his back and stared the man straight in the eyes. He wasn't going to give him the satisfaction of losing his rag and his voice was soft, non-threatening. 'Wildlife film makers pay more for filming endangered species, Jaco. You can still use her but go careful is all I'm saying. Let Willem handle her. She knows him.'

Jaco snorted. 'I've been handling wild animals all my life, boy. The trick is to show them whose boss. It's the same with the blacks. Now, if you don't mind, fella, some of us have work to do.'

The next time Quent saw Jaco du Plessis he was in a wheelchair.

The cake

The cake today was chocolate – Henrik's favourite. He arrived promptly at 10.30 a.m. and they took tea in the morning room – as Sofia liked to call it – but it was actually the sitting room – the only one in the house. This was their daily ritual and had been since Sofia's daughter had run off with that loathsome man. To begin with Sofia used these times to comfort her poor son-in-law but over time their roles had been reversed and now he was her mentor. It was only a half an hour chat and then he would drive the bible students back to Birkenheadbaai for their daily tuition in the Meeting House.

The moment Pastor Morgan saw Sofia he knew that something was wrong but he said nothing. It was important to follow the niceties of social intercourse. Henrik said a short prayer and swallowed his first mouthful of cake. It was delicious – almost as moist as his dear mother's. Finally he settled back in his chair and raised the cup of tea to his mouth. He smiled reassuringly at his flustered hostess.

'I did what you suggested, Henrik,' she blurted out, hardly waiting for him to put his cup down. 'But it didn't work. It was horrible. He...he shouted at me – in front of everyone – and now he's gone off,' she wailed. A tear escaped from the corner of her eye and rolled majestically down her round, plump cheek.

It was such a big tear drop Mr Morgan was tempted to put his finger out and catch it. Instead he laid a consoling hand on Sofia's knee. 'I think you're mistaken. I'm sure I saw your husband's vehicle parked behind the house. I took the liberty of looking before I came in.'

'They used her car.'

This did surprise him. 'You mean that woman had the audacity to come here?'

Sofia nodded and dabbed at her eyes. 'She confronted me, Henrik, on my own doorstep. It was dreadful. And she had the...child with her.'

'She has no shame.'

But Sofia wasn't listening. 'That old Renault's not road-worthy, Henrik. What if something terrible happens to them and it's my fault? I'd never forgive myself.'

Henrik watched Sofia carefully as he wiped an errant cake-crumb from the corner of his mouth. 'Take a deep breath, my dear,' he ordered and watched as she obeyed. 'There that's better, isn't it? Now, tell me everything.'

While she talked his mind was racing. It was he who had advised Sofia to sabotage Desmond's car and if there was an accident he would be culpable. He didn't like that one little bit. It went without saying that he'd done it with the best of motives. It was his duty to protect decent God-fearing members of his flock from sinners but would the authorities see it like that?

'Desmond was so angry, Henrik. It was horrible.' Sofia had a catch in her voice and Henrik covered her hands with his. Usually his cool, dry touch soothed her but not today, today his skin felt scratchy and cold and she moved her hands abruptly away. 'I was frightened of him, of my own husband. I thought...I thought he was going to hit me.'

Henrik leant closer to her. His breath was sickly sweet with cake and she turned her face away. He whispered, 'Sometimes, my dear lady, sometimes we have to be brave in the service of the Lord.'

Sofia's thoughts were in turmoil. 'We were right to stop him from helping her, weren't we? Only I'm not sure.'

'Of course you were right, Sofia.'

'But you told me to do it, Henrik.'

'Hardly. I would never suggest you did anything...illegal.'

Sofia wasn't listening. 'Desmond has a heart condition and it's not good for him to get worked up. The doctor said.'

'Um. Don't you see, Sofia? This is what happens when a good soul is contaminated by consorting with corruption? I'm afraid it might already be too late for Desmond to be saved.'

But Sofia wasn't interested in what Henrik had to say. 'I didn't know him. He was like a stranger.'

Henrik took another thoughtful bite into the cake. 'There is a solution to all this,' he said, spraying crumbs in all directions. 'The question is whether your faith is strong enough to do what is required? I think it is.'

'I'm frightened, Henrik.'

'Don't be, my dear, I would never allow anything bad to happen to you, whatever the cost to me. Now. You agree that we must expunge the festering wound root and branch?' He waited for her response but when there was none he continued. 'Your daughter uses candles doesn't she – one could almost say she's profligate with candles?' His eyes narrowed at the thought.

Sofia still said nothing.

'So? What would happen if one such candle fell, in that house on the kloof, and it caught fire? Um? Do you understand what I'm saying?' He saw the sudden look of alarm on Sofia's face. 'At a time when she's out of the way, of course, she and her child.'

Sofia stared at him in disbelief.

'I believe you said that she's destitute?' He took a drink of tea and eyed her over the rim of his cup.

'But if her house burnt down where would she live?' Sofia's voice was shrill. 'How could she look after her baby?'

'Forgiveness is a wonderful gift, Sofia. And if she was truly penitent then I would certainly consider taking her child into my household. I'm a forgiving man. That's the Lord's way, isn't it? Of course, you and I mustn't be implicated in the little ...accident, so all we need to do is find someone who would 'help' us...' he smiled, '...and keep his mouth shut? One of your husband's casual workers should do nicely. These illegals will do anything for a few rand.'

'And Raki?' Sofia hadn't used her daughter's name for such a long time it felt like a large pebble in her mouth.

He raised his eyebrows at her. 'Oh no. Just the child.'

Sofia stared down at her hands for a few moments as if deciding what to say in response.

263

Henrik knew it would be hard for Sofia to agree but the child was an extra incentive. He sniffed and settled back in his chair, a smile playing at the corners of his thin mouth. He wasn't going to rush her. He had all the time in the world.

10.20 a.m.

Someone is shouting in a hoarse, belligerent voice but Quent can't make sense of the words. It's just one long rant of abuse. Is there someone in the room with him? Are they here? He screws up his eyes but all he sees is the outline of the kloof house door and the patterns of light and shade like cardboard cut-outs on the floor.

'Who's there?' Quent rasps into the prickly silence. 'Show yourself.' Then the dog's muzzle brushes his hand. 'Hey, Bullseye,' he croaks, through parched lips. 'Were you talking to me, man?' His high-pitched giggle sends him into a coughing fit. 'Or was it me?' he asks, when he can speak again. 'Don't tell anyone my secrets, boy. Okay? You have to swear on the bible. Don't tell them what I did.'

A couple of days passed before Quent left Cape Town in response to Gail du Plessis. He was in no hurry. Let the bastards wait. He took the last of his painkillers before setting off. Jaco would pay for the next batch. He felt on top of the world as he drove. Both windows were wound right down and he breathed in the fresh air. Bullseye was on the passenger seat, head thrust out of the window, jowls ballooning out in the wind. The Anatolian didn't like towns either – too many conflicting scents and no recognisable territory.

Quent smiled as he drove. One thing was certain. He was going to make Jaco pay for humiliating him. He might even ask for more than double what he'd been paid before. It all depended on how much they wanted him.

He stopped in a small town overnight – there was a woman he knew there – and the next morning he drove on to Jacos's. He arrived at midday and went straight to the shack looking for Willem. The place was deserted. He felt uneasy about Florentina's money. Willem would be okay about it but he couldn't relax until it was sorted. It was strange that no one was about. Quent could have checked the house but Du Plessis could wait.

He parked alongside Willem's car then he went inside the shack and found something to eat and drink. Bullseye padded off. Afterwards, Quent decided to go up to the farm store; see if Madam was about. On his way past the leopard's enclosure he looked for Gauta. There was no sign of her but he guessed she'd be sheltering from the noon day heat. Quent shielded his eyes against the glare and looked more closely amongst the trees. He was about to walk on when he felt a light touch on his shoulder.

'Quent?' It was Willem.

'Hey, Willem. I thought you were out on a shoot.'

'No,' Willem shook his head. 'Not today, bra.'

'Where is everybody?'

Willem shrugged. 'Waiting.'

'What for?' Quent laughed. He was playing for time, trying to think how he could break the news about Willem's money. Now he was face to face with his old friend it didn't seem quite such an easy thing to do. Willem looked tired and drawn and there were deep worry-lines etched across his forehead.

'You okay, man? You look ill.'

'Not too okay, bra,' Willem said sadly, but then he smiled. 'Hey, Bullseye? Good to see you too, man.'

The animal was circling Willem, a pleased look on his face and there was an almost imperceptible twitch to his tail. Quent smiled to himself. Bullseye definitely liked Willem.

'Look, man,' Quent said, taking a big breath. 'The money you gave me for Florentina and the kids? Well, unfortunately, I never made it to Birkenheadbaai. Bloody leg wouldn't heal and I had to use your cash for med. I'm really sorry, man, but I'll pay you back with interest, promise, soon as Du Plessis pays up. They've offered me a big rise. Well, it wasn't Jaco it was her, Madam. Nearly fell off my perch when she rang, very polite, almost friendly. What's happening here? Must be something major.' He was babbling now. He glanced at Willem to see how he was taking the news. The man was looking down at the ground and fidgeting from foot to foot. 'You know what crap I am with money.' Quent smiled.

'Maybe you shouldn't have trusted me, hey?' He tried to make it sound like a joke but it didn't work.

Willem met Quent's gaze. 'It is always the same story with you. Maybe, I am the fool...for trusting you.'

'Oh, man. Don't say that. I promise I'll...'

But Willem waved his words away. 'No. No more promises, bra. Johannes and me,' he said, 'we are leaving this place. This is no job for a man. We have packed our things and we are going home, back to where we belong.'

'But Jaco says he'll pay me double. I can get more for you and Johannes. Stay, just until I can pay you back.'

Willem shook his head. 'Goodbye, Quent.' He walked a few paces away before turning to face Quent. 'Gauta is in the old pigsty at the back of the enclosures. Be very careful.' And with that he was gone, running back towards the shack, shouting as he went. Quent heard the urgency in Willem's voice. 'Johannes. Hurry, Johannes. We must leave. Come. Come now.'

Truth

'Why did you marry my daughter?'

The question came out of nowhere and at first Henrik thought he must have misheard. 'I'm sorry?'

'I said why did you marry her?'

Sofia's question was inappropriate and it took a moment for Henrik to regain his composure. He decided to ignore her. Sofia wasn't herself. 'As you are aware, my dear, I'm interested in the physical and spiritual wellbeing of young boys. I believe that an innocent child's immortal soul is more important to the Lord than yours or mine. I would see it as my holy duty to rescue the child from the evil influences that have beset him and endeavour to mould him into innocent clay, fit for the Lord's work.'

'You never loved her did you?'

Henrik was losing patience. 'This is ridiculous, Sofia,' he said, sharply. 'You know perfectly well why I married your daughter and you were happy with the arrangement. In fact, if I remember correctly, you actively encouraged me. Now, I think I should I ring for your maid – get her to bring you an aspirin? You're overwrought.'

'I admit it.' Sofia hung her head. 'I was partly to blame, may God forgive me, but you wouldn't have married her just for my sake. So why? I'm waiting.'

He sighed and set aside his cup and plate and then he moved his chair slightly so that he was staring straight into Sofia van de Venter's large eyes. 'You know that I never had feelings for your daughter. It was a marriage of convenience.' He laughed unkindly at the thought. 'Except it wasn't convenient was it? She was a barren woman with no sense of the importance of my ministry and possessed of a depraved, sinner's soul.'

'So, why?' Sofia was like a dog with a bone.

'You don't have to play the innocent with me, Sofia. We both knew what I really wanted.'

Sofia looked puzzled.

'I'm divorcing her. It's all in hand. I will be a free man again and eventually you will be free too but until then you can move into my house as ... housekeeper. You must see that you can't stay here – not now Desmond's become violent.'

Sofia opened her mouth in amazement and then she started to laugh uncontrollably. 'Me?' she roared. 'You want me to be your housekeeper?'

Mr Morgan's smile wavered slightly. 'And you could help with the child. Um? Help bring him up?'

Sofia stopped laughing. 'My grandson?'

'Exactly.' Henrik held up his cup for more tea but Sofia ignored it. Henrik frowned.

'Not many cuckolded husbands would take their unfaithful wife's bastard child into their home, Henrik. Are you sure it would be quite proper?'

Henrik flinched at the implication but held his peace.

'So? Let me get this straight. You want me to leave Desmond and move in with you?'

'As my housekeeper. I'm not suggesting anything immoral. Oh no, far from it.'

'So I am to be your housekeeper – cook and clean for you – and in return I'm allowed to look after my grandson?'

'Why are you so angry?'

'You stupid, stupid man. You think I'd leave my husband for you? You're mad, stark-staring mad. I'm not a maid and I'm certainly not your mother. What you suggest is insulting in the extreme. Now get out.' And she walked to the door and flung it open. If she'd not been so angry she would have seen the backs of the young men as they dashed up the stairs to their rooms.

'I think you may have misunderstood me, Sofia. I have something quite different in mind for you. And don't say you didn't know how I've felt about you. Older woman have always attracted me and I know my mother would approve.' He rose and swaggered towards her. He forgave her this uncharacteristic behaviour. His declaration was a shock, he understood her confusion. When she'd had time to think about what he was offering her she would be contrite. He looked forward to that. 'I'll see you this afternoon at the meeting? We can discuss this further.'

'I won't be there. I'm finished with you and your meetings. And, from now on, I will deliver my lodgers to the Meeting House. You're not welcome here, Henrik Morgan, ever again. Do you understand me? '

'But, Sofia, please, think about what I'm offering. I can assure you I would never pressurise you into producing a son for me. We will have the boy.'

Sofia was glaring at him in a most alarming way. 'I'm warning you. If you do anything to harm my grandson or my daughter, I will personally see to it that the police are informed. I have finished with you and your church, Pastor Morgan. You are a disgrace to your calling. A lascivious, evil little man.'

Henrik was speechless. He'd never been spoken to like this before. But as he herded his young men into the car he was already thinking about the future. There was a youngish widow who'd recently moved into Birkenheadbaai. Yes, she might do very nicely indeed. As it happened he was getting tired of chocolate cake – much too fattening and not a patch on his beloved mother's.

After he'd gone Sofia sent the surprised Elizabeth home early after paying her too much money.

Sofia was in turmoil as she washed up. She was so angry. How could she have been so stupid? It made her flesh crawl to think of Henrik Morgan in that way. Would she ever be able to forget the look on his face as he came towards her? He desired her. It was obscene. But worse than anger was the growing panic she felt about Desmond and the baby. What if they'd had an accident? She'd texted her husband three times but he hadn't responded. Maybe he was still driving, or he just didn't want to speak to her? She wouldn't blame him. She vowed that if he got home safely she would make it up to him – to him and her daughter.

As she was drying the last cup she heard the sound of several cars racing down the track towards the house. She ran to the kitchen door, yanked it open and watched in horror as two police cars swung into the yard. 'Oh my God. No!' she whispered. 'Please, God. Don't let it be them.'

10.25 a.m.

Quent stood looking down the path that Willem had taken, willing him to come back, but he knew he wouldn't. Quent had finally blown it with his friend.

He set off to find Gail du Plessis and give her his ultimatum. If they wanted him urgently then they'd pay for the privilege. He cut down the back of the estate, following the warren of lanes that snaked between the mainly empty enclosures. Bullseye followed him. 'Just you and me then, fella?' They passed great stinking mounds of animal dung – each heap pulsing with feasting feral-cats, carrion birds and rats that leapt away at their approach, scattering lumps of muck behind them.

Turning a corner Quent found himself in front of a small concrete building in a dark corner of a yard. One time they'd kept wart-hogs here. The smell was evil. So? This was Gauta's new home. Why in God's name would the leopard be here? Maybe she was ill? Quent hesitated for a moment, tossing up whether he could be bothered, but then he went through a rusty gate into the yard and shut it firmly behind him. Bullseye was showing a lot of interest and patrolling the wire looking for a way in.

Quent had to duck his head to get inside the building. He waited just inside the opening until his eyes adjusted in the dim light. There was a sliver of sunlight spooling into the space from a hole in the roof. After a few moments, recognisable shapes floated out of the darkness towards him. There was a movement at the far wall and he heard chains rattling. Some living thing was in there with him, something that was making a deep grunting sound, half growl, half despair. It was the noise that inhabited Quent's dreams. *Gauta*.

Quent wasn't the only one aware of the leopard. Quent heard the crashes as Bullseye leapt at the perimeter fence.

The leopard turned her head to look at Quent and the sun spotlighted the animal's face. Her eyes were fever-bright and her beautiful markings were dull and caked in shit. The short length of chain that shackled her to the wall was barely long enough to allow her to stand. 'Gauta?' Quent called softly, 'Gauta?' He looked into her dead eyes searching for some sign of recognition. But there was nothing there. She snarled, her lips curled back in a grimace, more pain than rage.

Quent stumbled back out of the sty and through the gate, where Bullseye was waiting. The dog charged as Quent came out but Quent managed to push him back. As he did so his leg slipped and he crunched his wounded thigh against the fencing. He bent over and retched and retched into the undergrowth. The dog was still going crazy. 'Leave it, man.' Quent croaked when he could speak again. He looked down and saw blood seeping onto his trousers. Quent limped away. Bullseye didn't want to leave the leopard but when Quent disappeared he followed.

When Quent got back to the shack he locked Bullseye in his bakkie, grabbed his rifle and stuffed his pocket with cartridges. His hand gun was in a holster strapped across his chest beneath his T-shirt– where he always kept it.

Back in the sty Quent talked softly as he loaded the cartridges. 'Forgive me, Gauta, please, forgive me.' But the rifle was only halfway to his shoulder when she launched herself at him. The range of her attack was measured by the chain but she came on as if she were a free leopard. The fury of her lunge took Quent by surprise and he leapt away. The chain stopped Gauta in mid air and she thudded onto the concrete floor but she was on her feet in an instant and coming on again. Her lips were curled back exposing long, strong incisors and her scream made the hairs on the back of his neck stand on end.

This time he got a decent shot off, right between the eyes. She was dead before she hit the ground. He stood for a shocked moment staring down at the animal. The most magnificent leopard he'd ever seen reduced to this evil-smelling corpse. Armies of flies were gathering on the body as he staggered out into the clean, bright day.

Quent heard a child's voice in the distance. She was laughing. 'No, Opa, that's cheating.' He heard the answering low rumble of Jaco's laugh.

When he turned the corner in front of the main house, the man and his grand- daughter looked up. They were seated together in the shade on the veranda playing cards. Quent knew the child, she lived on the estate with her mother. She was a pretty, blond little thing called Katie and the apple of Jaco's eye.

Jaco was in a wheelchair. He had a large tumbler of whisky in one hand and the other rested gently on the little girl's neck. She was standing beside him, her body pressed up against his and giggling at something he'd just said.

When Jaco saw Quent he looked so relieved that Quent almost kept walking. The man was smiling – genuinely smiling, like he was really pleased to see Quent. If it hadn't been so tragic Quent might have laughed.

'Hey, the great man at last,' Jaco said, hitching up a chair with his good leg. 'Take a seat, man. You look done in.'

Quent didn't move.

'Leg still playing up I see.' Quent was standing with the sun behind him and Jaco had to shield his eyes to see him. 'Not to worry. I'll get my doc to take a look at it. Get you some white man's medicine.' When Quent didn't laugh Jaco pointed down to his own leg. 'Don't talk to me about legs.'

Quent saw the long, livid line of stitches that snaked down Jaco's leg. It reached from his thigh to his ankle.

The man moved slightly on his chair and winced with the pain. 'At least I got done by a proper wild animal, not one of your cuddly otters. Oh no, only the best for Jaco du Plessis— an endangered species.'

'You used her?'

'Yeah, I did. A whole year I waited, did as you said, Byrant. Let you have your way but, hey? The day after I kicked you out I needed her. So I went into her enclosure, walked straight up to her and she backed away, like she always did. I followed her, smiling and laughing, acting big in front of the film crew. I said something like, *this is my little pussy. She will do whatever I say.* That made them laugh. But I made a mistake, Quent. I took my eyes off her and that's when she came for me. She got me on the ground, her jaws round my leg and she would have killed me if the guy with the tranquillising dart hadn't got her first. But I paid her back. She's in the pigsty with all the filth. She'll learn.'

Quent found his voice at last. 'What in Christ's name were you thinking of?' he yelled. 'Why didn't Willem handle her?'

'The day I ask one of my blacks for help will be the day I die, Byrant.'

Quent didn't want to ask the question but there it was, flying out of his mouth as if it had a will of its own. 'Afterwards – why didn't you shoot her?'

Jaco looked surprised. 'What, waste a bullet on a runt like her? You've got to be joking.' He was smiling again. 'And besides,' he added. 'The runt belongs to me and sometimes film people need a ...crazy animal. The punters like it.'

Quent kept his eyes on the ground.

'What's up, man?' Jaco asked. 'Not still sulking cause I bollocked you? Didn't she say? I'm gonna make it up to you – big time. Just name your price to run the business till I'm back on my feet. I need you, man. Never thought I'd say that but there you go.'

'Opa,' the little girl's voice was wheedling. 'Can I pat the cheetah? You promised.'

Quent moved a step closer to Jaco. 'Send her away.' Quent's voice was soft and the man looked up in surprise. 'What you say?'

'I said send her away.'

Jaco was about to protest but then he saw what Quent was carrying. He unwound the child's fingers from his hand and placed the protesting child on the ground. 'Go find Ouma,' he said firmly.

'But you promised, Opa.'

'I said git.'

And the child heard something terrible in her grandfather's voice, burst into tears and fled.

275

Journey to Cape Town

Desmond looked grim as he drove. Little Farnie was in the back seat, happily feeding currants to his teddy while Raki sat staring straight ahead. He rested his hand briefly on her knee.

'I thought you'd changed your mind about helping us.'

' Never. The bloody bakkie wouldn't start.'

'Oh,' she said, turning her head away. She wanted to believe him but she knew there was more to it than that. 'What about the other car?'

'It's in the garage getting serviced.'

'Well, you're here now. Let's forget it – '

' – No. I want to tell you. It was her – you mother – she drained the oil out of my car. She did it deliberately to stop me taking you and Farnie to the hospital.'

'What?'

'I promise you, it's the truth. I'll never forgive her.' He glanced at Raki. 'You live with someone all those years, you think you know everything about them and then something like this happens and your whole life's turned upside down.'

'She must hate me so much.'

'What sort of a human being is she?'

'It must have been a terrible shock for her to find out you'd been seeing me.'

'Don't make excuses for her. The plain truth is she knew that Farnie was going to hospital today and she sabotaged my car. It was a deliberate and evil act and she calls herself a Christian? Whatever she thinks about Quent Byrant the child's innocent.'

They were beginning the long slow climb up into the mountains and Desmond was forced to pull onto the hard shoulder to allow a long line of impatient drivers to overtake them. The Renault had no power on any gradient.

'She was never as bad as this before Morgan turned up. I could reason with her back then. I'm sure he's going mad and

276

taking your mother with him. He's got her and all the old nanny-goats praying and preparing for *The Second Coming*, so they can enter the New Jerusalem side by side with his *beloved* mother. They can't cope with life now Apartheid's gone. *It's disturbed the balance of civilisation*, that's what Morgan says. I've heard him spouting his poison.'

Raki had turned around in her seat and was rescuing Farnie's bear that had fallen onto the floor. As she faced forward again Desmond caught sight of her face. Her skin was so pale it looked almost blue and her nose was bleeding.

'My God, Raki, what happened? Did you have an accident?'

'It's nothing,' she said wiping at the blood with the back of her hand. 'I had a little bump that's all.'

But he saw her anguish and as soon as he was back on the main road he watched out for somewhere to park. Farnie was asleep and Desmond put his arms around his daughter and she sobbed into his shoulder. 'It's okay,' he said, patting her. 'Everything's okay, we're on our way and Farnie's going to be just fine. Try not to worry.'

She lifted her head and looked despairingly into her father's face. 'There's a leopard on the kloof.'

He was staggered. 'What?'

'I saw it in the forest.'

'Are you sure? There hasn't been one since he...

'...I promise you, Dad, it's there. There was a dead Bok hanging from a tree and the leopard was up there, watching us. It could have... I'll never be able to let Farnie out of my sight on the kloof again. It's our home – our only home – so what will happen to us? If I can't protect my own son what good am I?'

Her father still wasn't convinced. 'Maybe it was a caracal – they can get pretty big – or a big male baboon?'

'No, it was a leopard, no mistake, Dad, I saw her...,' Raki shuddered, 'and she saw me. My God, what am I going to do? I can't go back. What if...'

'...But he took the leopard, Raki. Everyone knows that.'

'That's what Du Toit said but he never had any proof did he?' She saw her father's expression. 'Just because he went away that day doesn't mean he had the leopard.'

Desmond spoke softly and reasonably. 'One day the leopard was there and the next it was gone and so was your man, plus three of Broot's farm workers – one who just happened to be Byrant's best buddy. When they searched the kloof the CLP workers found a dead leopard-cub on a ledge high up and a gin-trap had been tossed over the edge of the cliff. A mother leopard would never abandon her cub. Of course it was Quent. I'm sorry Raki but Pierre Montes and the others reckon he must have sold the animal to a wild-life farm or a hunting syndicate. There are mega bucks to be made from big cats.'

'But leopards were special to him.'

'A lot of things were 'special' to him.'

Raki closed her eyes. Her father was only repeating what she'd been telling herself. Quent was no good; he'd treated her with contempt and had disowned his own son. He hadn't even sent her money for Farnie. She should hate him. She did hate him.

Desmond glanced at his watch and started the engine. 'Best be on our way. We'll talk about this later, okay?'

She nodded.

'We can sort something out. You'll just have to come and live on the farm.'

That almost made her smile. 'That would be over my mother's dead body, I think.'

'I could find us a place to live.'

'Us? You mean you, me and Farnie?'

'It's time I retired. Now, try and get some sleep. You look done in.'

It was still two hours to Cape Town. 'Did I tell you my petrol gauge doesn't work?'

'Just out of interest, does anything work in this car?'

'Radio's good. CD player, sometimes, but I haven't got any CDs. Oh and the cigarette lighter works spasmodically.'

Raki closed her eyes. She wouldn't sleep but it was wonderful to feel safe and warm and have her father close. Talking about the leopard had eased that worry a little but she couldn't get her head around what her mother had tried to do. How could she square that with her religion? But Raki knew the answer. Sofia van de Venter's God was the Old Testament deity, who smote his enemies with hell-fire and damnation. Raki had always been drawn to the gentler, New Testament saviour, Jesus Christ, who preached love, forgiveness and redemption.

With that thought she fell into a deep, exhausted sleep. The first she'd had for days.

10.30 a.m.

The tears and the sweat running down his face are one to Quent – one channel of grief. The salty-cocktail stings his chapped lips. He reaches for a bottle but there are none left. Strange that he doesn't pee anymore. Maybe Jesus is working a miracle? Changing the water into tears? He would smile if he could but smiles are gone. The sadness is a pressure on Quent's head like a woman's touch. Not the old woman for sure, and he flinches at the memory. Not one of his women either – except for Raki. But this is another hand – a gentle touch like a blessing. *Good boy, Quent. There's a good boy for your Mama.*

And now he'll never know who she was – his mother, or his father or even who the old woman was, but it doesn't matter. None of it matters.

Traction

Raki opened her eyes when the car began the long, slow descent down the Sir Lowry Pass. Table Mountain was straight ahead with its rim of icing-sugar cloud, set in the line of mountains tinged with blue. It was a beautiful clear morning and several hot-air balloons sashayed through the sky above them, teasing the mountain peaks behind them. Planes circled lazily preparing to land at Cape Town airport. The plain below was green and lush except for the smoke-shrouded Cape Flats where thousands of blacks and coloureds lived in make-shift wooden shacks with corrugated iron roofs.

Her father smiled at her. 'Nice sleep, Raki?'

'I wasn't asleep,' she said. 'Just thinking.' She glanced at the sleeping child in the back seat.

'He's been thinking too,' said Desmond, and patted her knee. 'Nearly there.'

When the nurse opened the door into Farnie's room Raki had to hold onto the door frame, to stop herself from keeling over. All she saw was the cot in the middle of the room, like some cruel contraption from a torture chamber. There were four sides of metal bars with a spar running across the top – holding a large, blue plastic block and tackle. Threaded through this were two pulleys with what looked like little stirrups attached to one end with counter-weights on the other.

The nurse bustled about pulling back the curtains and allowing the sunlight to stream into the room, making it look less scary. Then she let down the side of the cot. She must have seen Raki's face because she patted her hand. 'Don't worry. Baby will get used to it long before you do, Mrs Morgan. Children adapt very quickly.'

Raki looked at her incredulously. Was the woman mad?

Her father followed carrying Farnie, who was wide awake now. The little boy stared around for a moment, his eyes wide with astonishment and then he made a *whoop* of delight. He'd spotted a whole menagerie of soft animals in the cot, attached to the bars with Velcro, and there were plastic cars and tractors and piles of picture books littering the mattress. There was even a kiddie's CD player and when the nurse pressed a button it played all the familiar songs and nursery rhymes. Farnie had never seen such treasures. His grandfather put him in the cot and he immediately started to play.

'Get baby undressed, Mrs Morgan,' the nurse said going to the door. 'Leave him in his nappy and T-shirt. It's very warm in here. Your bed's there,' she said, pointing to a day-bed on the other side of the room beside a door. 'Toilet and shower in there and we have a galley kitchen down the corridor where you can prepare food. There's a cafe on the ground floor.' She consulted her list. 'Doctor will be up this afternoon to see Farnie. Anything you need or any questions just ask at the nurses 'station' down the corridor on the right. I'll come back later and see how you're getting on. My name's Melanie and I will be Farnie's day-nurse while you're with us.'

Raki's hands were shaking as she undressed Farnie. He was busy playing with a bright red xylophone that made a tinny, loud sound and he objected to his mother interrupting him. When he was ready she made him some honey sandwiches and a bottle of milk and Desmond and she had some tea.

'You must be hungry, Raki,' her father said, hopefully. He'd missed out on breakfast. 'I'll get us something, shall I?'

Raki couldn't think about food. 'You go, Dad, I'll have something later.'

Desmond hesitated at the door. He smiled. 'So? It doesn't look too bad does it? This will be our home for the next three weeks.'

He had promised to come and stay over occasionally, to give Raki a break he said; although there was no way she was leaving Farnie – not for a moment. And whatever universe her father was on wasn't the same as hers. The nurses could pile the room high with toys but it would still be the place where Farnie was going to have traction.

Desmond lowered his voice so that Farnie couldn't hear. 'I know it's hard for you, Raki, but you must try not to let Farnie see you're scared.'

When she was on her own she unpacked and put things away in a cupboard under the window. The hospital was set in beautiful grounds and although it was in the middle of the city she could see Table Mountain in the distance. She stared at the view for a moment, breathing in and out rhythmically, feeling her chest rise and fall. She'd been tense for so long she felt like an over-wound clock. Her father was right she had to relax. Farnie was safe and they were in the hospital and everything was going to be okay.

When Desmond returned with a sandwich she forced a bit down for his sake. Shortly after this the young doctor arrived. Dressed in casual clothes, he had a friendly, easy rapport with Farnie. The little boy hadn't had much contact with men and was usually a bit wary – except for his opa who he'd loved from the first moment he saw him. But this doctor ran the toy car up and down Farnie's arms and over his fat little tummy making *brrm brrm* noises. Farnie shrieked with delight.

After a few minutes of play the man bandaged each of the little boy's legs – from just below the knee down to his feet. Farnie wriggled about a bit but didn't seem unduly bothered. When the doctor pulled the stirrups down from the pulleys and fixed them to the child's feet Farnie did kick up a bit but the young medic worked so quickly that Farnie didn't really have time to object.

In no time at all Farnie was lying on his back with both legs straight up in the air attached to the pulleys. The doctor added the counter-weights so that the 'bad' hip was pulled into the correct position. He explained that the weights would be changed regularly to allow the head of the femur to locate in the correct position in the pelvis. By now Farnie was really objecting. He wanted to 'read' a book, so Raki drew up a chair beside the cot and opened a book. Farnie soon discovered he could change his position and turn onto his tummy and grab the side bars if he wanted and soon he was happily listening and babbling at her.

The doctor checked the equipment to make sure everything was working properly and said *goodnight* and that he'd pop in the next morning.

Raki made Farnie his bedtime bottle and she stayed with him until his eyes closed. He was almost hidden in a mound of fluffy animals and she attached them to the bars and pushed the larger toys down to the bottom of the cot. She left his teddy beside him and a big soft blow-up duck that he'd fallen in love with. Finally she switched off the incessant loop of nursery rhymes. Peace at last.

Desmond got to his feet. 'I'll have to be going soon,' he said. 'But I'll be back first thing tomorrow, okay? Oh, and I bought a few things downstairs – just in case.' He pressed a plastic bag into her hands. Inside there was milk, tea and biscuits, toothpaste, soap and a couple of magazines.

She hugged him. 'Thanks so much, Dad. And please drive carefully.'

'Is there any option?' he grinned. 'Thank God I'll be in my car tomorrow. Sleep tight. I'll see you first thing – sixish, okay?' Then he kissed her and pressed some money into her hand. She started to protest but he put his finger to his lips and went out of the room, closing the door quietly behind him.

After her father left Raki pulled the mattress off the day-bed and dragged it beside the cot. She needed to be close in case Farnie woke up in the night and was frightened. She lay there wide awake for hours, aware of every sound the little boy made, but he didn't wake and in the early hours she fell asleep.

They are here

Quent's vision is blurred but he knows where the sun is because a brighter shade of grey indicates it and he feels its heat. Hard to tell where his fever starts and the sun begins. He is burning...burning.

Sight is going but his hearing is still there. There's a jackal buzzard close by – its *ka,ka,ka* fills his brain. There's something else in the background, a loud and repetitive noise – so familiar –yet his brain refuses to decipher it.

The only thing he knows is that it's getting nearer and that's when he recognises what it is. The barking of dogs.

They are here.

Thank God.

He stumbles outside. It's raining now– the cold, vicious rain of autumn, slicing into Quent's flesh like icy needles. The dogs are very close and Quent hears their mounting hysteria. He imagines them pulling on their leashes, eager for battle. Bullseye barks furiously in response. Quent sits on the chair facing downhill. His rifle is propped beside him against the railings. His hand gun is in his shoulder holster. He can't stand, not because he doesn't want to, but because every time he tries to rise he's so dizzy he knows he will fall over. Bullseye moves away and Quent tries to call him but he has no spit left and his voice is thin and reedy. Nevertheless the dog comes to him – as if he senses the man's desperation.

'S'okay. Nothing worry...' Quent slurs like a drunken man. 'Stay, Bullseye, stay with me, okay?'

Quent attempts to focus on the spot where the men's heads will appear over the rise but all he sees are black floaters. What does it matter if he sees them or not? There's nothing he can do about it. It's over. But he's going to get himself upright, whatever the cost. He can't be sitting down like some feeble old guy when they take him.

He presses both hands down on the arms of the chair and pushes himself slowly to his feet. The pain is unbelievable and he collapses back down, jarring his leg. He waits a few moments and then he grits his teeth and tries again. This time he manages to grab the railings and slowly straighten up. If he can wedge himself between the veranda rails and the chair it might be possible to stay on his feet.

When he's balanced against the wooden support, he turns his hip into the railings and leans his full weight against it. Sweat is streaming down his face now. He feels Bullseye's body stiffen. This is it, then. He hears the men shouting and their dog's hysterical barking. The sounds are coming at him from down a long echoing tunnel. A line of black, bobbing silhouettes moves slowly towards him. Quent attempts to separate the shapes into individual bodies. He thinks five and they have Dobermans, by the shape and size of the animals.

The full weight of Bullseye's body is pushed against him now. He is like a tightly wound spring waiting for release. 'No,' Quent slips a length of rope around the animal's neck and fastens it. 'S'not your fight.'

The dog drops to its haunches, the complaint stifled in his throat, but he never takes his eyes off the approaching figures. The Dobermans are baying now. They've spotted Bullseye and are waiting for the command to attack.

'Keep those dogs leashed,' Quent voice is hoarse. 'Look, surrender,' he says, grabbing the rifle with one hand and dropping it over the side of the veranda onto the turf. Then he raises his hand for a second, to show that he isn't carrying another gun. 'Inside. Some letters,' he manages.

Someone shouts, 'Get the other one up, fella.'

Quent shakes his head and attempts to make his voice sound friendly, 'No, can't.' He looks towards the house. 'Stuff inside for the woman. This is her place.'

'I said get your bloody hands in the air.'

Quent's legs are buckling.

'Keep standing you bastard,' screams another voice. 'Or I'll shoot.'

'Sorry...' he gasps as his legs crumple.

'Stand!' the same man, his voice shrill with panic. 'I'll kill you.'

'Do it.'

They are in a line facing him now, fifty or so metres away. He thinks he sees one of them bend down to the dogs.

'No!' But it's too late and the animals leap towards him like black arrows aimed at his throat. Bullseye rears up and the rope rips through Quent's hands like a line of fire. He clings on for as long as he can but Bullseye shakes him off as if he was nothing. Quent is dragged down the steps and falls heavily onto his knees, arms outstretched. The hand gun skids away under the stoep.

It is all over in moments. The Dobermans realise their mistake at about the same time Bullseye gets one of them, flips it over his head and comes on for the rest of them. The remaining dogs scatter back down the mountainside. There is furious yelping, barking and flying rocks. Then there's a single shot and silence – absolute silence, except for the *drip drip* of rain off the kloof-house roof.

Murderer

It's five a.m. when Raki opens her eyes. Farnie is lying on his tummy with his legs sticking up behind him and he's shouting at her, demanding she turn on the CD player. She obeys and then pulls back the curtains, flooding the room with the rising sun.

After changing and washing Farnie, she makes breakfast, and then Melanie bustles in and glances at the happily playing child. 'See?' she says. 'Nothing to worry about.'

The nurse spends a few moments explaining what will happen next and leaves Raki some forms to fill in. The cleaners come and go and one or two children, on the same corridor, come by to say *hello* to the new patient. Finally the doctor arrives to check on his little patient.

Raki is surprised when she looks at the clock. It's seven o'clock already. Her father should be here soon but when it gets to eight o'clock she's panicking. She knows she's working herself up into a state again but she has to find out if he's okay. The doctor is busy with Farnie, so she slips out into the corridor and uses her cell phone.

The phone is answered immediately. Her mother's voice sounds odd – strained. as if she's been crying. 'Hello, the Van de Venter household.'

'It's Raki. Is Dad there?' Raki speaks quickly before her mother can switch off.

'No.'

Raki's in no mood for her mother's games. 'Where is he?' she demands. 'I have to know. Is he okay? Has something happened?'

'Look, I'm sorry but I'm...I'm waiting for an important call.'

'Don't go, mother. Tell me what's happened. I'm so worried.'

There is silence and then a nervous cough. 'Your father's been arrested.'

'What?' Raki is horrified. 'But why? What's he done? Was it my car? Did he have an accident? Oh my God. Is he all right? Is he hurt?'

'He's not been home since you went to Cape Town yesterday. I got a call from him late last night saying he was helping the police with their enquiries. And he couldn't come home until they'd finished with him.'

'The police? But why?'

'It's that man – that terrible man – he's murdered someone.'

'Who are you talking about? What man?'

'They came here too and interrogated me, accused me of aiding and abetting a criminal.' Sofia is silent for a moment and when she speaks again her voice is angry. 'How long have you been hiding him up there?'

'I've got no idea what you're talking about.'

'Don't play the innocent with me. Byrant's up there on the kloof. He's been seen.'

'Quent? You're talking about Quent? He's murdered someone?' The words were only just percolating into her brain. 'Never.'

'Just send your father home to me, Raki.'

'It's a mistake.'

'Byrant will be arrested and tried for murder. Thank God your little boy isn't there. I'm switching off now, Raki. Desmond might be trying to reach me.'

'I haven't seen Quent for over a year, not since – '

' – I'm not interested. I just want my husband home.'

'I promise you, mother, Quent wasn't in my house when I left yesterday morning.'

'They sent a helicopter up this morning. He's there. Everybody knows – the whole town. The police questioned me for hours. I kept telling them I had nothing to do with him or you and, thank God, in the end they believed me. I said they should question his friends, like that black boy...?'

'...Willem?'

'And your cousin.'

289

'Mari? Why would Mari know where Quent was?'

'You and she have always been as thick as thieves.'

'That was cruel.'

Sofia's voice is pleading. 'I was frightened. I wanted them to leave us alone. I'm too old for all this worry. Just make it better. Tell the police your father's got nothing to do with it. Please. Send him home to me.'

'Did you tell the police where I was?'

Sofia's silence says it all.

'Oh my God, Mother. How could you? They'll come here and they might arrest me, then what would happen to Farnie? He can't be in the hospital on his own.'

'I'm sorry, Raki. I panicked. Is he all right? Your little boy? Farnie? Is he going to be all right?'

Raki mutters something and switches off. She's crying. Hurrying into the loo she splashes cold water onto her red-rimmed eyes before returning to Farnie's room. The doctor comes out at that moment, does a thumbs-up, and ambles off down the corridor.

Back inside, Raki busies herself making a drink for Farnie but her brain is in free-fall. Quent has murdered someone? No. Quent is many things, but a murderer? Never. She can't believe it – she won't believe it. She starts to dial the police station in Birkenheadbaai to explain but thinks better of it. They'll tell her to stay where she is until they get to her. She's frantically trying to decide what she should do when her phone rings. It's Mari. As soon as she hears her cousin's voice she jumps in. 'I'm so sorry. Mari. Mother said the police had questioned you about Quent. I can't believe it – any of it.'

'It's okay, calm down, everything's fine. How's my Farnie doing?'

'He's good, Mari. Look, can you do me a favour? You know Quent's friend Willem? Could you ring Martin Broot and get his cell phone number? Only I heard the police have taken Willem in for questioning and I wanted to check that Florentina and the kids are okay?'

'Sure, Florentina cleans for Anton's old lady. I'll pop by later.'

'Thanks. Look, I've got to go, Mari.'

'Hang on, Raki. What about...him? D'you know what happened?'

'They say he's murdered someone. But he wouldn't, Mari. There's been some mistake. Mother said he's at my house and the police are on their way to arrest him.'

'The cops were running around like headless chickens when I was at the station. You'd think they were planning a war.'

'Oh my God.'

'Raki? You're not going to do anything stupid, are you? Answer me. You don't owe him a thing. He walked out on you, remember? He left you pregnant, with no money. He's scum.'

'He didn't know I was pregnant.'

'Promise me you're not going up there.'

'He's in trouble, Mari, and he's come back to the kloof – to find me.'

'For God's sake, woman, where else would he go? Who else would take him in?'

'Goodbye, Mari.'

'Wait. Raki? Speak to me. Please, don't do this. The police will be armed and he's capable of anything. You could get hurt.'

'Quent wouldn't harm me.'

'Raki. If you don't care about yourself think about your little boy. What would he do if anything happened to you?'

Raki's voice is hard. 'That's strange coming from someone who suggested I give Farnie away for adoption.' And she switches off.

When the phone rings again it's her father, apologising for his lateness and saying he's almost at the hospital. He doesn't mention the police or Quent and neither does she. She's so relieved that he's coming. While she waits she busies herself with Farnie, reading him stories and playing farms.

When Desmond hurries in Raki hugs him as if her life depends on it.

'Sorry, Raki. Roads were mad.'

While he takes off his coat and says *hello* to Farnie she takes two bulging carrier bags from him and plonks everything down on her bed. Farnie is delighted to see his Opa, especially when he sees the sweeties and chocolate biscuits.

Raki has never left Farnie with anyone before. She watches her father with him. He is so loving and gentle. Will he understand? The unsaid words hang in the air between them.

When she can stand it no longer she takes a deep breath and speaks. 'I rang home, Dad, to see where you were.'

'I know,' he says, leaning back on his heels and looking straight at her. 'Sofia told me.'

'I'm so sorry to bring you all this trouble.'

'Did your mother tell you why the police are after him?'

Raki nods. 'I don't believe it.'

'There's no question, Raki, he did it. He shot an unarmed man in the head at point blank range. There were witnesses.'

Raki closes her eyes.

'It was a guy called Jaco du Plessis. Byrant worked for him.'

'Mother said Quent's at my house.'

'They sent a chopper up first thing and he's there all right, him and that dog of his.'

Raki takes a deep breath. 'Dad?'

Desmond shakes his head. 'Don't ask me.'

'I have to go.'

'No, you don't.'

'I do. Please. Will you stay with Farnie for me? Just for tonight?'

Her father shakes his head sadly.

'Please, Dad. I have to do this. And I must go soon. The police...'

' ...Yeah I know. Just one question. What's Byrant ever done for you but bring you misery?'

Raki looks at her little boy and then back to her father. He is staring at her as if he doesn't know her and she can't bear it. She kneels beside him and takes his hands in hers. 'I know it's hard for you to understand but this isn't about Quent, not really, it's about me. There has to be an end to it and unless I see him I'll never know.'

'What? What else do you need to know?'

'If it was ...real. What we had together, because if it wasn't, then...'

'...Then you'd be able to get on with the rest of your life? You're not alone now, you've got me and Mari and even your mother seems to be coming round. We'll always be there for you. Quent Byrant doesn't matter.'

'He's Farnie's father and I loved him, Dad.'

Desmond gives a helpless shrug. 'You want "real"? This is what's real. That man has ruined your life and now he's a murderer too. Apart from anything else you could get hurt and then what would we do?'

'Dad. Please. I'll never ask you for anything, ever again, but I've got to see him.'

Her father wipes a weary hand across his mouth then he stands up and goes to where he's thrown his coat on the bed. He searches in the pocket and holds out the car keys. 'Three rows back from the main entrance – row K.'

She reaches for the keys but he holds onto them 'One condition. Whatever happens up there, don't try to protect him from the police. Promise me.'

'I promise.'

'Just drive carefully. I need you, Raki.' And he glances at the happily playing child. 'We both need you.'

Raki ducks her head and takes a deep breath; then she kisses Farnie on top of his head and says, 'Be a good boy for Opa. Mama's going to bring you a nice surprise. Okay?' The little boy looks vaguely surprised but then Opa gives him another sweet. Raki clutches her dad's hand and then she's gone.

She walks quickly away down the corridor. As she passes the nurses 'station' Melanie calls out. 'Good idea, Mrs Morgan. Have a bit of freedom, girl.'

'My father's staying with Farnie tonight. Okay?'
'Fine, honey. Have fun. See you tomorrow.'

Now

From where he lies Quent hears the men's staccato breathing. They're shit-scared. If Quent had the strength their fear might amuse him but he's beyond all that. The rain moistens his lips and he stares up at the rolling clouds. She's not coming. If he had the gun he could end it here – three bullets. He curses himself for waiting too long. He should have done it while he still had the chance.

The men are shouting now. One voice rising above the others. 'Your bastard dog's killed my boys. I'll swing for you.' And that's when they come, anger giving them courage. They plough him face-down in the scrub. One of them sits on his back, pressing his face into the dirt, while another twists his arms behind his back. Their voices come from far away.

'No need to cuff him. He's not going anywhere. He's clean. Christ! Look at his leg. No one said he...' A silence and then awkward laughter. 'What's this he's wearing? A woman's skirt. Never knew Byrant was a poofter.' More laughter and then hands heave him upright and he is thrown into a sitting position, his back slamming against the veranda railings. His hands are still behind him and he feels the barrel of the hand gun, just within reach.

'Dog?' he mouths.

'Your dog's fine, now he's got a bullet in his brain.'

'Good,' Quent mutters. No one hears. 'Good,' he whispers again.

'Look, he's wet himself! Piece of shit. I thought the boss said he was dangerous?'

The men's jeering faces dance in front of him like a bunch of balloons. 'Bastards.' The word gurgles in Quent's throat and dribbles of blood bubble from the corners of his mouth.

Quent's gun is in his hand before anyone can move. He's aware of the men scattering and he points it towards the blurred movement. His trembling fingers curl around the trigger but he is too weak to hold it there and darkness closes in. The pain doesn't matter, nothing matters, and the gun drops from his nerveless fingers.

Real

Raki is on auto-pilot as she drives towards Pig's Snout. She doesn't know how she feels except she must get to the kloof house. This compulsion is as strong as that of a tiny frog, hopping blindly towards some far-away pool of stagnant water. The creature doesn't understand the impulse but it goes on nonetheless.

Raki has no memory of the drive but somehow here she is on the kloof. There are three police cars in the car park. They are parked haphazardly as if the drivers abandoned them in a hurry. It's raining – not the gentle rain of summer but the sort that scours the skin. All of Raki's concentration is focused on keeping to the path. The wind is coming at her from all directions – a freezing blast that hurts the back of her throat as she breathes in.

Just before the edge of the rise Raki sees the dogs. Bullseye and three Dobermans are sprawled grotesquely in the fynbos, their muzzles dark with blood. Bullseye has a bullet-wound in his head.

As she scrambles over the edge of the kloof Raki sees a group of heavily-armed policemen clustered around a body on the ground. Forgetting all her promises she runs straight at the men and forces her way through to where the man lies face down on the sodden earth. He is breathing with difficulty, each laboured breath sending an answering shudder through the length of his body. She can't see his face and she drops to her knees and raises his head off the wet ground and onto her lap. 'Quent?'

But there's been some mistake, this isn't him. This pathetic creature is an old, frail man, someone else – a stranger. She gently rolls him onto his back to get a better look and he groans. 'Sorry, sorry,' she says, touching his shoulder. 'Are you hurt? Can I help you?' And that's when she sees the leopard tattoo. She stares down in disbelief at the claw-slashing, teeth-ripping animal: so incongruous on the arm of this shell of the man – this man who used to be Quent Byrant.

One of the policemen rests a hand on her shoulder but someone says 'Leave her, man. It's her – the Morgan woman.'

She stares up at the circle of men. 'What have you done to him?'

'Nothing,' one says. 'We found him like this.'

She leans down and whispers in Quent's ear. 'It's me, Quent.' His eyelids flicker open but he sees nothing.

A policeman shrugs and shifts uneasily from one foot to the other. 'We didn't know he was sick. No one told us.'

'Dangerous criminal,' another chips in. 'That's what we were told. Had to wait for the dog unit before we came up and reinforcements are being sent down from Cape Town.' His voice drifts away. If truth were told, these men are bitterly disappointed. They'd been excited at the thought of capturing one of the most talked about villains in the neighbourhood. Quent Byrant, mercenary, big-game hunter, made a lot of money up North. Christ, this was the guy who stole a leopard right off this kloof from under the noses of the authorities. There weren't many men like Byrant in South Africa nowadays. These guys were legends, from the old days – some might say the glory days of South Africa. Even the two coloured and one black policeman had a sneaking admiration for this man. The Leopard Man had a reputation.

They'd been promised a risky mission. They dealt with murders and thieving all the time. It's what you expected up on the *Schema* or squatter camps. Coloured and black crime was routine work but this, this was to have been something they could have told their kids about – something to make them proud. A white man killing another white man was rare. They stare morosely down at Quent.

'He killed my dogs,' the dog handler whines. 'And he tried to shoot us.'

But it didn't amount to much, did it? And this 'dangerous' criminal was dying, up here, with the rain hammering down and the wind cutting them in half. One of the cops goes into the house and comes back with two blankets. He has the two letters in his hand and puts them in his pocket. He drapes one blanket over Raki's shoulders and lays the other across the dying man. As Raki tucks the blanket around Quent she sees his injured leg. The flesh is a bluish colour and covered in a mass of large flat, purple wounds. She feels Quent's pulse and turns a frantic face to the men. 'Why aren't you doing something? We've got to get him to the hospital.'

No one moves.

'Didn't you hear me?'

'He'd be dead before we got him down the kloof. Mrs.... It's septicaemia. Last stages by the look of it.'

She presses Quent's hand to her mouth and kisses it. 'Quent. What have you done?'

He can't speak but he knows she's there. He can smell her and feel her arms around him, her body pressed close to his – her warmth radiating into him. The sadness is lifting - her hand on his head, her blessing, her love. Nothing else matters now she's here.

He wants to tell her that he loves her and he's sorry. And the child? Of course the boy is his.

And then it happens.

A tear rolls down Quent's cheek as Raki rocks him in her arms. 'Shh, it's okay. I'm okay,' Raki talks rapidly. 'We're both fine, me and Farnie. He's in Cape Town at the hospital, Dad's there. I got the money, Quent. No need to worry.'

The men move away, giving the couple some privacy. The rain is coming down in sheets now. They stamp their feet and stare at the ground, their discomfort making them spiteful.

'Christ, all that bloody climb for nothing,' one says, feeling a finger of icy rain trickling down his neck.

'They should've left him to die on his own.'

'Yeh, now we've got to get the bastard down that bloody kloof.'

'We could always toss him over the edge,' another says. 'Watch him bounce all the way down.'

There's silence for a moment then uneasy laughter but Raki isn't listening. She has her mouth pressed to Quent's ear and is whispering urgently. They think they hear the word 'leopard' but then he slips sideways in the woman's arms and she lays him gently on the ground. She tucks the blanket tightly around his body crossing his arms across his chest. It is hard to see the leopard through her tears and the rain but she traces the shape of the animal with her finger then she lies beside him.

The cops stand awkwardly around her, willing her to get up from the wet ground. No one wants to be the first to speak but they've got to get going.

The man who gave her the blanket kneels beside her. 'It's over, Mrs Morgan. Time to go.'

'Please, don't call me that. I'm not Mrs Morgan. And this is my home so I'll leave when I'm ready and I'm not ready.'

The old guy is dead and the cops have a difficult woman on their hands. This day is going from bad to worse. They're mad with their boss for sending them on a wild-goose chase, mad with Quent for making them look idiots, mad about the loss of their dogs and mad for something they can never admit to – the pity of it all.

The path will be wet and treacherous by now and the woman says she wants to bury Quent up on the kloof. Raki isn't hysterical or anything just very determined. The cops know they have to get the body down the kloof but they can't leave the woman alone in this state.

They are trying to decide who should stay with her and who should take the body down the kloof when there's the sound of laboured breathing and loose-shale cascading down the mountain-side behind them. They turn their frightened faces towards the escarpment, hands on their guns, half expecting to see the monster dog coming at them out of the gloaming. But it isn't a dog it's a woman – a very wet, out of breath, red-faced woman, with wisps of blonde hair hanging lankly across her eyes.

Mari stands for a moment getting her breath back and then she looks cautiously about her. At first she's unsure of what she's seeing but then she spots Raki. Going to her she kneels beside her and takes her in her arms. 'It's okay now, sweet pea.

Mari's here.' And Mari works her magic. Within a short time Raki and she are heading down the kloof. They will wait in the warmth of Mari's car while the relieved cops deal with Quent. Mari hasn't got the slightest idea whether the authorities will let them bury a murderer where they want but she promises Raki that they will. And she'll do her best to make sure it happens.

Raki is in the lead as they descend. She walks quickly and confidently. The only time she stops is to wait for her cousin to catch up. Raki reaches the car park first and climbs into the driving seat of her father's bakkie. By the time Mari stumbles into view Raki has heated up the car.

Mari scrambles in beside her, 'God, I'm freezing.'

They sit in silence for a few minutes and then Raki turns to her cousin. 'Is it real, Mari?'

Mari puts her arms around her friend. 'Yeah, 'fraid so, Raki.'

'He's dead?'

Mari kisses Raki's head.

'I'm not dreaming?'

'No.'

After a moment Raki moves out of her cousin's arms and sits up straight. She wipes her eyes with the back of her hand, takes off her wet coat, throws it in the back and tucks her hair behind her ears. She glances at Mari. 'Can you come with me or are you working?'

'No way. I'm staying with you for as long as you need me.'

'Thanks. If we hurry, we can be in Cape Town before Farnie goes to sleep.'

'What?'

'He would love to see you. You can leave your car here and Dad can drop you off on his way home tonight. Okay?'

Mari is incredulous. 'But what about him? Quent? Don't you want to wait for them to bring him down?'

Raki shakes her head.

Mari stares at her cousin. 'I don't get it, Raki. What was all that about up there? I thought you loved ...the man.' She was going to say *bastard* but decided not.

Raki turns the key in the ignition. 'I do love him. I always will but I'm done with waiting for him.'

It takes Mari a moment to assemble her scrambled thoughts. 'So? You're going to Cape Town?'

'Um.' Raki is concentrating on reversing down the pot-holed track to the road.

'Now?'

Raki pulls up at the gate, waiting for the road to clear. 'Yes, now.'

'But should you be driving? Let me. Come on, shift over, Raki, be sensible.'

Raki sees Mari's worried face. 'Don't worry. I won't crash. I'm fine. Bit wet but fine.'

Mari shakes her head in disbelief then she shrugs off her wet things and tosses them in the back.

'This is the start of the rest of my life, Mari. That's okay, isn't it?' And then, before her cousin can reply Raki says, 'God! Isn't it great to have windscreen wipers that work?'

Mari turns her head away so her cousin won't see her smile but if she looked she'd see that Raki is smiling too.

* * *

Peace returns to the kloof as the light fades. Icy winds and rain lash the mountainside and the leopardess moves away from the edge and shelters beneath an overhang of rock. At last she can suckle her cubs and, as they wriggle ecstatically against her, their bodies' warmth calms her.

No need to hunt tonight. She has her prey in the tree below and she will go to it while her cubs sleep. She bends her head and licks the head of the nearest cub dislodging him from the teat. He growl-meows at her and latches on again. They are growing fast and will soon be big enough to hunt with her.

The leopardess has no memory except for this kloof. It has always been her refuge but there is a stronger urge now –

the overwhelming need to protect her young. And if she has
to leave this kloof, then she will.

Anne Ousby lives on the Northumbrian Coast in England. Her stories have been published in anthologies and broadcast on Radio 4 and her stage plays have been performed widely in the North East. A television drama, *Wait till the Summer Comes*, was broadcast on ITV. Her first novel *Patterson's Curse* was published in 2010 by Roomtowrite www.roomtowrite.co.uk

The Leopard Man is her second novel based in South Africa and has been inspired by the people and beauty of the rural Western Cape.

12911767R00182

Made in the USA
Charleston, SC
05 June 2012